*Praise for Daryl Gregory's*

# Revelator

"[Gregory] has a talent for writing outcasts, for conjuring empathy and sympathy for those left to toil in the margins. That talent is certainly on display in *Revelator,* where it's damn near impossible not to root for Stella but also for the family of choice she finds along the way."
                                                            —*Tor Nightfire*

"Smart, original, and scary as hell. . . . Gregory's novel is packed to the gills with action and suspense, and he has an enviable skill for characterization. . . . The Smoky Mountains of Tennessee become a character as well, and Gregory writes about them beautifully. This is an excellent work of horror, perfectly structured and dark as a Tennessee night."
                                                            —*Kirkus Reviews* (starred review)

"Full of matter-of-fact descriptions of unthinkable horror, *Revelator* is both weird and wonderful. . . . *Revelator* is full of surprises both fascinating and stomach-clenching."
                                                            —*BookPage* (starred review)

"An addictive tale of historical horror. . . . Gregory ratches up the tension in stunning prose. . . . A thrilling ride."
                                                            —*Publishers Weekly*

DARYL GREGORY

# Revelator

Daryl Gregory is the author of *Spoonbenders, Afterparty, The Devil's Alphabet,* and other novels. His novella *We Are All Completely Fine* won the World Fantasy Award and the Shirley Jackson Award.

ALSO BY DARYL GREGORY

Novels

*Spoonbenders*

*Pandemonium*

*The Devil's Alphabet*

*Raising Stony Mayhall*

*Afterparty*

*We Are All Completely Fine*

*Harrison Squared*

*The Album of Dr. Moreau*

Short Fiction

*Unpossible and Other Stories*

# Revelator

# Revelator

### Daryl Gregory

VINTAGE BOOKS
*A Division of Penguin Random House LLC*
*New York*

FIRST VINTAGE BOOKS EDITION 2024

The Library of Congress has cataloged the Knopf edition as follows:
Names: Gregory, Daryl, [date] author.
Title: Revelator : a novel / Daryl Gregory.
Description: First edition. | New York : Alfred A. Knopf, 2021.
Identifiers: LCCN 2020047832
Classification: LCC PS3607.R48836 R48 2021 (print) | DDC 813/.6—dc23
LC record available at https://lccn.loc.gov/2020047832

**Vintage Books Trade Paperback ISBN: 978-1-9848-9848-7**
**eBook ISBN: 978-0-525-65739-2**

*Author photograph © Liza Trombi*
*Book design by Cassandra J. Pappas*

vintagebooks.com

Printed in the United States of America
10  9  8  7  6  5  4  3  2  1

*For my dad, Darrell Gregory,*
*who taught me to love Cades Cove*

And when the seven thunders had uttered their voices, I was about to write: and I heard a voice from heaven saying unto me, Seal up those things which the seven thunders uttered, and write them not.

—*Revelation 10:4, King James Version*

If all the folks in Adam's race
were gathered together in one place
then I'd prepare to shed a tear
before I'd part from you, my dear.

—*"Little Brown Jug" by Joseph Eastburn Winner*

# Revelator

1

**1933**

STELLA WALLACE MET her family's god when she was nine years old. Later, she couldn't figure out why she didn't run when she saw it. It wasn't fear that pinned her to the spot, staring up at it, or even shock. It was something else. Awe, maybe. Wonder so deep it was almost adoration.

Pa said she'd been born in the cove but they'd left when she was too young to remember it. This was where her ma was born too, and where she'd come back to die when she got sick. Where all the Birches before her had lived and died. He'd never told Stella much more about it than that. He was a quiet man, could go days on a dozen words, like a camel crossing the desert. The day before, they'd spent twelve hours together in the truck going from Chicago to Lexington, then another four this morning driving into the mountains, and the whole time the only one doing any talking was the truck, engine whining up the foothills, brakes complaining on the way down. Then the biggest climb, to the top of Rich Mountain. At the gap Pa pulled into a gravel overlook. He poured water into the Ford's ticking radiator, then rolled himself a cigarette. Stella crept to the edge of the gravel and peered down at a valley spread open like a green pool.

"Is that it? This is the cove?"

Pa nodded.

"Where's Motty's house?"

Her father squinted. Stupid question, she thought. Probably couldn't see it from here. She didn't expect him to answer, and then he pointed his cigarette at a high mountain to the east. "That's Thunderhead. And over there . . ." The tip of the cigarette swung south, pointed at a high, round bulge. "That's yourn. Birch Bald."

My mountain, she thought. Not his.

"Motty's is straight down from there."

They followed the twisting road into a valley as bright and warm as a bowl of light. Pa pulled onto a rutted lane, finally rolled to a stop in a grassy clearing in front of a white, tin-roofed house. A short ways off to the side, a gray, unpainted barn sat askew as if leaning into a stiff wind. Her father stared at the house for a long minute, sighed, ran a hand through his black hair.

A gray-haired woman came out onto the porch. Scrawny neck and thick arms in a no-color housedress. A long nose like a hawk. She held a tin can, as if she'd just opened some beans.

Pa said, "Well." Got out of the truck and Stella climbed out after him.

The woman was old, and her skin was marked like Stella's, splotches of red on her cheek, her neck, her arms, like a map of an island empire. The old woman's stains were dark where Stella's were bright red, but there was no mistaking them. They shared the same skin.

The woman gestured for Stella to come forward. Stella glanced at her father, but his eyes were on the hills, as if he were standing here alone.

The old woman gripped Stella's chin, tipped her head sideways, examining those blossoms of red. Stella burned with embarrassment. She kept her arms and legs covered when she could, but nothing could hide the marks on her neck and face. She learned to avoid looking strangers in the eye, afraid to see their disgust.

Motty said, "You're a Birch, all right." Then she turned Stella's wrists and examined her palms.

"She ain't done hard work, if that's what you're wondering," Pa said. "I kept her in school."

The old woman grunted. "Town girl."

Pa said to Stella, "You stay here. Motty and I . . . need a word."

A word. Close to her father's limit. The two of them went up the steps to the porch, then inside.

After ten minutes of fanning gnats from her face, Stella climbed the porch steps. Harsh voices stopped her at the screen door. They weren't in the front room; must have gone to the back of the house. She thought about sitting in the porch swing but didn't want to make noise. She wanted to disappear.

She went around the side of the house and found a neighborhood of narrow gray houses. In the first, a ham was strung up like a prisoner. A row of miniature apartments turned out to be occupied by chickens. Then a trio of wooden boxes whose purpose she couldn't identify. And then a narrow little shack with a human-sized door. She smelled the shit before she opened it. An *outhouse*. She stared in horror at the hole in the bench. It was as wide as she was. They wouldn't expect her to squat over this thing, would they? She could fall in and never be able to climb out! And where was the toilet paper? There was nothing but a mail-order catalog on the bench.

No. No no no. There had to be a bathroom in the house. She slammed the door shut.

The yard ended at a high bank cut into the side of the mountain, curling forward like a wave. She followed the curve, running her hand along the red clay, until she was behind the house. A back door was wedged open, and she could hear the old woman talking. Demanding answers. A shadow moved in the doorway and Stella scooted out of sight, toward the barn.

Attached to that building was an open shed—a roof nailed to the barn at the low end and angling upward to two posts like stout legs. A fence of wood rails and barbwire guarded an expanse of churned-up dirt, a muddy puddle, and an empty steel trough. Then she realized that in the dark shade of that roof lay an enormous creature. A pig, unmoving, as big as a hippo. She put her hands on the fence. Could it see her? Was it even alive?

The beast moved. Stepped out of the shade, staring at her.

"Hey, piggie piggie."

It answered her with a sound like a cough.

She put her hand between the fence rails. "C'mere. C'mere, piggy."

It charged at her. She jumped back and its head slammed against the fence. She stumbled, fell back on her butt. The animal looked at her for a long moment, between the two lowest rails, its eyes even with hers. Then suddenly it turned aside. Scraped its bristly hide against the wooden rails. Ambled away from her.

Stella got to her feet, feeling stupid. It was behind a fence. What was she afraid of?

She went up to the fence and kicked the rail. "You go to hades, pig."

The animal ignored her.

She started for the mouth of the barn and stopped. The trees behind the pigpen had moved in a sneaky way. She went still, trying to detect what was in that thick brush. A bear? She'd like to see a bear.

She stepped toward a pair of trees leaning into each other like giraffe necks. A dirt path cut between them.

She looked back at the house, then at the path. No choice, really. She scampered between the cross trees.

The path turned steep, but the surface was smooth and the edges sharp. An important trail then, hundreds of years old, carved out by the Cherokee. Warpath! She followed it up, up, across an interruption of gray stone, and around a hairpin. She looked down and was surprised to see the roof of the old woman's barn, and the house's stone chimney. Kept climbing.

A white shape peeked through the trees—a building. The path led to it.

It was a steep-roofed house set into the slope of the mountain, all white clapboard, no windows in front and only a wide door set at the center. A long, deep scratch zigzagged along the door's surface like a letter from a foreign alphabet.

She pulled on the iron handle. It didn't budge. She set her feet and heaved. The lip of the door scraped over a stone threshold.

The light behind her showed her rows of church pews, four on each side of a center aisle. She'd gone to a church once, with a teacher who took pity on her, because Pa refused to walk into one. Where the podium should have been was a wide, blank stage with some kind of black carpet lying askew on it. The only window in the church was a small square thing high on the back wall.

Where was the cross? Seemed like there ought to be a cross.

The air smelled like sawdust. A lick of cold touched her face.

She crept forward, led by that feather of cold across her nose.

The black on the stage wasn't a carpet—it was a hole, swallowing the light. A wide plank that had covered it had been pushed aside. Was this one of those baptizing pools? Some of her classmates in Chicago had been baptized.

Stella leaned over it. Wooden steps led down from one end, into the black. Dank air whispered around its edges.

This was no pool. But she knew exactly what this was. She was a girl who read novels about castles. She'd been waiting her entire life to discover a secret passage.

She glanced back at the church entrance, which seemed farther away than she expected. Stepped down. Cold air swirled across her legs. Bit by bit she climbed down into the earth.

Sixteen steps, and her feet found the dirt bottom. The hole barely allowed any light; darkness surrounded her. The air smelled like a muddy riverbank.

She put out a hand and shuffled forward. Her fingers touched something cool and slick as toad skin and she yanked her hand back. Yet still she didn't leave. She could go up and pull that trapdoor over her and her father would never find her. He'd send for search parties and they'd comb the forests and even come into this church and never find this cave. Newspapers would print her picture. Years later men would scratch their beards and say, well, I guess the Indians got her.

She took another step, and something in the air changed. A trembling, a thrum she felt in her chest. She looked around, eyes wide against the dark. And then she heard another sound, penetrating the thrum: a scrape like a knife caressing a stone. She looked up.

Above her, a gleam like moonlight on a china plate. She reached toward it, unsure how far away it was, then froze.

The pale, smooth surface belonged to something very large. She could barely see it, and couldn't make out its shape. But she could feel it. The presence loomed over her, gazing down, listening to her—every breath a roar.

She couldn't move. The scrape came again. A limb—a long, chalky limb, flat as a blade—eased toward her. Other limbs unfolded. It descended like a spider.

Something seized the back of her neck. She screamed. A hand gripped her jaw.

*"How did you get in here?"* Her grandmother, shouting in her face out of the dark. So furious.

She pulled Stella toward the steps, shoved her up. She fell onto the altar floor. After the dark of the cave, the church seemed so much brighter. Motty climbed out of the hole, cursing. She picked up the plank with surprising ease, then dropped it across the hole with a *boom*.

Stella blinked up at her, afraid. "I'm sorry, I don't—"

"You *never* go in here, do you hear?" Stella nodded and Motty said, "Say it!"

"I'll never."

The old woman yanked her to her feet. "Your father's calling for you. Go."

She didn't know what she'd seen. Didn't have a name for it. She wouldn't know either of those things for a while.

HER FATHER WAS PACING beside the truck, scanning the trees. Stella's cardboard suitcase and her wicker basket of personals sat on the porch's front steps. She didn't want to go to him.

Then he saw her. Saw that she'd been crying. His face went hard, as if she'd disappointed him terribly. She rubbed the tears from her eyes. She wanted to tell him about what she saw. If he hadn't looked at her like that maybe she would have.

Instead she said, "How long?" She'd asked him this a dozen times. Usually he didn't answer. Sometimes he said what he said now: "Till I find work."

Tears popped into her eyes again, and she blinked them away. "And then you'll come get me?"

He didn't answer.

*"Promise."*

Pa and her, they never knew what to do with each other. He couldn't talk to her, and she didn't know how to draw him out.

He ran a hand across his jaw. "Your mama's people . . ." He looked at the house behind her, seemed to change his mind about what he was going to say. Her grandmother stood on the porch, hands on hips, watching them. "Motty'll take good care of you. She been waiting for you a long time."

Later, when she thought about this day, it wasn't the creature in the cave that most shook her. Oh, it should have scared her to death, and the fact that it didn't was a strangeness in herself she'd ponder about for years. What did frighten her was her father's coldness. Her pa was gone already, standing in front of her.

She wanted to punch him, just to wake him up. But her body betrayed her and went to him and hugged him. She didn't have a say in it. After a while he pulled her arms from his waist.

She watched the truck back up, turn awkwardly, and rattle out of the yard.

"Might as well come on in," Motty said. Pretending like she hadn't been ready to whup Stella a minute ago. "Supper's on."

But Stella wouldn't come in. She wanted her father to look back and see her standing there. When he got to the top of Rich Mountain she wanted him to look down and see her burning like a bonfire.

2

1948

**M**OST TIMES IT ONLY took that one sip.

Stella watched Willie Teffeteller start to put down the Mason jar—and then the second burn hit him. He looked at the jar like he was about to weep. Like a man in love. "God damn, Stella."

"This batch came out pretty well, I have to say." She said that every time, and Willie didn't mind, because she was always correct.

"God *damn*." He sipped again. "Is that peach I taste?"

"You know I can't share family secrets." She was leaning into the country accent and these boys were eating it up. Couldn't get enough of this hillbilly chickadee bootlegging the pure stuff, straight from Uncle Dan's still. "Let's just say it's two parts science and one part mystery."

Willie was still shaking his head at the wonder of it. It was after midnight and a dozen men sat in the tavern, most of them fresh off second shift at Alcoa and not ready to go home. The regulars knew Stella, but an elaborately Brylcreemed boy a couple of stools away was absolutely boggled to find an unattended woman in his vicinity. This was why she wore pants when working.

"You ready to finally stop fooling around with that swamp water you've been buying?" she asked. She'd been working on Willie for months to make her his sole supplier. He usually bought from Lester Mapes, whose hooch she knew firsthand proofed all over the map, from 190 to 100, and it went down like a mouthful of gravel. "I'll match his price, and you won't have to worry you might be serving watered-down shine."

"I don't know. I been with Lester a long time."

"I promise you a hundred fifty proof. Every gallon. Every time." She knew very well that he'd water it down himself. But at least he'd be able to do it with confidence. Dilute some 100-proof to 75 or 50 and your customers took exception.

"Can you get it to me before the weekend?"

Meaning tomorrow. She projected a smile. "How much we talking?"

"Let's start with two barrels."

A hundred and ten gallons! She nodded as if this wasn't four times what she'd been expecting. "That'll do. Uncle Dan told me he's got a private stash, aging as we speak."

"Is that so?" Willie had to suspect she was bootlegging for more than one distiller.

"And I'm sure he'd part with it if I showed him cash money."

"You reckon half now, half later would satisfy him?"

She gave him the smile he was waiting for. "I reckon it would."

Willie went into his back room to retrieve the money. From behind her a voice said, "Say, Stella! How's Uncle Dan doing?" It came from a broad-faced man in olive-green coveralls.

His drinking buddy said, "Yeah, what's that ol' rascal been up to?"

Stella laughed and shook her head. "He's doing just fine."

"Come on now, you got to give us a little news."

It'd be good business if she sat around with these half-drunk customers and started telling Uncle Dan stories. White southerners feasted on nostalgia, even the manufactured kind. They loved tales of true country folk, authentic and unsullied, running barefoot in the hollers and living life the way it was supposed to be lived. Nobody thought of *themselves* as a hillbilly, but they liked knowing they were out there somewhere, like the buffalo.

"Sorry, boys," she said. Alfonse was waiting for her, and they had a few more stops to make tonight. She told them, "Next time I'll have a report for sure."

Willie came back and passed her a paper bag.

"I'll have Alfonse drop off your order tomorrow," she said. "He'll knock twice at the back door."

"That colored boy?" Willie laughed as he tucked the jar under the pine-top bar. "I'll make sure to lock the door."

Stella didn't move. Willie felt the change in the air, looked up, confused. He tried a laugh. "What's going on? What are you—?"

Stella got ahold of herself. Took a breath. "Two knocks."

ACROSS THE STREET, Alfonse Bowlin leaned against Stella's '41 Ford coupe, cigarette in hand, making loitering look elegant. "How's Mr. Teffeteller tonight?"

"The same." She didn't mention the *colored boy* crack. "He'll take two."

"Two gallons! That God damn cheap—"

"Barrels." Laughed to see his face light up. "Top that, Mr. Bowlin."

"You're just trying to show me up." The next two stops were in Hall, Alcoa's Black neighborhood, and it would be Stella's turn to wait by the car while he made the sale. Alfonse was a hell of a salesman, but 110 gallons in one order was a career-high bar for both of them.

She took a Lucky Strike from behind her ear and lit it with her Zippo, just to be sociable. "I think he'll take even more next week if we don't mess this up."

"Where's all this whiskey going to come from? We already promised everything you said you could make. Pee Wee alone's on tap for seventy gallons."

"I know what we've promised. But between me and Hump, we can work around the clock and make enough for Willie *and* our existing clientele."

"Oh, they're clientele now?"

"That's business talk for customers who pay full price."

He chuckled and put up his hands. "You're the boss."

"Damn straight." Their customers thought Stella was just a bootlegger like Alfonse, running hooch cooked up by the mysterious Uncle Dan. Her secret, maintained for professional reasons, was that she was the sole distiller, with some assistance from Hump Cornette. That boy wasn't the brightest employee, but he was loyal and eager to please.

Alfonse started to ask a question, but headlights were coming up the highway. No mistaking the three beacons on the roof—it was a radio car, looked like a Plymouth. Not Alcoa police, then; they drove Dodge.

The car zipped past them, hit the brakes. Alfonse swore. They watched in silence as the car backed down the middle of the highway and stopped beside them. "Blount County Sheriff" on the door, the driver's window down.

"Jesus Christ, Bobby," Stella said. "You like to give me a heart attack."

Bobby Reed was Sheriff Whaley's deputy. Whaley was a pain in the ass and a worry to her business, but Bobby was all right, a longtime acquaintance who appreciated the occasional jar left on his doorstep. "I've been looking all over for you, Stella. I got a message for you."

He glanced at Alfonse. Bobby was good people, but he was still white people. Nobody around here cared for Stella driving around with a Black man. Alfonse had let it be known that he wasn't African but Melungeon—Dutch and Indian and a little Portuguese, probably more Caucasian than some of the sons of the Confederacy—but that didn't carry any weight with white folks: dusky skin was midnight black as far as they were concerned.

Stella said, "Whatever it is, you can say it in front of Alfonse." Alfonse raised his cigarette in salute, not quite disrespectful.

Bobby said, "It came through the prayer chain."

Stella grunted. She hadn't heard that phrase in years. A cold feeling came up in her stomach like rising water.

He said, "Abby Whitt wanted to get you word, soon as possible."

She blinked hard. "Get to the point."

The deputy spoke. Two words, and they were swallowed up by a roar in her head like radio static. Alfonse asked her if she was all right. She put a hand out to him, then stopped herself before she touched him. Bobby stared at her.

"What did you say?" she asked. The question was automatic, a delaying action. The words were there if she wanted to hear them, like the shout of a drowning man in heavy surf.

*Motty's passed.*


SHE DROVE ALFONSE back to his Chevy, tucked away behind the trees just off 129. Alfonse offered to stay with her, but she told him no, he could collect the rest of the orders in Hall, leave the white deliveries till morning. Nobody'd bother him if he stayed in the Black part of town.

To her consternation, he wouldn't get out of the car. "You sure you're all right?" he asked.

"I'm fine."

"Not convincing, Stel, not convincing. I was in France when I lost my mamaw and I cried like a baby."

"You won't see any tears from me. Motty was mean as a snake."

He laughed. "Is that why you looked so mad?"

"What are you talking about?"

"Bobby Reed told you she'd passed, and at first you looked like you was about to fall over—and then you got that look."

"Look?"

"Like you're about to punch a drunk in the throat."

Now it was her turn to laugh. "That wasn't anger, that was disappointment. I never thought she'd die in her sleep. I expected her to go down in a hail of bullets."

"So why you going up, right this minute?" Alfonse asked. "She'll still be dead in the morning."

That was the truth. And Motty would still be dead in a month and a year. Maybe in a dozen years Stella would be ready to go back to the cove. She said, "I got no choice."

He pursed his lips. "Care to elaborate?"

She didn't care to, no. Then: "I never told you much about my family."

"You never told me a thing about your family. That's all right, I figure it was your business."

"I got a cousin, living up there alone with Motty. She's just ten."

"She's alone in that house with a dead body?"

"Maybe." Uncle Hendrick, Motty's younger brother, lived in Atlanta, a day's drive away, and if he'd gotten word about Motty he'd be on the road already. She couldn't let him get to the house before her. "Though I'm hoping Abby's with her."

"This is the same Abby who taught you to moonshine?"

"You'd like him."

"I'd certainly like to shake his hand. Thanks to him I can make a living—bootlegging beats the hell out of the alternative." Alfonse had come out of the army with two options: go back to mining bauxite like he'd done before the war, or work in the Alcoa pot room with his daddy. Then he'd met Stella, and a third way appeared.

He reached for the door handle but didn't get out. "Anything you need, you call me, all right?"

"I'll be fine."

"Promise me."

No doubt plenty of people assumed she and Alfonse were screwing. And it was true the two of them had recognized straight off they were the perfect match—just not for romance. It wasn't color that made it impossible, though that might have been enough. And it wasn't that he was an unattractive man. But early on they realized they could do something much rarer than make love—they could make money. They called it their Moonshine Marriage.

She kissed his cheek. "My Hooch Husband."

"My Whiskey Wife."

She took out the paper bag of cash she'd gotten from Willie, then handed the whole wad to Alfonse. "Have Hump buy more supplies. We're low on everything—sugar, mash, malt. And tell him to buy white oak charcoal, because we're going to need to speed up the aging. Then as soon as he can, start running a batch."

"White oak charcoal. All right." Alfonse was a bootlegger and a salesman, and mostly stayed out of the way when Stella was cooking. "Has Hump ever run the still on his own?"

"First time for everything. I'll try to get back as soon as I can."

Alfonse didn't like the sound of that, but he was a gentleman about it. "Be careful up there, Stella. Those hillbillies are crazy."

"Not crazier than me."

"Fair enough." He got out of the car, then leaned through the window. "So what's her name? This girl cousin."

Stella put the Ford in gear. Suppressed a sigh.

"Sunny."


WITH THE NEW PAVED ROAD, it took most tourists over an hour to get from Maryville to the Great Smoky Mountains National Park. Stella made it in thirty-five minutes without even pushing the Ford hard. Not two months ago, she and Alfonse had dropped a brand-new engine into the old car, a Cadillac overhead-valve V8 with 190 horsepower. It was like jamming a cheetah's heart into a barn cat's body. She roared past the park gate without touching the brakes. A few minutes later she was deep in the cove.

Out of bootlegger's habit she cut the lights and the engine and coasted into the front yard. The house was dark except for a pair of hurricane lamps burning in the windows. She watched the front door until the steering wheel turned slick under her palms.

Ten years ago she'd told Motty she was never coming back to this place. It had never occurred to her that Motty would force her hand by up and dying.

Stella stepped up to the front door, knocked. After a while she pushed it open but didn't step inside. The room was lit only by those lamps.

She called out, "Sunny?"

She waited a mite longer, and then stepped in.

Even in the gloom the house felt the same as when she left. She knew without taking inventory that everything was still in its place. The hook rug under foot, the cane chairs, the rack holding three guns as familiar to her as family dogs: Motty's .22 single-shot, her Winchester Model 97 shotgun, and Long Tom, the ancient family long rifle, passed down from Russell Birch himself.

The house smelled the same, too; decades of wood smoke and tobacco and bacon grease had soaked into the timbers.

The only thing different was herself. She could see now how cramped and dark and worn out the house was, like a tiny wooden ship on a long voyage.

She walked down the short hallway that ran between the front room and the kitchen. Her old bedroom was on the right. She knocked on the door and said, "Sunny?" Eased the door open. The room was dark, but a few shapes were visible: her old chiffarobe, hulking in the same corner as always, and her bed, now against the north wall.

The girl wasn't there.

Had Uncle Hendrick already gotten there and carried her off? It didn't seem possible. Sunny had to be up the mountain, with Abby.

Stella went into the second bedroom.

Two lit kerosene lamps on the windowsill and one on Motty's Singer sewing machine, making the air shimmer. The iron-frame bed seemed to float above the dark floor. Motty lay in the center of the bed with her arms crossed over her belly and eyes closed. The patchwork quilt, the old blue star one that had been Stella's favorite, lay unwrinkled across her, the pillow placed just so under her head. Was this Sunny's work? It was worthy of an undertaker.

Stella stared at Motty's face for a long time. The flickering lamplight made it seem as if she might be breathing. At any moment she'd open her eyes and say, *What the hell you looking at?*

Motty's glasses and the jar containing her teeth were in their usual spots atop the sewing machine. A Bible lay on the seat of a chair, open to a page late in the New Testament, one verse underlined. It was Stella's own Bible, the one she'd left behind when she ran away from the place. She'd gotten it as a gift when she was twelve years old and remembered underlining that passage.

*Seal up those things which the seven thunders uttered, and write them not.*

Who set out the Bible? Motty wouldn't have been looking through it before she died; she'd never been one for scripture, of any religion.

Stella touched the back of her hand to Motty's cheek. She'd braced herself for the coldness, thinking it would feel like a slab of hog flesh—Stella had butchered and hung her share of hogs—but it was a shock just the same. This dead body was a mistake. A wrongness. When she first came to the cove as a child, Stella thought Motty was ancient, even though she couldn't have been more than sixty. Eventually she came to seem not old but ageless, permanent as the mountain.

Stella sat on the edge of the bed and folded back the quilt. Motty wore her old housedress, the one with the pink ceramic buttons. Stella turned the body's arm, ran a thumb over the palm. The skin was heavily calloused, crossed and recrossed with scars like a switchyard—but unbloodied. The other hand, harder to see in the dim light, also seemed unwounded, and as scarred as always.

For five years it had been just the two of them on this farm. There'd been no privacy, no modesty. They took turns bathing in a steel tub in the kitchen, went braless in the heat. When Stella went through puberty, it was Motty who explained her new body to her, who belted on her first sanitary pad. Stella rubbed the Jergens lotion between Motty's shoulders, massaged her blue-veined calves, buttoned her Sunday dress from behind. On the coldest nights they slept in the same bed. This leftover body seemed like some kind of trick.

She undid the first button of Motty's dress, and the next. Pressed a hand to the old woman's throat, then moved her hand slowly down, between her breasts, across her cold belly. It was a stupid gesture; the wound she was looking for would be near impossible to see in this light, much less find by touch.

She reached for the lantern. Set it on Motty's belly, holding the top of it with one hand. The woman's pale skin, exposed like this, was obscene.

Stella leaned close. There. A puckered bruise like a yellow-jacket's sting, surrounding a trio of dots. No one looking at it would take it for a killing wound. But Stella knew.

The God in the Mountain had killed her.

A sound. Stella jerked upright, glimpsed a shadow moving in the hallway. Then quick steps, running away.

Stella shouted and lurched into the hallway, still holding the lantern. The kitchen door banged open, and a figure threw itself into the backyard, small and rabbit quick.

Sunny.

Stella chased, calling the girl's name. Somehow Sunny had already crossed the yard. She vanished into the shadow beside the hog pen and seconds later reappeared, on the hill above the barn. Stella caught only a flash of a pale dress, a spray of dark hair. In the moonlight her arms and legs seemed strange, a swirl of light and shadow. Then the trees swallowed her.

Stella ran for the path between the crossed trees. As she passed the hog pen she glanced into the dark under that roof and it seemed empty, thank God. Then she started up the hill.

MINUTES LATER STELLA was bent over, huffing hard, sweat running down her back. It had been ten years and ten thousand cigarettes since she'd run up those switchbacks.

The front door to the chapel hung open. The arm of a shiny padlock was hooked over the handle.

Stella spit. Stood up, hands on hips. Summoned a yell. "Sunny! You don't have to run!"

She took a few steps into the building. "Did Motty talk to you about me?"

Only the nearest pew was visible; the rest were waiting there in the dark. The air smelled smoky and faintly sweet, like the inside of a charred whiskey barrel. She scanned the room, willing her eyes to adjust. Where was the high window in the far wall? She ought to be able to make it out against the dark.

"You don't have to be afraid," Stella said. She moved forward, hands out, thankful the aisle between the pews she remembered was still there. Her toes found the edge of the platform. She froze, put out a hand. Was the floor open? If she took a step she could plummet.

Stella knelt, reached out. Her fingers found a rough, stony surface. What the hell?

She ran her hand across the pebbly surface. It was concrete. She crawled forward, hands out, waiting for her eyes to adjust. The entrance to the God's cave had been sealed. When had Motty done this? It made no sense.

A sound like a breath. Stella jerked her head up. High up on the wall behind the pulpit, a silhouette in the frame of the small window, crouched like a gargoyle.

"Sunny?"

The shape moved and pushed backward out of the window. Stella shouted, jumped to her feet.

She ran toward the front of the chapel—and nearly collided with a tall figure walking in. A deep voice said, "Hey there, Little Star."

Abby! Stella grabbed his arm. "The girl—Sunny. She just jumped out of a ten-foot window."

"Yeah," Abby said. "She does that."

## 3

**1933**

FOR THAT FIRST MONTH in the cove Stella carried the secret like a snake wound around her heart. She couldn't speak to her grandmother about it, and she didn't know if she could confide in the only other person on the farm, Abby Whitt, Motty's hired man. He was the biggest man she'd ever met, twice the size of her pa, each naked bicep as wide as a ham. When he sweat he had to mop his bald head with a huge rag he kept in his back pocket.

The old woman had ordered Abby to bolt a latch on the chapel door and hang a huge brass padlock on it. Stella was to never go near it, and Stella obeyed. Whatever was in that cave didn't scare her, but her grandmother sure did.

Motty had worked her like a mule. Stella raked hay behind Abby as he swung the scythe, fed the chickens, braved the terrifying hogs. She collected the eggs and filled the cistern and scrubbed the sheets and dug up potatoes. Every Wednesday and Saturday she swept and mopped the floors and dusted the house with a damp rag.

She told herself she was as much a slave as Mrs. Shelby's Eliza. Only two things kept her from running away to find Pa. One was the promise of fall, when she could start school—a small, country school, far from the multitude of yahoos in Chicago. The other was Abby.

She'd attached herself to him like a burr on a dog, and whenever she was done with chores she followed him around the farm. Sometimes she'd catch him looking at her with a serious look, and then, seeing he'd been caught, he'd wink or laugh or widen his eyes, playing it off comic. She didn't understand what that was about.

One hot day he was getting into his beaten-down Model A and she climbed into the passenger seat without asking permission. "Where we going?" she asked.

"Get out now. I'm helping some folks move house. You can't come because we'll be working."

"I can work. All my chores here is done." Which was mostly true, and she kept arguing until he gave up and started the car. The engine roared when he hit the pedal. This old car *flew*, so much faster than Pa's truck. But when they hit a rough spot it liked to have thrown her through the roof.

Abby chuckled. "Heavy springs for heavy loads." And for sure he was a big man, hardly fit behind that steering wheel. His shirt was half open, exposing a potbelly barely restrained by a white T-shirt. He pointed the car west, up a road she didn't know. Then again, she'd hardly seen any of the cove.

Stella asked, "You think I'll ever run into a panther like Uncle Dan?"

He grunted, kept driving. She didn't let that put her off.

"I never seen a panther," she said.

A front wheel dropped into a pothole and the car lurched toward the trees. Abby yelled, "Fuck me!" and yanked on the wheel.

Ooh, Stella thought. That's a good one.

Abby straightened the car, slowed a bit. He glanced at her, looking chagrined. "You're too young for those words."

"Am not." She'd heard plenty of swears back home, though she'd never heard anyone say fuck *me*. It was practically polite, like offering to load the gun of the gangster robbing you.

"Well, I'd appreciate it if you didn't tell Motty I said that."

"Tick tock, close the lock, throw away the key." Stella tossed it out the passenger window. "Now, what was it you was saying about panthers?"

He squinted at her, weighing whether to go along with this blackmail. Finally he said, "You'd make a pretty snack."

"Not if I met Uncle Dan's friend," she said, egging him on.

"Y'uns better beware up in them hills," he said in his Uncle Dan voice, which came out like *yuns bare bewaaare up 'n em hae'l*. Stella laughed in delight. She'd never met Uncle Dan, but she was sure she'd recognize him by his voice, a slurry of vowels coming from so far back in his throat he sounded like he was shouting from a mile away. "Panthers, bears, bushwhackers—"

"Bushwhackers!" A new word.

"Oh lord yes," he said in his normal voice. "Motty didn't tell you about your great-great-granddad Russell Birch and those Carolina bushwhackers?"

She was dying to hear. "Well, this was at the tail end of the war." His voice carried easily over the wind noise. "The Rebel soldiers didn't care much for people in the cove. You see, this part of Tennessee had voted to stay in the Union." When the South started losing, he went on, renegade soldiers who were cut off from the main army would ride into the cove through North Carolina passes and steal cattle and take cove folks' stores. Russell Birch organized a home guard made up of women, children, and old men, and they'd try to scare off the renegades with nothing but hunting rifles.

"Like Long Tom," Stella said. Russell's famous rifle hung in the front room.

"Just so." The road had turned into not much more than a goat path, and he was going careful now.

"And one night," Abby said, "those bushwhackers decided they'd just murder Russell in his bed and solve that problem." He nodded at the hill above the barn, in the direction of the chapel. "Came down at midnight, right about there."

"What happened?"

"The next morning, Russell walked out and found their bodies all laid out in the yard. Four Rebel soldiers, stone-cold dead."

A squeak escaped her. "Who shot them?"

"They weren't shot. Not a mark on 'em."

"Then how?"

"Well now—" He caught himself. Started again. "You ought to ask Motty about that."

"Motty won't tell me nothing. She hates me."

"No she don't. She's just a tough old bird."

"Tell me."

"It ain't my place. I told you what everybody knows. Motty may have her own story."

This infuriated her. "I already know. I saw it."

He looked over at her. "Saw what?"

"I don't know what to call it," she said. "I saw it in the chapel. In that hole in the floor."

He looked back at the road. Said nothing. But she was used to men who refused to speak.

"The first day I was here," she said. "I walked to the chapel, and down those steps." Abby kept his eyes on the windshield. "And something came down out of the dark."

Abby braked the car, bowed up right in the middle of the road. The engine stuttered and died. "I was just telling a story," Abby said. "I shouldn't have done that."

"*I'm* not telling a story," she said. "It was there in the room with me. I know that down to my bones."

"You tell Motty about this?"

"She knows what I saw. She told me I wasn't allowed in there. Why else would she have you put a lock on the door?"

"Because it ain't no play house. It's a house of—it's not for children to run around in."

Stella balled her fists. She'd finally shown someone her deadly secret, and he'd told her it wasn't anything at all. He'd called her a liar.

Abby put up his hands. "I take it back. Stand down, soldier."

But he was still playacting, and she would not accept his surrender. Then he said, "How about you drive?"

A jolt went through her. "What now?"

"It's just a ways up the road." She scooched onto his lap and gripped the wheel with both hands. Her legs were too short for the pedals. He started the car with a complicated series of gestures.

"One more thing," he said into her ear. "These people we're going to help, the Ledbetters? They're losing the only home they know, you understand?"

"The park kicked them out because they don't have a life lease like Motty."

"Not many do. So they've got their own sadness going on. They don't need you telling stories."

I'll tell who I want, she thought. And someday she'd find somebody who believed her.

"Hit the gas," she said.

FOR THE NEXT few hours Stella wrapped up dishes in squares of burlap while Mrs. Ledbetter packed them into the trunk. The woman wasn't weeping, but her face was all dead like she'd been awake for a week. She barely spoke. Didn't even seem to notice all the colored spots on Stella's skin. Mr. Ledbetter and his skinny son, however, did nothing but bark at each other. All morning they'd been ferrying furniture out of that two-story house to a big hay truck, and they would have been at it all day if Abby hadn't shown up. He was a giant compared to them, fiercely strong, and he never took breaks. He even carried out their iron stove by himself—just hoisted it onto his back and held on to it with a belt across his chest. When it thunked onto the truck bed Mr. Ledbetter and his son hooted and clapped. Abby wiped the sweat from his gleaming forehead, went to his car, and came back with a jug. He took a long pull, then handed it to Mr. Ledbetter. He took a sip and grimaced, and Abby laughed.

Mrs. Ledbetter gave Stella a long look. "So you're staying in the cove and I'm leaving."

"Not for long. My daddy's coming back when he finds work."

"I'm sure he is."

Stella's cheeks heated. Stella had never met Mrs. Ledbetter before today, but Motty said everybody was always into their business.

"You stand up for yourself," Mrs. Ledbetter said. "People looked down at your mama for leaving you, and she paid the cost. But that ain't no shame on you."

Stella felt her eyes sting. *Paid the cost?* Did everybody in the cove think her mama deserved to die for her sins?

Before she could find words to defend her mother, a black horse trotted into the yard, pulling a small black buggy.

A tall man stepped down, and a boy a little older than Stella jumped out after him. The tall man shook Mr. Ledbetter's hand and said, "This is a sad day, a sad day."

Abby quietly set the jug on the ground behind him.

Mrs. Ledbetter came forward, and now, suddenly, there were

tears in her eyes. "You didn't have to come, Elder Rayburn. But I appreciate it, I surely do."

"And I will surely miss your singing voice," the man said. "I hope you'll be able to come back for a service or two. It would warm my heart." The adults kept talking, and Stella gathered that he was pastor at the Primitive Baptist Church, and the Ledbetters were longtime members. The whole time they were talking, the man's son was staring at Stella.

Finally Elder Rayburn turned his attention to her. "You must be Motty's granddaughter. Stella, is it? It's a pleasure to meet you."

Stella looked at Abby and he nodded. She extended her hand and the elder's bony hand wrapped hers like a bundle of sticks.

"This is my son, Lincoln," he said.

"Hi." He was still staring at her.

Stella didn't like it. She said, "Can I look at your horse?"

"Why?" the boy asked.

"Because it's a horse."

Elder Rayburn said, "Show her Miss Jane, Lincoln."

Stella walked up to the animal. It watched her with big eyes. Then she touched its neck, marveling at its warmth. The horse dipped her head.

The boy was staring at Stella again.

"What's your problem?" she asked him.

The boy said, "I ain't never seen somebody with skin like yours."

"And I never met a boy named after a car."

"I'm not named after a car!"

"Sure you are. The car came first, and you were named after. That's facts."

"I was named after Abraham Lincoln."

She looked at him. "Why didn't they name you Abraham,

then?" Before he could answer she said, "What's your middle name, Log?"

"What?"

"Don't you get beat up at school? I thought hillbillies didn't like Lincoln."

"He was our greatest president! The cove voted Union. We weren't no slaveholders."

"I don't believe it."

"We weren't! Just ask my daddy. Lincoln was a great man."

"Tell you what," she said. "I'll just call you Lunk."

He was shocked. Had no girl ever talked back to him? Then, suddenly, he laughed. "You're something, Stella."

"We're all something." She put her cheek close to the horse's neck. Breathed in.

"You going to school in the fall?" the boy asked. "You're my sister's age. Do you know how to read?"

"Of course I know how to read. Don't be ignorant."

"Well, you're living out there alone with Motty Birch." Stella thought, What does that have to do with anything? Then he said, "How about arithmetic?"

"Ask me one more stupid question," Stella said, "and I'll punch you in the nose."

The men finished loading the hay truck, and Elder Rayburn called for a prayer. Everybody closed their eyes, except Stella— and Abby. While the elder's deep voice droned on, Abby slipped the jug into the floorboard of the truck. He was back in place by the time they said Amen.


UNCLE HENDRICK AND HIS FAMILY visited for the first time that late August. Stella had never been in the presence of such fancy people. Uncle Hendrick carried a beautiful green suitcase—a color she didn't know leather could be. His blue suit was shot through with silver thread, and a silver bar yoked the wings of his collar and propped up the knot of a tie that was as vibrant and gaudy as a butterfly wing. She gawked at his black-and-white shoes and sheer socks.

Compared to Uncle Hendrick, Aunt Ruth was plain as toast, a sharp-eyed woman in a cream frock who kept her eyes on her husband like a hunting dog waiting for the gun to go off. Their daughter, though, was a princess. *Veronica.* Blonde, curly-haired. Couldn't have been more than five years old, but her gauzy lime-green dress was more expensive than anything Stella had ever owned. She sat beside her mother, kicking her little patent-leather shoes, sucking on a hard candy. No one had offered Stella candy.

Uncle Hendrick gestured Stella forward. She stood in front of him, not sure where to put her eyes. She wore her best dress, a thin cotton thing Pa had bought her last summer, with three flowers embroidered on it. Before the relatives had walked in with all their finery she'd been proud of it.

Uncle Hendrick went down on one knee. "Hello there, Stella." His voice was soft. He smelled like a barbershop. He put out his hands, asking for hers, and inspected her palms the way Motty had that first day.

"Are you sure?" he asked Motty.

"Lord almighty," Motty said. "Raymond Wallace brought her here. You think he just grabbed some speckled orphan off the street?"

He winced. "Now, Motty, I didn't say—"

"Look at her. Look at that skin. Tell me that ain't Lena's daughter."

Stella wanted to crawl away. She hated when someone pointed out the red blotches. And Uncle Hendrick was staring at her harder now, wouldn't let go of her hands. After a terribly long time he said, "It's you, isn't it?"

She didn't know how to answer that.

Then he asked, "Do you know how special you are?"

She didn't know how to answer that, either. The little girl, Veronica, said, "I'm special."

"Yes, you are," Aunt Ruth said.

"I thought all was lost when Lena passed," Uncle Hendrick said, as if he were talking to himself. "All lost."

Stella pulled her hands out of his. She could hear Mrs. Ledbetter's voice in her ear.

Hendrick said to Motty, "She hasn't been inside yet, has she?"

*Inside.* To Stella that meant only one thing.

"She's not ready yet," Motty said. "I told you that. Not till she's twelve at the earliest."

"We can't wait that long," he said. "It's been years since Lena. Perhaps we can—"

"*Twelve*, Hendrick. The age of accountability. I won't have it otherwise." Stella was thrilled to see Motty annoyed at someone besides her.

"We can't wait years, Motty. Who knows how many messages we'll miss!"

"Don't cross me," Motty said. "Don't you even try."

Stella thought, They don't want me to go into the chapel—for years? "I ain't afraid," Stella said.

"I can see you're fearless," Hendrick said.

"Hush, both of you," Motty said. To Hendrick she said, "You've set eyes on her, you want anything else?"

Uncle Hendrick took Stella's hands again, this time at the wrists. He pursed his lips, stared at her for close to a minute. Were his eyes misting up? "Stella," he said finally. "Oh, Stella." His voice was hoarse with emotion.

Stella nodded slowly. Yes, that was her name.

"I've brought you something." He nodded to Ruth, who opened the green suitcase. She handed him a leather-bound book.

"This is *The Book of Clara*," he said. "Do you know who Clara is?"

"My great-great-grandmother. She was there when the bush-whackers came."

Hendrick was delighted. "Ha! Yes, she was! But nobody knows what really happened—nobody but us." He put the book in her hands. It was thin, and the deep red cover was blank. On the first page it said:

THE BOOK OF CLARA
*Being the First Volume of a New Revelation*
*From the God in the Mountain*
*To Clara Birch, Recorded by Russell Birch, her Husband*
*with Commentary and Clarifications*
*by Hendrick Birch*

"Russell Birch kept a diary, documenting everything that Clara saw and experienced in those years. This isn't the original, of course, that's in safekeeping. But I've had it typed up, and this book includes the commentaries—special explanatory text that I've written."

Motty snorted.

Stella sat down and began turning the thin pages. The text was typeset like a library book. The first twenty or so pages were walls of text, and didn't look like a diary so much as a history book. Then the pages changed to have two columns.

Hendrick had moved to hover over her. "Those are the things Russell recorded on the left, and my commentary on the right." The right-hand column was much wider than the left.

"It starts with the story of the night the Rebels came to this farm," Hendrick said. "This is the story of the first time a Birch met the God in the Mountain."

The God in the Mountain. That was what she'd seen.

She began to flip through the pages, not reading, but looking at the diary entries. Phrases popped out at her: "the old woman of the cave"; "stone clad yet not stone cold"; "without a visible wound."

"She called it a woman," Stella said.

"Isn't that interesting?" Hendrick said. "Clara was confused. She didn't commune with it, not true communion as we now know it—that was Esther, her daughter—so of course she got some things wrong. That's why there are commentaries."

"Did you bring Esther's book, too?"

Hendrick drew back. "Aren't you eager! No, I want you to read *The Book of Clara*, and when I come back I'll answer all your questions. All right?"

"But there are more books, right? Does Motty have a book?"

"That ain't for you," Motty growled.

Hendrick glanced at his sister, and then said to Stella, "There are certain rules. We don't share the books of anyone living. Their story's not finished."

"What about my mama, then?" Stella asked.

"Her neither," Motty said.

This made no sense to Stella. Hendrick looked apologetic. "Motty's the eldest. She has say on what you're ready for. But for now, let's start with Clara! You're about to learn how special your family is, and the great things the God has promised us."

"One body, ever blooming," Aunt Ruth intoned.

"One body, ever blooming," Hendrick repeated. Stella had no idea what they were talking about, but she was alarmed to see that it had caused a tear to well up in his eye. "You don't even know what you're capable of, do you?"

She tried to answer, but then it happened: that fat tear blooped over his eyelid and ran down his cheek. He didn't even wipe at it.

"I'm ashamed to say it, I'm a little jealous of you, Stella. You have a great calling, and I'm just a . . ." He shook his head, unable to come up with a suitably humble word. "A disciple. I want to bring the word. But you, Stella, you're the one who can receive the word directly. Someday it will be *revealed* to you." He glanced at Motty. "Someday soon."

Motty said, "All right, all right. Everybody's very happy. Did you bring what was on my shopping list?"

Uncle Hendrick didn't respond; he was gazing at Stella with a rapturous expression that gave her the heebie-jeebies. Aunt Ruth said, "*Please*, Mathilda. The groceries are all in the car. Can't you give us a *moment*?"

Stella froze. Hendrick slowly turned his eyes toward Ruth. Even Veronica sensed that her mother had made a terrible, terrible mistake.

Motty didn't say another word. But in two minutes they were gone, driven like swallows before a storm.

Her grandmother stayed in a foul mood the rest of the day, but Stella was impervious to it. She went back to her chores, almost singing to herself, *You don't even know what you're capable of.*


IF IT HADN'T BEEN the night before her first day of school, she might never have heard Motty leave the house. But Stella had been tossing and turning, imagining cruel children and stern teachers. She was worried she'd get lost on the way to the schoolhouse. She was petrified that she'd look like a pauper in her cheap dress and worn shoes. She distracted herself by rereading her favorite passages from *The Book of Clara*.

Each thin page was split into two columns, everything done on typewriter so it looked official. The left was Russell Birch's words, and the right showed Hendrick's commentary.

Russell, Stella thought, wasn't much of a writer. He was vague when she craved details, and unrelentingly specific about things she didn't care about, like the amount of seed they'd planted in spring and the number of pigs they slaughtered in the fall. He also seemed pretty confused by what his wife was up to. Clara had found a cave a year earlier, the entrance "not much bigger than a bobcat's den." She'd spent hours widening the hole and exploring the chambers inside. Russell avoided the place and only went in as far as the first chamber. As the war progressed Clara spent more and more time there, maybe grieving for her son, who joined the Confederate army.

> *October 23rd, 1864*
> *Clara's worries continue and I cannot do much with her. Six or perhaps seven Rebels rode into the cove two nights ago and carried off much of D. Whitehead's stores as well as one ham. He rang the bell and several came running but we were too late. They are hungry and will return. Clara has said that our home guard of old men and women is inadequate and our root cellar no good. She has decided that the cave is to become our warehouse, unknown to the Rebels, even our son. She has already tucked away all of our potatoes and onions and cornmeal in this new hole. She means to put the pig in there too but I will not allow that. I think she would burrow in as well, with me or without me.*

Russell never said why he didn't go in, but Hendrick's commentary explained it:

> *Russell, unlike Clara, sensed the sacred nature of the place and was afraid, for good reason! Russell no doubt remembered the Lord's command to Moses to let no one go up Mount Sinai: "Whosoever toucheth the mount shall be surely put to death."*

Stella paged ahead to her favorite part, when the bushwhackers showed up to the Birch farm on a December night. It wasn't at all how Abby had told it. The four Rebels were led to the farm by Russell and Clara's own son, Cyril, which "about broke

Clara's heart." This was late in the war and her son and his fellow soldiers were a scrawny and scraggly bunch, without even a uniform between them. The strangers got angry when the root cellar was empty, and one of them pointed a rifle at Russell. It was then that Clara confessed where their food was kept and *led* them to the cave. Said, "Here, take it."

As the men climbed down into the hole, Clara put a hand on their son's shoulder and held him back. Russell wrote:

> *We heard a couple of them holler and laugh when they found our whiskey. Soon all talk ceased. We waited a long time over that hole, not hearing nothing. Cyril called down and started to go in after them, and Clara grabbed on to his arm and would not let go. She told him those boys weren't coming back. This place belonged to him now. Cyril asked who she meant, and she said its secret name.*

Oh, that secret name. Hendrick's commentary said that Russell never recorded the name, but perhaps it was one of the Hebrew names for God. Stella pondered the mystery for hours, trying out syllables on her own.

Stella was rereading that last bit of the diary—about the end of the war and Clara making the children promise not to talk about the cave—when she heard the back door creak open, then close with a careful *tock*.

Stella told herself it was just Motty heading for the outhouse, despite there being a night pan for exactly these emergencies. But it was strange that Motty had closed the door so quietly. *The Book of Clara* had put Stella in a suspicious state of mind.

Stella opened her door and crept to the kitchen. The air was cold; the wood floor colder. A cabinet drawer hung open, and a kitchen chair was out of place, standing by itself near the cupboards. That was strange. Motty liked everything in its place, and Stella herself had been the one to clean up after supper.

She went to the small window. Motty was crossing the yard in the bright moonlight. Her grandmother wore only her house-dress and a shawl. Her feet were bare, which must have stung on the cold ground; the grass gleamed silver, dew about to become frost. Just before she reached the tree line above the barn, she looked back at the house.

Stella jerked her head away from the window. For a terrifying moment she thought she'd been seen.

When she next had the courage to look, Motty was gone.

Stella stood there, shifting from foot to foot, studying that patch of moonlight. Motty didn't appear.

She thought, *You don't even know what you're capable of.* Then she ran back to her room and pulled on her shoes, not bothering with the laces.

The chapel door hung open. She stopped well back from the doorway, listening and trembling in the cold. Finally she crept forward.

At the far end of the room, two fat candles on the floor lit the edges of the cave mouth. The boards had been pushed aside. Motty was nowhere to be seen.

Stella tiptoed forward, imagining that her steps would be heard below. When she was almost to the platform, a sound arose from the hole. Motty, pleading. It was a tone Stella had never heard before in her grandmother's voice.

Stella took a step, then another. It was as if someone else controlled her body, someone braver. At the entrance to the cave she knelt down. Slowly leaned over.

Lantern light, swaying and throwing jagged shadows against the wall. Motty's voice floated out of the dark. "Please," she said. "Please—" And then she said a word, three syllables.

A chirp of surprise escaped Stella's throat.

The shadows at the base of the steps suddenly changed size. Stella jerked back her head. She ran, trying to keep her steps light as a deer's. Jumped through the doorway onto the slick grass. And in her head she chanted those syllables: *Ghostdaddy, Ghostdaddy, Ghostdaddy.*

Knowing that name changed nothing about her situation, but it made her feel differently about everything. It was not just that she shared a secret with Clara and Motty. It was that she knew something that Uncle Hendrick didn't.

The solution to the mystery so thrilled her that it was two days later before she stopped to wonder about a much larger mystery: What was it that Motty was asking the Ghostdaddy for?

1948

SEEING ABSALOM WHITT WAS like standing high above a fast river on a hot day. Stella wanted nothing more than to let herself go, but she couldn't help thinking of rocks.

"So," he said. Still filling that doorway. "I suppose the prayer chain's still working."

"The pony keg express."

He chuckled dryly. Back when Abby ran whiskey, up here in the cove with no telephone, there was a kind of postal service made up of moonshiners, drinkers, good ol' boys, guitar players, and Baptist backsliders that relayed orders from his customers and allowed Abby to let them know when he'd deliver.

"I appreciated you putting out the word." She walked toward him between the pews. He was tall as ever, but thin, so thin. Had prison done that to him? She didn't want to think about that. "I came as soon as I could."

"You sure did. Didn't expect you till morning, or, well . . ."

Or, well, if she'd come at all. He didn't have to say it for it to hurt. She said, "I saw the girl. At least I'm pretty sure."

"She's shy."

"And stays up awful late, too."

"It's true, she don't sleep much."

"So you been watching out for her?"

He stepped back out of the doorway, scratched the back of his head, looked off toward the trees. Abby had two speeds. Sober you couldn't rush him, drunk you couldn't keep up.

"She came up to my place, after what happened with Motty. I let her sleep on the couch."

"You got a *couch*? That's practically civilized."

"My bony butt got too old for wooden chairs all the time."

Stella wondered if that change came from prison, too. In the moonlight his face was haggard. He was the closest thing to a father she'd ever had, a man who'd paid a huge price to protect her—and in return she'd done him nothing but wrong.

"Uncle Hendrick's got to be on his way," Stella said. "I'd appreciate knowing how Motty died."

His eyes stayed on the treetops. There were two ways to Abby's shack from here—go up a ways to the ridge and follow that west, or head down to Motty's, cross the yard, and start back up the other side.

He said, "Let me walk you down."

Abby, being Abby, didn't speak till they'd reached Motty's barn.

"There's where she fell," Abby said, pointing to a spot behind the house.

"You found her?"

"I came down to check on them, saw her there. I carried her into the house."

"And there wasn't anything—anyone around?"

He gave her a look. Maybe he heard the tension in her voice. "It was just her," he said. "Figure it was a heart attack or a stroke. Hard to say."

Stella nodded at the house. "Who set out the Bible?"

"What do you mean?"

"Never mind." If it wasn't Abby, it was Sunny. Stella had plenty more important questions for Abby, and not much time before Hendrick spoiled everything. "You might as well stay up now," Stella said. "Let me make you some coffee."

"Naw, I better get back. Get that girl to bed."

He promised he'd be down in a while but wasn't sure if Sunny would come with him. "Like I said. Shy."

"Has Uncle Hendrick met her?"

Abby was surprised. "Of course he has."

"Really?"

"He stops by every few months. Like he does."

Fuck me, Stella thought.

"You don't have to worry about him," Abby said. "Hendrick is Hendrick, and he ain't—"

"Has he held a service for her? In this chapel?"

Abby gawped at her.

"Tell me," Stella said.

"I don't know anything about that. You know I don't get involved."

"You're involved enough to cement over that hole. Come on, I know Motty didn't do it herself, that's what she has you for."

"She asked me to do it, and I did it."

"When was this?"

"Just last week."

So Hendrick didn't know about that yet. "Did she say why she wanted to seal it off?"

"I didn't ask. I don't have anything to do with that Birchy churchy stuff."

*"Birchy churchy?"* Stella laughed. "Is that what you call it?"

He looked pained, and she regretted the laugh. Abby had never been a professional at hiding his emotions, but there was a nakedness to him now. She'd have to be careful with him.

He said, "You should talk to Sunny."

"Maybe if she stops running away from me."

Stella stepped onto the back porch. Stared at the roller washer, the bane of her childhood. She'd spent hours cranking that thing.

"So what are you going to do?" Abby asked.

Her breath caught. Stella waved a hand without turning around. "I'm just trying to get through the funeral." That wasn't what he was asking, and she knew it.

"You're all she's got," he said.

"She's got you."

"Stella."

She looked at him. "She obviously trusts you. We could work something out. I could help support her."

"It ain't my place," Abby said. "Motty wanted you."

"She say that in her will and testament? Otherwise . . ."

"You know Motty. She never wrote anything down."

"Well, *I* can't take her."

Abby didn't answer.

"Don't look at me like that," she said. "Besides, she probably hates me."

"Sunny don't hate you. She don't know you."

"Those're the easiest people to hate."

"You need to get to know her is all. Come over to my place with me, I'll introduce you."

Stella felt the back of her neck go cold.

"Stella?" Abby said.

"I'll come up in a while, when it's daylight. Go on home to her, before she gets eaten by your bears."

He didn't get the joke.

"Your menagerie of murder," she added.

He chuckled. "Forgot you called it that. Well, it ain't as much of a threat as it used to be."

He lumbered across the yard. He was a thinner man now, but he walked the same heavy-footed walk.

Stella said his name and he looked back. She couldn't see his eyes, but the moonlight glanced off his bald head. "Sunny. Is she all right?"

*All right.* 'Round here that could mean a lot of things. Abby considered.

"She's a little girl," he said.


THE SHERIFF ARRIVED at daybreak.

Stella heard the engine and went out to the front porch. It was the same radio car Bobby Reed had been driving a few hours ago.

To her right, the sun was edging up over the peak of Thunderhead. Light sliced across the valley, igniting the western hills opposite, the trees burning orange and red under a blue fog. It really did look like smoke, she thought. Autumn in the Smokies made for the world's prettiest forest fire.

Two men stepped out of the car. Tom Acherson from the passenger side, wearing his official brown park uniform. The right sleeve was pinned up where an elbow would've been. The other was Don Whaley, Blount County sheriff. He put a hand on the hood of her Ford, studying it.

"Stella! This is a surprise," Tom said. "I'm so sorry for your loss. Motty was, well, certainly a part of this place." His accent was straight out of Movietone News.

"She was that," Stella said. Whaley was looking into her back seat.

Tom nodded at the sunlit hills. "It's breathtaking, isn't it?"

"Practically a crime."

"We're getting quite famous for our fall colors." The park superintendent remained a smiler and a head-bobber, the happiest man she'd ever met. When she was a girl she'd found his relentless enthusiasm charming. "By noon the park will be full of visitors."

"Gawking at the last of the old-timey pioneers, too. Sheriff, you want to stop petting my car?"

Sheriff Whaley's hand rested on the trunk. He looked tired, but then he always did. He was one of those men prone to dark circles under his eyes, like he woke up every morning and lightly punched himself in the face. He said, "You mind if I take a peek inside?"

Whaley was the worst kind of cop: a solid churchman who didn't partake. He'd also grown up with Hendrick, and once they'd been bosom fucking buddies. Maybe still. She wished she'd parked the car in the barn. "You're a bit out of your jurisdiction," she said.

Tom seemed dismayed that the conversation had taken this turn. "We came to check on Sunny—and of course, offer help to the family."

"And check out your new property."

Tom's face fell.

"I'm kidding you," she said. "Come on in."

Whaley glanced around the living room like he was taking inventory—and maybe he was. Hendrick would've wanted Whaley there quick, in case Stella got into the house and tried to abscond with her inheritance. Stella had indeed been searching the house, but for Motty's will, on the slim odds that the old woman had reversed her lifetime habit and had actually written something down longer than a grocery list. She'd found not a scrap.

Tom said, "I was told Abby found the body?"

Stella passed on what Abby had told her: the yard, the possibility of heart attack.

"It sounds like it was quick," Tom said. "So that's a mercy."

"Where's the girl?" Whaley asked. "Sunny," he added, as if to prove he knew the name.

"Sleeping." Not necessarily a lie.

"I'd like to set eyes on her."

"You aren't waking her. The woman who was like a mother to her just died. Leave her be."

"Every girl needs a mother," Whaley said.

Tom's eyes widened. He'd seen something in Stella's face that alarmed him.

Whaley said, "So you're staying until Hendrick gets here?" And there it was: confirmation the sheriff had been talking to Uncle Hendrick.

"Don't you worry," Stella said. "I ain't going to run off with the family jewels."


IF MOTTY HAD DIED in the old days they would have tolled the church bell for every year she'd lived, and everyone in the cove would've sussed out who'd died. These days the cove was empty, the friends and family and former neighbors scattered across three counties, and the bells that summoned them were on telephones. Cars started rolling in soon after Sheriff Whaley and Tom Acherson left, and kept coming like troopships on D-Day, deploying Christian soldiers armed with casseroles and jugs of sweet tea.

Stella was forced to welcome the visitors, listen to condolences, and make table space for the dishes. Many of the first through the door were members of the Primitive Baptist Church, who still drove into the cove on Sundays to meet in the old building, just out of stubbornness. She doubted they'd come today because they loved Motty—there was bad blood there. But the Birches had founded the church, and forms had to be followed.

Baptists of other flavors made an appearance. A passel of Missionary Baptists, still carrying a grudge after splitting with the Primitives in the 1830s, Southern Baptists, Pentecostals, independents. Methodists made an appearance, and even a couple of Maryville Episcopalians. A good portion of these people were cousins. The residents of the cove had intermarried so much that every family tree was as tangled as a blackberry bush; those claiming to *not* be kin to the Birches probably hadn't checked the fine print in their family Bibles.

Everybody was curious about Sunny—Stella could see it in the way they scanned the tiny house—and several got around to asking about her. They called her "that poor girl" or "that poor little thing." Only a few knew her name, and no one seemed to have met her. Motty, evidently, had kept her out of school and, even worse, out of church. The whiff of disapproval hung over every covered dish.

Stella told them all the same thing: "She's staying with family."

Upon receiving her third green bean casserole—"Just heat it up in the stove, honey"—Stella walked out of the kitchen, slipped into her old bedroom, and put her back to the door.

She fished out her pack of Luckies. Lit one with her Zippo. Smoking in her bedroom was something she used to dream about. She wondered how long she could hide. Folks would assume she was grieving, wouldn't they?

The room was very different in daylight.

When she'd searched the house in the predawn hours she'd spent only a few minutes here, because she couldn't imagine Motty hiding anything of worth where Sunny (or Stella, in her day) could get at it easily. In the half dark the bedroom seemed pretty close to the way Stella had left it.

Now, though, it was clear that Sunny had made the room her own. Starting with the books—the shelf had been decimated. Her biology journals were gone, the remaining novels were all jumbled—the Nancy Drews stacked helter-skelter!—and worse, *The Book of Clara* and *The Book of Esther* were nowhere to be seen.

Surely Sunny hadn't thrown those out. Had Hendrick repossessed them?

Stella started pulling the mysteries off the stack to place them spine out, but stopped when she found a small cardboard box tucked behind them.

She didn't recognize the box, so it had to belong to Sunny. The shelf was a good hiding place because Motty didn't have much interest in books. When Stella lived here she hated how the old woman would go through any of her things, no privacy at all. Stella thought, I really ought to put this back.

She lifted off the lid.

Her chest cinched tight. Inside lay a square of lace, a handkerchief, folded to show Stella's initials, "SW." Lunk had given this to her for her fourteenth birthday.

And Motty, God damn her, had given it to Sunny.

Someone knocked on the door. "Stella?" A voice she didn't recognize.

"Just a second."

"Your uncle Hendrick's asking for you."

Hendrick? Fuck.

She closed the box and returned it to the shelf. Pushed a palm across her eyes. Dried her hand on her pants. She was not about to meet that man with tears in her eyes.

UNCLE HENDRICK STOOD in the front room, talking with an old man who used to live in the cove. Behind Hendrick stood three men in almost identical blue suits, their hair slicked back, awkwardly holding their hats and hanging on to Hendrick's every word. The biggest one was pale as an uncooked biscuit: white hair, white eyebrows, pink lips. Most definitely not from around here.

Hendrick had never looked like he was from the cove. Her great-uncle looked so fucking dapper, his suit somehow appearing neatly pressed despite the drive from Atlanta, smug as King Richard back from the Crusades.

She wasn't ready for this. Not after Motty's sneak attack from beyond the grave. She didn't know whether she was about to run from the house or drive the bastard out of it.

Before she could decide, the men in blue parted and Aunt Ruth and Veronica stepped to Hendrick, Ruth already mad about something, Veronica looking sleepy. Then Veronica spotted Stella and her eyes lit up. She strode over on high heels, arms open. Stella accepted her hug.

"Oh law, I've missed you," Veronica said. She smelled of hairspray and Shalimar.

"It's good to see you, Vee." They'd been girls when they last saw each other, Veronica not even a teenager, but they'd exchanged letters over the years. She was the only family member Stella had cared to stay in touch with.

"Are you okay?" Veronica asked. "You look all broke up. I'm so sorry it had to be like this. Poor Motty."

"You're upset too, huh?"

"Of course I am." Veronica looked to the side to see if anyone was listening to them. "You remember that navy veteran I wrote you about?" She held up her hand to show an engagement ring. "Look!"

"When did this happen?"

"Last May. We're going to get married next June."

"I'm surprised you'd go that long with a ring on your finger. That's like leaving your turn signal on for a year."

"Stop it! We're taking our time."

Stella had been watching Uncle Hendrick; he'd finally seen her. Stella kept nodding as Veronica chattered on about wedding plans.

Hendrick glided up. "Stella," he said in that warm fog of a voice. His hair had picked up a dusting of silver, but he was as handsome as ever. Maybe more so.

He moved in for a hug and Stella shook his hand instead. "How was the drive?"

"We made good time," he said. "Though not as good as yours."

Veronica said, "Daddy wanted to hop in the car by himself as soon as the call came in, but Mommy wouldn't have it. She had to pack the car like we were crossing the prairie—half a dozen egg salad sandwiches and a case of Coca-Cola. We checked into a new hotel in Gatlinburg an hour ago and freshened up."

The men in the blue suits watched all this conversation. Stella nodded at them. "You pack those boys, too?"

Hendrick glanced behind him. "Oh! These are members of the church. They kindly came with me." He introduced them and Stella promptly forgot their names. She was thinking, What church?

The pale one said, "It's a pleasure to meet you. Pastor Hendrick's told us a lot about you."

Pastor Fucking What?

Aunt Ruth squeezed around her husband and looked at Stella with an anxious, searching expression. "Someone just asked if— what are you wearing?"

"How you doing, Aunt Ruth?" Stella said pointedly.

"You couldn't put on a dress?"

"I don't think Motty's going to mind."

"Someone just asked when the service will be. You haven't called a funeral home yet, have you?"

"I haven't decided anything. No arrangements."

Her aunt's relief lasted only a second. "Hendrick, we have to call Smith's in Maryville."

"Whatever you think, dear," he said distractedly. To Stella he said, "Is Sunny in her room?"

"She's up at Abby's."

A flash of annoyance crossed his face, and then he covered it. "This house is probably too crowded for her. She's a sensitive soul. We'll get some of this food to her."

Stella wasn't sure what irked her more, Hendrick's familiarity or the fact that he'd thought of the obvious kindness. Stella should have run food up there already.

"Hendrick, the funeral home!" Ruth said.

"Darn it, Ruth, let me see my sister first."

STELLA HAD KEPT Motty's door closed all this morning. She opened it for Hendrick and then kept it open behind her.

He stood over Motty's body, and he didn't seem to know what to do with his hands. He kept passing his hat from one to the other. He didn't look closely at her body. She was relieved by that.

Without turning he said, "Had she been sick?"

Stella almost said, Your god murdered her, you idiot. Motty's health don't enter into it. But there were too many people in the house to say it aloud—and she wanted to be sure before she put that idea in his head. Instead she said, "Don't ask me."

"You never came to see her?" Putting on a hurt tone.

"When I left I said I was never coming back. I never came back."

He turned. "You came running over here pretty quick this morning." Oh, yes. He *was* mad she'd beaten him here.

"I didn't want Sunny to be up here alone."

"That's so kind of you. To take an interest."

He'd kept his voice low. The small house was growing more

crowded, and Ruth was hovering six feet away—giving them their privacy without quite respecting it.

Stella said, "You want to explain what's going on with those boys in the suits, Pastor Hendrick?"

He shook his head, pretending not to understand.

"What kind of church we talking about?" she asked.

"The same one you grew up in."

He couldn't be serious. "That—that stays in the family. That's what you always said."

"It was time to bring in others. The mission of the church continues."

"How does that work? We're in the middle of a national park—one that's about to seize all the land."

"We'll figure it out."

We. Meaning, not her. "You and your followers can't stay," she said. "John Toliver already sued the government, and he lost. *You* sued and lost. The park gets this farm, and they'll tear it all down. The house, the barn, the chapel."

"We should talk about this later," he said.

"Just answer one thing," Stella said. "Has she gone in?"

He flinched. She'd put him on edge by saying as much as she had within earshot of so many nonbelievers. She stepped closer. "Has she?"

Stella was taller than him, she realized, and not because Hendrick had shrunk in the ten years since she'd seen him. Stella had gotten all her height by the time she was fourteen, so even then she would have been taller than her great-uncle—but it hadn't felt that way. In her memory he was always the adult and she was the little girl.

Hendrick looked away. "No. She wasn't of age yet."

"Hendrick."

"And Motty wouldn't allow it."

Stella took a breath, stepped back. That rang true. Motty had always had final say on who went into the chapel. Even now she was calling the shots. That concrete over the cave entrance was a Fuck You from beyond the grave.

"What is it?" Hendrick asked.

He'd seen the smile on her lips. She considered telling him about what Motty had done, then decided it'd be more fun for him to find out.

"I want what's best for Sunny," he said. And then added, smooth as a knife sliding into the belly of a fish, "I will not abandon her."

STELLA STALKED OUT of the house, feeling stunned and ashamed. *I will not abandon her.* Went to the barn where she'd moved her car, thinking: Fuck them. Let the God take them all. I've got work to do.

Veronica came up behind her. "Are you all right? What did Daddy say?"

"Nothing I didn't have coming."

"Well all right, then." Vee looped an arm through Stella's. "You know where a girl can get a drink around here?"

"It's ten in the morning."

"And I've been up all night. You too, from the looks of it."

"So you're saying this is a nightcap."

"Exactly!"

Stella stepped to the Ford and Veronica said, "Oh heavens, have you been transporting demon liquor?"

"Sheriff Whaley nearly opened my trunk this morning."

"Oh no!"

"Not to worry—the trunk's empty. However . . ." She opened the driver's side door, flipped the hidden latch, and lifted the back seat. Inside were twenty jars of moonshine, packed in straw to keep them from clinking against each other.

Veronica was delighted. "You've always been my favorite outlaw."

Stella opened a jar and raised it. "Here's to your impending nuptials."

"And I'm not even pregnant! That must be a first in our family." She took a sip. "Law!"

"This batch came out pretty well, I have to say."

"I take it back. That jar just knocked me up. I'm with child now." That got a smile out of Stella. How did Vee do that? Her letters had come every few months, so chock-full of vapid cheeriness and admiration for her older cousin that Stella had allowed herself to write back.

Stella said, "I just hope Hump doesn't ruin the next batch."

"Hump? You know someone named *Hump*?"

"One of my employees. Doesn't matter." That boy had better be cooking by now. Willie Teffeteller wanted those barrels before Friday night. If Hump screwed up, it could fuck this new deal with Willie and screw her existing customers to boot.

Veronica fished a locket from her cleavage. Trapped inside was a young man in navy whites, glaring at the camera. "That's Rickie. He's Italian but doesn't look it."

"He's handsome." And looked very Italian.

"Daddy's going to give him a job at the furniture store. My job, actually."

Stella raised her eyebrows.

Veronica shrugged. "I handled all the accounting since I was sixteen, and I've been doing the inventory, too. But Daddy says the war's over, and he doesn't want me to work once I'm married."

"So Rickie's going from the navy to retail. He must be so excited."

"Alas, we can't all be criminals."

"Maybe you can rob a bank or something while he's at work."

"A housewife does need a hobby." Veronica drank and passed the jar back to Stella. "I tell you what, I don't want to be broke again."

"I used to think y'all were so rich."

Veronica blew out her lips.

"I did! Your clothes were so fancy."

"That's about all we had. You know Daddy lost near everything—nobody was buying living room suits in the Depression."

"You were city poor. Country poor's a whole 'nother thing."

"We did have indoor plumbing."

"There you go. Does *Riccardo* know you're a flush-toilet kinda girl? He'll need to provide all the facilities to which you've become accustomed."

"You can ask him yourself. He's driving up tomorrow."

"Have you told him about the church? Because it looks like Hendrick's told half of Atlanta."

Veronica smiled in faux embarrassment; she wasn't capable of the real thing. "Mostly."

"What's that mean?"

"We've told him a lot, just not . . . everything. Rickie's family is Catholic."

"But he's not?"

"He's flexible."

"He damn well better be."

Veronica laughed. "Don't worry, Daddy knows how to lead people gently."

"By the nose." Stella could almost believe that Hendrick and Veronica could bring this sailor boy into the fold without spooking him or letting him squeal. But strangers? What the hell was Hendrick doing talking to outsiders? "Do those city slickers in the suits know how fucking weird our family is? They haven't read the books, have they?" Stella had been raised to believe that the knowledge of the Revelations stayed in the family. Secrecy above all else.

"You'd be surprised how popular it is," Veronica said. "People are hungry for something, I don't know, a little more *real* than two-thousand-year-old Jesus in the sky."

"But they can't know it's real," Stella said. "They're just taking Hendrick's word for it."

"You know Daddy, he's so *sincere*. Folks eat it up." Veronica had always been happy to mock her father, though never to his face.

"This is crazy. He can't hold services, or—" She stopped herself from mentioning communion. "There are already tourists tramping through here every day, and pretty soon this whole farm will be gone."

Veronica sighed. "I know, I know. And I think Daddy knows it, too. He's always talking about the life of the church *after* the cove. With him in charge, of course."

"How is the church supposed to survive without the cove? You can't just . . ." She searched for a word, couldn't come up with it. "Without this mountain, without what's *in* the mountain, you don't have anything. There's no going forward."

"Tell Daddy that."

"I tried. Do you know what he's got planned for Sunny?"

"Besides treating her like a princess?"

"He likes her, then."

"He *adores* her. I hope he's got some precious attention left over for when his actual grandchildren show up. Rickie and I have already talked about children."

So Hendrick wanted to treat her like a princess. But would he love her if she couldn't help him with this church? Stella couldn't picture it.

Veronica was saying something. Stella asked her to repeat it.

"I said I was sorry, I don't mean to lord it over you."

Stella shook her head in confusion.

"With my engagement," Veronica said. "My good fortune. You never got that chance."

Stella felt a rush of emotion. Anger, shame, guilt, and maybe a dozen other feelings she couldn't name. Nothing that couldn't be burned out.

"No," Stella said. "I'm happy for you."

Hendrick had appeared in the backyard, holding a casserole dish in one hand and a sack in the other. He crossed the yard, heading for Abby's.

Stella took a hard pull on the jar, then set it on the roof of the car. "Fucking elated."

"Where are you going?" Veronica asked.

"Back in a bit."

STELLA WENT UP the same path as Hendrick. He was well out of sight, and she didn't yell for him or try to catch up. Kept her steps quiet in the dry leaves. Considered, over and over, whether she should turn around and finish that drink.

She came in sight of Abby's shack and stopped beside a tree, watching through a scramble of foliage. Hendrick approached the door, called out.

The door swung open. Abby stepped out, not smiling. Stella thought, That's right, big man, don't give that bastard the time of day.

Then Abby turned back, pushed open the door wider. Sunny stepped out.

Her skin, in sunlight, was a shock: swaths of dark and light, like a pinto horse. Last night those dark patches had seemed almost black, but in the daylight the color was a deep scarlet. The red swirled up her pale arms, arced across her face. Her condition was more striking than Stella's, deeper by far than Motty's. Anybody in the cove would know her for a Birch woman.

Hendrick and Sunny stared at each other for a long moment. Stella held her breath. Then Sunny flew across the grass, running for him. Hendrick put up his hands, protecting the food. Sunny threw her arms around his waist.

Hendrick's delighted laughter carried through the trees.

## 5

**1936**

O N A SATURDAY a few weeks after her twelfth birthday, Stella stood on the front steps, ignoring the chill in the air, watching the road, ears straining. She would not wear a coat, or even sit, for fear she'd wrinkle her dress.

This morning Motty had opened a box to reveal it, an old-fashioned ivory gown with a high collar, stiff and crinkly, fancier even than the one Veronica had worn. After Stella put it on she wished the house had a full-length mirror to see herself. For three years she'd lived her life like the Man in the Iron Mask, and now she was about to assume her rightful place in the world.

She and Motty had long ago worked out the terms of her sentence. Stella would do her chores without complaint, and when she was finished Motty would leave her alone to do as she wished. Mostly she wished to read books and pester Abby. She visited him often at his cabin, and he'd trusted her with the secret of how he made his money.

School was another kind of prison. She hiked alone to the Carter School at the west end of the cove, what they called the consolidated school, since there were only a couple dozen families left in the cove now. But even in those close quarters her fellow students were cruel to her. Birches had a bad reputation, Motty particularly. The girls said she cursed people, and put evil spirits into stray animals, which was why she didn't go to church no more.

The proof that Stella was just as bad? Look at her diseased skin, that permanent rash, like Motty's but even worse! Her first day at school three years ago the girls had looked her up and down and said, "Yep. She's one of them." It hadn't got much better since.

The only person who showed her any positive regard was her teacher, Mr. Whitehead, who allowed her to borrow as many books as she could carry. Most were on loan from the library in Maryville, and Mr. W put no restrictions on her reading—at least when choosing among the books he'd allowed into the schoolhouse. The Count of Monte Cristo rode in her satchel alongside Nancy Drew, Odysseus, and Tom Swift. Uncle Hendrick had told her she was special, and she was preparing herself by reading about special people.

The most special person of all, of course, was Clara, the first woman to meet the God in the Mountain, the protector of the Birch clan. But Stella had read The Book of Clara so many times her eyeballs had scoured the words from the page. Hendrick wouldn't give her the next diary, however. Said it was Motty's rules. Stella couldn't read The Book of Esther until her first communion.

While she waited for her life to begin, Stella drew strength from one thing: whatever was waiting for her in the cave, Motty wanted it too, and Stella would take it from her.

The rumble of a car engine made Stella hop down from the porch. Three cars rolled into the yard and parked. Uncle Hendrick stepped out first, and he beamed at her.

The men—seven of them, all of them decades older than Hendrick—one by one shook her hand as they entered the house. They acted like they were meeting royalty, and in a way they were. They were the elders of the Church of the God in the Mountain, her uncles and cousins, all Birches by blood—and she was their Revelator.

HENDRICK HAD BROUGHT in a big trunk full of robes. Vestments, he called them. The men chatted casually as they put them on, like a team suiting up for the big game. The Holy Uncles. The collars and sleeves were embroidered with strange symbols: crescents and stars and human eyes and balancing scales. Hendrick's robe was extra special. The cloth was shot through with gold thread, and stitched across the right breast was a five-point star blazing with sunrays, fit for a sheriff of Oz. Stella was awfully glad she was wearing her special dress.

Motty watched from the doorway, scowling, her arms crossed.

The oldest and most desiccated of the men moved his hand, summoning Stella. His mouth was a toothless cavern. Stella was reluctant to go to him. Uncle Hendrick put a hand on her shoulder. "Stella, this is Morgan Birch. He's Esther's brother—he wrote much of her book!" A nudge moved Stella closer to him. His carp mouth widened into perhaps a smile.

Stella looked to Motty, but her face was impassive.

The old man reached toward Stella's face with fingers stained a sickly yellow. She pulled back in revulsion. He didn't seem to notice. "The God in the Mountain." His eyes searched hers. "Tell me what he said."

"Not yet, Morgan," Hendrick said in a solicitous voice. "She hasn't gone in yet."

He looked up at Hendrick. "What did he say?"

"*Not yet,*" Hendrick said, louder.

One of the men brought in a chair from the kitchen and set it in the middle of the circle. Hendrick made her sit and then, alarmingly, knelt in front of her, his legs under the robe. He looked like a mushroom.

"Stella, tonight's service is sacred," Hendrick said quietly, as if only she could hear him—but the men and Motty were so close there was no keeping it from them. "We don't talk about this with anyone who's not in this room, right now. Do you understand?"

She nodded.

"Good, good," he said. "Are you ready?"

She nodded again, though she had no idea what she was agreeing to. One of the Uncles handed him a copper bowl filled with a shimmering liquid. He set it on the floor between Stella and himself.

"And let him call for the elders of the church," Hendrick said in a strange, foggy voice. "And let them pray over him, anointing him with oil in the name of the Lord."

The men gazed at her, waiting. Hendrick directed her with his eyes to look at her hands. What did he want her to do?

Hendrick said over her shoulder, "Did you not talk with her?" He was annoyed.

Motty said, "Get it over with."

Hendrick pursed his lips. In a low voice he said to Stella, "Hold out your hands, dear. No, palms up. That's it."

He held her left wrist and dipped the fingers of his other hand into the bowl. Lifted them, dripping.

Stella's arm trembled. She tried to pull back but Hendrick gripped harder. "Open your fingers," he whispered.

She felt like she was about to vomit. Tears filled her eyes.

"It's all right." His thumb combed her fingers open. "Everything's all right."

Oil dripped onto her hand, and she jerked. A dollop of oil fell onto her lap. The gray stain widened like an eye.

Her hand was fine. She thought the oil would burn, but it felt like . . . nothing.

Hendrick rubbed the substance into her palm. "Behold his daughter, the child of God." The men murmured their approval.

She felt flushed by all this attention. It was like being onstage, exciting yet terrifying, because no one had told her what to do, what to expect. Again she glanced back at Motty. Her grandmother met her gaze and then walked into the kitchen.

Hendrick winked at her. They were sharing a joke, a joke on Motty, though what was so amusing Stella couldn't say. But she liked it.

In that same velvet voice Uncle Hendrick said, "And when Clara had offered her gift, the God in the Mountain said, On the day I step into the light . . ."

"The world will know my name," the Uncles answered in unison.

"And I will give unto my children . . . ," Hendrick said.

"One body," the men said, "ever blooming."

Hendrick dipped his hand again and held it over her right hand, and this time Stella cupped her palm.

"So that the poison of this world . . ." Hendrick's voice rose.

"Shall never corrupt us," the Uncles responded.

"Amen," Hendrick said.

The oil touched her, and she held her arm steady. She didn't want to spill a drop.

THE NEXT STEP COULDN'T happen until nightfall. The Holy Uncles took off their vestments and crowded around the table in the small dining room, waiting for the food and complaining loudly about the new park and the damage those CCC boys were doing. Camps of workers "reforesting" and tearing down farms, but at least no Black workers, thank the Lord.

In the kitchen, Stella perched on a stool, the skirt of the white dress spread out prettily. As she eavesdropped she traced the contours of her palm, trying to feel where the oil had touched her.

At the stove, Motty dropped pieces of battered chicken into a skillet of hot oil. Stella asked for a drumstick.

"This ain't for you," Motty said.

"What, I don't get to eat?"

"You'll thank me later."

In the next room the men were talking loudly to each other, but Stella lowered her voice anyway. "Tell me what's going to happen."

"You'll find out soon enough."

"Suppose I don't go in."

Motty dropped in a big thigh, and the skillet erupted in applause. "Suit yourself."

"Did my mama go in?"

"She did."

"And you went in?"

Motty speared a piece of browned chicken in the skillet, shook it, and dropped it onto the plate.

"Just *tell me*," Stella pleaded. "Tell me what I'm supposed to do!"

"Stop fussing. I'll be there with you."

"You will?"

"I'll walk you in. I decide how long you stay in there, when you get to go back in."

No one had told Stella this. She thought she would be going in alone. For a moment she was relieved. Then she thought, Did they not trust her? Did they think she'd run away?

"Why do you get to decide?" Stella asked.

"I'm the eldest Revelator. I have say. Now go on, take in the side dishes." On the counter sat orange and green glass bowls holding corn, green beans, mashed potatoes, beets soaking in juice.

"I can't do that," Stella said. "My dress." She didn't say that she'd already stained it with the oil.

"Get your princess hind end off that stool and get to."

Stella was offended. Was she blessed or not? This was *her* day. She wasn't supposed to share it with Motty, and she sure as heck wasn't supposed to ferry dishes like a slave girl.

"You're jealous," Stella said.

"What did you say?"

"You wish you were the Revelator. Like you used to be."

Motty set down the fork. The chicken kept sizzling.

Stella said, "You wish they were here for *you*."

Motty walked to the counter. "You think these men care about you? You think they'll be *offended* if you wait on them?"

Stella said nothing.

Motty picked up the bowl of beets. "Take this out."

Stella didn't move.

"Take it to them."

Stella set her mouth. Raised her eyebrows in mock innocence.

Motty upended the bowl. Two quarts of deep-purple juice slapped her knees, soaking her lap. Stella screamed, jumped up. Red chunks of beet plopped wetly onto the floor. The dress was awash in violet.

Ruined. Ruined. Ruined.

Hendrick called, "Everything all right in there? We're getting hungry."

"Just a little accident," Motty said.

No one came to rescue her.

WHEN THE SLIVER of moon finally rose over the mountain, the men put on their robes again, which made Stella feel terrible; she was wearing her old dress now, the one with the three flowers. It was too short for her, and she was mortified. If any of the men had remarked on it she'd have run into her bedroom and hid.

The Uncles went on ahead, leaving only Hendrick and Stella in the front room. Motty was cleaning up in the kitchen. Stella could not sit down, and her insides were quaking.

"You don't have to be nervous," Uncle Hendrick said. "You were born to this." She didn't feel any better.

After a while Hendrick called out, "Motty, it's time. We got to go."

"Don't you tell me when to go," Motty said. She appeared a couple of minutes later. She'd taken off her apron, but she was wearing the same housedress she'd spent the day in. Stella eyed her, thinking, You're going to wear that to my ceremony? But she knew better than to say it aloud.

Uncle Hendrick took her hand and walked her up the mountain, Motty trailing. The door to the chapel hung open, spilling yellow light onto the grass. Inside, more than a dozen lamps burned. The Uncles waited there. Hendrick directed her to walk down the aisle between them. The men said things as she passed: "Amen" and "Blessed child" and "Thank you, God."

The panel of wood covering the stairs had been moved aside. Motty picked up a lantern and sighed. "All right. Let's go."

Motty stepped through the hole, and Stella stood at the top, watching that swaying light turn her grandmother's body into frantic shadows. Motty reached the bottom and looked back at her.

"You wanted this," Motty said.

Stella looked at the pews. All eyes were on her. Uncle Hendrick touched her between the shoulders.

Stella looked at the first step. Put her foot down, gently, half expecting the wood to crack. Took another step, and another.

At the bottom, Motty's lantern revealed a room barely wider

than the smokehouse. How had the thing she'd sensed that first day fit into this space?

"Let's get to the table," Motty said. And Stella thought, What table? But Motty was clomping forward. Her light found a gap in the rock, a narrow passage, and she moved into it.

Stella looked up. At the top of the stairs, the light kept shifting; Hendrick and the men, waiting. She wanted to run up and out, to Abby's cabin. But she didn't want to be the only Birch woman to let down the family. Motty wasn't afraid. Lena and Esther and Clara Birch had all gone into the cave, too. If Stella ran out now, she'd break a chain of generations.

She followed Motty, into that constricted passage. The air grew chill. The ground tilted up and the tunnel turned, turned again, then suddenly widened into a cavern.

Motty held the lantern high. In the center of this space, a stone platform rose out of the floor. It looked half natural, half constructed, as if a bulge of rock had been sculpted into a pedestal.

The table.

Stella turned, taking in the ridges and furrows and shadowed nooks like the burrows of underground animals. Was the God here? She tried to remember what it felt like that first time in the cave, when she felt the presence. Nothing seemed to lurk in the dark.

"Climb up," Motty said.

"What?"

Motty nodded toward the table. It was almost four feet high. How did they expect her to climb up on this thing?

Stella ran her hands over the table's surface. It was ice-block cold, and smooth except for a few shallow grooves. She pushed up on tiptoes, and with elbows and forearms levered one knee onto the surface, then hauled herself up. Rolled onto her back.

"I'll come back for you," Motty said. The lantern moved away.

"Wait! No!"

Motty stopped. Her hand touched Stella's forehead. Brushed back her hair. "I won't be far," she said softly.

Stella heard Motty move away, and the light vanished. Stella lay on the stone, breathing hard—and every breath sounded enormously loud. She couldn't see anything.

A minute passed. Then five. Something was wrong. Or Stella had done something wrong. She started to sit up, and then felt the stone rumble beneath her. The vibration moved into her chest. She lay back and put a hand to her heart and stared up into the dark. Her left hand gripped the edge of the table. The mountain felt like it was coming alive around her.

The God was here. Somewhere in the room, somewhere above her.

The air felt heavy as water. Moving only her eyes, she searched the dark, longing to detect any movement. Each breath she took seemed impossibly loud.

And then, a sliver of white. It slipped down toward her through the dark—a limb, flat as the foreleg of a praying mantis. Its torso became visible, a pale mass gleaming like mother-of-pearl. Half a dozen limbs fanned out behind it, gripping the rock.

Stella's throat tightened. Her limbs clenched, paralyzing her.

The God's foreleg stretched along the length of her body. Its serrated tip drifted close to her face, then abruptly withdrew. Then its entire body receded into shadow. Alarmed, she sat up and reached toward it.

The arm drifted down again. The tip opened like the bulb of a flower. The interior gleamed, white and pink.

Stella opened her hand. Spread her fingers wide.

They touched. A spike of pain. She cried out—and a heat spread through her hand as if she'd plunged it into a hot spring.

The heat rose up through her arm, to her shoulder, then warmed her cheeks like a fever.

She gasped. The air had become milky violet. She could see the God now, as if the room were lit by a dozen red lamps. It leaned out of a hole in the rock above, limbs delicately holding it in place. Its head—she could only think of it as a head—was a smooth boulder, eyeless and mouthless, yet it tilted gracefully as if to take her in.

She'd never seen anything so beautiful. So fragile.

The limb gently pulled back a few inches. She felt a tugging inside her palm. The limb pulled back farther and white threads stretched between them, crisscrossing and stretching like a cat's cradle.

"Oh," she said. She extended her left hand, and another limb came down to kiss her palm.

The pain was just as sharp but seemed to come from a great distance. Stella looked up at the God, and its thoughts blossomed into her head.

STELLA AWOKE in her room. Motty sat beside her on the bed, touching a damp washcloth to her forehead.

Stella reached up and was surprised to find her hand bandaged. The other hand as well. Blood spots marked the cloth covering her palms.

"Did I do okay?" she asked. Her throat was sore.

"You did fine. How do you feel?"

How did she feel? She closed her eyes. Strange shapes folded and unfolded behind her eyelids. Scraping at her. There wasn't enough room in her mind for them.

She opened her eyes again. "He's alone. He's dying."

Motty said nothing.

"We have to protect him." Another memory came to her. The interruption. Stella had been yanked away from the God before he had finished. "You stopped us." Tears sprang to her eyes. "Why did you stop us?"

"Tiny sips," Motty said. "Tiny sips."

"I could have done more."

"And you will. When you get stronger." Motty folded the washcloth and laid it across Stella's forehead. "The men are waiting in the front room to hear from you. But I told them you're too wrung out, so Hendrick's going to come in here and record your words."

"What do I say?"

"Tell him what he gave you. As best you can."

She sat up and her head swam. Beside her was a book. *The Book of Esther.* She'd been waiting for years to read it, but her head was too full to make room for words. The God was moving inside her, trying to make room for himself.

"I need to go back," she said. "I need to talk to him. Her. I need . . ." She didn't know what all she needed.

"You're drunk on him," Motty said. "It'll pass."

## 6

**1948**

THEY CALLED IT the sittin' up. The good Christians, by tradition, sat inside, drinking coffee, occasionally going into the deceased's room to tut-tut over the body. The bad ones sat out back around a fire, doing as they pleased. Tonight that was drinking cans of Goldcrest 51 and passing jars. Stella had firmly aligned with the bad Christians. They were all young people happy to partake of Stella's liquor supply, produced mysteriously from the barn.

She and Veronica were the only girls at the fire. The boys were distant cousins, most of whom she'd never met. Veronica had her hand on the knee of one of them. So—engaged but not yet dead.

Stella watched the house, waiting for Hendrick to appear. She'd slunk away from Abby's without revealing herself, and thought about driving home to check on Hump Cornette and the progress of the batch. Yet, she stayed. For the rest of the afternoon she avoided Hendrick. She knew he wanted to talk, and she knew she'd have to face him eventually. She just wanted to make up her mind before she did. The constant flux and flow of yammering relatives and nosy neighbors made it near impossible to be alone, which was a boon, but also made it impossible to think.

So, she kept drinking. After several hours of that the only thoughts moving in her brain were a few hard absolutes, turning and scraping against each other like millstones. Stay. Go. Take Sunny. Leave her.

Across the yard, a figure emerged from the trees. Abby. She recognized that lumbering gait. He walked straight toward her. She tossed her cigarette into the fire. Got to her feet. Steadied herself.

Abby said, "How you doing, Little Star?"

"I'm all right."

"Are you?"

"Where's Sunny?"

"Up at the cabin. She doesn't want to come down, not with all these people." He started to say more when Vee swept in, threw her arms around him. "Abby!"

"Golly bum," Abby said. "Look at you, all growed up, and still as pretty as a peach blossom." His drawl had stretched into pure *Gone With the Wind*. Veronica had that effect on men.

"Are you all right?" she asked. "I know this must be a blow. Motty thought the world of you."

"She thought plenty of things about me, I'll tell you that."

Veronica laughed. "Daddy says Motty couldn't have gotten by without you."

"She helped me more than I did her," he said. "She held the line out here for years without me. Even after, I barely did anything. Mow the lawn and drop off groceries, that was about it. Said she was done with farming."

"I don't know why anyone ever starts," Veronica said. "Do you know what you're going to do now?"

"Leave him alone," Stella said. "Abby, you thirsty? I've got some of your recipe. Not as good as what you used to make."

"I doubt that," Abby said. "But none for me, thank you."

"What the hell? Abby Whitt turning down a drink?"

He shrugged. Veronica said, "Come sit by the fire. I think you know some of these delinquents."

Abby went around the circle, shaking hands. Everyone seemed to know him. Somebody asked, "How's your uncle Dan doing, Abby?"

Abby chuckled. "He's doing fine."

"Have a seat and tell us the news."

"Naw, there ain't much to tell." But they begged him and finally he said, "All right, all right. Let me see . . ."

Abby started with the story of Uncle Dan building a still out of a hollow tree and siphoning the liquor like it was sap, and the cousins were laughing as if it were the first time they'd heard it.

Stella stood outside the circle, nursing her beer. How the fuck were these people so easy with each other? It all seemed so fake. Desperate, even. A bunch of human beings huddled up like dogs in a den, pretending they wouldn't turn on each other if they got the chance. Stella had learned to do a passable impersonation of a normal person, but she couldn't keep it up for long. Not like Veronica, who could charm your pants off all day. Even Abby— even this older, sadder Abby—had a talent for being liked.

"I remember this one time," he said, and launched into a story about one of Dan's batches. "Once Ol' Dan had finished, of course, he had to make sure it was up to snuff. After about a gallon or so he figured that corn likker was just fine, and it was time to head home. Now Dan's pure country, you know, mountain-raised. He don't need a light to get out of the woods 'cause his bare feet always carry him home, even when he's feelin' top-heavy."

Tears sprang into her eyes. She stepped back, dizzy. He's telling my favorite story, she thought. He's doing it for me.

"Well wouldn't you know it, he bumps into someone in the dark as they was coming up the hill. Dan apologizes immediately, of course. 'I'm sorry, neighbor!' he says, 'cause his mama raised him right. 'I've had a bit to drink.' But just about then—did I mention it was a cloudy night? Just about then the clouds part and the moon shines down and there stands Dan, looking at a panther three times his size, with bright yaller eyes. That big cat growls and shows his teeth. And I tell you what, that offended Uncle Dan. He throws up his hands and hollers, 'Dagnabbit, I *said* I was sorry!'"

The boys fell over laughing. It wasn't the story, or *just* the story. It was Abby throwing out his arms and bellowing in that Uncle Dan voice. Also, they were drunk.

"Now that panther," Abby continued, "that panther, he wants nothing but to transfer Uncle Dan to the inside of his belly, and he bites down on Dan's arm—chomp! Now, Dan, he's pretty well lit, and didn't feel a thing. But oh, that panther! See, Dan's blood was about ninety-eight proof by this point. One bite and that big cat was as drunk as a deacon on a Saturday night."

"What happened then?" asked another cousin. "He shoot that panther?"

"Naw, Uncle Dan wouldn't harm a drinkin' buddy. He opened a jar and they sat up partakin' till the sun come up. Then they shook paws and went their separate ways. To this day, that panther's one of his best customers."

Yep. Drunk definitely helped.

Stella went to Abby, feeling weak in her chest. She bent over him and kissed his bald spot. "Nicely done, old man."

Abby reached up and touched the back of her neck.

They called for another story. Stella stepped back, and realized she was being watched. Hendrick stood a dozen yards away, holding a Coleman lantern. He turned and walked between the trees.

WHEN SHE REACHED the chapel door, Uncle Hendrick was kneeling beside the new concrete but not looking at it. He was staring up at the back wall, the lantern on the floor beside him. Stella could picture herself kicking over that lantern and setting the building alight.

"You praying to the wall now?" she asked.

He didn't answer.

"There's precedent for that," she said. Took a sip of beer.

"Did you know she did this?"

"Portland cement and river rock," she said. "Pretty thorough job."

"Why would she do it? It makes no sense."

Stella had been wondering that herself. She had two ideas, and spoke the one she most hoped for. "Maybe because it's dead."

"What? Don't be ridiculous."

"It was always dying. Been dying for years. I hope to hell it's kicked off. What a relief that would be."

"Don't blaspheme," Hendrick said. "She did this to spite me."

"She sure as hell didn't trust you. She know about this God damn sister church you've started? You can't have people trooping up here. The park's taking the farm as soon as we empty the house. If that thing's not dead—well, fuck. What happens when the park rangers find out about the hole?"

"Why do you have to use that word?"

"Fuck? Because they'll be fucked. Any tourists go in that hole, they'll die."

"I'll make sure that never happens."

Stella blew out her lips.

Hendrick pushed himself to his feet, straightened his sleeves, not looking at her. Oh, he was angry.

"Motty didn't go far enough," Stella said. "We got to make sure nobody ever finds this place."

"This is a holy site," Hendrick said. "Sacred as Calvary. For centuries to come, pilgrims will come here to—"

"Pilgrims?" She burst out laughing.

"Get ahold of yourself."

"Pilgrims!" It was hilarious.

He waited for her to finish.

She took a breath, held up a hand. "Fine, yeah. Shit." Dropped into the front pew with a grunt.

Hendrick shook his head in disappointment. That would have worked on her, years ago.

Stella said, "You must be happy to have a bunch of followers calling you 'Pastor.' How much've you told them?"

Hendrick didn't answer.

"Whatever you said, they're going to be awfully excited to see this patch of cement. That'll make true believers out of 'em."

"After the God makes himself manifest, there won't be any such thing as believing, or not believing. There'll be no such thing as faith. He'll be a fact."

"*Makes himself manifest,*" she repeated derisively. The Birch family had been waiting a hundred years for the Ghostdaddy to announce itself to the world. Right now she was the only person alive who'd seen it in person—and she was damn sure going to be the last.

"I don't know why you're so angry." His voice sad now. "What happened to the girl who loved the God so much she'd do anything for him?"

"I used to love horses, too. I was a girl."

He crouched in front of her, and his knees popped. "Come back into the fold. I know you went through some dark times, but don't blame our God. Help us do the work."

"You just want to fill out my book." He'd never shown her what was written in *The Book of Stella*. "And start Sunny's."

"Ah."

Finally they'd arrived at the heart of the matter.

Hendrick straightened. "It's true. I did want Sunny to commune with the God. But it looks like that's not meant to be. The park's closing before she's reached the age of accountability, and I won't go against that tradition."

"So you don't need her."

"Stella! This isn't about—I meant what I said. I won't abandon her. Ruth and I will take her in."

Stella stared up at him. "You will, huh?"

"Hear me out," he said. "I have a plot of land, five hundred acres, well outside Atlanta. It's wooded, plenty of privacy. She won't have to go to school, unless she wants. I'll pay for tutors, and anything else she needs."

"You don't know what she needs."

"You're probably right—but I'm willing to find out. I have the resources, the time, and the desire to take care of her."

"If I wanted custody, you know a judge would give her to me. All I have to do is say a few words."

"That's probably true," he said. "But do you want to be her guardian? I imagine your . . . business doesn't allow for raising a child."

"What the hell do you know about my business?"

"Not a thing. And that's what I prefer."

Stella let her head fall back to rest on the top of the pew. Hendrick waited.

"Motty would have a fit," Stella said.

"My sister and I didn't agree on much, but she didn't doubt that I loved Sunny. And I think it's fair to say the girl has grown fond of me, as well."

Stella pictured Sunny running across the grass, embracing him.

Hendrick said, "Abby's already told me that he's not comfortable with my plan unless you give your blessing."

"My blessing."

"Just a few words."

Stella heaved herself upright. Looked at the cement. "This only works if Sunny never goes in there."

Hendrick didn't answer. She turned to face him.

"I'm not fucking around. Sunny goes in there without me to guide her, she'll be . . . hurt. Bad hurt." *Tiny sips.*

He put up his hands. "I know what Motty's told me. And I know what happened with your mama."

"Promise me," she said.

He looked at her. His eyes were moist. "You're the eldest now. You have say. Sunny won't go into that cave unless you take her there."

Stella thought, Do I tell him? The girl was never going in. Stella had come back to make sure of it.

Hendrick was watching her. "So you'll allow it? Sunny will come back with me?"

"Let me think it over."

HER BODY JERKED awake as if she'd nodded off behind the wheel at fifty miles per hour. A face hovered outside the dewy glass of the passenger window. An angry face, yelling at her.

Stella scrambled upright. She was in the front seat of the Ford. She'd fallen asleep in her car—not for the first time and surely not the last. Her head felt like a cracked walnut.

The door was yanked open. It was Ruth—her face like ten

pounds of bitter in a five-pound bag. How did Hendrick cope with *that* every morning?

"Where is it?" Ruth demanded. "Where's the ring?"

"What ring?"

"Don't play innocent. First the will and now her *jewelry*? She wore a diamond ring around her neck and you did something with it!"

"I don't know what the hell you're talking about." Motty had never worn a ring around her neck, and Stella would have seen it when she looked over the old woman's body.

"Don't lie to me," Ruth said.

The Ford was still parked in the barn, but the big wooden doors had been opened and light filled the car's rear window. "Can we do this later?"

"No! The mortuary men are here for the body."

"What? They're already taking her?" Stella leaned out the door. Stood up. The planet moved under her like a barge.

Ruth followed her out of the barn, hissing meanness. "This is a ploy of yours, isn't it? You think because Motty never married that somehow her things are yours?"

There'd been a man in Motty's past, but no husband. Private Ronald Whitehead, distant kin to Stella's old grade school teacher, had died in Nicaragua or somewhere during the Banana Wars. Motty never talked about him except to say he'd left behind an unborn child—that would be Lena—and nothing else, not even a picture. Certainly no diamond ring, if that's what Ruth was going on about.

"Hendrick is her brother, and as the closest male relative—"

"Jesus, Ruth. If there was a ring in the house I'm sure it'll turn up."

Last night's fire circle had burned down to ash. Beer cans littered the yard.

A Pontiac hearse with curtained side windows had been

backed up to the porch steps, the rear doors spread open, ready to receive the body. Hendrick was in the living room, arguing with the jowly mortuary man, whose young assistant watched nervously.

Hendrick said, "I don't see how it can be one person's decision!"

"I'm so sorry," the mortuary man said, and meant it. "But we can't force Elder Rayburn to let her in."

"What's the matter?" Ruth said. "What is it now?"

Only one of the Georgians was in the living room—the beefy pale man. His jacket was off, and there was a holster on his hip. He saw Stella looking at it and nodded at her. What the God damn fuck?

"They say they can't bury her at the church cemetery," Hendrick said. "John Rayburn won't allow it."

"But why?"

Stella knew why. He was still wounded, and lashing out. His only son was dead, and he wanted payback.

"I'm sure you can work something out," the mortuary man said. "There are other churches—"

"No," Hendrick said. "There are no other churches. Our family *founded* the Primitive Baptist Church. I was a deacon before I left. It's our right—her right—to be buried with her ancestors."

"You have to talk to him," Ruth said.

"God damn it," Stella said quietly. Her hangover was chiseling at the inside of her head.

Hendrick and Ruth looked at her. The mortuary man glanced away.

"I'll go," she said.

Hendrick was surprised. "You will?"

She recoiled at the idea of facing John Rayburn. She'd avoided him for ten years. But she'd be damned if she'd let him have the last word on where they put Motty. And Stella was the only one who could fix this. "Motty's owed her spot—next to my mother. With all the Birches."

Hendrick nodded enthusiastically. "We'll both talk to him. He has to know he's facing the entire family." He was swole up with capital-H Honor.

Last night, Stella hadn't given Hendrick an answer on his plan to raise Sunny in Georgia—at least she didn't remember giving one. She'd walked back to the fire and sat up for a few more hours, passing moonshine. But Hendrick was acting, well, avuncular, which worried her.

The pale man pulled on his jacket. "I'll ride with you."

Hell no, Stella thought. Then said, "Give me a sec," and walked out of the room.

"What about the ring?" Ruth screeched.

Stella went into Motty's bedroom, Ruth right on her ass. The air was heavy with perfume—Hendrick and Ruth overcompensating. The body couldn't smell that bad yet, could it? A blue dress Stella didn't recognize lay across the foot of the bed, the price tag still on the collar. Stella could feel Ruth behind her, bristling, almost eager for her to object.

Stella gazed at Motty, waiting for sadness or regret or *something* to poke its way up through the fog of the hangover. Anger would at least be familiar. It was the emotion they'd most often brought out in each other. It would be nice to argue one last time—say, about this diamond ring that Motty had evidently been hiding from her all her life. Or about the benefits of cremation. Or how Hendrick, despite being an asshole, was Sunny's best chance for a good life.

"What do you say, Motty?"

Motty didn't answer. Her face seemed more caved in than yesterday, her skin grayer, but otherwise the same as when Stella first saw the body. Death took some time to assert itself. Maybe grief did, too.

Stella leaned close. "Speak now," she whispered. "Or forever hold your peace."

JOHN RAYBURN HAD TAKEN the government's money and moved into a humble frame house on the edge of Townsend. Stella pulled into the driveway happy that she'd never been there. No memories to get in the way of the job.

Uncle Hendrick and the bleached Georgian were waiting in Hendrick's car. Her uncle had been hurt that Stella had wanted to drive separate. Weren't they family? But even though she was cooperating with him on Sunny, the thought of getting trapped in his car with a pistol-packing deacon made her feel itchy. Ruth was staying back at the house to "receive visitors" and take care of Veronica, who was probably still sleeping off her sins in what used to be Stella's bedroom. The rest of the Georgia boys were staying somewhere in town.

"I thought we should go in together," Hendrick said. "Present a unified front."

"Uh-huh." He was afraid of Rayburn, always had been.

"Just . . . try to be respectful. You get more flies with honey."

"What about him?" Nodded to the man in the car.

Hendrick said, "Brother Paul will wait for us out here."

"Suits me."

Mary Lynn, Elder Rayburn's daughter, met them at the door. "Stella? Oh my goodness." She was surprised, but there was a warmth in her voice Stella hadn't expected. They'd hardly seen each other since Lincoln died. Mary Lynn had moved to Maryville, working at the diner a couple of doors from the police station, and Stella made it a point to avoid both places. Mary Lynn was a few years younger than her brother, a grade below Stella, in fact, and had never looked or acted much like him.

Lunk had been solid and forthright, but she was soft and watchful as a mouse.

"Hey, Mary Lynn."

Hendrick said, "It's good to see you, Mary. Is your father in?"

Mary Lynn winced. Looked back into the dark of the house. A voice said, "I thought you were going to sit out there all day, Hendrick."

Hendrick forced a laugh. Mary opened the door.

Elder Rayburn was a silhouette in an armchair set up by the front window. Sentry duty. The only place for Stella and Hendrick to sit was side by side on the pebbly couch.

Mary asked them if they wanted coffee and Stella said, "Lord yes."

Hendrick shot her a glance. What, was "Lord" too close to taking His name in vain? Her hangover didn't leave room for worrying about blasphemy.

Hendrick and Rayburn talked about the weather in the cove, and Georgia weather, and the new road going in. This was a southern home, and even blood enemies wouldn't draw swords before coffee and corn bread. It may have been a new house, but everything in it was old—the armchair, the elaborately scrolled wooden clock, the rugs, even the drapes—no doubt hauled from the Rayburn farmhouse in the cove, jammed together in this unfamiliar place like refugees.

Stella downed a cup and asked for a refill. Mary Lynn poured it silently, then hovered at the doorway between the kitchen and the front room. Where was Mrs. Rayburn? It was odd for Mary Lynn to play hostess.

"How's your mother?" Stella asked Mary Lynn.

"She's . . ." She gestured toward the back of the house.

"Resting," Elder Rayburn said. Gazing into his coffee cup. He'd yet to look at Stella or address her.

Hendrick said, "Well, please give Elsa our regards. You know, I always loved to hear her sing."

A silence descended. Hendrick gazed at the clock. Rayburn noticed something out the window.

Stella sighed, set down her coffee cup. "We're here about Motty."

Hendrick shifted uncomfortably. Rayburn looked at him, not her.

"There seems to be some confusion," Hendrick said. "The boys from Smith Mortuary . . ."

Rayburn pursed his lips.

"The boys were under the impression that they weren't allowed to bury Mathilda at the church."

"You can see how that wouldn't be proper," Rayburn said.

"Proper?" Hendrick said.

"The cemetery is for church members in good standing."

Hendrick glanced to the side, performing his confusion. "Motty was a member of the church, John. We both grew up in the church, both baptized there. I may have transferred my membership to Georgia, but Motty—"

"I said, in good standing."

"What does *that* mean?" Stella asked.

Rayburn finally looked at her. "Don't pretend you don't know what I mean."

"I'm not pretending. All the Birches are buried there. My *mother's* buried there."

"In hindsight, that may have been a mistake."

"*What?*"

"Lena barely attended. And Mathilda outright rejected the church."

"Oh come now," Hendrick said. "Motty never rejected the church. She just stopped going. She got old."

"She followed other ways."

Mary Lynn inhaled sharply. Her father was practically calling Motty a pagan. Or worse, a Catholic.

"That's—" Hendrick bit off what he was going to say next. Took a breath. "I know my sister. I know she was rough around the edges—"

"She was a mite more than rough."

"She was still a Christian! One of the Elect. I don't see how gossip and made-up stories . . ." Hendrick was flustered. He couldn't say what the stories were without lending them credence. But everybody in the cove had theories about the Birches. You couldn't stop them from talking.

Stella was about to come off the couch, but she kept her voice steady. "You still believe in eternal security, don't you, Elder Rayburn? Once saved, always saved?"

"Even the devil can quote scripture," Rayburn said evenly. "You always had a talent for it."

"There's one I remember about *God* granting eternal life," Stella said. "And no man shall pluck them out of My hand."

"Only God knows if she was in His hand to begin with."

"You're making my point."

"And *my* point," Hendrick said, "is that we've always been a congregation-led church. Perhaps the other elders—"

"We?" Rayburn said. "You left for Georgia, to sell chairs."

"I went where there was work." He forced a smile. "The world needs a place to sit."

"What we're wondering," Stella said, "is if the other elders would be more impartial."

That got to Rayburn. But he wouldn't respond to Stella. He turned to Hendrick and said, icily, "Impartiality has nothing to do with it. This is about the Lord's plan, not mine."

"The Lord's plan," Hendrick said. His voice dropped and slowed. "The Lord's plan."

"That's what I said."

"I sure wish we knew what it was. I think about what happened to Lincoln . . . it doesn't seem fair. That was a tragedy."

"Don't you talk about my son."

There was a time people couldn't stop talking about it. Everyone in the cove knew the story of the preacher's son, good and true, who drove his daddy's new car to see the wicked Stella Wallace. That girl made him dance in the moonlight and drink whiskey straight from Abby Whitt's still and sent him on his way with her lipstick on his cheek. The next morning they found that new car wheels-up in the icy-cold Little River.

Hillbillies did love a good murder ballad.

"He made a mistake a hundred boys made before him," Hendrick continued. "They all lived to tell the tale. Some of 'em might even brag about it—though Lincoln was not that kind of boy. We all know that."

"He was tempted," Rayburn said. Hendrick put up his hands, allowing the point.

Stella thought, I'm sitting right here, you bastards.

"Now, I'm a father myself," Hendrick said. "But even I can't imagine the pain of losing your son. No one would be surprised if you let your personal feelings about my niece . . . let them cloud your heart."

"Your niece," Rayburn said. He was so angry, barely holding on to himself. "I don't care a whit about your niece. My feelings, my *concern*, is for my progeny. Given your family history—"

Mary Lynn suddenly swept in. "Can I get anything for anybody? More coffee?"

No one responded to her. "The whole cove knows about the Birch women," Rayburn said. "The string of children born out of wedlock."

Hendrick said, "John, I don't think—"

Stella held up a hand. "You said *progeny*."

Rayburn's eyes didn't leave hers. "You ran away," he said.

"Days after Lincoln's funeral, you ran away. Now my wife, she has a kind heart. Even after what you did to her boy, she was ready to forgive you. But then, you vanished. You *hid*." Stella realized she'd gotten to her feet. He said, "And then that girl appeared in Mathilda's arms."

Hendrick's mouth was agape. The conversation had taken a turn he didn't understand. "Sunny is an orphan," he said. "From the North Carolina Birches."

"A family no one's ever seen or heard from," Rayburn said.

Stella said, "Is that what this is about? You won't let us bury Motty because you want something from me? You want to *trade*?"

Rayburn blinked hard. Good lord, was the man going to cry?

"We want to do right by her. You owe us that much."

"Let me tell you something," Stella said. "Sunny Birch is not Lincoln's. There's no grandchild for you or Elsa."

"We can pay you."

Her body jerked. She'd stopped herself from slapping him, the movement arrested as violently as a stick jammed into bicycle spokes. Her right arm had already come up, her hand open. A hot wire burned from her neck to her palm. She could picture Rayburn bent sideways in the chair from the blow.

Mary Lynn cried out as if she'd seen it too. Rayburn's eyes were wide, his mouth open. He'd suddenly become ancient, frail as paper.

Stella closed her fist. "Keep your God damn graveyard," she said. "I'll bury her myself."

Mary Lynn ran outside before Stella could climb into the car. She was crying, too. Before she could speak Stella said, "Tell your father he's right. Motty was a pagan. All the Birches—we're all God damn devil worshippers."

The Georgian—Brother Paul—watched her as she backed out at full speed.

She drove fast, wiping at her eyes, cursing. After three minutes she pulled over, leaving the car running, and popped open the back seat compartment. Ran a hand through the straw packing material. Jesus Christ, they couldn't have drunk it all, could they? Then her fingers touched a jar and she pulled it out, unscrewed the cap.

The whiskey hit the back of her throat and burned. She took another pull. Got back behind the wheel. She was ready to leave the cove again, funeral or no funeral. But there was one person she had to see first.

## 7

## 1936

ELDER RAYBURN WAITED until Stella was twelve years old before he paid a visit, perhaps finally worrying about her immortal soul. A month after Stella's first communion, he drove up in the black buggy, his fool son, Lunk, by his side.

Stella was out by the hog pen when they pulled up. She was perched on the fence rail, pouring feed over the rail and into the trough. The sow was gigantic. She'd been growing all that winter, but suddenly, in the month after Stella's communion, the beast had somehow taken on a hundred pounds. Usually the sow watched her whenever Stella climbed the fence, glaring at her with those eyes that looked too much like a human's, as if Stella were her next meal, as if the corncobs and chestnuts and the pounds and pounds of suet she consumed every day were not enough for her, would never be enough. Stella was sure if she fell over the fence and went down in the mud, the hog would squash her and then calmly chew her limbs off.

But not today. The sow wouldn't come to the trough. She was

walking in circles around a pile of straw she'd made, squealing low and plaintive.

Stella dropped the feed bag and hopped down. Elder Rayburn and Lunk were already striding toward her. She looked at her filthy hands and hoped her scars didn't show through the dirt.

"Miss Wallace," Elder Rayburn said in that deep voice. "So good to see you."

"Afternoon, Elder," she said. "Hey there, Lunk."

Elder Rayburn raised his eyebrows.

"It's what we call him at school," Stella explained.

"No it's not," Lunk said. To his father he said, "It's what *she* calls me." Lunk had grown a couple of inches, and his hair was combed with a straightedge part just like his daddy's. A white box was tucked under his arm. She didn't see much of Lunk these days. Since he'd turned fourteen he started going to a fancy high school in Maryville. But the elder showed up often enough to give his daughter, Mary Lynn, a ride home.

"That sow looks ready to drop," Rayburn said.

Stella thought, Is that what's going on? "She has been acting strange," she said.

Rayburn asked for Motty, and Stella ran to get her. Motty was suspicious. Then she saw the white box in Lunk's arm and grunted. "So it's this."

"I've been meaning to visit for quite a while," Rayburn said. "The church has a gift for Stella."

"She don't need that," Motty said.

Stella looked up at Motty, projecting a mental plea: Please don't run them off! She hardly ever got gifts. An orange for Christmas, a new pair of shoes for her birthday. Motty said anything else was a waste.

"We've brought something every child your age should have," Elder Rayburn said to Stella. "Your very own—"

"Bible," Motty said. "It's always a Bible."

"Yes, well," Elder Rayburn said. "Son, why don't you . . . ?"

Lunk handed over the box. His expression was serious, as if he were applying for early elderhood.

Stella lifted the lid. Inside was a book, with a black leather cover. It said "Holy Bible" in gold script, and the thin pages were gilt-edged.

"That's the King James Version," Rayburn said. "The inspired word of God in English clothing, passed down to the true church."

"Red letter edition," Lunk said solemnly. Stella had no idea what that meant.

"Thank you," she said earnestly. "I'll read it cover to cover."

Elder Rayburn smiled indulgently. "Well, that's quite a task you've set yourself."

"She'll do it," Motty said. "You can't keep her from anything with words on it."

"That's fine, that's fine. Now, Stella?" She looked up from the book. "I want to invite you to church. Motty hadn't brought you yet, and I wanted to make sure you knew you were welcome."

"I'll bring her," Motty said, "when I decide to bring her."

"Of course, of course." Rayburn decided to focus on Stella. "Has Motty told you that you might be one of the Elect?"

"Uhm . . ."

"She doesn't know what that is," Motty said tiredly.

Elder Rayburn seemed to relish this news. "Well now, the Elect are the souls going to Heaven. Jesus Christ died for your sins so that you might be welcomed there, but it was God the Father who would have picked your soul to be one of the Elect, way back at the dawn of Creation."

Stella didn't understand. "God already chose me?"

"Perhaps, perhaps. He gives His children eternal life—and neither shall any man pluck them out of my hand."

"John 10:28," Lincoln said.

"I don't have to do anything?"

"Exactly! If you're one of the Elect, the work's already done for you. Grace is already yours."

This didn't correspond to anything Stella had read about Christians. "But if God's already decided everything, why did Jesus have to die?"

"For your sins," he repeated. "For God so loved the world, that He gave His only begotten son, that whosoever believeth in Him should not perish, but have everlasting life." She thought, Have these Rayburns memorized the whole book? "You see, Jesus was the sacrifice."

Stella knew all about sacrifices—she'd read *The Return of Tarzan*. "Who was God sacrificing Jesus *to*?"

"Pardon?"

"I thought you made a sacrifice to get a god to do you a favor."

"There's only one God."

"So God sacrificed His son to Himself?"

Motty barked a laugh. Stella didn't know why that was so funny.

"Not exactly," Rayburn said. "Jesus *is* God, and He's also the holy spirit."

Stella was amazed. "So God sacrificed *Himself* to Himself."

"Keep going, Elder," Motty said.

"How about the other gods?" Stella asked.

"Thou shalt have no other gods before Me," Lunk said. "That's a commandment." Elder Rayburn scowled at him. The boy wasn't helping.

"But not *all* the gods, right?" Stella asked. "How about—?"

Motty seized Stella at the back of the neck. Stella yelped and dropped the Bible.

"Get inside the house," Motty growled.

"But—"

"*Now.*"

STELLA SPENT THE REST of the day in her room, stewing. She'd thought everything would change once she'd had communion, but as soon as Hendrick and the Uncles had left, life went back to normal, and Motty treated her like a peasant. She refused to tell Stella when, if ever, she'd be allowed to commune again. "I'm the eldest Birch woman," Motty said. "I say when you're ready."

And Stella would decide when she left her room. Let the old woman do the chores on her own.

Stella was curious about the Bible, but at least she had *The Book of Esther*.

She'd been reading it every day since she'd received it, dipping into her favorite passages every chance she got, going so far as to whisper aloud her favorite passages. Now she turned again to the first page, the entry for March 3, 1865, and said, "God has seen fit to give us a daughter."

The book, thick despite the thinness of each onionskin page, contained twenty-two years of Esther's life, as told by Russell Birch and then, after Russell's death, by his youngest son, Morgan, now an old, old man. It was the most delicious thing she'd ever read—and she'd thought nothing was better than Nancy Drew. Days after the communion, the God's thoughts had faded from her mind, but every time she read *The Book of Esther* it was like crawling into that cave again.

Well, almost. Nothing was like touching the hand of God. But this was the closest thing she'd found—that feeling of being part of a mission, a captain riding atop the machine of history.

She turned the page. Here was baby Esther in the arms of Clara. Turned again, to young Esther bleaching her gown white.

Then a teenage Esther commanding her brother to build a church. She could picture Esther pointing her finger at him.

Hunger finally drew Stella out of the room. Motty had made biscuits and greens for supper. Stella was happy to see her looking worn-out.

"You take care of that sow yet?" Stella asked.

Motty gave her a sharp look. "What are you talking about?"

"It was walking around in circles," Stella said. "Elder Rayburn said it was about to drop."

"Why the hell didn't you tell me sooner?" Motty said. She cursed and went out to the pen.

Stella smiled to herself. She reached over and took one of Motty's biscuits, got out her book, and went back to her reading.

When Stella heard the gunshot an hour later, it almost seemed to have come from *The Book of Esther*. She scrambled into her coat and pulled on shoes. Outside it was already full dark. A skiff of snow lay across the yard. The tractor was backed up to the hog pen, engine rumbling, but there was no one at the wheel. What was happening?

She heard Motty cursing. Stella peeked around one of the big metal tractor wheels. A lantern sat atop a fence post at the hog pen. The pig lay on its side, and Motty stooped over it, looping a rope around the animal's front legs and neck. The air steamed with the heat from its body—an alarming amount of steam, as if it lay on a cook fire.

Suddenly Motty straightened and grabbed the rifle, which had been propped against the fence. She walked toward the tractor, dragging the other end of the rope with her. Her dress was stained with blood.

Then Motty spotted her, her murderous glare like a shout.

Stella realized she wouldn't be safe in the house. She sprinted away from Motty, across the yard, and then up, into the woods.

. . .

MOONLIGHT DANCED AHEAD of her like a will-o'-the-wisp, but she would have known her way blindfolded. She pushed through Abby's door without knocking and slammed the door behind her.

Safe!

"Abby?"

He didn't answer, and neither did his menagerie. She was surrounded by wild animals. Heads, mostly. Four spectacularly antlered deer who looked like they'd just burst through the wall and couldn't back out. A trio of decapitated bears, mouths agape, teeth sharp, permanently ravenous. A manic-eyed bobcat head.

A few lucky critters had retained their bodies. Trout swam the walls. A small wolf howled. A fat raccoon squatted in the corner, tiny black hands in the air, begging. And everywhere skeletons: coiled snake spines, fleshless birds with wings spread like a fan of tiny daggers, gape-eyed elk skulls.

Warming itself by the embers in the fireplace stood Abby's crowning achievement as a taxidermist: a long-snouted Russian boar, ready to charge, grinning with mischief.

This was her secret home. When Motty was acting cruel, when Stella was feeling so lonely she could die, this cozy shack was where she ran to. The front room was barely twenty feet long, both sitting room and kitchen, though "kitchen" was a grandiose word for a single-burner cookstove and a metal tub full of dishes. His water came through a spout fed out through the wall to the cistern.

Motty would have called it a God damn mess. Stella loved it, especially the stuffed animals, though at the moment that boar reminded her of the sow Motty had just shot.

Stella called Abby's name again, just in case he was asleep in the back room, the only other room in the cabin. She didn't even think about opening that door. Never had. She knew without being told that it was a Man Place, private to Abby.

She knocked, but there was no answer. If he wasn't here this time of night, she was pretty sure of the one place he'd be. And that gave her some time.

She dragged one of his rickety chairs to the fireplace and climbed up. The "mantel" was a few rocks jutting out of the stone chimney, but on it sat what were surely Abby's two most valuable possessions.

First was an ornately carved wooden box. The items inside had taken on a magical significance for her: an ivory-handled jackknife, a handful of silver and gold foreign coins, and the prize, a bronze war medal with a rainbow ribbon. On the front of the medal was an angel holding a sword, and on the back were six stars, a fancy shield, and the names of a dozen faraway countries: France, Rumania, China, places she'd only read about. The box conjured an entire life of war and adventure and distant travels. She often pictured Abby in the trenches as his best friend was shot and fell to the ground with a surprised expression. Or on a navy destroyer, loading shells into a giant artillery gun. In a port, kissing a beautiful red-haired woman. Then sitting alone in a Paris café, writing love letters that never received a reply. (The woman had died tragically by a sniper's bullet when she left her house to find a baguette.) Stella could never ask Abby to tell her the real story, because then she'd have to admit she'd peeked.

Beside the box leaned an unframed black-and-white photograph of three people that had been painted to add color. Abby and Ray Wallace wore cowboy hats and vests. Between them was a skinny, sharp-nosed woman dressed like an Indian in fringe and feathers. Tourist costumes. The three of them stared without smiling at the camera, but their expressions spoke of deep friendship; she was sure of it. In pencil on the back of the photo it said, "Cherokee NC Feb 3 1924."

She knew that the woman was her mother. Nobody else had kept a photograph of her—not Motty, not Pa. She promised herself that if she ever ran away from the cove she was going to come here first and steal that picture.

STELLA WENT FARTHER UP the mountain, following the smell of smoke to a hidden spot she'd visited many times.

Abby and another man sat beside a fire—two fires, actually. One to keep them warm, the other to boil the mash in Bessie, Abby's big copper pot. Abby spotted her. "Stella! What are you doing up here so late?"

"Stars do come out at night," the other man said.

Abby laughed. Both of them held tin cups. She understood what was happening; she'd seen Abby drunk.

The stranger offered his hand. "Pee Wee Simms. I've heard a lot about you, little miss." He spoke with a nasal, northern accent. He was a long, tall man with oiled hair and a pencil mustache that made him look like William Powell. "We heard a gunshot. You haven't turned us in to the revenuers, have you?"

"Leave her be," Abby said.

"What, have you managed to keep this activity a secret from her?"

"I been up here plenty of times," Stella told the Yankee. She couldn't quite believe that his name was Pee Wee. "I know what a still is."

"Do you now?"

"It's a machine that turns corn into money."

Pee Wee laughed so hard moonshine sloshed out of his cup. Stella had stolen the line from Abby. She didn't think it was *that* funny.

Abby said, "Does Motty know you're out of bed?"

"The hog's sick and Motty's riled up," she said airily. "She chased me out of the house." Stella didn't want to talk about it, or be sent back.

"What's wrong with the sow?"

Before she was forced to answer, Pee Wee said, "I hope you appreciate that you are in the presence of genius. Abby is a miracle worker—and this, my dear, is his miracle machine."

"It's not a miracle," she said. "It's just . . . science."

"Damn straight," Abby said.

Pee Wee sat up straighter, suddenly intrigued. "And what does a little girl like you know about science?"

She resented his tone. Abby said, "She knows this machine backwards and forwards."

"Challenge accepted," Pee Wee said. Stella thought, What challenge? "Question One: Tell me about . . ." He surveyed the still, pointed at the small barrel between the pot and the larger condenser barrel. Copper pipes connected all three containers. "This piece."

"Thump keg," she said.

"Is this the doubler I've heard so much about?"

Abby had called it that once. She nodded.

"And what does this doubler double?"

"Well, the pot boils the mash, so that's the first boil, and this is where you get the second boil."

Pee Wee nodded sagely. "And how does that happen?" He waved a hand. "In detail."

"The fumes from the pot go through the arm—" She pointed to the copper pipe connected to the thump keg. "And then in the keg they cool down and turn into a liquid again." She glanced at Abby, but he was watching with his hands over his belly. "So then more fumes come in, and they start heating up some of the alcohol, and that's where you get the second boil."

"And where do these vapors go from there?" Pee Wee asked. He kept using that teacher voice.

"Out to the condenser—excuse me, the flake stand condenser." She wasn't going to lose points for imprecision. The condenser was a barrel full of creek water; a copper tube wound through it, giving the fumes time to cool and turn back into liquid. It was such a crazy process. One thing turning into something else, then back into its previous form, over and over again—but at each step it got a little closer to its perfect state.

"And then?" he asked.

What more did he want? "And then the whiskey comes out the worm," she said. That was what Abby called the final bit of pipe, where it dripped into the catch pan.

Pee Wee wasn't yet satisfied. "Back to the doubler. Why go to the trouble of doing it an extra time? What's the point? Scientifically speaking."

Stella glanced at Abby. She'd always been a little foggy on this part. "Well, it gives the bad stuff a chance to fall out of the vapors."

"Bad stuff?" Pee Wee asked.

"Nefarious chemicals. That's what Abby calls them."

Pee Wee said, "That's just a fancy way of saying he doesn't know."

She looked at Abby, alarmed. Was that true?

Abby shrugged. "It's the same reason we throw out the foreshot." That was the first few ounces that dripped out of the worm. "Some things you just do because that's the way it's done."

"But . . . you have to know *why*," she said.

"I agree completely," Pee Wee said.

Stella hadn't even known she was ignorant. She'd trusted that Abby, an adult, knew the answers, all the way down. But he was just using words to hide what he didn't know.

Abby said, "Tradition means you don't have to think everything up from scratch. If it works, it works."

"My goodness, we're in transubstantiation territory," Pee Wee said. "Abby's invoking faith to explain his miracle."

Stella was frustrated. Pee Wee was the one who started out talking about miracles, and Abby was on her side about moonshining being science. Now they'd flipped around.

"What I have faith in is this still and this recipe," Abby said. "Doubling makes it taste better, that's objective fact."

Pee Wee waved a hand. "Fine, fine. Final question." He nodded toward the catch pan. "What's that pale thing sticking out of the worm?"

"Pee Wee . . ." Abby warned.

"A scientist should know!"

Stella frowned. Abby had never told her its name. "It's a stick. It keeps the whiskey from running back along the bottom of the pipe and getting wasted."

Pee Wee laughed. "That is not a stick, my dear, that's a coon dick!"

Abby slapped Pee Wee in the shoulder, who laughed harder. "What, you never told her?"

Stella didn't like to feel dumb. "Y'all are lying."

"Not at all!" Pee Wee exclaimed. She wished he'd stop laughing. "That is indeed the penis bone of your North American raccoon. Evolution has shaped it for this exact purpose."

She checked with Abby. He was embarrassed, but finally admitted to it. "Don't believe him about the evolution part."

Stella thought of the begging raccoon in Abby's cabin. Maybe it was pining for its missing pecker.

"So what do you think?" Pee Wee asked her. "Are you going to make your own moonshine someday?"

"Absolutely not," Abby said.

"That depends," Stella said.

"On what?" Pee Wee asked.

"How much money we talkin'?"

Stella had never felt so good, getting a grown man to listen to her and laugh that hard.

. . .

THEY LET HER SIT with them for another couple of hours. Every time the pan filled she helped Abby swap it out and fill jars, and in between she sat by the hot fire and ate goober peas and listened to them talk. Pee Wee had opinions on life insurance (against it), something called the proletariat (it was complicated), and belches (enthusiastically and repeatedly pro). He also believed that Stella ought to be allowed to taste the night's product, seeing as how she was helping, but Abby forbade it.

Stella thought, I ought to tell this to Uncle Hendrick, so he could write it in my book.

*April 24th, 1936. Stella demonstrated her knowledge of whiskey distillation to the disbelieving Yankee, Pee Wee Simms.*

Part of what thrilled her about *The Book of Esther* was that it was someone else recording these events, a man paying attention to the lives of his wife and daughter, even if he didn't seem to understand everything that was going on. Starting with that first line: "God has seen fit to give us a daughter." That "seen fit" struck Stella a bit testy. In the commentary for the page, Hendrick noted that Russell was about to turn seventy and Clara was only a few years younger. Their children—including the Confederate betrayer, Cyril, and Morgan, who also lived in the cove— were grown and were raising babies of their own. But then Clara found an orphan girl whose parents were casualties of the war and decided they'd take her in.

*Clara has named her Esther, which is fitting. She is beautiful but for the blemish that covers one side of her face. Clara assures me it will shrink and fade as she grows.*

Hendrick wrote: "It won't."

Hendrick also explained Russell's comment about the fitness of the name: the biblical Esther was an orphan and was so beautiful that the king of Persia took her as his wife, not realizing she was a "Jewess." (Stella had never seen that word before opening the diary, and for days after she'd find herself saying it aloud: jew-*essss*, jew-*ess*.) Esther was such a stunner that when the king's advisor was about to decree that all the Jews in Persia be killed, Esther convinced the king otherwise and, even better, put out an alternate order that allowed the Jews to kill anyone who threatened their families. A few days later, seventy-five thousand people were dead!

Most of the early part of the diary was about Russell's wife, Clara. Russell seemed confused and cowed by her. When she demanded he build a shelter over the mouth of the cave, so that Clara could sleep near the entrance with baby Esther, he didn't understand it, but he did it. Word got out, though, and Russell worried that their neighbors were looking askance at these old folks taking care of an infant.

Russell never got very good at storytelling—he was no Abby, in other words—and Stella wished Clara would take over the diary. Key details were missing, like why *did* they adopt the girl? Surely their grown children, who all lived nearby, could have taken her in. And why did she insist on sleeping over the cave?

Esther came more to the fore as a character, and she seemed just as stubborn as her mother. In the late fall of 1876, when she was twelve—Stella's age!—the girl announced that she was a Revelator, just like John in the Bible, and that she alone was allowed to go into the cave. Clara didn't take this well. Poor Russell, now in his early eighties, was distressed:

*I cannot bear all this bickering and backbiting. Mother and Daughter have turned on each other like the Rebels versus the Union.*

So Russell went hunting.

Before the war he'd built a round stone hut on top of Birch Bald, and he could stick his gun out a slit and shoot whatever walked into the clearing, though mostly he just watched and waited. He filled two pages of the diary with all the wildlife he *could* have killed. Again, he was no Abby.

When Russell came back a week later, his wife and daughter had stopped fighting. Esther was in bed with a "fever," her hands bandaged as if they'd been burned.

*I demanded to know what had happened to put her in this state. Clara at first refused to answer, but finally she said, "The God has spoken. Listen up."*

What followed were scores of pages, documenting all the times Esther went into the cave for communion, and what she said, after. Everything she said under the God's influence remained mysterious and poetic, though after Russell died and Esther's brother, Morgan, took up the transcription, the words took a turn toward the King James: *The God has made his home among the rocks and stones; The first child shall breathe poison yet survive.* And the kicker, delivered several times over the course of her Revelations: *This is promised to the children, on the day the God steps into the light: thou shalt have one body, ever blooming.*

Sometimes Stella grew weepy just reading it.

But the end—the end was terrible. The book just *stopped.* There was no note to say what Esther went on to do, or if she ever left the cove, or how she died. Nothing.

The first time she got to the last page, she couldn't believe it. She had an urge to throw the book across the room, and only barely stopped her arm from doing it. Her arm was an excellent critic.

BY THE TIME they doused the fire under the still, Pee Wee was snoring in his chair.

"Well," Abby said, drawing it out so it came out *whaaaale.* "It's about time I walk you home." The moonshine had brought out the Uncle Dan in him.

"I can get there myself," she said. "What about Pee Wee? Is he all right?"

"He's not going anywhere. In the morning I'll walk him back down to his car."

"How'd you get to be friends with a *Yankee*?"

"He married my sister."

Abby had a sister? The night was full of surprises.

He said, "Come on now, let's check on that sick hog."

"There's nothing to check on." Stella tried to keep her voice steady. For a short while she'd forgotten about the pig. "Motty shot it."

"What? Why'd she do that?" He was more shocked about a dead farm animal than she expected.

She told him she didn't know for sure, but that the sow looked sick, walking around in circles. Abby stopped talking and moved faster.

The gate to the hog pen hung open. The tractor had been driven a few yards past the barn door, a rope running from the back hook to a wooden pallet, which now lay just inside the door. Motty was bent over the pallet, sawing through the pig's carcass.

She saw them and stood up, one hand still holding the saw. Blood splattered her dress. Her face hung slack with exhaustion.

Abby looked down at Stella, as if weighing what he could say in front of her. Then he said, "You haul that beast by yourself? I could have helped you."

"Don't need help." She removed her spectacles, tried to find a clean patch on her dress.

"You want me to call the butcher?"

Motty's face jerked up. *"No."*

"I could—"

"Go back home, Abby. And *you*." Her attention turned to Stella. "What did I tell you?"

Stella was banished to the house. She stomped to Motty's room, found the Bible, and took it back. She thought, I ought to pack up right now and go move in with Abby. She'd change her name to Whitt, run whiskey, and keep the money for herself.

## 8

1948

THERE ARE BACKROADS in the cove, and backroads to the backroads, rutted tracks, barely wide enough for a car, that followed the old Cherokee trails up into the mountains and along the ridges. The park service hadn't mapped them—can't map what you don't know about—but Stella had learned to drive on these roads. Abby Whitt had told her that when you see the revenuers coming up the hill, you best have an escape route. Yet when the police did come for him, he didn't run.

Stella took the road slow, fighting the ruts and easing the Ford's wheels over roots and rocks. Tree branches scraped the paint from the doors.

After thirty minutes she nosed into a small clearing and set the handbrake.

This was the spot where Abby used to run his still. The only clue that this was home to the greatest moonshine ever made was the nature of the trash: broken Mason jars, cornmeal sacks, a spool of black rubber hose, a split wooden barrel. Bessie had been hauled away while Abby was in prison, the copper too valuable to go to waste.

There ought to be a historical marker here, Stella thought.

She had another ten-minute hike ahead of her. It would have been much faster to walk to Abby's place from Motty's house, but she hadn't wanted to deal with Veronica and Ruth.

She was a hundred yards along the old path through the trees when she heard a rustling, something big in the undergrowth. She froze. Black bears didn't bother people, mostly, but she didn't want to blunder into one.

After a minute of silence, she started moving again, head swiveling. Thirty feet farther along she saw a white-tailed doe, lying on its side. The animal wasn't moving except for one twitching back leg, the hoof scratching at air.

She'd heard no gunfire—maybe it had been shot a while ago? The hunter ought to be beating the bushes for it. Unless he got spooked—hunting in the park was a federal crime. Or maybe the deer was diseased.

Suddenly it thrashed, a full-body spasm, but its legs weren't working. It collapsed back onto its side and went still.

The doe's huge dark eye regarded her. It was still alive.

"God damn it."

She didn't own a gun. Didn't trust herself with one.

She walked back up the trail, scanning the ground. Finally found a good-sized rock. Carried it back, hoping the animal had expired in the minute she'd been away.

No such luck.


ABBY SAT ON a stump in his front yard, a metal tub between his knees, washing bones. The finished whites were laid out on a cloth on the grass, a few long bones among a score of small ones. Stella tried to reconstruct the creature in her mind.

"Raccoon?" she asked.

"Possum."

She raised her eyebrows and he said, "It's a fine and noble creature. I was thinking of mounting it hanging from a branch by its tail."

"Artistic."

"I owed it to a fella. Thought I'd finish up."

He seemed happy to see her. He'd cleaned up his yard a bit in the last ten years, but there was still plenty of garbage in the gully a few yards away. Thirty years of dumped trash didn't just disappear. And that stump—it had always been the throne of the yard. She remembered sitting there alone one night, heartbroken, when a single snowflake drifted down in front of her. Then another fell, and another. She held out her arm and caught them in her hand.

Ugh. She hadn't thought of that night in a long time.

She grabbed a paint bucket and sat down across from Abby. "See?" she said. "Patio set. I've just increased the value of your real estate."

"You mean Motty's."

"Shit. Right." The shack wasn't his, never had been. It sat on Birch land, and belonged to the park service now. They'd demolish it when they tore down the rest of Motty's buildings.

She offered him a cigarette, knowing he'd decline, and lit it for herself with her Zippo. The door to the cabin was ajar, but the girl was nowhere in sight.

"There's a dead deer back there," she said. "A doe. She was twitching and couldn't get up. I had to put her down."

He thought for a moment, hands working a wire brush. The air smelled of bleach. "Any idea what was wrong with her?"

"I didn't see a wound, so probably disease or parasites. Screwworm, maybe? I wouldn't butcher it for meat, but she might make a pretty trophy."

He nodded. He knew she was here for a reason but was content to wait. He said, "You all right? You were hitting it pretty hard last night."

"I'm feeling it."

After leaving Hendrick in the chapel she'd opened a new jar and drank most of it herself. She didn't remember saying goodbye to Abby last night—wasn't even sure when he'd left. Hell, she didn't remember climbing into her car. She was a drinker, no refuting that, but she didn't usually overrun her headlights.

"Where you thinking of going?" she asked. "After."

"Haven't quite worked that out."

"Ah."

"Don't you worry. I've got a few irons in the fire."

It was selfish of her to ask him to take on Sunny. He'd already done enough for her. After Lincoln Rayburn's body had been found, he told the police he was to blame for the liquor Lunk got ahold of, not Stella. The seven-year sentence was severe, considering most other moonshiners got off with fines and deferred jail time. But Lincoln was well loved, and his father highly respected—justice was going to come out of someone's hide. And now Abby was practically indigent, with no equipment for making whiskey even if he had the desire to do it. There couldn't be a lot of money in preserving dead animals.

He lifted out the little wooden tray that held the possum's spine, let the water run off. Gently slid the bones onto the cloth. A lovely snakelike thing. When she was young she hadn't realized how few taxidermists worked with skeletons. It was tricky work, a puzzle of bone and wire, but Abby had a head for anatomy and he was meticulous in taxidermy, as he'd been in moonshine.

She said, "You ought to wear gloves." His hands were pink and raw from the bleach.

He nodded. Still waiting for her to do what she came to do.

"Tell me about the girl and Hendrick," she said. "She likes him?"

He glanced back at the cabin door. "You know how he is."

Charismatic, she thought. Charming in the way a little girl couldn't see through. But that wasn't the question.

"Does he love her?"

Abby reached into the water, came up with a handful of tiny bones.

"Abby?"

"He dotes on her a bit."

Stella sighed. "You mind if I talk to Sunny?"

He stood, and she said, "By myself."

He said, "I suppose I could check on that deer."


SUNNY SAT ON the hearth of the fireplace with her arms around her knees, staring at Stella with a hawklike intensity. She was all angles: bare skinny arms and shins, a narrow face, long fingers and toes. That strong Birch nose. The tips of her ears poked from her long black hair.

Stella suddenly remembered holding this child when she was hours old, the heat of her against Stella's skin. A decade vanished, and just as suddenly opened again like a chasm.

The girl said nothing. Studied her.

Stella tried not to stare at her bare skin. Sunny was more scarlet than white, and that red was unnaturally vibrant—nobody'd take her for Cherokee. Stella's own blemishes were a ragged pink rash, but the patches of ruby swirling across Sunny's legs and arms and face seemed almost poreless, like painted glass.

Finally Stella said, "You know who I am?"

"You're the apostate Stella Wallace." Her accent was as thick as Uncle Dan's. "Abby says I got to talk to you."

"Yes, you do."

"Don't see why."

"I'm the eldest Birch woman," Stella said. "That means I have say over what happens to you."

Stella looked around for a chair, pulled one over to the girl. She was alarmed at how empty the cabin felt. There was indeed a couch—good for you, Abby—but most of his trophies were missing. A single bear head remained on the wall, next to a buck. The raccoon no longer begged in the corner. Saddest of all, the Russian boar was gone. Had he sold them off, or was he robbed while he was in prison? She hoped a few of them were in the back room. As always, that door was shut.

"But actually," Stella said, "I'm here to ask you what you want to happen next."

The girl tilted her head, skeptical. The red of her cheek seemed to flow like wine in a glass.

"When I was little, nobody asked me what I wanted," Stella said. "They thought I was too stupid to decide for myself."

"Maybe you were," Sunny said.

Stella laughed, and it sent a twinge into her hangover-abused skull. "Maybe so."

"Since you're *asking*," Sunny said. "I'll be staying with Uncle Hendrick."

So she did know why Stella was here. Stella said, "Abby said Motty wanted me to take you in."

"So?"

"So I've got to figure out if you're smarter than I was at your age. I need to know what Motty's told you, what Hendrick's told you."

"He's told me he'll have a big house for me, and I won't have to go to school."

"I see the attraction." The girl scowled and Stella said, "School wasn't a great place for me. Too many children. They aren't nice to people who look different."

"So you got the same stains I do," Sunny said. "Don't mean nothing."

"It runs in the family," Stella said. She didn't add, And your skin's even stranger than mine is. "People 'round here treat it like the mark of Cain, but in Georgia, well, you'd have it easier."

"I don't care what people think."

"Good for you," Stella said—not believing it for a second. "So what else has Hendrick told you?"

"About what?"

"Why don't you start with that necklace?"

Sunny looked down at herself. On a cheap metal chain hung a thin gold ring. The prongs held a speck of a diamond. The girl put a fist around it.

"It's mine," she said. "Motty gave it to me."

"And where'd she get it?"

"How the hell should I know?"

So. She swears already. Motty and Abby remained excellent influences.

"Well, Aunt Ruth's heard about it," Stella said. "If you want to hold on to it, I suggest you keep it hid."

Sunny dropped the ring back into the neck of her dress. One question answered, but it was still a mystery where Motty got the money for a diamond ring, even one with such a tiny stone. It was possible the old woman had hidden it from Stella all the time she lived there, but not likely. The house was too small, and Stella too much a snoop. So, something the old woman had picked up in the last ten years.

"My turn," Sunny said.

"You don't get a turn."

"Why'd you run away?"

"None of your business. Show me your hands."

Sunny folded her arms.

"Have you gone in the cave?" Stella asked.

"No. But you have. Show me yours."

Stella hesitated. She showed no one her hands.

"Fair's fair," Sunny said.

Stella stretched out her right arm, loosened her fist.

Sunny leaned forward. Her eyes narrowed. Her face was almost all red except for a swirl of pale skin from her left eye to her chin.

She pressed a finger into Stella's palm. Traced the scars.

"Does it hurt?" Sunny asked.

"Not anymore. Now you." The girl frowned. "I have to know, Sunny. You don't get to run off to Georgia until I see."

Sunny thrust out her arm. Stella opened the girl's fingers. Her skin was warm, and wine dark, except for a pale bulge at the center of her palm, as if the skin covered a tiny egg. Stella ran her finger over it. Her skin was smooth, unbroken.

"Now the other."

The girl sighed, but did it. There were no scars. No scars. The Ghostdaddy hadn't touched her. Motty had kept to the age of accountability. And Sunny was innocent.

"Why, you look like you're gonna cry," Sunny said.

"I'm fine. I just thought—" Stopping herself before she said: I thought you'd done something terrible.

"You miss it, don't you," Sunny said.

Stella took a breath. Pushed away the start of tears with the back of her hand. "What?"

Sunny leaned forward. "What was it like for you? Touching him."

"It was . . ."

Like standing in the sun and being the sun at the same time, Stella thought.

"I'll admit it felt pretty good," she said. "At first."

"*Pretty good?*" Sunny said. "I read the books, Stella Wallace. I read your book."

"You . . . ?"

The girl looked smug.

"I thought that was against the rules," Stella said. "He shouldn't have given it to you—I'm still here. I wasn't allowed to read *The Book of Mathilda.*"

"But you ain't *been* here," Sunny said.

"Motty would never have allowed that."

"Motty didn't have to know every little thing."

"Hendrick gave the books, without telling Motty?"

Sunny was enjoying Stella's shock. "He thought I should know what you done. All your conversations with the God are in there."

"They're not conversations, they're—" Stella shook her head. "You shouldn't read that. And you should know, it ain't *my* book. It's something Hendrick wrote about me. You need to know the difference."

"But it ain't lies! You loved the God, that's in there. And it loved you. I know you felt it."

"It ain't love. I thought it was."

Sunny wasn't buying it.

"The thing in there wants what it wants," Stella said. "It *takes* what it wants. There's a reason we wait until we're of age. Why we don't go in alone. You got to be strong enough, strong enough to hold on to yourself, and you got to go bit by bit or the Ghost-daddy will just—never mind."

"Say it." Sunny's voice was eager. "I ain't never gonna know unless you tell me."

That's right, Stella thought. I ain't never going to tell you. They've already fed you on too many stories about the glory of the God in the Mountain.

"Here's all you need to know," Stella said. "It doesn't care about little people, like you and me. Not like a person cares for a person."

"That ain't true! Uncle Hendrick said that—"

"Uncle Hendrick don't know what the hell he's talking about. He's got this big story he's selling, and he's leading you on. That thing in there will hurt you. It hurt me, and Lena before me." She made sure the girl was looking her in the eye. "It hurt Motty, too."

The girl shook her head. "No. Uncle Hendrick told me—she died of a heart attack."

Stella took a breath. She couldn't tell the girl what happened, not yet. She'd run to Hendrick. And Stella had a lot to do before the shit hit that particular fan. If it all worked out, Sunny would never have to go through what Stella did. She'd grow up normal—or nearer to it than Stella had been allowed.

"That's their best guess," Stella allowed. "We can talk about it later."

Sunny said, "So now do I get to go to Georgia?"

"You really want to live on some ranch down there?" Stella asked.

The girl's face lit up. She'd thought she'd won. Then she added, "Of course I'd rather stay in the cove, if—"

"You can't."

"I know! The park the park the park. I ain't stupid."

The girl wasn't. And that gave Stella hope that she was smart enough to see through Hendrick's bullshit—eventually, if not right now.

Stella got to her feet. "For now, you can stay here with Abby."

At the door a wrenching feeling stopped her. She looked back at the floor around Sunny's feet. "I shouldn't have stayed away from the cove. I shouldn't have left you alone with Motty. That way you wouldn't have had to learn about me from a book."

Stella looked her in the eye. Sunny hadn't moved. She was

holding on to herself, her jaw tight, burning. Stella remembered being that angry.

"If we do this, *if,* I'm going to come visit you," Stella said. "Check on you, regular, you understand?"

"Fine, fine."

"I'll talk to Hendrick when the funeral's over."

Sunny blinked hard, holding back some emotion. Abby was right. No matter what Sunny was, she was a little girl.

Abby wasn't in the yard. Stella hiked back uphill to her car, and was thankful she didn't run into him along the way.

The deer was gone.

## 9

## 1936

ONE SATURDAY MORNING in early May, a few weeks after Motty killed the sow, the old woman announced that Decoration Day was tomorrow, so they'd better get started. Stella didn't know what she was talking about and was in no mood for newly invented chores. She had a book to read.

Motty marched her up into the woods past Abby's shack to a hillside covered with wildflowers. She started pointing out ones to collect in the basket: purple irises, pale yellow bloodroot flowers, three different kinds of trilliums with their white leaves and mouths of different colors like candy with secret centers. She sent Stella into the brush to find fire pink (which wasn't pink but was indeed fiery), lone trout-lilies with their drooping yellow heads, violets and azaleas and blue phlox. Motty fussed at her for picking the wrong ones, or the older ones, or the insect-damaged ones, and sent her back for replacements.

"What are we doing with all these?" Stella asked.

"They're for the dead."

"Why're they so picky?"

"Show some respect. You can afford to think about more than yourself once a year."

Stella wondered if Motty cared so much, why hadn't they decorated in the three years she'd been here?

After lunch they walked for almost four miles, Stella carrying the basket while Motty arranged bouquets and tied them with string. They arrived at the Primitive Baptist Church, an austere white frame building alone in a clearing on uneven ground; it rested on stacks of rock like gray ankles to keep it level. A horse, still attached to its buggy, nibbled grass outside. That was the Rayburn horse, Miss Jane. The face of the church was practically a blank wall, with no windows and one narrow door, which hung ajar. A figure moved inside.

Motty didn't go through the door, but headed for the graveyard behind the church. The yard was empty—of living people, anyway.

"These are your kin," Stella said. And there was the tombstone for Russell Birch, 1795–1878, DEFENDER OF THE COVE. Stella wished it mentioned bushwhackers. Clara lay beside him, with no words on her marker to note she was the first person to meet the God in the Mountain.

Motty chose the right bouquet for each resident, then had Stella pin it to the ground with a nail and string. "Not that it'll do any good," Motty said. "People steal the nice ones and put them on their own graves."

It seemed they were related to everyone in the row. Stella worked her way down to the end, Motty fussing at her the whole time. At the next tombstone Motty handed her the largest bunch of flowers yet. Stella looked at the stone and saw her mother's name: Selena Birch Wallace. The date was August 5, 1926—ten years before this year. And just two years after Stella was born.

Stella said, "Pa told me she got sick when I was a baby. That's why she came back here, for you to take care of her."

Motty was staring at the tombstone.

"So she was sick a long time?" Stella asked.

"Did your pa tell you what she died of?"

"Tuberculosis." She'd studied the word.

"Well. That's a lingering disease."

Stella thought, Do I have tuberculosis? Is that why Pa dropped me off? How long does it take to know you're just . . . lingering?

Stella asked, "Do I get to be buried next to her?"

"Nope. That's my spot there." Meaning the empty patch next to Lena.

"But I want to be next to Ma!"

"Not much room. Guess they can turn you sideways and bury you at our feet."

Stella marched away, and Motty didn't call her back. Maybe she was as tired of Stella as Stella was of her.

She looked at a few gravestones, and most of the last names were familiar. Then she circled around the other side of the church and there was Lunk, hoeing out weeds that had sprouted under the church.

"Saw you over there," Lunk said.

"But you didn't come over?"

He shook his head. "Afraid to. I never met a woman as mean as your grandmother."

"You should live with her."

"Ha! No thanks."

"So your daddy makes you do chores around the church?"

"He says it beats whipping me."

"Oh! So you've been misbehaving? What'd you do?"

He flushed—red as cranberry!

"Come on, you can tell me," she said.

"I'd worry about your own soul. You read that Bible all the way through yet?"

"I read a fair piece." She'd read all of Genesis, Exodus, and Leviticus, and had lately run aground in Deuteronomy. "I like that serpent in the garden. He's 'subtil.' Never knew that word."

"You would like the serpent." He shook his head, smiling. "Daddy's worried about you. Though he says it's not your fault, you just got put into the hands of . . . never mind."

"Come on. Say it."

"A heathen."

"Motty ain't a heathen." Was she?

"He thinks she's going to lead you off the straight and narrow path."

"And your daddy, how does he know what path that is? I thought only God knows if I'm one of the *Elect*."

"God speaks to him."

Stella blew out her lips.

"He does!"

"About *me*?"

"About all kinds of things. All the time."

"How about you?" Stella asked. "Does God speak to you?"

"Sure He does. Well, sometimes." Then: "He does, but—" His face cinched up.

Stella waited.

"It's not like he does with Daddy. It's not . . . clear."

"What do you want Him to tell you?"

"Whether I'm good or not."

Her surprise showed. Suddenly he got embarrassed. "I shouldn't have said that."

"No," Stella said. "I think that all the time."

"You do?"

"Good" and "bad" were the wrong words. More like "damaged" and "undamaged." There was a flaw in her. Her mother had seen it early, and then her father sussed it out, something nearly invisible, like a pinhole leak in a copper kettle. The only thing was, she didn't know what her flaw was yet. She knew it was there, and she knew it would come out at some point, and then everybody would see her for what she was.

"If God hasn't answered," Stella said, "maybe we should make a sacrifice. Get His attention."

Motty came around the corner, mad. "Don't you walk off from me." She grabbed Stella by the elbow. At the road Stella glanced behind her. Lunk had stepped out to the front of the church, watching her. You big lunk, she thought.

A FEW WEEKS LATER, deep into the pocket of a warm June, Uncle Hendrick came back to Motty's, carrying a couple of suitcases, one of them that green case that had carried *The Book of Clara*. She thought: More books!

No men with him this time, and no Ruth or Veronica, either. Alone he seemed more courteous and somehow shyer. He asked her how she was doing.

She proudly showed him her palms. "See? All healed up."

Motty grunted.

"And how do you feel about . . . what happened? In the cave? Did you remember what it said to you?"

"Mostly."

Hendrick was surprised. He looked at Motty, and she said, "Tell the truth."

She remembered the communion. She'd never forget the hard bite of the God's hands on her, or those long minutes of connection, his thoughts rushing into her, carrying her away like a log on a raging river. She remembered the bone-deep pain when Motty yanked her hands away from the contact. She'd passed out, and Stella realized, just now, that Motty must have carried her out of the cave and up those stairs. Stella had woken up in bed aching from the loss of that connection, the God's jagged thoughts still echoing in her head.

What had slipped away from her was the nature of those thoughts. They were so foreign to her, so oddly shaped, she couldn't hold on to them. Hendrick had come to her bedside, and she'd talked as fast as she could while he scribbled in his notebook, but every word she spoke seemed to shred the God's thoughts. How could human language capture what the God had imparted to her?

Yet the *feeling* behind the thoughts remained, like a sore tooth she couldn't stop touching. Sometimes in the weeks that followed she'd stare at her hand and think, This is not my body. Or she'd wake up in the middle of the night, her arms spread, and realize that she was vast, a mountain rising up from the plain—and then suddenly everything would flip and she was ant-sized, the room's dark ceiling impossibly far away. Little, big, little, big.

"I'm fine," Stella said. "I'm ready for the next communion."

"She's not," Motty said.

"I am!"

Stella had asked Motty a dozen times about when she could go back, and every time she replied, "When you're ready." But she'd never explain what would make Stella ready, or how long it would take. It was infuriating.

"It's Motty's choice," Hendrick said quietly. "She's the eldest Birch woman."

Motty was eldest everything, Stella thought. She was twenty years older than Hendrick, and could have been his mother.

"Damn straight," Motty said. "I won't be rushed again."

"It's no one's fault, Motty."

"I know whose fault it is. And your part in it."

The adults had forgotten her. She didn't know what they were talking about—some kind of old grievance. Stella had so many questions, but she wasn't brave enough to step between them. The cross fire would kill her.

IT TURNED OUT there was no chance she was going into the cave today—Hendrick had come for another reason. Motty made a show of unlocking the chapel door for him, then tucked the key into her bra. Her lock, her key. Stella hadn't figured out where she kept that key when it wasn't on her.

Hendrick strode through the door with that green suitcase under his arm. "What's he doing?" Stella asked Motty. She was gripped with jealousy. Was Hendrick seeing the God in the Mountain without her?

"None of your business. Leave him alone."

She wasn't about to leave him alone. When Motty got busy in the kitchen about an hour later, Stella snuck out to the chapel. Hendrick looked up and smiled. "You shouldn't be in here."

The stairs to the cave were covered by that door in the platform. She was very aware of that door, like it was the muzzled jaw of a dangerous dog.

Hendrick sat at a chair with a writing board across his lap. A leather notebook lay open atop a barrel—a makeshift reading stand.

"You're making a copy?" she said.

"No, no. I'm writing commentary."

She didn't want to admit that she didn't know what that meant. "Is that my book?"

He nodded. "It is indeed."

"Can I read it?" She stepped closer.

"I'm sorry." He put a hand over the page. "I can't tell you the commentary, it would prejudice you." He saw the confusion on her face. "If I told you how I interpreted your communion, you might be tempted to echo it, give us what we expect."

"I wouldn't lie about what the God said."

"You wouldn't mean to. But such knowledge might, um, *color* what you report. You see, what we need from each Revelator is the pure message, undiluted, unpolluted. Like a mountain stream, clear and straight from the source. It's my job to write explanations of what was said, to expand on it, so that it'll make sense to others."

"Will you put them in a library?"

"Someday they'll be in every library in the world. When the God makes his presence known, the world will change forever, every person on Earth will know your name—and all the Revelators who came before you. But for now . . ." He smiled indulgently. "It's for family only. Just for us."

"But not me." Stella was offended. *She* was family. Who else deserved to read it more? "You could at least show me Motty's book. Or Lena's."

He winced. "I told you the rules. No reading the word of any living Revelator. But don't worry, someday, when you've laid your burden down, and Motty has—well, you'll read them all. You can even come to Georgia and read the original handwritten manuscripts. I keep the originals safe with me, but I do like to come here to write the first draft of each commentary. I can feel the difference in my work, and I believe future generations will sense the difference too." He smiled. "You commune with the God, and I commune with the text."

"I don't understand—why can't people just read what I—what the God said? It seems like the God can speak for himself."

"I wish it were so. It's very complicated, Stella."

"Show me, then."

He laughed. "Oh, Stella, you're a persistent one."

"One line. Please."

He put on a serious face that had a grin hiding under it. "You can't tell Motty."

"I promise."

That made him even happier. "All right then, let me see." He flipped back a page, then another. "Ah, here's an interesting passage." He cleared his throat. "A white fire, it moves, it moves, cold under skin, like a light under glass in the dark." His voice was sing-songy. "It cannot—*I* cannot. We starve without speaking, alone."

She thought, *I* said that?

Hendrick inhaled deeply, as if savoring the words. "Now, then," he said to her. "What do you think it means?"

This felt like a test. She desperately wanted to succeed. "When I said that thing about the white fire, I must have been—"

He was shaking his head before she'd finished her sentence. "The *God* is talking. That's the first thing you have to understand. He's speaking through you, to us."

She started again, flustered. "So the God is talking about the fever he gave me when I communed with him." She'd woken up with Motty pressing a damp cloth to her forehead.

He shook his head again, and she winced. "The fire's a metaphor. It stands for the secret knowledge that he's trying to share—a *transformative* knowledge, capable of changing everything it touches, but so hot you can forge steel in it. We can build new things with it! Normally we don't have the tools to understand this knowledge—it would look like a dim light, that 'light under glass.' Now that's a divine idea, there, that we know from First Corinthians. We mortals see things through a glass darkly, which means we always have incomplete understanding. Have you read your New Testament?"

"I have a Bible. Elder Rayburn gave it to me."

"Of course he did."

"He wants me to come to church."

"Motty didn't mention that."

"Well, she doesn't want me to go."

He seemed relieved to hear that. "There's nothing wrong with the Christian faith. I'm a Christian. But it's incomplete. It's . . ." His eyes went wide. "It's exactly like the glass darkly that we're looking through. What we're creating, what the God is giving to us, is a third testament, and a fourth aspect—do you know what that means, aspect?" She hated not knowing a word, and was going to say Of course I do, but he saw her hesitation. "Trinity, then—have you heard of that? There's God the Father, God the Son, and God the Holy Ghost."

"Yes! Elder Rayburn told me about that."

"Did he now. Well, that's what most of the church believes. They all look like separate beings, when viewed through our mortal perceptions, but they're really three views of the same God. The three *known* views."

"So the God in the Mountain—"

"He's the fourth aspect, revealed just to us. He's not *antithetical* to Jehovah—how can he be? But like Jesus, he can bring a new message that the world wasn't ready for before now. He adds, he clarifies, and when the great day comes that he emerges from the mountain, the whole world will hear it. Do you understand?"

She nodded, just to keep him going.

"Where was I? A glass darkly. That mention of skin—that fire that moves under cold skin—tells us that the God can only share what he knows through the medium of the flesh—that's to say, through a human Revelator."

Stella felt like an idiot. Uncle Hendrick had gotten so much more from those words than she did—and she'd been the one to speak them. "What does it mean that it's starving because it can't speak?" she asked. "Is that . . ." An idea came to mind. ". . . loneliness?"

"Yes! He longs to communicate with us, just as a starving man longs for food."

The praise lit her up.

"When the God says, it cannot, and *I* cannot," Hendrick said, "that means that neither the God nor we mortals can survive, unless the message is transmitted."

"Golly bum," Stella said. She wished she could tell Abby about this.

As if reading her mind, Hendrick said, "I hope you realize now how important you are to the church. You have to hide this light inside yourself, telling no one."

"I understand, but . . . why don't we just tell people now? If they knew he was in there, that he was *real,* then . . ."

"No! That would be terrible! Stella, if we let strangers into that cave, and they discovered the God before he was ready, imagine the chaos. The government would swoop down upon us like locusts. You've heard of revenuers, haven't you? This would be a thousand times worse. Why, they'd probably lock you up just to stop you from talking to him."

"Oh! That would be terrible!" Again, Stella felt so stupid. She wasn't thinking through the consequences. But other questions popped into her head, such as: How could a God ever not be ready? Why did it need people to defend it and hide it?

"Don't worry," Hendrick said. "The time is coming soon. The God's getting ready, and when he steps into the sunlight the world will know all about you and the other Revelators, the sacrifices you've made—you, Motty, Lena, her especially, going back to—"

"Why especially?"

He grimaced. "Another time. Let's just say she had a hard time of it, your mother. But history will know of her, and perhaps even remember my small role in bringing this third testament to the world."

"Okay . . . so we'll be famous. That's why we're doing this?"

"Oh, Stella, no. No, no, no. We're not doing it for glory."

"Then what do we get from the God?"

"His love, of course. And, well, a sense of purpose. There's nothing more fulfilling than knowing what we do will help the world."

"I mean, what do we *get*. Like, will he protect us from our enemies, like those Carolina bushwhackers? Or, say the government tries to take the farm from us. Will he stop them, or, I don't know—"

"The God doesn't work like that," Hendrick said. "He loves us, he wants to keep us safe, but we can't expect him to, well, *slay* people on our behalf."

She was disappointed. "So what, then?"

"There is one promise it has made to us. It comes from *The Book of Esther*. The God has guaranteed that when he emerges from the mountain to reveal himself to the world, his children will receive a new body. Not in heaven—here on Earth. An immaculate body that never grows old, never suffers from disease, and never dies. It will be as immortal as the flowers that come back every year."

"One body, ever blooming," Stella said.

"That's right!"

The chapel door banged open. It was Motty, and she was in a rage. One look at Hendrick told Stella he wasn't going to get in Motty's way. The full brunt of her punishment was about to fall.

And Stella thought: It's worth it. Hendrick had listened to her. He'd talked to her like a person. He'd opened a book for her—that vast story of the Birch family and the God in the Mountain—and she'd stepped inside it.

"Excuse me," Stella said to Hendrick, with the grace and dignity of a royal. "I have to go break off a switch."

EARLY IN SEPTEMBER, Motty walked into her bedroom without knocking, wearing a scowl. Stella said, "Don't get on me, I already slopped the hogs." New pigs had arrived over the summer, and Motty cared about nothing more than those animals.

"Sit down," Motty said.

Stella frowned. Looked at her bed like it was a trap. Sat gingerly.

"We aren't like them," Motty said finally. "You, me. All the Birch women."

Stella waited for her to say more. Motty was worked up about something. Finally the old woman said, "We walk a tougher road. These men, they only know what they've heard. It's all secondhand, might as well be gossip. Do you understand?"

Stella didn't. But she nodded. "Hendrick said that my mama paid a sacrifice. What did he mean?"

"She's dead, isn't she?"

"Yes, but—?"

"Never mind him. You're responsible for your own soul. Just remember that."

What a crazy thing to say, Stella thought. Who else would be responsible for it?

Motty went to the door. "Hendrick and the Uncles are coming in the morning."

A thrill ran through Stella's body. *Finally!* It had been six months since the communion.

"You best take a bath tonight," Motty said. And slammed the door.

. . .

STELLA WAS WAITING on the front lawn when Hendrick and the Uncles got out of their cars. She greeted each one by name, and old Morgan Birch cackled when he shook her hand. And then, after supper, she led Motty and the old men to the chapel. The door had been set aside for her.

Motty held out her hand, but Stella ignored it. She stepped down through the hole on her own, her head high. Then she reached the bottom. She hesitated, letting her eyes widen in the dark.

"Go on," Motty said. "You want to lead, lead."

Stella held out a hand and made her way through the dark. She found the narrow passage, and then reached the stone table.

"Climb up," Motty said.

Suddenly Stella was afraid. What if the Ghostdaddy didn't show up? What if he rejected her?

Motty gasped, and Stella looked up and saw a glimmer of white. A shape leaned down out of the dark. Joy erupted in her chest, and she raised her hand.

Here I am, she thought. Here I am.

## 10

**1948**

S TELLA DROVE the hour back to Maryville, following her
headlights but seeing nothing but Sunny, that crazy-quilt
skin, those sharp eyes.

In the dark her home looked as small as a doghouse.

It was just a six-hundred-square-foot cottage on red clay and
spongy lawn, but it was hers, paid cash for it. She had a telephone, electric heat, and her pride and joy, a Speed Queen automatic washer. None of that back-porch handwringer bullshit.
Never again.

The house was clean, too: no still, no mash, no moonshine
paraphernalia of any kind. The law wasn't going to have any
excuse to seize it from her.

First thing she took a hot shower. Heard the phone ringing for
her number—two short rings, one long—and ignored it. When
she was done she wrapped herself in her robe, went out to the
kitchen. She was starving. Her tiny fridge was empty, though,
and there was nothing in the cupboards but half a sleeve of saltines and of course the Final Okra. She hated okra, and that

unopened canning jar, a gift from one of her customers, was the last bullet in the chamber, the one you saved for yourself for when the enemy overran the barricades.

Not today, Final Okra.

The saltines pack was already open. The top cracker was stale, but that was nothing that bourbon and Lucky Strikes couldn't fix.

The phone rang again, for her number. She shared the party line with five other households along the road.

"Hello, central," she said.

"How you doing, Stella?" It was Alfonse.

"Today's been a hell of a week."

He asked about her cousin and she told him the girl was fine. Everything was going to be fine. He had something on his mind, though, and she suspected what it was.

"Did you make the delivery?" she asked.

"I ran into a problem."

Stella heard a breath on the line. "Georgette, is that you?"

"What?" Alfonse said.

"Just a second," she said. "Georgette, quit rubbernecking or I swear to God I'll march over there and smack the receiver out of your hand."

There was no answer. But the click was clear.

"Maybe we should meet in person," Alfonse said. "I've got a hell of a sample for you."

"It's that bad?" She didn't have time for this. "Can you handle it?"

"It's not something in my bailiwick."

"Oh, your *bailiwick*. Don't want to offend your wicks."

"I'm just the bootlegger."

"So where's the kid?" Meaning Hump.

"I stopped by the farm but he wasn't there. I think you're going to have to go up there to suss out the problem."

"Not tonight," Stella said. "I can't."

"Yeah, you're probably going to need daylight. Tomorrow, then?"

She poured two fat fingers of bourbon and tossed it back. Looked hard at the bottle. She'd probably had enough for tonight, especially if she had to get up in the morning.

Then she thought, At least Hendrick doesn't drink. Sunny'd be better off with someone more stable than a moonshiner. She sure as hell would be better off growing up far away from here.

She poured another glass.

ALFONSE TOOK A HAND off the wheel and reached under his seat, came up with a jar. "See what you think."

She unscrewed the lid, keeping it away from her lap. They were bouncing along an unpaved county road three miles outside of Alcoa. She sniffed. A faint smell, like smoke—not a good sign. Took a sip.

"Good lord," she said.

"Yup."

"Tastes like . . ." She searched for an accurate description.

"Shit?"

"I was going to say burnt tires."

"Burnt tires rolling through shit."

"There ya go. Is it all like this? Is this from the foreshot? I told Hump he has to throw out the first few ounces."

"Nope. It's the whole batch, near as I can tell."

"Fuck me."

"Bartender Willie couldn't reach you, and word got back to me. He's plenty mad. Wants a refund."

"Of course he does. But we already spent his money on supplies."

A night's sleep in her own bed had brought her halfway back

to life, which is to say, merely miserable. And now Hump Cornette had fucked the batch and her along with it.

As usual they parked in the trees. No other cars were tucked in there, which was mixed news. Annoying that Hump wasn't working, but a relief nobody else was snooping around.

They walked up through the brush, taking a meandering route—she didn't want to wear a path, and they needed to finish their smokes—until they were atop the hill behind the Acorn Farm. Maybe a dozen people had heard of the farm. Eight knew it was real. And six knew it was located here.

It wasn't much to look at: a 1,500-square-foot warehouse in a stand of oaks, a half mile from any other house or barn. The only things tethering it to the outside world were a rogue power line illegally piggybacking off the main line, and a narrow track that used to be a road. Stella had used it to haul truckloads of lumber during construction of the farm, then let it grow over. Nobody had any good reason to come down that road.

"All right then," she said. "Put out your cigarette."

She unlocked the side door and flipped on the main lights. Her heart quickened every time she walked in. The building and everything in it had been built to her specifications. If a still was a machine for turning corn into money, this was a money factory.

At one end was a set of bay doors and a small window that faced the old road—her lookout. At the other end of the room sat Queen Bess—a glorious, eight-hundred-gallon steel vat, whose throne was a brick and iron hearth. A thick copper pipe exited from her top cone at a right angle and ran to the custom-designed thump keg, then to the condenser, where a coil wound down through 110 gallons of water in a long steel tube. High-capacity pipes could suck up a hundred gallons a minute from an underground stream running beneath the hill, send it through the still, and dump the warm water back underground, all without pumps—the whole system ran on artesian pressure. She'd picked this location for the farm because of that stream—and because it was at the ass-end of nowhere. The factory ran on water, heat, sugar, microbes, and privacy.

"At least he didn't leave it running," Alfonse said. The industrial iron burners directly under the queen's bottom were off, the taps to the oil tank closed. Good thing, because the fans in the huge vents were off, too. Run an indoor still without ventilation and you were asking for either asphyxiation or conflagration. The air in the building smelled only faintly of alcohol, which was fine, and the sour smell of stewing mash, which was typical.

She said, "Let's check the mash first."

There were forty fifty-five-gallon barrels in the room, two holding just water, and a few filled with cracked corn, but the rest, wrapped in electric blankets and industrial heat strips, contained mash at various stages of fermentation. The newest smelled mildly of puke, as usual, but the aging barrels were bubbling along nicely, soupy and golden, with ground corn floating on the surface like gold cream. She resisted the urge to start stirring. "Keep eating that sugar," she said, just loud enough for the yeast to hear. She loved her busy fungi the way other women loved babies.

She did a cursory check of the rest of the still. The queen's vat smelled clean, the crossover pipe was clear, the condenser intake valves grime free. The catch barrel was damp but unobjectionable.

"Hey, the mice have gotten in again," Alfonse called. He was scrutinizing the floor around the south wall where they kept their supplies: crates of quart jars, dozens of brown gallon jugs, bags of dried corn and sprouted malt; and sugar, lots and lots of sugar. Alfonse gestured to the stack of twenty-five-pound Domino bags. "They've chewed through and there are turds along here."

"God damn it. I told Hump to watch that." A drawback of

being out here in the woods was that the mice had home field advantage. She'd told Hump to mix up sugar and baking soda in hopes it would kill the little fuckers, but he hadn't followed directions.

This was the problem with trying to make money from whiskey—you had to trust too many people, and trust cost money. Over the years she'd recruited five moonshiners, each with his own setup, work schedule, and capacity, each a unique pain in her ass. She insisted on them using Uncle Dan's recipe, and her methods. They didn't like taking orders from a girl but they were happy to take her money. Quality control, however, was a nightmare.

The farm was supposed to be a solution to all that, but so far it had cost her more to build it and get it running than she'd made back. She'd had to hire a discreet contractor, a morally flexible power company linesman, and a plumber who owed her a favor, then pay them enough to keep everything off the books. Then she had to find an assistant to run the still when she couldn't be there, buy the supplies, and not fuck the batch.

She moved on to the aging barrels, the last step before being decanted to bottles. The first one she opened, the burnt smell hit her. There was something floating in the moonshine, half submerged. No, lots of somethings. She reached in, fished one out. It was a lump of black. Then she recognized it.

"Alfonse," she said.

"Yes?"

"Bring me the head of Hump Cornette."

TWO HOURS LATER, Alfonse came back to the farm, dragging with him a tall, skinny white boy with unfortunate teeth. Hump Cornette knew he was in trouble, but didn't know how much.

"Hey, Stella."

"Don't you hey me." She nodded at the chair opposite her. "Sit down."

He dropped onto his butt quick, as appropriate. Alfonse stood behind him, arms crossed. Hump said, "I can explain."

"Explain what?"

The three mental gears in his possession seized up. "Um . . . everything?" His eyes were darting around, looking for clues. They were in the part of the warehouse Stella called her office—three walls of sugar bags around a workbench and her tools, an army cot, alarm clock, and automatic percolator.

"What's my rule?" she asked.

"Knock before I go in the bathroom."

"The other rule."

He drew a blank.

"The rule when we're running a batch."

"Oh! Stick to the recipe." He could see she was seething, and knew he was in deep trouble. "Please, Stella, if you just tell me what I done."

She opened her fist. Inside was the hunk of black material. He blinked at it.

"What's this, Hump?"

He shook his head. She tossed it at him. It bounced off his chest and he had to scramble to retrieve it.

"I found them floating in my hooch like black turds."

"Charcoal's in the recipe! You said it smooths out the shine, absorbs the last of the, the—"

"Nefarious chemicals," Alfonse said.

"Those!"

"That's not charcoal," Stella said.

"It is!"

"Sit your ass down," Alfonse said.

Hump sat, looking at the lump. Now tears were in his eyes. "The bag said . . ."

"This bag?" Stella asked. An empty ten-pound bag, brown with red lettering, lay across the workbench. She'd found a dozen just like it, crumpled and empty, stuffed into the split barrel they used for a garbage can. On the front of each it said:

FORD CHARCOAL BRIQUETS—

THE MODERN FORM OF CHARCOAL—

PERFECTED TO BURN TWICE AS LONG AS COMMON CHARCOAL

"Jesus," Alfonse said.

"What the recipe *says*, Hump, is to soak overnight with white oak charcoal. Hardwood chips."

"We were out! You told me to buy more."

"And you decided to buy charcoal fucking *briquets*?"

"But it's charcoal!"

"No. No it's not. You know what they put in briquets?" God, she hated that made-up word. "Sodium nitrate, borax, tar, dirt—"

"Burnt tires," Alfonse said.

"Burnt tires, and actual shit."

"I didn't know!" Hump said.

"And that, hammerhead, is the only thing saving your ass. See, I blame myself. Because I did not think that you were such a God damn idiot. What I blame is my lack of imagination."

"Oh. Okay. I'm glad that—hey!" Alfonse had smacked him in the back of the head.

"You fucked up, and now you owe me. Hours and hours of owe me, to make this right."

He nodded. Squinted at her. Zero lights were going on in that noggin of his.

"We have to dump everything," she said. "Everything from that batch that's already in jugs, everything in the soaking barrels. You're going to scrub those barrels, too. And then you're going to help me run a full batch, right now. And a hundred and sixty-five of it's going to Willie Teffeteller."

"Fifty free gallons?" Alfonse said. "That's generous."

"I'm not losing his business because Hump thought he was going to a God damn picnic barbecue. This is an apology delivery—think of it as long-term investment."

"Where are you going?"

"To buy some fucking white oak charcoal."

WELL AFTER MIDNIGHT and Hump was laid out on the cot, snoring. She would have woken him up as punishment, but that meant she'd have to talk to him, and she needed time to think. Time alone with her machine.

She loved the farm when a batch was running. The roar of the fans and the hissing burners beneath the vat were as soothing as a South Carolina beach. The air swam with alcohol. The smell of mash was so sour it became sweet in her lungs, a miracle the papists would have called transubstantiation.

There was that dark year, the first after she left the cove, when she had no idea how to glue together her broken mind. The idea of humans had repelled her, and the outside world seemed like chaos. She became a Dorothy who wouldn't leave the house because it was spinning through the air.

Fuck Kansas. Fuck Oz.

In the end it was whiskey that had saved her. Not the drinking of it, though she came to love that, too. The work of it. The chemistry and engineering and art of it. Distillation burned away the impurities and made something beautiful that people would pay good money for. Money was the only shield a woman could count on in this world. Oh, she'd had to go into debt to build the Acorn Farm, but that was short-term risk for long-term security. And in the meantime if anybody came for her or what she'd built, they'd get a fight.

She checked the catch barrel but it was only half full. Distilling was a slow business, but that was soothing too—usually. It pissed her off that her thoughts kept turning back to the cove, and Sunny. While she was out shopping she'd learned that Motty's funeral was tomorrow—they were going to bury her on the farm. After that, Sunny would be in Hendrick's care.

What choice did Stella have? She couldn't raise the girl herself. Stella was a God damn moonshiner.

Stella pulled up a chair next to Queen Bess and stared up at her bright steel belly. Stella's proudest moment had been when she welded the last seam on her. The metal was vibrating gently the way it did when cooking smooth. She closed her eyes.

Willie would accept her apology, and the free gallons. Tomorrow morning they'd pour the last of the new batch into the jugs, and she and Alfonse would deliver it to him. She'd save this business. She'd save Motty. And the deer—the bushes shook, moved by a hidden shape. An animal? No, a girl. Sunny. She was holding the deer's neck, squeezing—

Stella jerked in the chair, suddenly awake. A hand lay on her shoulder.

Alfonse said, "Easy now, didn't mean to startle you."

Had she been dreaming? She reached for her thoughts and they fled like fish.

"What time is it?" she asked.

"Three in the morning." Thank God. She'd only been asleep for a half hour at most.

She checked the barrel. Three-quarters now, and it smelled clean. The still had stopped working, so the batch was finished. She cut the burners but kept the fans on.

Alfonse tasted a spoonful. "*There* it is. The pure recipe. Your work here is done."

"We've got to get this to Willie."

"I'll do that. Go home. You've got a funeral to get to."

"About that."

He raised an eyebrow.

"I was wondering if you could do me a favor. After the delivery, come with me."

He looked skeptical. Weren't many Black folk in the cove. "You want me to come to the funeral, I'll be there."

"Yes—and after. There's something I got to do that may go south. I'd appreciate you having my back."

"How south we talking?"

She thought of the pale man and his non-pale pistol. "Georgia, maybe."

"Hmm," Alfonse said. "As you know, I have a firm policy against people messing with my business partner."

## 11

## 1936

ONE NOVEMBER WHEN Stella was twelve years and eight months old, she snuck out of the house to meet a boy. It was a Sunday morning, and the boy was a God-fearing Baptist, so maybe a waste of a good sneak.

Lunk was waiting for her on the road, looking nervous with his hands jammed in his coat pockets, black Bible tucked under one arm. Then he saw her and he jogged to her, which was sweet.

"I didn't think you'd make it," he said. His breath clouded in the chilly air.

"It's not even eight yet."

"I mean, I didn't think Motty would let you come."

"I'm in charge of my own soul."

They walked side by side back the way he'd come. He was so much taller than she was, all that baby fat squeezed to make inches of height. He looked extra handsome with his hair combed. She knew he was working up the courage to hold her hand. Not that she would have let him, for a couple of reasons. She kept the Bible in her hand between them, and he noticed.

"I'm glad you brought it," he said. He mentioned that Bible every time he saw her. On Fridays, when he was off from his fancy Maryville school, he mooned around the cove schoolyard in the afternoons, supposedly waiting to walk Mary Lynn home. "Did you read it cover to cover yet?" He always brought that up, too.

"I may have skipped some of the begats."

"So you really haven't gone to church before?"

"I have, just not among the *primitives*. Y'uns are cannibals, or . . . ?"

"That's not what it means! It's the one true church, directly descended—"

She laughed. "Relax, Lunk." He'd never objected to her name for him. He either liked it or was happy she called him anything at all. But law! the boy was nervous. She bumped him, and the back of her bare hand touched his. "Besides, I'll try anything once."

Oh, that got him all flushed.

"There are some rules I better explain," he said.

"Sure, I can follow rules." He made a noise and she said, "Did you just snort at me?"

"The first thing is, you have to sit with my mother." The men and women sat on opposite sides of the church. Also, she shouldn't expect any piano playing or guitar, because that wasn't biblical. Neither was Sunday School. There'd be lots of singing, though, and then a sermon delivered by Elder Rayburn. "Whatever you do, don't say anything. It's not allowed."

*"What?"* She stopped there in the road. The church lay just up around the bend.

"It's in First Corinthians," he said. "Let your women keep silence in the churches."

"I'm not your woman. And didn't you just say there was singing?"

"What's that got to do with it?"

"So only the men sing?"

"No! Women can sing, they just can't talk."

"Well that's a load of horse pucky."

"Stella!"

"This is a bad idea. I'm going home."

"No! Please. Just give it a try. One service."

"It's that important to you, huh?"

"It's important to you. Your soul, I mean. You said you was worried about it, right?"

"I'm not *worried.*"

Well, she was a little worried. In all the books she'd read, there was no mention of the God in the Mountain, nor the Ghost-daddy either. But she'd read enough Nathaniel Hawthorne to know a woman could meet the devil out in the woods.

"Maybe I'm just curious," she said.

Truth was she feared she was becoming unfit for human company. She had no friends, no true friends, like the ones she read about. The children at school seemed like another species, dumb as chickens, and the school building a clattering henhouse. They made fun of her for the blotches on her skin and the blots on her family record—the Birch women were suspect.

As for Abby, well, she loved him, but he was a grown man, a criminal, and a drunk. Which meant that most of the time she was trapped in a house with a crazy old woman.

She could speak to no one about the most important thing in her life. The second communion, a couple of months ago, had left her brains scrambled again, so full of the God's thoughts that she felt he was looking out of her eyes. She had to lay out of school while her hands healed. She lived two lives that didn't intersect, one as a revered conduit to God, the other as a farm girl who slopped pigs. She wondered if teenage Jesus felt this way when Joseph told Him to clean up the carpentry shop. The thrilling strangeness of one existence did nothing to reduce the dreariness of the other. Those were accounts in separate banks.

She was confident Lunk had no clue about her other life as a Revelator, because, when she wasn't being anointed by Uncle Hendrick, she barely believed it herself. She was going into his church like a spy from a foreign country.

The church bells started ringing the call to worship. Stella had heard those bells for years from Motty's house, but they were more impressive up close. Lunk started hurrying up the road, and then they topped a small rise and there it was, the blank white face of the Primitive Baptist Church. Folks were loitering outside—maybe the women were getting their last words in.

"Anything else you want to tell me?" she asked.

"Um . . . don't fall asleep? Daddy can preach for a while."

IT SEEMED COLDER inside the church than out, and the stove near the front door was not up to the job. Unfortunately, the Rayburn women liked to sit up front in the second row, left side, practically looking up Elder Rayburn's nostrils. They boxed in Stella between Elsa Rayburn, Lunk's mother, and his little sister, Mary Lynn. Lunk sat across the aisle in the men's section. He kept leaning over to get a glimpse of her.

At first it wasn't bad. Stella liked the singing—four-part harmony blasted at wall-shaking volume, and Elsa hitting the high notes like a trumpet—and the announcements, which were interesting because of their alternating specificity ("Mrs. Meyers asks for prayer about the swelling in her leg") and vagueness ("The Childress Family asks for your prayers during this difficult time"). But then Elder Rayburn opened his big Bible and eased into his sermon. He began with a supposedly true anecdote of a farmer who mistreated his cattle, took a left turn into the parable of the sower, then meandered through a few Psalms.

In the months since Elder Rayburn had gifted her with that Bible, Stella had fallen in love with the poetry of the King James Version, and Rayburn was a good reader. Still, she was disappointed. She'd expected a little more fire and at least a whiff of brimstone, but the elder's deep voice was ferrying them to the Promised Land by slow boat. He seemed more of a teacher than a preacher. Church, it turned out, was a lot like school, except you weren't allowed to ask questions.

She was gazing up at the ceiling beams when she noticed handprints pressed into the wood of one beam. Mary Lynn leaned close and whispered, "Those are angel's hands."

"Sorry I missed its appearance," she whispered back. Mary Lynn giggled. Elsa Rayburn shushed them.

The handprints were just about the only things to look at, which she supposed kept the focus on the sermon. There were no pictures on the walls, not even of Jesus, which seemed rude considering it was His house. Would it kill them to put in a stained-glass window or two like in the cathedrals she'd read about? She would have appreciated a few angels, or a Jonah-swallowing fish, maybe a naked Adam and Eve addressing the snake. But no, there wasn't even a cross. If it weren't for the steeple and bell on the roof you could've taken this place for a barn.

After forty-five minutes Elder Rayburn finally got to something interesting—Abraham calmly plotting the murder of his son. "And Abraham rose up early in the morning," he read. "And saddled his ass, and took two of his young men with him, and Isaac his son, and clave the wood for the burnt offering, and rose up, and went unto the place of which God had told him." Rayburn's deep voice added a necessary hint of menace. It was like a scene from a gangster movie: *And lo, Cagney told the henchmen to warm up the car, and they did throw Isaac into the trunk and departed with him unto Hell's Kitchen.*

Poor Isaac had no clue. He was sweating it, asking his father where the lamb is, but Abe's busy talking to angels. It took another fifteen minutes of sermon for the ram to show up in the thicket and save Isaac's hind end. Elder Rayburn gushed about the devotion of Abraham and how God was going to reward him by spreading his seed all over the nations, but Stella was annoyed. If Abe was such a great guy, why didn't he offer to sacrifice himself rather than his own boy? And why was this God so het up for people to burn things in His honor that He sent the ram in there, like somebody showing up for dinner with their own chicken and demanding you cook it? It was the Jesus thing all over again.

By the time Stella resumed listening, Rayburn had jumped from Abraham's promised nation to "the present indignity" of the park service seizing the land of the cove's residents. Seemed like every week another family was evicted. "The *government of man* seeks to erase us, my friends. The *government of man* wants to wipe out our family farms, destroy generations of hard work, and let the land run wild. The *government of man* wants to disband this church and make this sacred building into a museum exhibit." In his mouth "museum exhibit" sounded like the two dirtiest words in the dictionary. "But I have news for the government." He looked out across their faces, and liked what he saw. "This congregation shall not be moved." He received back a chorus of amens—from men only, of course. The women nodded, just as fervent as the men, but bound by silence.

AFTER THE SERVICE Stella realized she was either famous or notorious, and it wasn't clear which. Folks were milling around outside, and quite a few took time to shake Stella's hand and welcome her, but others kept their distance. Elsa, Lunk, and Mary Lynn stayed at her side; Elsa especially seemed ready to strike down anyone who'd dare to be rude.

Elder Rayburn stepped away from a group of men and said to Stella, "I hope you enjoyed the service, Miss Wallace."

"It was . . . nice."

She sensed Lunk freeze up. What's the matter? she thought. Was nice not good enough?

Elder Rayburn smiled. "Well, I'm sure it's different than the churches in Chicago."

"Sure is," she said, though her father had never taken her to church.

He smiled. "Well, we follow what's in the Bible. If it's not in the scripture, we don't do it."

"So no pipe organs."

He laughed. "That's right. Other churches may change with the times, but God doesn't change."

"What if something new happens? Let's say there's a situation that never happened in the Bible? Like . . . cars?"

"An automobile's just a machine, and man's always inventing machines. We just have to make sure that the *way* they're used fits with biblical teachings. A car is nothing but a fancy plow, and we know enough about plows not to work on the Sabbath. When you look at each new innovation of man, when you look *thoughtfully*, you realize that what the Bible says is true—there's nothing new under the sun."

Lunk mumbled something about Ecclesiastes.

"How about other suns?" Stella said.

Elder Rayburn laughed. "You can't surprise God. He created everything."

"But God didn't *tell* us everything."

"But He did! Everything we need is right there in the Bible. It's whole and complete—we like to say that it's a holy book, not a book full of holes."

He thought that was pretty clever. Stella said, "What about the seven thunders?"

"The seven—?"

"It's in Revelations." She glanced at Lunk. "Chapter ten, verse four."

"That's true," Elder Rayburn said. "However—"

"So what was it that was so scary that God couldn't let it be written down?"

"I don't know that it's anything *scary*. Maybe it's glorious. There are undoubtedly many things we aren't meant to know."

"But y'uns are basing your decisions on a book that's incomplete. It's *told* you there are holes. How do you know God hasn't been telling somebody else new scripture—a *new* New Testament?"

Mary Lynn squeaked.

Elder Rayburn said, "You sound like a younger and prettier Joseph Smith."

Don't "pretty" me, Stella thought. "You can't know," she repeated.

Elder Rayburn thought for a moment. Members of the congregation hadn't moved any closer, but none of them had moved away, either.

"The Bible said that there will be false prophets," Rayburn said. "I think it's much more likely that unscrupulous men would make up things for their own benefit, rather than God suddenly deciding He had more to say. We already have our salvation—we don't need anything else."

"But what if God—?"

"You're confused," he said, cutting her off. "I don't know what kinds of things Motty's told you, but I welcome you to come back to church and *listen*. Not for your salvation—that's assured, if you're one of the Elect—but for your edification."

She wanted to shout at him: You don't know what I know!

Elsa was staring at her. Mary Lynn had covered her mouth

with her hands. And Lunk was saying nothing in her defense. And why would he? This was his father, his family, his religion.

Elder Rayburn said, "You're welcome back anytime, Stella."

LUNK INSISTED ON walking her home. She was too mad to speak, but that didn't stop him from yammering at her. Kept saying "That sure was something" and telling her she was like no girl he'd ever met. "Daddy's never talked to me like that."

She heard the envy in his voice. "Like what?" she asked.

"Like I was worth talking to."

Oh, poor Lunk. Jealous of an argument.

Suddenly she felt sorry for Lunk's entire congregation. All that talk about God, and they never got to see Him. Their whole religion depended on faith—faith that He was real, that He was coming back. But for her, and for Motty and her mother before her, belief wasn't required, any more than she needed to believe in gravity for the rain to fall. The God in the Mountain just *was*.

Lunk reached for her hand, and she didn't pull away. If he was startled by the rough scars he didn't mention it.

She thought, Could he be the one? Could I tell my secret to him? It was delicious to think about. She might do permanent damage to his Baptist brain. But if he wasn't broken by her secret, she would have someone who wasn't Motty or Hendrick to finally talk to.

When they'd almost reached the curve that would put them in sight of Motty's house, Lunk said, "Stella Wallace, would you let me kiss you?"

Damn it. She'd already told him she'd try anything once. And she *was* curious. "Make it quick."

His lips were dry. It didn't feel like much. Lunk, though, was staring at her with shining eyes.

"Happy?" she asked.

He tried for a second one and she slapped him lightly with her Bible.

"I have to protect my immortal soul," she said.

He laughed like that was the wittiest thing he'd ever heard. God damn, she thought. He's giddy.

TWO WEEKS LATER, on a frigid night, Stella awoke, blood whooshing in her ears and her heart beating fast. She'd been dreaming—but of what? Sweat dampened her neck. Her body knew something her mind had already forgot.

She went out to the front room. The fire had retreated to the coals. Motty slumped in her chair, eyes closed and mouth agape. Her left hand held a glass with half an inch of moonshine in it. A miracle it hadn't slipped from her fingers. The ashtray was full of the butts of hand-rolled cigarettes.

Whatever had woken Stella was not in this room. She heard a distant sound, a cry like an infant's. She went to the kitchen and out to the backyard.

A great pale shape, a dozen feet tall, crouched beside the pig-pen, his hinged legs holding his pale torso aloft like a cocoon.

The God had left the mountain.

One of his limbs was extended over the top of the fence rail. The sow was pinned beneath it. It was the animal's cry she'd heard. Suddenly the limb raised and the sow scrambled to her feet and ran for the darkness under the shelter roof, squealing.

Stella held a hand to her throat. She hadn't made a noise, but the God knew she was there.

He swiveled on complex joints, limbs scissoring—and then he was moving toward her. Stella was paralyzed.

He stopped in front of her. She gazed up at him, her eyes watering.

The God hovered over her, and she stood her ground. She realized now that it was Motty and Hendrick's rules that had filled her with shame. Their religion. Her fear of breaking their commandments had sent her flying from the cave. But those rules had nothing to do with the God.

The Ghostdaddy loved her.

The Birches can't control me, she told herself. I will not be bound by human rules.

She reached up to his torso. His skin was so warm. The air around her began to vibrate as if she were inside an engine. He shifted so that he sat on an array of back legs, presenting his belly to her. His arms surrounded her.

She couldn't speak. She didn't have to. This wasn't a communion, like the ones Uncle Hendrick and the men had witnessed. It was something simpler, and better—because later she could recall every moment of it.

He seemed to gaze down from that eyeless, mouthless boulder at the top of his torso. Her fingers found a long crease alongside that bulge and clung there. His body thrummed. She leaned into him, and now *her* bones were thrumming, resonating with him. Warmth traveled through her.

She wanted his hands. She wanted to press her palms to him. She wanted to bind herself to him, feel the rush of his thoughts. She reached behind her, where his limb was pressed to her back.

Suddenly he tightened his grip and her feet left the ground. The God spun her about, and laughter bubbled out of her.

Sometime later he set her on the ground. One limb pulled back, then another. His smooth chest slipped from her fingertips. She reached forward and found only air. He was gone.

My God, she thought. My God is a living god.

## 12

**1948**

I T LOOKED LIKE half of Tennessee wanted proof Motty was dead. Cars and trucks lined both sides of the road and were parked all over the lawn.

"Fuck me," Stella said. She made no move to get out of the car.

"Fuck *me*," Alfonse said. "I didn't expect this many of y'all. I feel like Fleet Walker."

"Who?"

"The Jackie Robinson of Jackie Robinsons."

"You can back out."

He sighed. "Come on now."

"There's some things I haven't told you about my family. Strange things. You might hear about a few of them."

He raised his eyebrows and dipped his chin, a look that meant, You waited all this way to bring this up?

"I know. I'm sorry. I'd like to ask you to ride it out, and I promise to explain it all afterward."

"Fair enough. Could you open the glove box for me?"

They'd taken his car, breaking her personal rule. But she wanted him to have an exit in case he had to leave without her.

She opened the box and handed him the pistol, a Colt 1911. A serviceman's weapon.

He checked the safety and put it in the pocket of his wool topcoat. "You'll point out which one is Brother Paul?"

"You'll know him. He's so white he's cellophane. You didn't happen to bring any of the batch with you, too?"

"I always carry a flagon of whiskey, in case of snakebite. I also carry a small—"

"A small snake. Got it, W.C."

They traded sips. Climbed out of the car.

The sky bulged with gray clouds, threatening rain. Her old tweed box coat wouldn't stand up to much weather, and the black dress—one of her few dresses—was no help. She hated going into battle wearing a dress.

"Mind if I keep this?" She holstered his flask in her jacket pocket. "I'd like us both to go in armed."

"You mean loaded."

The porch and yard were overrun with chattering humans. A lot of them were cousins—Birches and Whits and Martins and Whiteheads—and members of the old cove families. She wondered how many had shown up just to retrieve the dishes they'd brought the other day. Most of them were old people, but it was surprising how many children were running around—girls in dresses, little boys in untucked shirts, incapable of suppressing their good mood. Why bring them to a funeral? Did their parents want them to witness the end of an era? Take note, kids: one of the last of the cove residents is dead; soon this place will be home only to deer and bears.

More surprising was the number of strangers, standing around in formal clothes. They were clumped together, talking among themselves, giving the side-eye to the local hillbillies. Then Stella saw Brother Paul with them and realized who they were: more of Hendrick's God damn Georgian disciples. They were multiplying. Even more alarming, one of them was cranking a handheld movie camera.

A voice yelled her name. Stella looked around, spotted Veronica, or rather her hat, a floppy-brimmed extravaganza of bright flowers. She was talking to a dark-haired young man in a too-tight suit. Stella made her way to her, Alfonse trailing.

"I want you to meet Rickie!" Veronica's voice was too loud for a funeral, even an outdoor one. "My fiancé." Hitting that last syllable hard.

Rickie shook her hand. "I've heard a lot about you."

"You don't know the half of it," Stella said. "This is my friend Alfonse."

Rickie looked him over, but dropped his hand to the side.

Oh, Stella thought. So he's an asshole.

Veronica did take Alfonse's hand in her gloved one. "I've heard a lot about you. Stella says you drive like lightning."

Alfonse glanced at Stella. He was surprised she'd mentioned him to this Georgia peach. "Well, I do *drive* lightning."

Veronica laughed and said, "Your product liked to kill me!" Rickie looked confused.

Stella said, "I see you recovered."

"Barely!"

The Georgians nearby were watching this exchange. They seemed to know who Stella was—and didn't like her much. Behind them, the Pontiac hearse that had taken away Motty's body sat parked on the grass. Rows of folding chairs were set up nearby, and in front of them was a line of people making their way past a pearl-gray casket. Uncle Hendrick was shaking hands with people. She couldn't see the hole behind the casket, but she could feel it.

Veronica said, "We're supposed to sit down front, right next to the grave." She glanced at Alfonse. "Just the family, I mean."

"I'm fine back here," he said.

"Thanks," Stella said to him quietly, and went to join the line.

The top half of the casket stood open. Inside lay a shrunken gray figure carved out of soapstone, wrapped in baggy blue cloth—that new dress Ruth had brought. The figure didn't look much like Motty. That was the thing about the funeral process; by the time you buried someone, days after their death, the body looked so little like the person you knew that it had become something else: *remains*. It was a gift, really. A necessary distancing. It felt immoral to put a loved one underground, but to bury some husk they'd left behind? No problem. It's easy to throw out leftovers.

Someone coughed behind her and Stella realized she'd been standing there too long. She had little choice but to take the seat next to Ruth.

Veronica sat on her other side. "So what do you think?"

"She looks horrible," Stella said.

"No, about Rickie!"

Ruth shushed them.

"Congratulations," Stella stage-whispered. "You've snagged yourself a handsome boyfriend."

"Fiancé."

"Have you seen Sunny? Or Abby?"

"Daddy said the funeral would be too much for her. She's . . ." One white glove fluttered. ". . . shy."

"Well no wonder with these strangers taking pictures. What's with the movie camera? It's disrespectful."

"It's a historical moment."

"What's historical about it?"

"Goodness gracious, Stella. Have you been up all night with that friend of yours? Look at your eyes." Her drawl had stretched into full Vivien Leigh. "I've got concealer for those bags. Let me—"

"Shhhh!" Ruth said.

The folding chairs began to fill with ancient family members, anxious to get started before their own funerals began. Hendrick nodded to the two boys from Smith Mortuary standing by the hearse. They fiddled with something inside the casket and then closed the lid.

Stella had a moment to wonder who Hendrick had gotten to preside over the service—and then he stepped forward, holding a Bible. Of course he was doing it himself. He thought he was Billy Sunday.

"Thank you for coming here, on such late notice," Hendrick said. "It warms my heart that you, our friends and family and church family, have gathered here, at our ancestral home, to say goodbye to my beloved sister, Mathilda Birch."

Jesus. He was pretending he loved Motty. Worse, he was pretending he *liked* her.

"Mathilda and I were lucky to grow up here in the cove. Our daddy called it paradise on Earth. But Mathilda, praise God, has gone to a far more glorious place."

Quit calling her Mathilda, Stella thought. God, she was tired. There were pins and needles behind her eyes. Gray clouds roofed the sky, but the rain refused to fall.

Hendrick rolled on, following the Standard Baptist Funeral Script, a time-honored string of bromides, Bible verses, reassurances, and evangelism. The loved one's suffering is over, their race has been run, Jesus has called them home, and have you got right with the Lord? The main message was that you were a sucker for grieving. Why shed tears over someone who's crossed over River Jordan into the Promised Land? And don't you want to be there too? The whole point of the sermon was not to honor the dead, but to use that death to remind sinners their own souls were in jeopardy. The corpse on display was merely a motivational prop.

What offended Stella most about the script was that it erased the woman they were talking about. Stella didn't expect him to talk about Motty's service to the God in the Mountain, but where was any mention of her regal stubbornness? The way she sailed on despite the gossip, like a ship in heavy weather? Someone needed to remind this crowd how Motty refused to take shit from any man, whether he was a preacher, cop, or government flunky.

Stella sighed, and Ruth's head whipped toward her. Oops— that was louder than she intended. Veronica put a gloved hand to her mouth, stifling a giggle. Hendrick glanced at Stella but kept talking.

She thought, I'm going to run across the pews.

Lunk had said that to her. She hadn't thought of it in years. They used to worry about whether or not they were good people. Lunk's death had settled the question for both of them. The only thing she had to worry about now was who else she'd hurt, how badly, and in what order.

She wondered what Elder Rayburn had said at Lunk's funeral. Probably the same platitudes as Hendrick was spouting now, but with a tragic spin: God called Lincoln home far earlier than we wanted, but we can't blame the Lord, no sirree Bob. He has a plan. God works in mysterious ways.

All gods do.

"I believe Mathilda is with Him now," Hendrick was saying. "She's looking down on us, and if there's one thing she would want us to—" He stopped, surprised by something behind his audience. Heads young enough to turn, turned.

Absalom Whitt was making his way slowly through the crowd. People got out of the way and Stella saw the girl at his side, his hand resting lightly on her shoulder. Sunny, in a white dress.

No one spoke.

The pair walked alongside the chairs. Sunny touched Abby's

arm and then she approached the casket alone. She was wearing the dress that Stella had worn for her first communion. There was no trace of the beet juice.

"Sunny, I'm so glad you're here," Hendrick said. "Do you want to take a seat?"

The girl's expression was hard to read. The swirls of red and white across her face acted like camouflage.

Ruth leaned across Stella. "Veronica! Have her sit down!"

"Open it," Sunny said.

"What's that?" Hendrick asked.

"Open it," Sunny said, louder.

"Oh, honey, I don't think we should—"

Stella stood up. Veronica squeaked.

Sunny looked at her. Stella stepped to the casket, tugged at the lip, but it wouldn't open. She gestured at the mortuary assistants.

They hustled forward, did something under the lid, and lifted it. Sunny looked inside. "Huh."

Then she walked away, toward Abby. The cameraman, a skinny, nervous fellow, pointed his lens at the girl and cranked away. She ignored him.

Abby whispered something to Sunny, and she nodded. The two of them walked away, heading for the trail that led to his cabin.

Hendrick abandoned his sermon. He called for them to bow their heads, declaimed a few words, and then brought Polly Ledbetter forward. Stella hadn't seen her since she'd helped her pack up her house, fifteen years ago. She sang "The Old Rugged Cross" in a high warble and some woman right behind Stella's ear hummed along off-key.

Hendrick said "Amen" and the service was over. The guests started assaulting the family with condolences.

"It's such an honor to meet you," one of the Georgian men said. He took her hand between his and shook it. Good lord, was there anything worse than the hand sandwich? "I've heard so much about you, but to meet you in person—and now to see Sunny!"

She pulled free from him. All around her, Georgians and cove people were saying Sunny's name.

A dozen feet away, Mary Lynn Rayburn stared at her with a mournful expression. It was a shock. For a moment she looked exactly like her brother.

Mary Lynn started toward her and Stella thought, No, no, no. She looked around for an escape route and spotted Merle Whitt and Pee Wee Simms, standing on the other side of the yard with Alfonse. She marched up to them, resolutely not looking in Mary Lynn's direction.

"Why, it's Stella Mae Wallace." Pee Wee, projecting devilish charm with his Errol Flynn mustache, hands in the pockets of his deeply pleated slacks. Her middle name wasn't Mae, and his grin was not funeral-appropriate.

"Hey, sweetie," Merle said. She was tall and thin, wearing slacks almost identical to her husband's, but she looked better in them. She stood with her arms away from her body, open to a hug, but not forcing it on Stella; she knew better. But Stella surprised herself. She stepped in close, reached up to wrap her arms around the woman. Breathed in that familiar scent of Lucky Strikes and Drene shampoo. Stella had met Merle when Stella was thirteen, and it was comforting to think Merle would always be the adult—taller, yes, but smarter and more sophisticated too.

"How are you doing?" Merle asked. "You eating?"

Jesus, how bad did she look? First Veronica's crack about her eyes; now this. It only made it worse that Merle's concern was sincere. "Been better. Life's complicated."

"We've had a long night," Alfonse explained.

Merle still looked worried. "How is Sunny? I'm glad she got a chance to say her goodbyes."

"At least identify the body," Pee Wee said.

"That was something," Alfonse said. Poor guy. That bit with the casket wasn't even the weirdness she'd been warning him about. It was only going to get worse.

"I think she'll be fine," Stella said—and then laid out a collection of words that, if assembled correctly, clearly meant the opposite. She didn't know if the girl was sad about Motty's death, happy about it, or just ready to leave for Georgia.

"Motty never allowed the girl to come to our house," Merle said. "Being a bad example and all. When you finish with all this, you should bring her by the house."

Stella's throat closed. This was the moment to tell her that Sunny might go live with Hendrick.

"Or . . . just you," Merle said.

Stella hadn't been to see Merle in months. There was no excuse for it. She and Pee Wee lived in Switchcreek, a short drive from her house in Maryville. These people had provided a home when Stella was thinking hard about following her mother into the air. They'd anchored her, and after the heavy weather of the dark years, they'd launched her into a new life. There was no one whose opinion meant more to her.

Yet: Sunny.

"I'm so sorry," Stella said. "I've been pretty busy with work."

Pee Wee arched an eyebrow. "Alfonse was telling us about a recent mix-up."

"I mentioned we just dropped off a major apology," Alfonse said.

"And how did it turn out?" Pee Wee asked.

Stella said, "You got your seventy gallons, right?" Pee Wee was her long-distance distributor. He didn't so much run moonshine as gently escort it across state lines. He kept to the speed limit, and drove only late-model sedans, relying on the appearance of propriety and affluence to avoid police attention, and his personal charm on the rare occasions he was stopped.

"Alfonse did indeed deliver it to my garage," Pee Wee said. "Though I haven't had a chance to taste it yet."

"Then let's not delay." She slipped him Alfonse's flask. He scanned for watching eyes like a practiced tippler, then tippled. Merle took the flask next. She coughed but held it in.

"Excellent apology," Pee Wee said. "Heartfelt."

Merle said, "I don't know how you two drink this stuff."

Stella was conscious of Mary Lynn's presence and moved so her back was to her. "So . . . how's the semester going?" she asked Merle. "Keeping the freshmen in line?" The first-year biology class generated Merle's best stories.

"Most of them don't believe in evolution, and I'm starting to see their point. How can they get stupider, year after year?"

"That's sexual selection," Stella said. "Those boys won't get laid by Christian girls if they start using big ol' science words."

"So they have to display their ignorance."

"Like peacock feathers," Stella said. "But for stupid."

"We should write a paper together."

"I'll have my grad students call your grad students."

Pee Wee shook his head in mock confusion. He loved their verbal badminton matches but kept to the sidelines.

Stella was relieved to see Mary Lynn walking toward the road. She'd given up. There were still plenty of people milling about the yard, some of them the Georgia visitors, but the rest locals. But why weren't they leaving? Thanks to Elder Rayburn's disapproval, the Primitive Baptists hadn't provided lunch, and no other church had crossed the picket line. Usually the quickest way to get rid of a Baptist was to tell them you were out of fried chicken.

Then she saw who Uncle Hendrick was chatting with.

Merle noticed her distraction and frowned. "What's wrong?"

Stella said, "I have to go, but I'll be seeing you soon, I promise."

Merle squeezed her arm. "Take care of yourself."

"It's not me I'm worried about." She exchanged a look with Alfonse: You all right? He nodded.

Stella ambled over to Hendrick to start the negotiations.


HENDRICK, TOM ACHERSON, and Sheriff Whaley were huddled like the triumvirate dividing up Rome. It bothered her to see them all so chummy.

Stella took a breath. Walked forward at ramming speed.

"How you boys doing?" she said. Ignoring Hendrick.

Tom Acherson took off his hat, tucked it under his right armpit, and extended his left hand. "That was a beautiful service." He wore a brown suit and a tan tie. Stella wondered if the outfit counted as dress browns.

Sheriff Whaley offered his condolences—something he hadn't bothered to do when he stormed the house the other morning.

Stella said, "I'm sure Motty was a pain in all your asses." Whaley chuckled, and Tom went red. He was too decent for his own good. Hendrick looked disapproving.

She said, "Thanks again for allowing us to bury her here, Tom. I appreciate it."

"The least I could do," Tom said. "I told Hendrick that whatever grave marker you put up, the park service will always make sure it's maintained."

"Really? I thought the plan was to erase all evidence of our existence."

"What? Oh no!"

"You're not going to tear down this farm?"

Hendrick said, "That's not the plan, Stella. You haven't kept up."

She tried to stifle her anger. "Well by all means, fill me in."

Tom said, "It's true, the original idea was to return the cove to its natural state, but the park service changed its mind years ago. We're going to preserve select homes and barns, for educational reasons."

"Select homes."

"Sure!" He was the most naturally happy man she'd ever met, and not even a funeral could suppress his cheerfulness. "We're focusing on homes built before, say, 1910—cabins, frontier constructions. You know, to show people what the cove was like for the southern highlanders, back in the day. The Birches were one of the first families, of course, and this house—well, it's not the original 1823 cabin, that was torn down in 1845 when the current cabin was built, and then there were the expansions in 1875 and '80—"

"It's old. Got it."

"The point is," Tom said cheerily, "I'm sure the service will want to keep it."

"When you say you're sure," Stella said, "that means somebody else ain't."

"Oh. Well. Yes, there is a committee—a good group of people, not just administrators but historians and anthropologists too. They'll decide. It's a tough job. You can't keep everything. You have to pick and choose. You have to curate."

"You mean burn away everything that doesn't fit the product you're selling."

Sheriff Whaley said, "You may know something about that process." He was watching her face. Hendrick too. As for Tom, he looked freshly embarrassed. Or maybe confused. He must have heard the rumors about her business—even a Yankee couldn't be that clueless.

She decided to laugh. "I may know something about distillation at that. I'm Motty's granddaughter."

"And Abby's apprentice," Whaley said. "The apple doesn't fall far."

Hendrick said, "The sheriff was saying you've got a reputation as quite the lady businessman."

"I think the word you're looking for is *madam* businessman."

"Ha!" Tom said. Then seemed to regret it.

"Alfonse and I are going into the house before this rain comes down," she said to Hendrick. "See you inside?"

"Alfonse?"

"Her boy," Whaley said.

"That *boy*," Stella said, "served in the 452nd Artillery on the front lines. Where were you all during the war? Tom excepted."

"Uhm, thank you," Tom said. "But—"

"I'll be inside in a minute," Hendrick said. "It'll be good to say our goodbyes before you head back home."

RAIN HAMMERED the tin roof, a whooshing racket as familiar to her as the roar of blood in her ears. She'd fallen asleep to that sound a hundred nights. Now it filled the kitchen like steam, making the small room even smaller, yet somehow more private too.

Uncle Hendrick sat across the table from her, both of them with their hands on coffee cups like dueling pistols. Veronica and Rickie sat between them. Brother Paul and half a dozen more of Hendrick's disciples surrounded the table, watching a little keenly for Stella's taste. She was happy to have Alfonse leaning against the wall a few feet away—with his hands in his pockets.

The rest of the house was full of Georgians, at least a dozen of them, nowhere to go in this rain, and for some reason not going home.

The skinny man started to raise the 8-millimeter camera and Stella said, "Touch that crank and I'll shove the whole camera down your throat."

He looked shocked that a woman would talk to him that way.

Hendrick said, "It's all right, Stanley." But his eyes were on Alfonse.

Stella liked that Hendrick didn't know how to judge Alfonse's presence. She wanted all of them wondering if this Black man was armed or not, if he was dangerous, and most especially, if he knew about the church. They'd have to watch what they said. They'd have to be careful how hard they pushed her.

"Let's all remember this isn't an argument," Hendrick said. His voice had shifted to the tone of a kindly patriarch. "We're just here to talk through some issues, as family."

Sure, just a family discussion, Stella thought. There were less people at Lee's surrender in Appomattox.

"If there's anything you want from the house, I'm happy to discuss it," Hendrick said. "Or pay you fairly for it. For personal and historical reasons, I'd like to preserve as many keepsakes as possible."

"You sound like Tom Acherson. You making a museum?"

Brother Paul said, "As a matter of fact, we are."

"I'm not here to talk about keepsakes," Stella said. "This is about Sunny."

"Of course, of course," Hendrick said. His sleeves were rolled up, tie loosened. He should have been as tired as she was, but he was keyed up, excited. Was it because he'd finally stepped out of Motty's shadow? "The important thing is that we both want what's best for the girl."

"The important thing," Stella said, "is that we agree what the hell 'best' means."

"I'm sure that—oh."

She liked throwing a swear into a sentence when dealing with the devout. Knocked them off their game.

"Why's Brother Paul here carrying a pistol?" she asked. "You a cop, Brother Paul?"

"A man's allowed to carry a weapon," Hendrick said.

"Aren't we all," Stella said. She reached into her pocket. Brother Paul stepped forward—and she showed them the flask. Poured the last of the moonshine into her cup.

Alfonse chuckled quietly.

"I don't understand," Rickie said. "Why is *he* here?"

Stella said, "Vee, could you tell your boyfriend to keep a lid on it?"

"Fiancé," Veronica said quietly.

Hendrick said, "I know you can be emotional, Stella. Whatever I can do to soothe your fears, I'm willing to do."

How fucking thoughtful, Stella thought.

"I just want you and Abby to be comfortable," he said. "He's not family, but Sunny listens to him."

Right. The blessing.

"I want to make sure you have the means to take care of her," Stella said. "Not just a year, but until she's old enough to be on her own."

"We have the means," Hendrick said. "Don't you worry."

That "we" was telling.

"Let's start with this ranch of yours," she said. "Where'd you get the money for five hundred acres?"

Hendrick smiled to cover something that looked like indigestion. "I think you've gotten something wrong. It's not my ranch. It belongs to the church."

She looked at Brother Paul in exaggerated surprise. "Holy shit, did Hendrick convince you folks to *tithe* to him?"

"We tithe to the church," Paul said.

"I bet I know whose name is on the bank account."

"That's none of your business."

Ooh, she thought. Paul's getting angry. She wondered how much money he'd sunk into this deal.

"You're right, I don't care where the money comes from,"

Stella said. "What does matter is that as long as Sunny's at this church ranch of yours, I have the right to visit her at any time, without notice. And she has the right to call me at any time."

"Why is she taking an interest now?" Brother Paul asked Hendrick. "I thought she washed her hands of the girl years ago."

"Because now Motty's dead," Stella said. She addressed the devout. "Sunny'll need a Birch woman in her life. I already told her, she's going to have questions as she grows up, questions you can't answer. That's why I need to be able to see her, at any time she wants, or any time I say."

"Stella's right," Hendrick said. It was annoying to have him agree with her. "She's now the eldest, and that's an honored position. Clara guided Esther, Esther guided Motty, and so it goes." He was still using that pastor voice. God, he loved performing. "Now Stella, I don't approve of all the choices you've made the past few years. Heavens no. But whatever my personal qualms, I will not be the first Birch man to break that tradition."

He gave in a little too easy, and Stella smelled bullshit. Maybe he figured she'd never take him up on a visit. After all, she'd avoided Sunny for ten years. It wouldn't be unexpected if she avoided her for ten more.

Stella had to consider how to phrase her next demand. She sipped from her cup, letting the taste of weak coffee and strong liquor sit on her tongue. Strange to taste it at night; coffee and whiskey was usually a breakfast item.

"Second," she said. And here, at last, was the moment for which she'd brought Alfonse. "Till she's of age, Sunny never sets foot back in the cove without me here. No picnics in the park. No services in the chapel. Nothing."

"*What?*" Brother Paul, taking umbrage—and he looked like a man who liked to take it by the barrel. His fellow Georgians started mumbling among themselves.

"That's the deal," Stella said. "Nothing happens without me."

"This is ridiculous," Paul said. "This woman can't dictate terms."

"Let me spell it out," Stella said. "If you try to bring Sunny here without me, I'll tell the park service about the chapel, the cave, everything. You'll never have access to it again."

Fresh consternation rolled through the Georgians.

"You wouldn't do that," Hendrick said.

"Of course I would."

"You can't pretend you don't love our God. You were the Revelator," Hendrick said. "Once you've touched the divine, that mark doesn't fade." He spoke with confidence, but he'd never experienced the Ghostdaddy direct. He'd heard a story about fire and thought he knew what hot was. "I'm sorry your fiancé died. I'm sorry that you—"

"Boyfriend," Veronica said.

"—felt the need to run away. I thought it was a mistake to run from your family, but I respected your decision."

"Because Motty told you to."

Hendrick smiled. "True enough. She was a force. And you! You take after her quite a bit. Sunny, too, if I'm honest."

If, Stella thought.

"Here's what I need to know," Hendrick said. "What will you do when Sunny comes of age?"

"Then it'll be her choice," Stella said. It wasn't even a lie—by the time Sunny was twelve there'd be no choice for her to make. "If it comes to that, I'll do my best to get her through the communion, safe and healthy. Not for you. For her. The Ghostdaddy's more dangerous than you men know."

Alfonse grunted in surprise. Hendrick and Veronica were looking at him, no doubt wondering how much Stella had told him. Not near enough, she thought. She was going to have *so* much to explain after this.

"So we have a—an agreement?" Hendrick asked.

"Depends on Veronica."

Veronica looked up, surprised.

"I need you to promise me you'll look out for her," Stella said. "You'll make sure she stays safe. Can you do that, Vee?"

Veronica played at flighty, and she was as vain as a Broadway actress, but she'd never been dumb. She knew this was serious. She reached across the table and squeezed Stella's hand. "I promise."

Stella stood up, and Alfonse straightened. They exchanged a look. You good? I'm good.

"I'll talk to Abby," Stella said to Hendrick. "I'll make him feel all right about it."

Hendrick clapped his hands. "Praise God." He rose to his feet. The men in the room looked to him. Brother Paul may have the money, but Hendrick was the God damn prophet.

"We've waited a hundred years," Hendrick said, raising his voice. "We can wait two more." He was looking at Stella but he was talking for the history books. He'd be writing this speech down tonight. "In the meantime, we study the Revelations, we take care of the Revelator. The God will reveal himself when it's time, when the world needs him. And on that day, the church will stand ready. Do I hear an amen?"

"Amen," Brother Paul said, reluctantly. A chorus of prayerful amens followed.

When she was a girl, Stella once asked Uncle Hendrick, What do we get from the God? And he'd told her about love and a sense of purpose and vague promises of an immaculate body. Nothing concrete. Nothing now.

But Hendrick had figured out how to leverage the God for something more immediate. First use divine access and mumbo jumbo to acquire followers, then soak the followers for money, and then spend the cash on real estate and whatever the hell else you wanted. Political power, even. It was the oldest trick in the book.

Hendrick extended his hand to Stella. "It's good to have you on our side again," he said.

She looked at that hand and thought, He doesn't know. He doesn't know how easy I could kill him.

She gripped his hand and he winced.

"One more thing," Stella said.

Hendrick suddenly seemed worried. "Yes?"

"The iron skillets."

"What?"

"You mentioned keepsakes. I want Motty's iron skillets. Do you know how many years she's been seasoning them?"

ALFONSE DROVE IN SILENCE, eyes on the narrow, twisting road. The car was loud with the drumming of the rain and the slap of the automatic windshield wipers.

Then they reached the highway. Alfonse hit the gas and said, "What the actual motherfucking fuck?"

"Thanks for being there," Stella said. "It went better than I thought." Hendrick had given her everything she asked for. The three nested skillets lay heavy on her lap.

"What the fuck is a Ghostdaddy?"

Stella sighed. "A made-up god for a made-up religion."

"That's insane."

"I tried to warn you."

"That's crazy hillbilly shit."

"Again—warned."

"You want to explain what kind of deal you struck? Because I do not know what the fuck was going on in there."

"All you have to know is I got what I wanted."

Alfonse shook his head. "You sure about that? I'm not sure I trust that uncle of yours."

"Hendrick?" Stella laughed. "I don't trust him as far as I can throw him."

"Then what the hell?"

"I had to put up a fight. Make it look painful, even threaten him a little, or he wouldn't trust the deal. You know how it is when you're negotiating with some son of a bitch. They ain't happy unless they feel like they've screwed you."

"Yet I have no idea what you were selling."

"More like what I was buying—time."

"To do what?"

Kill a god, she thought.

Aloud she said, "I needed Hendrick to go, get out of the cove, just for a while. Make him think everything would go his way if he waited a couple years."

"And what're you going to do in the meantime?"

She put a hand on his shoulder. "I do have one more favor to ask."

"Here we go." But he was grinning.

"You still got cousins working that mine in Chattanooga?"

"The Bowlins are everywhere."

"Think they'd sell you some dynamite?"

Alfonse looked at her. Put his eyes back on the road. "How much we talking?"

"Enough to—let's call it a significant geologic event."

"Shee-it. Is this about that cave you was talking about?"

"Maybe so."

"How soon you need it?" he asked.

"Think you could get it in a week?"

"I'll make some calls." They talked over the amount, the probable cost. They didn't talk about the legal ramifications. Then he asked, "What about that girl, Sunny? You going to let her go with your uncle?"

"Hendrick adores her. More than that, he needs her. He won't hurt her."

"But if she's—"

Alfonse stopped himself. She waited for him to ask the question. But if she's yours . . . ?

He said, "She looks an awful lot like you."

"It's the skin condition. Runs in the family."

"Mom or Dad's side?"

"What? No. The man I called my *pa* has got fuck all to do with any of this."

## 13

**1937**

ABBY CAUGHT HER staring into the woods, an open book on her lap. "You all right, Little Star?"

She didn't know how to answer. For the past six months she'd been living somewhere between all right and all wrong. The God hadn't come to her again, but she'd gone to him—Hendrick and the Uncles had let her commune three more times. Each recovery took longer. She'd lie in bed for days, dizzy with foreign thoughts. Now she didn't know what part of her still belonged to her, and what belonged to the God in the Mountain.

"I'm fine," she said. "Just . . . daydreaming."

"It's okay if you miss your daddy."

"What's he got to do with it?"

"I just thought—"

"Motty told you about the letter." It had come two days ago, postmarked Cook County, Ill., all of six sentences, most of it how cold Chicago was in the winter and how muggy in the summer, and how much better it was in Tennessee. He'd ended with a sentence like a confession finally beaten out of a gangster:

*In November I married a woman named Marie, she is very nice and I
hope youll meet her soon.*

—*Pa*

"It don't matter to me," Stella said. "Ray Wallace can jump
in a lake."

Abby blew out his lips. Sat beside her. She pretended to read
her book.

The silence didn't last. After a while he asked what she was
reading, trying to sound casual. Then more questions: How were
things going at school? Did she like any of them boys? She wondered if he'd heard about Lincoln Rayburn coming to call on
her after her visit to his church. Motty had run him off, but Lunk
kept coming by the school, kept asking her out, hoping to wear
her down. She was thirteen and all the other girls her age at
the consolidated school were boy crazy, couldn't figure out why
she wouldn't pair up with such a handsome boy. Stella remained
unconvinced and unconsolidated.

"I'm fine, Abby."

He was so worried for her. Had been for a long time, probably.
Motty had been watching her, too, as close as she watched her
sow, a burly sweet-faced pig who was mean as spit. That animal
could move quick as a blacksnake even though she'd been packing on pounds for a year, her body turning into a new shape.
Stella knew how she felt. Her own body was out of control. Her
legs ached, what Motty dismissed as growing pains. Her thigh
bones were stretching her muscles like guitar strings, tighter and
tighter, ready to snap with a *plink!* Spots had broken out across
her forehead.

But worse was her out-of-control brain. Sometimes in the
middle of the night she woke up with a head full of sharp, word-
less thoughts, her pulse racing.

She hated that it was so hard to hold on to what the God communicated to her. The beginning of each communion was clear: the long wait as she lay on the table, the cold stone under her back, staring up into the dark. And then, when she'd almost convinced herself the God wasn't going to appear this time, she'd glimpse movement in the dark and her heart would jump. The God always moved slowly, descending like a spider on a thread, and then he would reach for her. A quick sharp pain as their hands met. Then he would withdraw his limbs, slowly, slowly, and her arms would ache as that strange, gleaming sinew stretched between them, trembling and tugging. She was a puppet, a fish on the line. And then a wave of thoughts and emotions would strike her. And then, at some point, she'd pass out.

Later she'd wake up in her bedroom like a drowned sailor washed ashore, worn out and gasping and amazed at her survival. Of course it was Motty who carried her out of the cave each time, Motty who took care of her. She'd bind up Stella's hands and mop her brow as gruffly as a cowboy branding cattle. Stella would spend days in bed, sleeping fitfully and dreaming something else's dreams. When she opened her eyes the room quivered with *meaning*. Each mundane object, each book and floorboard and windowpane, seemed to be revealing itself to her: The dinner plate Motty brought her was both itself and something purer, some original form as it must have existed when God whispered the world into existence. The ruby slice of tomato came straight from the Garden of Eden.

The constant blast of secret knowledge was exhausting, yet she cried when it began to fade. And when it disappeared completely, when every object turned dumb and forgot its true self, she ached to get it back. She longed to see the God again.

But the God hadn't come to her. Hendrick and the Uncles kept their own schedule. And she couldn't get into the chapel on her own, because Motty had hidden the key. Everyone controlled what Stella did and when she did it, and she had no say.

Adults could do what they wanted, men especially. Hell, they could go off and marry some floozy named *Marie.*

Abby said, "You want to go watch Tom Acherson knock down the Ledbetter house? He's got a big backhoe."

"No." That sounded too sad for words. She remembered the day she helped them pack up, and how dead Polly Ledbetter had seemed.

"Aw, come on," Abby said. "Not every day you see a one-armed man tear down a house."

"You go." For months he'd been trying to draw her out. He'd offer to take her hunting, or invite her to help run batches of shine, but she'd lost all interest.

"Wait! I got it!"

"I just want to read, thank you."

"Oh, this is miles better than any old book." Then he made her an offer she couldn't refuse.

SHE PERCHED AT the edge of the Model A's high front seat, practically standing up, her palms slick on the steering wheel—and the car hadn't even started yet. They were on level ground, about a mile from Motty's. "I don't think I'm ready for this," she said.

"Pfff. You're thirteen," Abby said. "Uncle Dan learned to drive when he was in diapers."

"Did he now?"

"Course, he was forty years old."

"Abby!"

"Ah, there's that smile. You ready to start 'er up? It's very simple."

"I'm listening."

"Pull back on the handbrake—safety first! Good. Now step on the clutch and put her in neutral—wiggle the gearshift so you know it's free, there you go. Make sure the fuel line is open. See that fuel line running under the dash? That little valve by your knee, turn it vertical, that lets the gas flow. This here's the choke, you're going to pull up on that when we start it, but not just yet. See that knob on the top of the choke? That's the air–fuel mixture valve, turn it left, nope, not all the way, just three-quarter open—you want a pretty rich mix to start. The starter button is there on the floor, just find it with your foot—nope, that's the gas, the little button, but don't step on it yet. Up there on the steering column, that lever on the right, that's your hand throttle, bring that down a couple notches to give it extra gas for the start. Now that doohickey on the left, that's the spark lever—push it all the way up, that's full retard. We'll advance that when the engine's running, get the timing right so the fire explodes when the piston's on the upstroke, you follow?"

She glared at him. The car still wasn't started. This device required as much ritual as running a full batch on the still.

"Here we go," Abby said. "Press the clutch. Turn the key. Press down on that starter. Pull out the choke and push it back—just once!"

The engine thumped and shuddered. "Advance the spark! Give her some more throttle!"

The engine died with a sound like it had swallowed a chicken bone.

"Forget it," Stella said.

"You're doing fine. I think we gave it too much choke. Let's try it again."

Five minutes later she released the handbrake and got the car rolling. They went ten whole feet before it started lurching so hard it was throwing her against the steering wheel. "What's going on?!" she shouted.

Abby laughed. "You've got it in rabbit gear!"

"There's a *rabbit* gear?"

"Hit the clutch." She had to pull against the steering wheel to push her foot all the way down. "Okay, let 'er out easy, easy! Give her more gas. Too much! Now advance the spark. Left hand, left hand."

"Stop yelling at me!"

"Press the clutch, shift back to neutral, then clutch again—"

"Slow down!"

"Now shift to second—" The car slammed to a stop. "—gear."

The engine died. Stella burst into tears.

"I think that went pretty well," Abby said.

"Don't mock me."

"I wouldn't do any such thing." He opened the passenger door.

"Where are you going?"

"I've taught you the basics. The rest you can figure out on your own."

*"What?"*

"Just bring it back before it runs out of gas. And stay between the fence posts." He started walking back the way they'd come. He was whistling. *Whistling.*

Stella stared at her hands, then at the wheel, then at the 1,400 levers, buttons, valves, pedals, and dials. Clutch, spark, throttle, starter, choke. Clutch, spark, throttle, starter—

The engine coughed to life. She slid out the choke, increased the hand throttle, and got it up to a fast idle. Then stomped the clutch, pushed into first—and killed the engine.

She screamed into the windshield. Gosh damn it, she'd never learn to drive this thing!

. . . AND THEN SHE WAS flying down 321 at fifty miles per hour. Abby lounged in the passenger seat with one arm behind his head and the other holding his flask, his eyes closed. The car was rattling and the wind was roaring and she was singing "Big River Blues" at the top of her lungs. Then a police car passed her going the other way. She saw it brake hard in the rearview.

"Uhm, Abby?"

He was hardly more awake when the cop ambled up to the driver's side window. The policeman looked her over, then saw who was next to her.

"Absalom Whitt," the cop said.

"Hey, Bobby."

Stella said nothing. She'd broken into a sweat.

"I was surprised to see your vehicle out in daylight. Who's this young thing?"

"My niece. Stella, say hi to Officer Reed."

She lifted a hand. He was a handsome, narrow-faced white man with brilliant green eyes. "How old are you?" he asked.

"Sixteen," she lied.

He raised his eyebrows.

"Short people are allowed to drive," Abby said.

"God almighty, Abby, are you corrupting a minor?"

"She's not corrupt! This girl knows Shakespeare! Stella, tell him a sonnet."

"So you aren't making a delivery?"

"Bobby, you think I'd put an innocent girl at risk of committing a felony?"

"I wouldn't put it past you."

Stella stared straight ahead. Felony?

"Show me your license, miss."

"Bobby, you're making her cry."

She glared at Abby. She wasn't crying. He made a face that said, Would it kill you to try?

To Officer Reed she said, "My grandmother doesn't let me travel with it."

"How's that?"

"My license. She says it's too valuable. She keeps it in the family Bible."

"Family—? That's the most—no. Who's your grandmother?" His eyes widened. "Not—?"

Abby nodded.

"Yeah," Stella said sadly.

"Motty and Bobby have a fraught relationship," Abby explained to her. "Motty took a shot at him 'cause he killed a squirrel on her land."

"I was ten years old!"

"I'm sure she's forgiven you," Stella said.

"But not forgotten," Abby added.

"Open the rumble seat," Bobby said.

"I told you, I'm not working today."

"Open it."

Abby got up and levered it open. The seat was empty. Officer Reed walked the perimeter of the car. Then he looked at Stella and saw that her face was crumpled like she was going to burst into tears. "Fine, fine."

Stella went through the starting ritual and pulled back onto the highway. Officer Reed didn't follow her.

A minute passed. Abby said, "Family Bible?"

"It was the only thing I could think of."

"You're a born bootlegger," he said admiringly. "I'm taking you with me every trip."


ABBY HAD PROMISED HER a hamburger and a movie—an Edward G. Robinson gangster flick was playing at the Palace theater—but they weren't going there directly, it turned out. Five miles before Maryville, Abby guided her off the highway and down a series of winding roads, to a town almost as small as the creek it was named after. Had her pull in to a pretty little blue frame house with yellow shutters. Pee Wee Simms came out to meet them.

"Holy shit," Pee Wee said in nasal Yankee. "This little girl's been driving your car, Abby!"

"She's sixteen now. Had three birthdays while we were on the road."

"Congratulations, Miss Wallace."

"Thank you, Mr. Simms."

Abby asked, "My sister's not here, is she?"

"She's inside working. Don't worry, a bomb could go off and she wouldn't hear it. Even so, perhaps we should, uhm, move quickly?"

Abby lifted the high front seat and exposed the two cases of moonshine, packed in straw.

"Go on into the house," Pee Wee said to Stella. "We've got lemonade in the icebox. But perhaps don't mention . . . ?"

"Don't worry," Abby said. "She can keep a secret."

Outside the house was neat as a pin, but inside . . . inside it looked like two libraries had collided. A bookshelf filled each wall. The furniture was covered by the rubble of books, more books, and stacks of white papers. Here and there a dinner plate or wine bottle topped a pile. On a couch there was a space carved out between two precarious mounds for a skinny person who didn't jiggle much. Stella picked up one of the books on top, a slim, pale thing with notes sticking out of its pages like feathers. *The Genetical Theory of Natural Selection* by R. A. Fisher, Sc.D., F.R.S.—a name that came with its own secret code.

A voice said, "Are the boys hiding the hooch?"

Through the gap between a pair of French doors she could see a white woman leaning back in a swivel chair, her legs up on a rolltop desk. Legs in *pants*. A notebook lay open on her lap. Glasses hung from a chain on her neck.

Stella didn't want to lie. "They're doing *something*."

The woman liked that. "You must be Stella." She swung her legs down, stepped over a knee-high wall of books, and offered her hand. "I'm Merle Whitt."

Stella didn't raise her arm. There were scabs on her palms. Merle smoothly turned her handshake into a wave at the room. "Sorry about the mess."

"No!" Stella said. "This is—" She struggled for a word. "Perfect."

"No one's ever used *that* word for here." Merle produced a cigarette from behind her ear, lit it. She was as tall as Abby, but with curly hazelnut hair and olive skin. She wore what looked like a man's leather belt with extra notches to cinch her waist, and a thick wristwatch. Stella was confused by her last name. How could she have kept Whitt if she'd married a Simms?

Merle said, "Are you a student of evolution?"

Oh. The book in her hand. "I'm sorry, I shouldn't have moved it."

"Or maybe they don't teach that in the cove."

"My teacher says it's not godly."

"He's right about that."

"Can I ask why're you keeping a frog?"

Merle turned to see where she was looking and laughed. "C'mere."

On one of the few bookshelves not crammed higgledy-piggledy with books was a set of glass objects, lined up smallest to biggest, from small rectangles to that jar containing a spotted frog, floating in clear liquid. "*Rana pipiens*," Merle said. "The northern leopard frog. It starts off as just one little cell, and then . . ." She picked up one of the smallest glass rectangles and put it in Stella's hands. "That slide holds a single blastula, just thirty-two little cells. We'll have to get my microscope out to see it."

Stella was scared she'd drop it. "You have a microscope?"

"Oh sure. The little fella takes about thirty hours to get to the gastrula stage, then the neurula . . ." More slides. "And then after eighty-four hours you get the tail bud—can you see that?"

Inside a tiny vial was a dark shape as big as a splinter. The next biggest jar was a tadpole; Stella had seen plenty of those on her own. But it was amazing to see one so clear, so still. "Is this water?" Stella asked. "How do you—?"

"Alcohol, nearly pure. There's more than one use for it, you know." She laughed. "I don't know why I hold on to these. I made them for a project in grad school. It's nice that you noticed them."

"Can we . . . ? If it's okay . . ."

"Get out the microscope? Of course. First, let's get something to drink. What'll you have?"

"I shouldn't. I have to drive."

Merle's laugh was a bold-print exclamation mark.


ABBY DROVE BACK to the cove. Stella walked into the house carrying a paper sack that held three science books. Three!

Motty was waiting for her in the living room, a glass in one hand and a willow switch across her lap. Rumors of Stella's near arrest had beaten them back to the cove. But how? Motty didn't even have a telephone.

"I'm too old for a switch," Stella said.

"You think so, do you?"


THAT NIGHT she lay in bed reading from her new stock, one ear cocked to the sounds of Motty moving around the house. Two of the books were biology textbooks, and one was a journal with different articles in it. All of them were hard reading, but the journal especially. Her favorite article so far was called "Artificial

Transmutation of the Gene," which was all about using X-rays to mutate genes in fruit flies, real mad scientist stuff. She was on her third run at the text when she finally heard the old woman go to bed. Stella waited a half hour more, then eased open the door.

Find the key. The thought had been echoing around her head all night.

Stella had already searched Motty's room a few times, finding nothing but old clothes and an even older carpetbag, disappointingly empty. For a while she fantasized that it was Esther's bag, somehow returned to the family after Esther's disappearance. She'd never figured out how to ask Motty about it without giving herself up as a snoop. The only remaining place to check was the kitchen.

Stella moved into the room like a thief. She slid open drawers, moved aside spoons and forks and cutlery, all as quietly as possible. She searched behind the store-bought canned goods and home-canned vegetables, lifted aside the bags of dried beans and salt and cornmeal. Nothing. She checked under the apple corer, inside the ice cream bucket, under each of the three black laundry irons, through the cleaning rags. Then she remembered the night four years ago, when she first saw Motty with the chapel key.

Stella picked up one of the cane-back kitchen chairs, set it down quietly in front of the cupboards, and stepped up. The highest shelf held the specialty glass, the "Princess Pink" dishes and bowls, Motty's most precious possessions, after the guns. Stella reached—and from the front room came a grunt. She froze. Waited. Twenty, thirty seconds later, Motty began to snore.

Stella found the key in the sugar bowl, half buried. Ha!

She wet the steel between her lips and dipped it again, then slipped out of the house sucking on it like a lollipop.

·  ·  ·

ONCE IN THE CHAPEL she didn't dare light a candle. She moved through the dark, hand touching each pew back, until her feet found the raised platform. It took a while to find the recessed handle in the panel that covered the hole, but then she pulled with both hands. The screech of wood was thunderous. She froze, suddenly afraid.

If Motty heard that noise, she'd tan Stella's hide. Motty had warned her, over and over, not to go into the chapel—and certainly never to go into the cave alone.

Yet . . .

She heaved again on the panel. Scooched it aside far enough to make a space wide enough for her body. Cool, wet air licked her face.

She went down.

At the last step she felt her way to the narrow passage, then followed it into the twisting heart of the cave. Then the air changed and she went still. She strained to—hear? feel?—the presence of the God.

"Hello?" she called softly.

She looked up, because in communion he always came from above. She climbed onto the table and stood, arms out. It made her dizzy to stand like that in the dark with nothing to orient her. She lifted her hands.

The hole in the ceiling, the chimney he descended from at the start of each communion, was too far above her head. She couldn't go to the God—he would have to come to her.

"I'm here," she said. And then, like Motty had done years ago, she said, "Please."

The dark ignored her. And she thought, What if the Ghostdaddy doesn't want me here?

She told herself to be steady, to be patient. On the night before Judas betrayed Him—according to the Bible Elder Rayburn had given her—Jesus went to a garden and prayed all night while the disciples kept falling asleep on Him. He wakes up Simon Peter and says (in red letters), Could you not watch just one damn hour? Or close enough, in King James–speak. He'd spent the night asking God if there was any way He didn't have to be crucified, and He prayed so hard that He *sweat blood.* Compared to that, this was nothing. She'd prove to the Ghostdaddy that she was worthy.

After another minute she sat down, feeling embarrassed. A cold knot of dread grew in her. She was wrong to be here. Wrong to bother him. And come to think of it, Jesus never got an answer either. God didn't appear in the garden, and Jesus ended up being crucified. A sacrifice to Himself, from Himself. So stupid.

The floor vibrated beneath her. She hopped up, and now the air was trembling. Joy tightened her chest.

"I'm here," she said.

# 14

## 1948

INTRUDER.

Stella sat up in bed with that thought in her head and a mental echo of a noise—the sound gone like a car over a hill. Then the smell hit her, and she realized it was the kind of intruder who cooked bacon.

Merle Whitt stood in front of the stove, cigarette in one hand, spatula in the other. She flipped a fried egg onto its belly and said, "Coffee's ready."

Merle didn't do this kind of thing. She'd never just dropped by. She hadn't even been in the house but once, the day Stella bought it, and Merle had arrived with spare furniture, extra kitchen goods, a brand-new shower curtain—enough supplies to set up housekeeping. After that, she'd stayed away, respecting Stella's privacy.

Till now.

"What's going on?" Stella asked.

"I hope you don't mind I used your kitchen to make myself breakfast."

"Always happy to help a friend out of a jam." Stella was

pleased to see Merle was using Motty's skillets. Stella plucked a strip of bacon from the pan—hot! Clenched it between her teeth and wiped her fingers on her robe. "Eh ehh?"

A bouquet of flowers sat atop her little kitchen table. Huge yellow Maximilian sunflowers, purple asters, blue gentians like rockets ready to take off—fall plants evolved to surge into bloom right before the first frost, like come-from-behind Thoroughbreds.

"Don't look at me," Merle said. "Those were leaning against your front door when I got here. There's a note."

A little white card with a hole punched in it, tied to a stem.

*Dear Stella,*

*Please accept my sincere condolences. I hope you know that there are some Rayburns who remember your love for Lincoln, and still hold you in their hearts. I'm sorry we have lost touch over the years. I wanted to speak to you at the funeral, but of course you were overwhelmed by family. It was a gift to see Sunny. I regret if my father's words about her caused you distress, but all we want is what's best for her. I very much hope we can visit together soon.*

*With Love and Great Affection,*
*Mary Lynn*

Jesus Christ, Stella thought. One more play for Sunny, one more attempt to shame Stella into doing "what's best." Well fuck you, Elder and Younger Rayburns, fuck you *very much*.

Stella poured herself a cup of coffee, and one for Merle. "Um, I don't have any . . . anything."

"Milk's in the fridge," Merle said. And not just milk, a host of breakfast and non-breakfast groceries: a head of iceberg lettuce, jam, a chunk of cheese, mayonnaise, baloney. Someone else might have thought the shelves still seemed empty, but for Stella they looked as crowded as Wrigley Field bleachers. Take that, Final Okra.

Stella poured enough milk into Merle's mug to turn it her preferred color. Stella kept her own black. They ate together at the
little kitchen table.

"So," Merle said. "What are your plans?"

"For today? Get back to work. Keep the farm running."

Merle gave her a look. That hadn't been her question, and
Stella knew it. "What about Sunny?" Merle asked.

"I worked out a custody arrangement." As they ate she laid
out the deal she'd struck with Hendrick—the visitation rights,
the rules about the cove. Merle's frown grew deeper.

"This is good for her," Stella said. "Hendrick's going to get
tutors, so she won't be bullied for how she looks. She'll get an
education and a stable home."

"And you get off the hook."

"I ain't off the hook. I'm involved."

"From a distance."

"That's probably best for her. The more distance, the better."

Merle ignored the joke. "You could pay for tutors, too. You're
making money."

"Not as much as you think. And it's not legitimate money. At
any moment it could all go away. That's no way to raise a kid."

"I can help."

"You've done your part." Before Merle could reply Stella said,
"Besides, Sunny *loves* Hendrick, and he loves her. He can handle
her."

"What if she hurts herself?"

"Jesus Christ," Stella said. Merle was so direct, and so persistent. When Stella was fifteen it drove her crazy that Merle
couldn't be distracted when she wanted an answer—and partial
answers didn't satisfy. The only way Stella had ever managed
to keep things from her was to go silent. She'd never told Merle
about the Ghostdaddy, never described communion. When she
left the cove she decided to never speak of it again, never *think*

of it again. These past few days had been a nightmare of talking and remembering and talking and remembering. Every time she looked at Sunny she saw herself.

"She's not going to do that," Stella said. She brought her plate to the sink. "She hasn't gone through what I did. She's never going to. I'm going to make damn sure of that."

"That doesn't mean she doesn't have her own hurts. Stella, please, look at me."

Stella turned, folded her arms. Merle had shifted her chair, but her hands were in her lap. "I know how hard it was for you when you left the cove. I didn't understand everything that had happened, but I tried. I'm just asking you to think about Sunny, what it was like for her to grow up alone, without a—"

*"Stop it."*

Merle's eyes widened a fraction.

"She's not my responsibility," Stella said harshly. "That was settled long ago."

"Sweetie." Her voice soft.

"She's not mine," Stella said, "and I'm not . . . *fit*. Do you understand? I can't be trusted with her. I can't. So back the fuck off."

Merle looked off to the side, eyes moving, as if considering arguments and putting them aside. Finally she sat back in her chair. Her eyes were shining.

Stella felt sick to her stomach.

This was the moment to make repairs. Stella would apologize, Merle would say she understood, and Stella would go on about how wonderful it was to wake up to breakfast, and so on, one phrase overlapping the other, until the wound was stitched closed. Merle had taught her how to do this—Motty had taught her only how to cut, and parry, and cut again until they both were exhausted.

But Stella said nothing, and so Merle could not reply. Merle said nothing until she'd reached the front door. She looked back and said, "Have you told Abby that Hendrick's taking Sunny?"

Stella drove west toward the Acorn Farm. Sunlight filled the car but her hands were cold on the wheel, and every bump in the dirt road made her clench her jaw.

Her foot had come off the gas. She accelerated again, blinking. Slammed on the brakes.

Screamed: "Fuuuuuck!"

She jammed the gearshift into reverse.

THREE CARS WERE PARKED in Motty's yard, all of them late-model sedans. All of them with Georgia plates.

Stella went into the house and was surprised to find it empty—or nearly so. Veronica was asleep in Motty's bed.

"Where is everybody?" Stella asked.

Veronica opened one eye. Her smile was goofy. "Stella. Stel-lala." She yawned dramatically. It was unclear if she was wearing anything under the blanket. "What time is it?"

"Near eleven. Hendrick's not here?"

"Daddy said last night he had to go into Knoxville to see . . . I don't know, Knoxville people."

"There are a lot of cars in the yard and nobody around."

"Well, Rickie *was* here—he slept in the other bedroom last night, I swear." Drawled that last word out to five syllables.

So Sunny still hadn't slept in her own bedroom since Motty died. Stella wasn't sure what that was about. Still too many strangers in the house?

Stella walked to the kitchen. Noted the dirty plates in the sink. These crackers were barbarians.

She walked out to the backyard. No one. The barn was empty, too.

And then she thought: Shit.

. . . .

FIFTY YARDS FROM the chapel, she heard the thrum of an engine. Thirty yards away she heard the bright sound of metal striking stone.

Jesus H. Christ.

The chapel door hung open. A few feet in front of it were a line of ten-gallon cans of gasoline and a Delco generator rumbling away. Stella followed the power cord inside.

The sanctuary was brightly lit. At the far end of the room stood a set of electric lights on tripods. A clump of men stood in their glare. One of them aimed a camera at the floor, while another man—fuck, it was Rickie—lifted a sledgehammer and swung down. The bang was tremendous. Cement chips flew and clattered against the wall.

"Hey!" Stella yelled. Faces turned her way. She marched toward them. "Get away from there!"

Rickie straightened. "Morning, Stella." Standing a few feet back from him and the skinny cameraman were Brother Paul, holding a shovel, and a balding, moonfaced cracker she recognized from the kitchen last night. Now he was in shirtsleeves, holding a microphone in one hand and a cigarette in the other. A reel-to-reel tape recorder sat at his feet.

"What the hell are you doing in here?" A stupid question. They'd chopped apart a chunk of the surface, and in the center was a hole as wide as a manhole. It wouldn't take long to open the cave completely. She planted herself close enough to Rickie that he couldn't swing that hammer. "Get the hell out. Now."

"We'll be done soon," Rickie said. He seemed to think this was a simple misunderstanding. "We're almost through."

"Through? You moron, you can't go *in*."

Brother Paul said to the other men, "Stop filming." The man with the microphone knelt to punch buttons on the recorder.

Paul stepped toward Stella. "I think it's best if you head up back to the house." In the harsh light his pale skin glowed. "Hendrick will be back soon, and he'll explain everything." He reached out as if to guide her to the door. She batted his hands aside.

"Out," she said.

His face contorted. He didn't like being touched by a woman. "We can't have this," he said.

Paul grabbed her again, and the balding man fastened a hand on her other bicep. "Get your hands off me, you fuckers!"

Their hands dropped. Jaws too.

It wasn't just the language. Her right fist was bloody. No, both fists were bleeding, the blood seeping through her fingers. She opened a hand. The wound in her palm had opened.

Brother Paul gasped. She looked up. His mouth hung open, as if he'd witnessed a miracle. The skinny man raised his camera.

Stella turned and stalked out, burning with embarrassment and rage and confusion. She hadn't bled like that in a long time.

Away from the chapel, she knelt on the ground, wiped blood on the grass. Her palms ached. Then she heard the sledgehammer strike rock.

The boys were back at it.

She slammed through the house's back door. Veronica, now in a robe, stood before the woodstove. "Do you know where you light this?"

Stella marched into the front room, went to the gun rack, and took down the Winchester 97.

"What's going on?" Veronica asked.

Stella pressed the release, racked the slide. The tube was empty. She grabbed a box of shells.

"Is there an animal?"

"Yeah," Stella said. She pushed a shell into the tube. "A bunch of them."

. . .

THE FIRST PERSON to see Stella was the cameraman. He was waddling down the aisle, a load of rocks pressed to his chest. He squinted into the light. She couldn't have been much more than a silhouette to him.

Stella lifted the shotgun.

He stepped back, somehow holding on to the rocks. The three men behind him straightened.

Brother Paul held up his hands, aggrieved. "Miss Wallace, please. This is going too far."

"Move over." She gestured with the barrel. "Away from the hole." Her hands were tacky with blood but that didn't affect her grip.

Rickie laughed. "God damn, Cousin Stella!"

The moonfaced man—he'd picked up the shovel—frowned at Rickie and then fixed on Stella.

"Go on," she said.

Nobody moved.

"I'm saving your lives, you idiots."

Rickie smiled quizzically. "Um, you're pointing a shotgun at us, so how does that work?"

"You don't understand a God damn thing. Now move."

"Enough." Brother Paul drew himself up. His right hand moved toward his waist. "I'm warning you. Put down the gun and get out of here before we—"

A pew back exploded, throwing splinters. Paul ducked and covered his head. Maybe he cried out. The skinny man dropped the load of rocks and jumped to her right, behind another row of pews. A tripod fell backward and a lamp popped.

"Out!" she shouted. Racked the shotgun. "Out! Out! Out!" Her ears were ringing and she could barely hear herself. She stepped aside and the cameraman ran out.

Rickie was looking down at himself. He lifted his undershirt, reached gingerly toward his ribs. He pulled out a splinter the size of a finger. Looked at it in amazement. Tossed it aside. Blood welled from the wound.

She aimed the barrel at Brother Paul's gut. "Out," she repeated. She wasn't eager to pull the trigger again; she was grateful the Winchester hadn't blown up the first time. It was fifty years old, and no telling how long since it had last been fired.

Paul said, "I'm going to speak to Hendrick about this."

"You do that, Paul."

He hesitantly moved toward the exit.

"Wait," Stella said. "Where's the other guy?"

Paul and Rickie looked around. The bald man wasn't in the sanctuary. He hadn't run past her. There was only one place he could have gone. Her stomach went cold.

Rickie started for the hole and Stella said, "Stay back!" She didn't like how high-pitched her voice sounded. "I fucking mean it."

Rickie put up one hand. The other was pressed to his bloody shirt.

She went to the hole, peered through, and it was like leaning over a high cliff. Her heart beat in her throat. The wooden stairs were still in place.

No, she thought. Do not go in there.

"Hey!" she called. "Fuckhead! Get out here."

There was no answer. She glanced over her shoulder. Brother Paul and Rickie were watching her—and the shotgun.

"Answer me, damn it! I'm not going to—I'm not going to fucking shoot you."

Still no answer.

Brother Paul was staring at her. Something in her face frightened him. "Let me go get him," he said softly.

She shouted wordlessly, furious now.

"Listen to me, you son of a bitch!" she yelled into the hole. She put one leg through, onto the first step. "If you try to jump me, I *will* blow a hole straight fucking through you."

No answer. She stepped down, and the shotgun barrel smacked the edge of the entrance. She moved her finger off the trigger. Ducked under. Her body blocked most of the light.

The last time she'd been in the cave, she'd sworn to herself she'd never return, except for one reason. Saving a Georgia redneck was not that reason.

"Listen . . . you," she said. She'd never caught the man's name. "It's dangerous to be in here. Just walk toward my voice."

Somewhere in the dark, a clattering of pebbles. "Please," she said. "Come on out."

He was not in the anteroom. Somehow he'd found his way deeper into the cave.

She shuffled forward, gripping the Winchester. Then she heard the rumble. That deep, deep sound as if the mountain itself was speaking to her.

"Fuck me," she said.

She threw herself forward, into pitch dark. For a dozen steps her body remembered the way. Her outstretched hand found the opening of the narrow passage that led up to the stone table. She turned sideways to keep the shotgun in front of her, moving as quick as she could, that bass vibrating her skull.

When the Winchester's barrel struck rock she knew she was at the hairpin turn. She followed it around, and suddenly the thrumming stopped. The change in the air told her she'd reached the table room.

"Hey," she whispered. "It's okay. It's Stella." She wasn't sure if she was speaking to the disciple or to the Ghostdaddy. She shuffled forward, and her shoes struck something. Not a stone.

She crouched. Extended a hand. Found flesh. An arm? No, a leg.

· · ·

SHE HALF CARRIED, half dragged the body to the bottom of the stairs and called for Rickie and Paul. They looked at each other, unwilling to step into the hole, and Stella thought, Yes, you sons of bitches, *now* you're nervous.

She circled her arms around his chest, backed up one step. Heaved. His head lolled to the side. She could smell his after-shave. She stepped backward again, yanked him up with a grunt. One heel caught the edge of a step, and the shoe popped off like a bottle cap.

Again.

Finally she got high enough that Brother Paul and Rickie could reach down to him, and they hauled the body into the electric light.

"Oh dear Lord," Brother Paul said. He knelt over his friend. "Oh dear Lord."

Rickie's eyes were wild. "What did you do to him?"

"I told you," Stella said. Her voice shook. She was sweating, breathing hard. "You wouldn't fucking listen."

She went back down the hole and retrieved the shotgun.

Brother Paul carried the dead man over the threshold like a bride. The sunlight hit like a hammer. The skinny man was crying.

"Stay the fuck out of the cave," Stella said.

She stood in front of the chapel and watched them carry the dead man down the hill. Her body quaked as if she stood waist deep in freezing water.

It's alive, she thought. It's fucking alive.

She felt someone watching her, in the trees. There was no one there.

· · ·

STELLA CLIMBED UP, to the high ridge. She followed the narrow trail west and came down again, into the clearing—and there stood Abby, throwing broken wood into a high fire. It was the spot where he used to cook mash.

"Abby—where's Sunny?"

He tilted his head. She realized she still clutched the shotgun. She pointed it at the ground.

"What's going on?" he asked.

"A bunch of Hendrick's friends busted through your floor," she said. "They went at it like the God damn Seven Dwarves. I tried to scare them off."

"You shot at them?" Abby said.

"I discharged in their direction. But one of them ran for the hole."

"Did—they didn't go *in*?"

That question told her he knew more about the church than he let on.

"I tried to stop him."

"God damn." He rubbed his jaw. All around him lay lumber, old sheets, wooden crates—every piece of junk from his house that could burn. He was preparing to leave.

She said, "Did you know they were planning this?"

"Stella! Of course not!"

"Hendrick had it in mind the whole time. Played me like a fish."

"I never wanted Sunny to go with him, you know that."

"Yet you let him come up here and woo her like a God damn girlfriend."

"It's not my place. I try to steer clear."

"You were always part of it. You were there with Lena. With me."

"I was just trying to take care of you girls."

"Playing the good shepherd."

He winced. "I tried."

And like a good shepherd, Stella thought, you kept us fat and happy until it was time to turn us over for the slaughter. No wonder he stayed drunk half the time.

"Where is she?" Stella said.

ABBY SAID HE KNEW where she liked to play. He led her to the crick that used to feed his old still. The water was low this time of year, maybe a foot deep, winding through rocks. They walked alongside the water for a few minutes, and then Abby pointed to a wide spot in the creek, where the opposite bank was five or six feet high. Sunny stood in the creek bed, her bare feet planted on a rock, facing that high bank. Terraces had been cut into the clay, and dozens of small objects rested there. Sunny was talking to them.

"What's she doing?" Stella asked.

"She calls it her church."

Of course. Church was all the girl knew.

"Sunny!" Stella called. "Can you come up here?"

The girl didn't turn around. Stella called her name, and the girl ignored her again. Stella handed Abby the Winchester and stepped down into pebbly mud at the edge of the stream. She plotted a path of stones, and stepped onto the first of them. The cold radiated off the water. She moved to the next stone. When she got within ten feet of the girl, Sunny nonchalantly skipped to another rock, farther away.

"Sunny, please."

The girl ignored her.

Stella hopped to another rock, and her foot slipped into the water with a splash, soaking her pants to the knee. The girl laughed without turning around, jumped ahead.

Stella looked back at Abby, still onshore. "Little help?"

"Sunny," Abby said. "Come on now."

She paused, twirled on one bare foot to face Stella. The cold didn't seem to bother her. The skin of her legs was like these half-wet river rocks, a swirl of pale and dark.

Stella moved carefully, finally reached the site of the "church." The objects in the terrace were stick dolls—twigs bound up in yarn, with fuzzy heads. One of them had fallen over, and Stella reached for it.

"Don't touch them," Sunny said.

"Sorry. These your babies?"

"Your hands are bloody."

Shit. Yes. Stella crouched carefully and dipped her palms into the frigid water. Dried her hands on her pants.

"Uncle Hendrick said you ran back to Mar-ee-ville." Exaggerating it like a Yankee. "What'd you come back for?"

"For you," Stella said. "I need you to come with me."

"Naw." Then: "Why's that?"

"Because you're in danger."

"Don't seem like it."

"Can we talk on land?"

"Nope."

Jesus Christ, Stella thought.

She stepped into the water, tried to ignore the shock of cold that ran up her leg. Thought of Esther, and her coat full of rocks.

"Uncle Hendrick's been lying to you," Stella said. Took another step. The rocks were slick beneath her shoes. "He said he's taking you to Georgia, but he wants you to do something that'll be bad for you."

"Oh yeah?" A trace of a smile on her face. "What's that?"

Did she know about Rickie and Paul breaking open the cave?

"We don't have time," Stella said. "I need you to come with me, and I'll tell you all about it."

"Tell me now."

It was probably good the girl was ten feet away or Stella would've strangled her.

If she told Sunny that they'd opened the cave, she might want to run down there and jump in. Hendrick and Motty had no doubt filled her head with Destiny, just like they'd done Stella. But if she didn't mention the excavation, and the girl knew about it, she'd never believe another word Stella said.

"I'm like you," Stella said. She held up a hand, palm out. "You know that. I'm the only one left in the world who knows what it's like to go into communion, and what it does to you, and how to survive it."

The girl was listening.

"Uncle Hendrick don't know. Veronica don't know. And Motty's dead. So I'm it, kid."

Stella took another step through the water, barely lifting her feet. Sunny didn't run.

"You and I are the last remaining Birch women," Stella said. "There are secrets we know, that we pass to each other, that aren't written down in any scripture. Motty didn't tell you, because you were too young. But if you're considering going in that cave, you need to know some things, right now."

Sunny looked skeptical. "Like what?"

"You need to know how we die."

## 15

1938

A MONTH BEFORE Stella turned fourteen, Motty caught her coming back from the chapel. The old woman was sitting at the kitchen table, facing the back door. The sugar bowl sat in front of her.

Stella stopped in the doorway, paralyzed. The chapel key in her fist felt like a hot coal.

Motty said, "Close the door."

Stella did as she was told.

"Did the Ghostdaddy come to you?" Motty asked.

"Don't call him that." It sounded disrespectful. She preferred the language of the church.

Motty slammed the table and the glass bowl jumped. "Answer me!"

Stella had never seen Motty so mad. And scared.

"How many times?" Motty asked.

"A few," Stella said quietly.

"Don't you lie to me."

"A dozen." Stella raised her eyes. "Maybe more."

Motty looked distraught. "Do you not know—didn't I tell you? You can't go alone, or he'll . . ."

"He'll what?" Stella asked.

"Show me your hands," Motty said. "Get over here!"

Stella came forward. She opened one palm, then the other. Her old scars were there, but no new ones. "Nothing happened," Stella said.

"What the hell were you doing, then?"

"We just . . . visit."

This made no sense to Motty. "He ain't touched you?"

They touched, Stella thought. The God would let her place her hand on his pale skin. The vibrations ran through her, comforting her. But their hands didn't connect. He didn't fill her with his thoughts.

"He ain't touched me," Stella said.

Motty still couldn't understand it. "Sit down, damn it. Tell me what you do."

"Didn't the God ever do that with you?" Stella asked.

Motty scowled. "You just go to him, and he comes out?"

"Every time. Sometimes I got to wait an hour, but if I'm patient, he shows up."

"Tell me what happened," Motty said. "This time, and all the times. Leave nothing out."

"Are you going to tell Uncle Hendrick?"

"This ain't for Hendrick. None of the men. This is ours."

Ours. That word went off like a firework.

"We pass down our own story," Motty said. "From Clara to Esther, all the way down to you."

Stella could barely breathe. All this time, there'd been secrets not in Hendrick's books? "I want to see the stories."

"There's nothing to see," Motty said. "We don't write it down."

"What? Why not?"

"Think. Where are the Revelations?"

"In Georgia?" Then she understood.

"Under lock and key," Motty said. "His lock. His key. But our stories, nobody can take those away from us."

"Did my mother tell you her story?"

"Not enough of it. I waited too long. That was a mistake, a grave mistake. I'm not doing the same with you."

"What's that mean? Did Lena visit the God on her own, too?"

Motty said, "Promise me you won't commune with him on your own. The God, he's too strong for a person alone. You need me there, you understand? To stop him when he goes too far."

She's jealous, Stella thought.

"You can't have secrets from me," Motty said. "No sneaking off on your own. You understand?"

They stared at each other. Stella said, "And what about your secrets?"

"When you're ready," Motty said.

"No. Tell me one thing from *The Book of Mathilda*. Don't look at me like that! Just one thing."

"I'll give you one question. That don't mean I'll answer it."

"Okay, tell me . . ." Stella wasn't sure what she could ask for. "Tell me what happened to your aunt Esther. Her book just *ends*. It ain't fair."

Motty lowered her chin. "You want me to tell you how she died."

"Yes!"

"There ain't anything to tell. When I was six years old, she took me down to the river. It was January, very cold. I remember the spray of water hitting my face, sharp as needles. I didn't mind. I used to follow Esther around like a baby duck. And Esther said, Let's play a game. I hunted for rocks, big as I could carry, and she put them in her pockets. We filled up her coat."

Stella's throat went tight.

Motty said, "And that's why we don't try to do this job alone."

FIVE YEARS ON THE FARM had taught Stella a few things. One: Everything dies. Two: Eat it if you can. Three: Everything that ain't dead, shits.

The day Lunk decided to drop by for a public visit, she was ankle deep in chicken shit. She was raking out the mounds under the chicken coops, an archeological exercise. Goop on top, hard as coal on the bottom, and every gradation of viscosity in between. Esther herself had probably raked this same shit-trough. No wonder she'd jumped into the river.

Lunk yelled, "Hey there, Stella!" Came walking up the drive, spiffy and scrubbed in a wool coat and Sunday pants. In his hand was a small square wrapped in butcher paper and tied with a red ribbon.

"What the hell are you doing here?" she said. He'd pestered her for months, and then finally she agreed to spend time with him—but only in the woods or down at the store, never here. And now, to her irritation, she was conscious of how she looked. Her arms were coated in muck up to the elbows, and she was wearing waders and overalls and one of Abby's old hats.

"I brought you something." He thrust his package at her.

"This ain't another Bible, is it?"

"What? No! It's your birthday."

"Am I supposed to open this now?"

"If you like."

She sighed elaborately but was secretly pleased. She pulled off the ribbon and folded open the paper. "Oh!"

"Is it all right?"

It was a folded white, lacy cloth that looked like a doily. "I can't take it out, I'm covered in chicken shit."

"Let me." He took it from her, then unfolded the lace. "It's a handkerchief. And it's monogrammed, see?" Stitched into one corner in pale blue thread were her initials, "SW." "I didn't know what your middle name was. Mary Lynn didn't, either." Lunk consulted his sister on everything, seemed like.

Stella said, "You spent money on this?"

His face fell. She hadn't meant it to come out so harsh but now he was hurt and she wanted to slug him in the shoulder.

"I . . . I bought it in Knoxville," he said defensively.

"Ooh, Knoxville." Like it was Paris. "I can't see blowing my nose in it."

"It's not for blowing your nose, it's a *girl's* hankie!"

"Girls don't blow their noses?"

"Not in—they just—it's—" He shook his head like he was trying to shake the words loose. "It's *decorative*."

Good lord. Wait till she told him girls farted. "All right, put it away. I don't want to touch it with my hands like this."

"So it's okay?"

He was suddenly relieved, and looking . . . hopeful. She glanced toward the house, and the kitchen window.

"It's lovely, Lincoln. Thank you."

She'd lit a candle inside him. It took her a couple of minutes to get him to go, and that hopeful expression didn't leave his face the whole time—until she sent him away without a kiss.

She hid the package inside the bib of her overalls and walked into the house. Motty was at the sink, plucking a chicken in hot water.

"So," she said. "Lace."

"Leave me alone."

"That boy trying to get into your panties?"

"No!" But of course he'd been trying, with the determination of a forty-niner.

Motty said, "You can't trust a preacher's son."

. . .

STELLA HIKED UP to Abby's cabin in the rain to tell him Motty had invited him to dinner. "She killed the fatted chicken so better not skip."

"What's the occasion?"

She made a face and Abby laughed at his own hilarity. He might have already been a little soused. But it was true that Motty had never cooked a chicken for her birthday—that was usually for guests.

"I've got something for you," Abby said. He vanished into the mysterious Man Place of the back bedroom and returned a minute later. "From Merle and Pee Wee."

Merle had sent a stack of journals and a leather-bound notebook. Inside the notebook she'd written:

*A scientist ought to have her own materials. Write clearly—you'll thank me later.*

*With Affection, Merle.*

*P.S. Start with Muller in Science, #1699. One article can kick off a golden age.*

"They're mine?" Stella asked. "To keep?" Finally someone was treating her like an adult. Hendrick was hiding his books, Motty hiding Stella's Revelation. Only Merle trusted her.

"You get to keep these, too." He handed her a fresh pack of Lucky Strikes and a small box. "Pee Wee sent these."

"My brand. He's so thoughtful." She opened the box. Inside lay a brass mechanical lighter. "A real Zippo! Just like Pee Wee's!"

"He thinks the way to a woman's heart is through her lungs."

"Well, technically . . ."

"One more thing." He went to the mantel. "I had this framed."

It was the picture of Abby, her father, and her mother, dressed as cowboys and Indians. "I think you ought to keep it."

Out of nowhere, tears. Her chest was tight and she couldn't see. Abby looked flummoxed. "Aw, sweetie . . ."

She turned away from him and waved a hand. "I'm fine, I'm just not used to these—" She was going to say gifts, but it wasn't that, it was the idea of these people *thinking* of her when she wasn't around, having ideas about her, probably picturing her face when she finally unwrapped the present. It was intrusive. Didn't matter that it was an attack of love—it was still an ambush.

She pushed the tears from her cheeks. Laughed at herself. "Y'uns are messing me up."

Abby grinned. "I apologize."

Stella ran a thumb across the glass. "She seems to get younger every year."

"I know what you mean. She was only twenty when we took that."

"Were you here when she died?"

He didn't answer and she looked up.

He admitted it with a nod.

"Did she suffer? I mean, at the end." She'd read a novel about a poet who was dying of consumption. "Did she cough and cough?"

He looked away. Ran a hand across his stubbled jaw.

"You don't have to talk about it," she said.

"She didn't suffer," Abby said. "Not at all."

Stella put her arms around him, still holding the frame. "I love this picture. I always have. Thank you."

"You're welcome, Little Star."


IT WAS STELLA'S BIRTHDAY but Abby brought Motty a gift, too—several. Motty unscrewed the top off the first jar, sniffed.

"This batch came out pretty well," Abby said.

An hour after supper they were both tipsy and Stella was holding one of Merle's new journals in front of her face. She'd read it front to back but didn't want to get up to retrieve another. She'd learned that adults were more likely to say interesting things when they forgot she was there or thought she wasn't listening. *Drunk* adults would say almost anything. Unfortunately, they'd decided to argue about pigs. Abby was very much in favor of harvesting the sow and getting another litter.

"I decide when I harvest and when I restock," Motty said. "Not you."

"But it's spring. If you get some shoats now, they'll be fat by the fall. And this time, I'll help you do it right."

"Do it right?" Motty said icily.

"You step in too early. Pigs give birth all the time—the trick is keeping the piglets alive while they're weaning. The mamas just roll over on them. Suffocate them."

"I know how to raise my stock."

"But your sows keep having problems birthing, it makes no sense. Let me help. I've helped birth cows and this ain't much different."

Stella kept her head down.

"I told you," Motty said, "it's none of your business."

"Or we could call the vet."

"Nobody's calling a vet! You don't talk about this with anyone, you hear me? No gossip about what I do here."

"When have I ever gossiped?"

They kept arguing, a sloppy tug-of-war greased by whiskey. On schedule, Motty brought up the fact that Abby was not paying a dime of rent, and Abby pointed out that she was drinking her rent, not to mention all the work he did for her, and besides, didn't Hendrick send her money every month?

"That's none of your God damn business. You got to know your place, Abby Whitt. You ain't better'n me."

"What are you talking about?"

"I'm no fool," Motty said. "I know how people whispered about me after Lena."

Lena! Stella went still as a stone. Kept her eyes locked on the page.

"I never talked to anybody about her," Abby said.

"You told that brother-in-law of yours, and Merle, and—"

"Merle's my sister!"

"Who knows who else. Just had to let everybody know you wanted to drive her to town and go see a doctor, when we both know that would do no good. But no, you went around crying like a baby."

Abby lurched to his feet. "I loved her like she was my own!"

Stella thought, No doctor could treat her?

"Next thing I know the whole cove thinks I killed her, all because you're making a big show. You worried they was going to blame you?"

"That's too far, Motty. Too far."

"Aw, get the hell out of my house," Motty said to Abby. "You're nothing but a freeloader."

Abby stormed from the room, banging every doorframe and door on the way out. But Stella's eyes were on Motty.

"What are you looking at?" Motty said. She was planted in her chair like a queen under siege.

"You lied to me," Stella said. She squeezed out the words.

"What? Get off to bed. You should have gone long ago."

"You lied." The room had narrowed to just the tunnel between them. "Lena didn't die of *tuberculosis*." Enunciating every ridiculous syllable. "There was no lingering disease."

"Oh, it was slow."

Stella forced herself to ask the question. "Did the God kill her? Or did you?"

Motty said nothing. Then, very deliberately, took a sip of

whiskey. Stella waited, a fluttering feeling high in her chest. If Motty was ever going to admit to anything it was now, when she was drunk and mired deep in memory. In the morning she'd be sober and daylight would stitch her shut.

"Tell me," Stella said.

"She went too far," Motty said. "And I didn't stop her."

*Too far.* "How many communions?" Stella asked.

"Fifteen, sixteen," Motty said. She started describing them, each one longer than the last. Near the end Lena was staying with the God for over an hour.

"I shouldn't've let her," Motty said. "It was more'n I could ever do. But she was better than me. And the things she brought back . . . it was like she had a direct line, a holy—" Motty shook her head. "Nobody got as deep as she did. Not even Esther."

Stella didn't speak. She thought, I could do an hour. I could do an hour, easy.

"Then the last time . . ." Motty was gazing into some memory. "Oh Lord."

"What happened?" Stella asked quietly.

"She stayed with the God for nearly two hours. She wouldn't let go of him."

"You mean the God wouldn't let her go."

"I mean what I say. Lena held on. And then finally she passed out, and the Ghostdaddy left her. I carried her to bed, laid her down like always. Bandaged her. I did everything the same. But she just lay there. Staring at the ceiling. Sometimes her mouth moved but she wasn't saying nothing. I couldn't get her to eat, could barely get a sip of water into her." Motty took a ragged breath. "I should've called a doctor. But we don't do things like that. We always thought . . ."

Stella waited. Motty drained her glass. Set it down with a *thump.*

"Five weeks," Motty said.

Stella stopped herself from speaking.

"I took care of her body for five weeks. Then she died, and that was that."

Motty leaned forward in the chair, pushed up with her arms until she was on her feet. Swayed there.

"What did she do wrong?" Stella asked.

Motty's head came up. "She didn't do nothing wrong. She did her duty. You should be proud of her."

"I'm stronger than her," Stella said. "You know I am."

"Sure you are." Motty shuffled out of the room. "Just keep telling yourself."

## 16

1948

TWO FIGURES STEPPED onto the lip of the road like hesitant animals. It was near dusk, and their bodies threw long shadows down the pavement. Stella stopped the Ford and jumped out.

Abby held a satchel in one hand and Sunny's hand in the other. Sunny eyed the car skeptically.

"No trouble getting to your car?" Abby asked.

"They were in the house," Stella said. "I could hear 'em worrying about Rickie's terrible terrible wound." One of the Georgians had been standing on the porch when she pulled out of Motty's yard, but he didn't get in her way and as far as she knew, nobody had followed her. Still, they could change their minds at any moment.

"Go ahead and get in," Stella told the girl.

"Where we going?"

"I'll tell you when we get there." She didn't want to say in front of Abby. The less he knew, the better.

Abby waited till the girl was in the car before he said to Stella, "He'll come after her."

"I know." As long as there was a God in the Mountain, there'd be the church, and as long as there was the church, Hendrick would want his Revelator. She'd always known that—she'd only fooled herself into thinking he'd changed. Hendrick had lied to her, and Veronica—well, Veronica had either lied too or been fooled herself.

She said, "He'll come for you first."

Abby shrugged, handed her the satchel. "I can take care of myself."

"Keep that shotgun close." She'd left him the Winchester 97.

He went around the car, leaned through the window. Kissed Sunny on the side of her head. "You be good, now."

The girl scowled. "Come with me."

"Wish I could."

"You can't leave me alone with her."

"You're going to be all right," Abby said. "There's nobody you can trust more."

FOR THE NEXT HALF HOUR, Sunny sat with her arms folded across her chest, stewing. Stella was grateful for the silence. Once they hit 321 Stella gave it some gas, but kept to the speed limit. She remembered the first time she'd driven this road with Abby, her first brush with the police.

A sign for Jimmy's Market came up on the right and Sunny said, "Coke-drinking bear?" She sat up. "We have to stop!"

"Sorry, kid."

"They have a bear that drinks Cokes!"

"You can't believe everything you read." The sign wasn't lying in this case—Jimmy did keep a black bear in an outdoor cage, and if you bought a Coca-Cola or a Nehi, Jimmy'd hand it through the bars. The bear would grasp the bottle in both paws and tip it up like a toddler.

Half a mile later they passed the market and Sunny saw the cage. She screamed. Stella screamed back, louder. The girl jerked back in surprise.

"I promise you," Stella said. "We'll come back someday and see the bear."

"When?"

"Someday."

"There isn't *time*. I need to see it *now*."

"What do you mean, there isn't time?"

The girl growled and looked out the window.

Stella said, "You aren't going to Georgia. You know that, right?"

"You don't know what's what, Stella Wallace." Sunny slumped dramatically against the door. "Nobody knows how anybody's going to die."

Stella sighed. "Did Motty tell you about Esther at the river?"

She could see the answer in Sunny's blank expression. Stella told the story of how Esther drowned herself. Then she told how Lena's story ended—the Revelator overwhelmed by the Ghost-daddy. The stories took them all the way to Maryville. Sunny had gone silent, absorbing each new detail like a blow. A pocketful of stones. Motty watching from the shore—and decades later watching Lena waste away. Five weeks.

Finally Sunny said, "But you're all right. You ran away."

Stella stuck out her right arm. "Pull."

"What?"

"Pull my jacket off."

The girl sat up. Tugged on the sleeve, and Stella shrugged out of it.

"Push up on my shirt. There you go."

Sunny stared. The scar meandered along the inside of the arm, from wrist to elbow. "Did the God do that?"

"No, I did it to myself."

"*Why?*"

"When I was fourteen, I wanted nothing more than to get out of the cove. So I got out. And then I began to think, What good am I, if I'm not a Revelator? What if I'm nothing but what the church made me?"

"Maybe you weren't good enough."

Stella felt a flash of anger. Tamped it down. "Maybe not. But maybe none of us are. Including Motty."

Stella glanced at the girl, and her eyes were wide with fear, her lips tight. As if she already knew.

"The Ghostdaddy killed her," Stella said.

"You can't know that." Her voice strained.

"The wound was right here." Stella touched a spot above her breast. "Three tiny holes. Needles, straight to her heart."

Sunny put a hand to her mouth.

"I don't know why the Ghostdaddy would do that. I don't even know how it got out of the cave to do it."

Sunny stared at her. She was scared. And Stella thought, Good. She ought to be fucking scared.

"There's no way to know what a god does or doesn't do," Stella said. "Yahweh sent a flood to kill everyone but one family. Later He sacrificed His own flesh and blood. Human rules don't apply."


SHE PARKED DEEP in the trees, then led a quiet Sunny up and over the hill, until they reached the side door of the Acorn Farm. The interior was dark, and silent.

"Fuck me," Stella said. She flipped on the lights. Hump Cornette was nowhere to be seen.

"What's the matter?" Sunny asked.

"A boy who works for me is supposed to be here. I thought I'd put the fear of God into him, but shit, now I got to fire his ass."

"What is *that*?" Sunny was gazing at the eight-hundred-gallon vat.

"You never seen a still before?"

Sunny turned defensive. "It's different is all."

"Sure it is. That's Queen Bess. She rules this kingdom."

Sunny walked around the big space, looking at everything, smelling barrels, but refusing to ask questions.

"Abby taught me," Stella volunteered. "He's the best durn moonshiner that ever came out of these here hills."

"Are you mocking my voice?"

"No! That's Uncle Dan. Never mind."

Sunny's eyes lit up. "I love Uncle Dan."

"When I was your age I wished I could meet him."

"Me too."

"Let me show you something," Stella said, and walked her to the window. "See that dirt road through the trees? Anybody who comes down that road is no friend of mine. If you see a car, you hide."

"Hide where?"

"That's the second thing." Behind Stella's desk was a false floor. Stella knelt and pulled up a section of boards.

"That's just like the chapel," Sunny said.

Huh. That had never occurred to Stella. But yes, it was exactly the same. Down below was a hidey-hole, about three feet square. Stella reached down and pulled out an ancient carpetbag. Its reds and blues were faded long before Stella had taken it from Motty a decade ago.

"What's in that?" Sunny asked.

"None of your business. If someone comes to the window, you crawl in here, and pull the panel down over yourself. You understand?"

"Where are you going to be?"

"I've got to run an errand. I'll leave this partly open so you can hop in quick."

"You can't leave me here!"

"We need food. You're hungry, aren't you?"

"Wait," Sunny said. "You didn't tell me."

"Tell you what?"

"How *I* die."

Ah. Fuck.

"That's up to you," Stella said. "If you want it, you can have a life that's bigger than the cove. You're more than just a girl they send into a hole."

SHE DROVE INTO Alcoa just as the sun was dropping over the tar-shingle roofs of the company-built houses. Her moonshiner's mind saw the process of distillation everywhere. The Aluminum Company of America had distilled its name down to an acronym, cooked it down further to title case, and the town name followed suit. A few more decades and company and town both would be reduced to the letter "A," and then nothing at all.

Stella turned off Bessemer into the neighborhood the company had carved out for its Black employees. It used to be called Black Bottom, but after the Great War the company built new houses and named the area after Charles M. Hall, Alcoa's cofounder and the inventor of the aluminum reduction process. Named all the new streets after inventors, too—Newton, Kelvin, Edison—as if to remind the residents of all the great things white men had created for them.

The frame houses were all alike but for their paint, long and narrow with peaked-roof porches. The house she was looking for was easy to spot, however, because the bushes out front were near-exploding with pink and white flowers. Mrs. Bowlin liked her camellias. What she didn't like was Stella.

Stella parked the car on the street. She waved at the Black man sitting on the porch across the street—one of Alfonse's uncles—and he returned the wave. He worked for the company, too, as did every Bowlin she'd met. Alfonse's grandfather had joined up thirty years ago, after Alcoa sent recruiters across the South to round up Blacks and Mexicans to do the dirtiest, hottest jobs in the company, whether digging bauxite ore in their mine in Arkansas or working here at the reduction plant, turning that ore into alumina powder and then aluminum. The pot rooms where they poured the molten aluminum were the hottest work areas in the plant, and splashes of metal could kill a man or, almost worse for his family, wound him so grievously the company would fire him. The Mexicans were all but gone completely by the time the plant unionized, just over ten years ago. Now the Black members had a better choice of jobs, and better pay, though still not equal to a white man's. It was still America.

No wonder that Alfonse, about ten days after he met Stella, quit his job at the mine and became a full-time moonshiner. That made Stella either popular or unpopular with each family member, depending on their attitude toward alcohol.

Stella walked past the camellias and knocked at the door. Mrs. Bowlin answered, already scowling. "What are you doing here, Stella Wallace?" She glanced pointedly at the bag in Stella's hand. "I won't have you bringing liquor around my house." She was a small, thin-boned woman, but heels and an expensive updo made her taller than Stella. She was a teacher at Charles M. Hall School and wore A-line dresses so starched they could have been fabricated in the Alcoa plate room.

"Is Alfonse home?" Stella asked.

"I told you I didn't want you around here. You're a bad influence."

"I wouldn't have come if it wasn't an emergency. This is the last time you'll see me."

"Last time?"

"I promise," Stella said. "And I'm not carrying whiskey."

Mrs. Bowlin looked her up and down. Nothing she saw impressed her. Finally she said, "He's out back."

THE ONE-CAR GARAGE WAS set thirty feet from the house. The door was up, and Alfonse was bent over the engine of his Chevy. He'd always been a meticulous mechanic, making sure his trip car was ready to burn rubber and break policemen's hearts.

"Your mother just tore into me," Stella said.

He chuckled. "Bless her heart." Set his wrench on a cloth draping the fender and straightened. He was wearing an old tan Alcoa workshirt. His father's name, ANTOINE, was stitched over the pocket.

"I haven't got much time," Stella said. "I've gotten myself into some trouble."

Alfonse raised an eyebrow. "Moonshine trouble?"

"Not as such," Stella said. "You remember the girl?"

"The one who opens coffins."

"I changed my mind about letting her go to Georgia. I've got her over at the farm, but I can't stay there forever. I'm going to have to go on the road with Sunny, find a place to stay."

"On the road? Why? Because you're taking custody?"

"That's what I'd call it. Sheriff Whaley might call it kidnapping. You know him and my uncle is pals."

"So you're going to Myrtle Beach."

It was their private slang for laying low. Every time an unfriendly cop seemed to be hanging around one of their favorite spots, or a customer got caught with a few gallons of their hooch, one of them would say, I was thinking of going to Myrtle Beach, and then they'd shut down the farm and stay out of sight for a few days.

"Maybe you should go too," Stella said. "Just for a while." She handed him the carpetbag. "This is the working cash. I took out some, but the rest is yours. When you feel like it's all right, I'd like you to start up the farm, and keep it running, as you see fit."

"Stella, no." He tried to give back the bag and she raised her hands.

"Hump will be able to run the batch, if you can find him. He bailed out on me again. I thought he'd have gone out to the farm this morning, to run a new the batch, but no. I'm sorry to put you in this spot. But you know the routine—you can run the still."

"Not like you. Come on, let me help you out. You don't have to run."

"Discretion is the better part of valor. Though I've never understood what that means."

"It means fuck those crackers. If they bother you, you know I've got your back. Last time I didn't even get to whip my pistol out."

"I already may have taken a shot at them."

Alfonse was amazed and happy. "You kill that one boy? The one that looks like a chalk drawing of a chalk drawing?"

"Brother Paul. He's alive, but angry."

"Let's go talk it over with him."

"I have to do this on my own," Stella said. "But there is something you can do for me."

"That TNT."

She was relieved. Alfonse had always been the easiest person to talk to.

She said, "Soon as you can get it. Please."

"I reckon this car could make it to Chattanooga pretty quick."

"Oh God. Thank you. I wouldn't ask if I didn't need it."

"Just don't tell my mother about it," Alfonse said. "She'll kill both of us."

．　．　．

SHE WAS TWO MINUTES from the farm when she saw the radio car. The sheriff's vehicle sat at the fork in the road, lights off, facing her.

Stella slowed her car, trying not to panic. If the car was here, the police knew where the farm was—or at least knew it was somewhere close to here. Stella could drive past the cop to the left, and that would take her to the back way to the farm, to try to grab Sunny. But that would tell them exactly where the farm was, and she couldn't picture getting away.

Or, go right. That road led to the farm's front door, where Sunny was hopefully watching the window. The girl could hide, and Stella could keep driving, maybe lose them in the back roads, and circle back for her.

Or she could slam on the brakes, wheel about, and run, back to the city.

None of those were good choices. She rolled to a stop, a hundred feet from the squad car. Kept her foot on the clutch. Waited.

"Come on," she said quietly. "Make your move."

The sheriff car's headlights flicked on, filled her windshield. Stella gripped the gearshift in one hand, the wheel in the other.

The car eased toward her. She thought, If he fires, I can duck. Go right.

A few yards from her front bumper, the police car turned, came up on her driver's side.

Bobby Reed, Sheriff Whaley's deputy, sat behind the wheel. He glanced at her, then drove on.

She watched his taillights in her rearview mirror.

"Shit." Stella punched the accelerator. "Shit shit shit."

．　．　．

THE LIGHTS WERE ON, the big room silent. No cops, not yet.

"Sunny!" Stella shouted. "We've got to leave! Now!"

Was she hiding under the floor? Stella ran to the desk, then saw her on the other end of the room, by the supplies—she'd been partially hidden by the stacks of sugar. The girl's back was to her.

"Sunny! Hey. We got to go."

She didn't turn around. Her arms were stretched in front of her. Stella walked quickly toward her, then froze.

A mass of glossy threads blossomed from each of the girl's palms. The tendrils, a yard long, caught the light like spun glass, weaving and unweaving about each other. Impaled on the frayed end of one mass was a small animal—a field mouse. The creature thrashed silently.

"Sunny. Sunny, look at me."

The girl glanced over her shoulder. Her expression was unreadable.

"Put it out of its misery," Stella said. "Please."

The girl sighed. A twitch of the threads and the animal went still, its tiny legs splayed in the air. Another twitch and the body slipped free and dropped onto the floor. It didn't move.

Stella stared at the mouse. Remembered the doe, its black eye gazing back at her.

The girl turned. The gleaming filaments danced in the air. "Why're you looking at me like that?"

"Put them away. Can you put them away?"

"What's the matter, Stella Wallace? They bother you?"

"Please."

She lifted her right hand, and the gossamer vanished—pulled back inside her. Her face was sad. "Motty was scared of them, too." The girl stepped toward her. The tendrils from her left hand drifted ahead of her like seaweed in a current.

"Sunny, listen to me. Those come from the Ghostdaddy, but

they ain't you, you understand? Just because they're in you don't mean—"

"Shush. Of course they're me. As much as my arm. Motty told me this big story—you were my mama, and a boy named Lincoln Rayburn was my daddy, la-di-da. But I always knew that wasn't true. I always knew I was the God's daughter." Her mouth worked, then she shook her head. "The first day I met it, I knew."

Stella took a step back. "You've gone into the cave?" Her voice was hoarse.

"Didn't have to. It came to see *me*. Couldn't wait."

"But did you—did it touch you? On your hands."

The filaments danced over Sunny's hand. "I know what communion is, Stella Wallace. It ain't happened yet, but I'm ready. I knew as soon these came out of me."

"That's not possible," Stella said. "Your palms. I touched them."

"Aw, that's nothing." Sunny held up her right hand. The skin there looked smooth as glass. "I can do things none of y'uns could do. That's why I'm the one who's going to save the God."

The strands drifted close to Stella's face.

Stella flinched, but held herself from moving back again. "Could you put those away?"

"I read the books, and I know it needs me—right now. Ain't no time to wait for no *age of accountability*. Nobody's going to stop me. Motty couldn't."

Stella saw it all in a flash. Motty threatening the girl. Sunny screaming back at her. Motty commanding Abby to cover the hole. The next fight.

Motty could be violent when pushed. And Stella knew now that Sunny could, too. It ran in the family like their painted skin.

"You killed her," Stella said.

Sunny threw out her hands. The filaments whipped the air. "I didn't know she'd go all crazy!" Tears filled the girl's eyes. "She was stopping me from doing my duty!"

All this time, Stella thought the God had done it. Told herself it couldn't be Sunny; those unmarked palms were proof.

"You need to listen to me," Stella said. She hated the shakiness in her voice, but there was nothing she could do for it. "You need to put those away, and we have to go."

Behind Sunny, the window lit up with flashing lights. Multiple squad cars.

The girl turned her hand and the threads vanished into her skin. "Uncle Hendrick's come to take me home."

## 17

1938

THE MOUNTAIN WAS frantic with new growth. The suddenly warm days made every bush and tree light up with green. Wildflowers punched out of the earth.

The nights were still cold, but that didn't stop Stella and Lunk. In the two months since her fourteenth birthday, Stella had snuck out to meet him once a week, sometimes twice, and hike a ways up the mountain. It was a relief to get away from Motty, and get away from herself. Lunk had other things on his mind.

One night at the end of May, she told him she wanted to go way up, halfway to the bald, an hour's walk. At a certain clearing they laid out an old Rayburn family wool blanket, then pulled it up to wrap around their shoulders. Stella was staring through a break in the trees at a gauzy, cloud-draped moon. Lunk was looking at her. His arm lay across her back, under her coat, and his fingers grazed the side of her breast, though she could barely feel them through her shirt and bra. His other hand was on her bare knee. She could feel that, all right. Every few minutes his hand crept a little higher.

"Why'd we come all the way up here?" he asked.

"No reason," Stella lied. Then: "You know, my mama was named after the moon."

"Her middle name?"

"No, Lena. Selene. She was the goddess who drove her chariot across the night sky."

"Huh." He didn't know where to go with that. "It's awful secluded."

"I didn't think you'd mind the walk."

"I'll go anywhere with you, Stella."

"You're sweet." She thought about stepping to the edge of the rock, just to get a closer look at that moon.

"You okay?" he asked. "You seem all . . ."

"I'm all right." She didn't want to be sad in front of him. She hadn't told him what she'd learned about Lena's death. Hadn't told him how she couldn't shake the picture of her mother lying there, wasting away, for day after day . . . No. Lunk had nothing to do with any other part of her life, and she liked it that way. Her next communion was coming soon, and she planned to make big changes. Uncle Hendrick and the elders wouldn't be happy with her. But she had to do that on her own, and Lunk couldn't help even if he wanted to.

"Here," she said. "I brought something to keep us warm."

The jar was in her pocket. She fished it out, unscrewed it. Took a sip. Let out a long "Ah . . ." like Abby did.

Lunk was about to lose his mind. He stammered for a few seconds and Stella said, "You're an older man, you never took a sip of moonshine?"

"Never."

"Then you're long overdue." She took his hand off her knee and put the jar in it. "Go easy."

He took a pull, then immediately coughed and spat. "Good lord!"

"That's Barbwire Honey. It'll put hair on your chest."

She cajoled him into another sip. He held it down this time. "Sure does burn."

"Told you it would warm you up."

They sat for a while, passing the jar. There was an image in her mind, vivid as these trees, the moon. Lena, dressed like a pretend Indian girl, standing on that cliff.

Lunk was oblivious to ghosts. Soon enough his hand was back on her knee.

"You think you'll ever leave the cove?" he asked her.

No, she thought. Never. The God lived here. Why would she leave? She wouldn't fail, like Lena. She knew this in her bones.

"How about you?" she asked.

"We'll have to. They're kicking everybody out." She couldn't argue with that. Only a couple of folks had a life lease like Motty. He said, "My daddy's family has land in Townsend. Not as big as what he has here, but enough. He's going to build a house there, and one for me, and one for my sister."

"Rayburn Estates."

Lunk laughed. "I suppose so. I'd have room for a family."

"Would you now?"

"I'll become an elder and start preaching, and you—"

"You're so determined to be a preacher. I don't get it."

"It's a calling. When God knocks on the door, you gotta answer."

"What if it's the devil?"

"I'd know if it was the devil."

"So you've got a peephole. Smart move."

"You shouldn't joke about Satan," he said. He believed in Lucifer as firmly as he believed in God.

"I just hope you can tell the difference," Stella said. "Both are supernatural fellas looking to own your soul. You might get confused."

"Goodness gracious, Stella." He decided to laugh. "You're definitely called to be a theologian."

Lunk loved to talk and talk. And she was grateful for the distraction.

He shook his head, took another sip. "You're the smartest girl I ever met. God gave you those smarts and it would be a sin to waste 'em. He wants you to go to Maryville College and become—"

"Maryville, not University of Tennessee?"

"Definitely Maryville, He's very clear on this." Lunk was getting downright hilarious. "Then you marry me and become a preacher's wife."

"Hold up. God gave me these smarts, but He still doesn't want me to speak in church?"

"We'd work it out."

"Tell you what, I'll let you come to my church, and you can sit there quiet."

"You going to start your own church?"

"Why not? It don't look that hard."

"If I had my own church I'd let you talk."

"Ha."

"I would! Can I tell you something? I never told this to anybody."

"All right."

"Sometimes when I'm sitting in church, I look out across all the rows of people and I think . . ." He slowly shook his head. "I think, I'm just going to stand up and run over the top of the pews."

Stella laughed and lost her balance, pulling the blanket off him. The jar bounced away.

"Come on now, it's cold!" He helped her up.

"I'd like to see you do that," she said.

"I can picture it, so clear. I'm sitting there, listening to Daddy, and I can see myself atop those pews and I start to think, Oh no, it's going to happen. Sometimes my legs start to tremble because they're getting ready to jump up. It's like I can't stop myself."

"But you do."

"So far. Does that sound crazy?"

She thought, You don't know crazy. "Next time you should just do it. Seize the moment."

"Seize the moment."

"That's right."

"You mind if I kiss you?"

"I suppose I wouldn't mind."

He leaned in. Her lips were chapped but he didn't complain. His hands moved under her coat.

She backed away from him, pulling him, toward the moon. Her heel caught a root and she stumbled.

"Easy now," he said.

They stood on a lip of rock hanging over a hundred feet of black air. The moon was close enough to touch.

"Stella?"

"I was just thinking."

"Me too."

He brought her in close. They swayed like dancers. He was tipsy now, drunk on infatuation and alcohol both. Numb to the sadness rising in her like a tide.

His hand bunched the side of her skirt, pulled it higher, and then his hand was hot on her skin.

She said, "You trying to reach the promised land, Moses?"

"Moses! Ha!"

"Maybe I'll let you see it one day, but you'll die before entering."

He groaned. She chuckled and touched his cheek. He lowered his head and kissed her neck. His hand hadn't moved from her thigh. Oh, this poor Christian soldier, she thought, stranded in foreign territory.

She took pity on him and pressed his hand to her. He made a tiny sound, like a boy startled awake.


THE HOLY UNCLES WERE dying off. Uncle Hendrick came to the next communion with only five elders. They'd lost Calvin Whit—no relation to Abby's double-T Whitts—just three weeks ago. The survivors who gathered around her in the living room were a creaky, paper-skinned bunch, dry as kindling. She wondered how long it would be before Hendrick was forced to come alone.

Hendrick knelt before her chair as always, the bowl of oil set between them. Just seeing it made her palms itch. He started to speak and Stella held up a hand.

"I have some questions."

The room went quiet. Prickles ran up the back of her neck, but she steeled herself to keep going. She'd been practicing in her head for this moment all week.

"Questions?" Hendrick said at last. "Let's do the anointing and then perhaps after dinner you and I can—"

"Why can't I read the other Revelations? My mama's dead, there can't be any harm in letting me see *The Book of Selena*."

He looked over her shoulder where she knew Motty was standing, but he received no support. "We've talked about this," he said.

"I'm the one who talks to the God in the Mountain," Stella said. "I deserve to read what came before, with Lena and Motty both."

Hendrick looked toward a few of the Uncles as if to say, What can I do with this child? To her he said, "Mathilda's book is not closed, and Lena's story can't be revealed until the one before it is known. You know the rules." One of the men offered an "Amen."

"My own book, then," she said. "I have to know you're getting it correct."

"Pardon?"

"How do I know you're writing down the truth—what it *really* means?" To the Uncles she said, "I've read *The Book of Clara* and *The Book of Esther*. I don't believe Hendrick has properly understood the God's message."

The portion of old men who could hear were alarmed. Hendrick got to his feet. Stella glanced behind her. Motty was staring daggers at her. Ha! The old woman didn't know what Stella was going to say next, but she wasn't going to interrupt. Not yet.

Hendrick said, "The commentaries are as divinely inspired as the words spoke through the Revelator."

"You don't know that," Stella said from the chair. "You're just guessing."

"I'm not *guessing*. God speaks through me. Writing the commentaries involves reflection, and prayer, and—and study. You're too young to understand."

"I think I understand better than you. I'm the one who communes."

"You commune in a delirium! You can't know what was said, much less what it means."

"Sure, I'm in a fever while it's happening—but you're one more step removed than I am. At least I can *remember* what the God intended. I may see through a glass darkly, but you're staring at a brick wall." She'd thought of that line last night, when she was preparing for this service. "Even if I don't remember what each word means, I'd know how he felt when he spoke to me. I'd know what he wants." She addressed the Uncles. "Do you know what the God wants from us? Do any of you know?"

"He doesn't want anything!" John Headley Martin said.

"Except our faith," Donald Birch said.

"Yes, of course."

"And our service."

"Faith and service, yes—"

"And love!" Porter Martin added.

"What?" Morgan Birch asked.

"Love, Morgan, love!"

"Fine," Stella said. "And what do you get in return?"

"Love!" Porter said again.

"I know he loves me," Stella said. "I can feel that he loves me. But how do you know he loves any of you?"

"He's told us so in the Revelations," Uncle Hendrick said.

"Did the God say that?" she asked. "Or you?"

Hendrick lifted his hands. "Motty, what's going on here? What have you been saying to her?"

Stella thought, It's my own words that transformed me. My own thoughts.

"Answer her question," Motty said. "Tell her what you get from the God."

Stella looked at Uncle Hendrick. Waited.

"On the day the God reveals himself to the world," Hendrick said carefully, "he will reward us for our faith and devotion. The children of the God will be given a great gift." He'd taken on the same tone as Elder Rayburn when he preached. Stella wondered if he'd intentionally copied him, or if every man around here grew up knowing how to sound as condescending as Moses. "Eternal life. Not in heaven, not in some world after this. Right now. In *The Book of Esther* it was first promised that the God will provide 'one body, ever blooming.' Like a flower that blooms every year, but continuously rejuvenated."

He was performing. Stella looked around at the Uncles and said, "You think he's going to give this to you? You men?"

"If we keep the faith, yes," Hendrick said.

"Why hasn't he, then? Cousin Calvin just died. Any of you could die before the next communion."

"Stella! What's gotten into you?"

"Can we get on with it?" Morgan Birch asked.

"I'm not going in," Stella said.

The men were too old for an uproar, but they gave it a shot. A few of them managed to get to their feet.

"I'm not going in," she repeated, "until you promise me I can read the Revelations. All of them, including my own. Talk about it over dinner. But you can't force me. You think the God will come if I'm kicking and screaming?"

The Uncles weren't about to discuss it—not over dinner, not ever. Hendrick loomed over her, called her a child. Worse, a *girl*. One of the old men said, "Take the belt to her!"

"Go ahead," Stella said. "I been whipped plenty."

"We'll send you back to your father!" another one said.

An empty threat. Her father wouldn't have her, and they wouldn't let her go. She knew she was the last Revelator.

"Please, everyone, calm down," Hendrick said. When all of them were seated again, he asked, "What about the God in the Mountain? You'd do this to him?" His voice hoarse with dismay. She wanted to laugh at him. At all of them. Did they think they could come between her and the God? It was ridiculous. They didn't know about her visits, or about the hogs. This secret knowledge glowed in her like a fiery sword.

The Uncles battered her with words, growing more mystified and angry each minute she failed to collapse. Even John Headley, one of the oldest, was shouting. "Drag her in there," he said. "Drag her in there and tie her down!"

Stella glanced back at Motty. She stood at the edge of the room, arms crossed, face closed like a book. Would she protect her? Or let this play out?

"All you have to do is one thing," Stella told the men.

"That's not going to happen," Hendrick said. "You're not giving us a choice. Gentlemen? Help me hold her down."

She jumped up and shouted, "Stop!"

The men exchanged smug glances.

"You'll comply?" Hendrick said.

"I won't." She stared him in the eyes. "And if you don't give me what it's my right to know, I'll leave. Just like Lena."

"What, run away with Lincoln Rayburn?" He laughed at the shock on her face. "I know you've been making time with that boy. I'm not stupid."

She couldn't summon a reply. She hadn't practiced anything like this.

"I've got news for you," Hendrick said. "Lena came back."

"I'm stronger than her—strong enough to walk away for good."

Hendrick looked at Motty. "You told her?"

"I'm dead serious," Stella said. "Do not force my hand."


THEY DIDN'T TRY to stop her when she walked out of the house. In the backyard Veronica nearly bowled her over, threw her arms around her, crying hard. Of course she'd been listening, hovering outside the front room window.

"What are you crying about?"

"Daddy's so mad at you!"

"He'll get over it. Most of that was for show." She didn't know if either of those things was true.

"You've got to make it up to him. Please tell me you'll apologize." Even in tears Veronica was adorable. Ten years old and on the verge of movie-star beauty: clear skin, huge eyes, blonde curls, that God damn button nose. She'd certainly never made Daddy that angry, and may have never even seen him blow his top. It was good for her.

They hiked up a short ways to the spring, holding hands. Stella said, "They brought up that boy I told you about."

"Lunk?"

Stella looked down at her. "Come on. Did you tell your daddy about him?"

Veronica was horrified. "You said it was a secret! I'd never tell him a secret." She burst into fresh tears.

Motty, then.

Veronica liked to drink the cold milk they stored in the springhouse. Stella hauled it out of the water and let her sip from the jug. Then they sat on top of the cement and waited. Stella didn't feel like talking. She pictured her mother at the top of a cliff, shining in the moonlight. In her mind's eye Stella was standing a dozen feet away, too far to stop her. Lena glanced back, smiled, and then stepped off.

Veronica touched the tear on Stella's cheek. "It's okay," she said. "Daddy will forgive you."

"I ain't worried about that."

"Tell me about having a boyfriend. Do you pet?"

"What do you know about petting?"

Veronica smiled bashfully. "What's it like?"

"It's . . . all right," Stella said.

Vee drilled for details, and Stella moved them on to other topics, and waited for the elders' meeting to end. Stella had expected it to break up immediately after her declaration, but it was nearly an hour before Hendrick called for Veronica.

Stella said, "You better go or he'll leave you behind."

Veronica laughed.

"Trust me, it happens."


STELLA CAME BACK after the last set of headlights had pulled away. The plates were still on the table, littered with chicken bones. Not even outrage could convince them to drive home hungry.

"Any left?" Stella asked.

"There's a plate on the stove."

Stella ate the chicken standing up while Motty sat with a coffee cup in her hands. Dirty skillets sat beside the sink, waiting to be salt-scrubbed and oiled. It wasn't like Motty to let a mess sit.

After a while Motty said, "You proud of yourself?"

Stella bit off a chunk of meat. Couldn't keep from smiling as she chewed.

"It doesn't do any good to confront them," Motty said. "You don't embarrass them."

"Why not?"

"Because they're *men*. They can't take it."

"Somebody had to do it."

"Watch your mouth."

"You were just standing there," Stella said.

"Watching you act the fool. You weren't ever going to get them to give you the Revelations."

"Then they weren't going to get me into the cave."

"You wanted to tell them about your visits, didn't you? You were itching to."

"I didn't say a thing."

"I would have whupped you upside the head if you had. What were you thinking?"

Stella considered the bone in her hand. "I'm thinking I been lied to enough."

Anger flashed in Motty's face. "I told you when you was ready."

"You don't get to decide that anymore," Stella said. "It's time I wrote my own Revelation."

"That ain't what we do. The books don't matter."

"Oh, they do. And it matters who writes them. All those Baptists reading the King James, without thinking how it was one man who decided what made it in and what was left out. Whole books were cut out. The king's men decided what to—"

"There ain't nothing left out!" Motty barked. "What's in the Bible is all that's supposed to be there, no more, no less."

"You sound just like Elder Rayburn."

"Who put all these thoughts in your head? His boy, Lincoln? Merle Whitt?"

"All our church has is Hendrick's version, and you know that's not the whole story. But because it's all the Uncles read, it's what they use to make the rules."

"Their rules don't matter. The books don't matter. We know what's true."

"No, *we* don't," Stella said. "Not the whole truth."

Motty tilted her head. Like she was waiting to see if Stella would take a swing.

"You got any more big secrets, you should tell me now before I find out myself," Stella said. Thinking: It better be more enlightening than the story of a suicide. Stella had come to think that Motty had made the whole story up. It was too much like some banjo murder ballad.

Motty leaned back in her chair. Crossed her arms.

"Fine," Stella said. "I'm done getting yanked around by you people."


THE GOD CAME to her when she called, as he always had. She sat on the stone table, feeling that deep rumble of the stone. And the shape loomed over her.

Flickering lantern flames and shadows brought out features in his blank, boulder face. He was like a manikin, or a homemade doll, that needed her attention to become fully alive.

"I'm not here just to visit," Stella said. Her heart beat fast, but she told herself, I'm stronger than Lena. Stronger than anyone. "They ain't up there. This is for me, just for me, all right?"

The Ghostdaddy moved, or almost moved. A deep moan filled the cavern, rumbling her bones.

Stella lay flat on the rock and lifted her left hand, palm open. It was the first time she'd ever asked to commune without the Uncles hovering in the chapel above, or Motty waiting back at the house to bind her hands. If Stella bled out through her God wounds, then so be it.

"I want to know everything," she said. "Tell me what you're trying to do. Let me help."

His limb drifted close to her outstretched hand. She reached with her other hand and pulled it toward her. Its smooth skin slapped her palm.

"Do it," she said. She pressed harder. "Please."

The spike of pain arched her back.

## 18

## 1948

F IVE HOURS IN the auxiliary wing of the Blount County Jail and Stella couldn't stop moving. She'd try to sit on the cot and then she'd imagine what was happening in the cove and she'd be up again, pacing the six-by-ten cell, checking her wristwatch, cursing. Picturing that field mouse, floating. The girl was dangerous. The girl was a danger.

Tomorrow Hendrick would lead her to the chapel and send her down into the hole, without Stella to guide her. Whoever Sunny was before she went in would be gone. The God would roll over her young mind like a tide.

Sheriff Whaley hadn't driven Stella to the main jail, or taken her fingerprints, or done any paperwork whatsoever. He wasn't arresting her—he was putting her on ice. Almost literally—the cinder block building he'd thrown her into was cold as a spring-house. Whaley had taken away her flask, so the only thing left to keep her warm was her anger, bubbling away on a low boil.

To soothe herself she contemplated homicide. She nursed a vivid fantasy of shooting Whaley with his own gun. Uncle Hendrick featured heavily in several scenarios, as did Veronica.

Sheriff Whaley had waltzed into the Acorn Farm with Hendrick at his side and Bobby Reed behind them, dragging Hump Cornette by his arm. They picked up the moron at his mama's shack, and he'd led them straight to the still. And how'd they know about Hump in the first place? Veronica. Stella had mentioned the boy's name and she'd squealed to her daddy.

Stella was furious with herself. She'd fallen for Veronica's game like that lonely sailor. All those letters over the years—Vee constantly bringing up their shared childhood memories, expressing her concern for Stella's situation, "worrying" that her daddy was a fool—had lulled her into forgetting that Veronica was Hendrick Birch's daughter. Then came their reunion, and that friendly night of drinking at the sittin' up, and Stella thought she'd found a fellow sinner to confide in. She still didn't know if Vee was a true believer—she'd never touched the God in the Mountain, or seen it in person—but she'd picked her side.

Her father had opened the cave, and tomorrow night, Sunny was going in.

Hendrick had looked so smug when he walked into the farm. Sunny ran to his arms, acting like she'd been rescued from pirates. That was the moment she knew Hendrick had no clue about Sunny's nature—that he didn't know about the God's tendrils that could run him through like needles. He wasn't afraid enough.

"Big day tomorrow," Hendrick said. He looked at her over the top of Sunny's head. "Everything we've waited for. I'm almost sorry you're going to miss it."

Then she understood. The cameras and lights. Hendrick's willingness to agree to whatever deal she proposed as long as it kept her out of the way for a few days. This desperate move to get Sunny back, even for a day.

The God was coming out of the mountain.

"You can't do this," Stella told him. "She's not ready. She can't go in alone."

"This is the God's daughter. He's already appeared to her. And tomorrow night, the God will come greet us all."

"You idiot," Stella shouted. "You fucking—"

That's when Sheriff Whaley grabbed her by the back of the neck. Next thing after that she was on her stomach, Whaley's knee in her back. Soon as she got her breath back Stella started shouting. "The Ghostdaddy don't take orders! It won't listen to you."

Sunny looked back at her without letting go of Hendrick's waist. "It's all right," she said. "He'll listen to me."

SOMETIME IN the thin hours of the morning, the outside door banged open. Deputy Bobby Reed came in, steering a loose-kneed white man in a floral shirt. Bobby dropped him onto a cot in the next cell. The man swore and complained in fluent Drunk.

Stella was at the bars, but Bobby started to walk out without looking at her.

"God damn it, Bobby. Tell me what's going on."

He seemed embarrassed. "Hey, Stella. Sorry about this." More quietly, he added, "I tried to warn you."

"I appreciate it." And she did. She would have appreciated it more if she'd gotten the warning more than a few minutes before Whaley arrived, but that was more her fault than his. "I need to know about Alfonse. Did you arrest him, too?"

He sucked on his teeth. "Whaley said not to talk to you."

"Did he also say I should just piss all over your jail?"

"What?"

"I got to pee," she said patiently. "I'm allowed to pee, aren't I?"

He had to think about this. Bobby was just seven or eight years older than she was, which she hadn't realized back when she met him, the day he pulled her over in Abby's car. He'd plumped up a bit over the years, but he was still handsome, and those green eyes remained a marvel, even in bad fluorescent light. He'd never married.

"Okay, okay." He walked her to a one-holer. By the looks of it the previous prisoners were unable to aim their dicks.

Bobby was still looking nervous when she came out.

"I'd like to make my one phone call."

"Come on, Stella." He was anxious to get her back in the cell.

"Tell me about Alfonse."

"We couldn't find him. His family said he left town, so he must have gotten wind of us."

Thank God, she thought.

Bobby still looked nervous. Maybe worried that she'd tell Whaley that he'd tipped her off, or worse, that he'd been looking the other way for years.

She thought, I could grab his gun. Lock him in her cell and ride off like an Old West bandit. But hours later she'd have every cop in the South chasing her.

After he closed the cell door she said, "Just do me one favor."

He groaned.

"Call Pee Wee Simms. Tell him where I am."

"I can't do that, Stella. The sheriff would have my head."

"Head? *Head?* How 'bout your balls—does he got them too?"

The drunk laughed.

SHERIFF WHALEY CAME IN the next morning and released the drunk, who was walking a lot straighter now. A little after that Whaley let Stella into the restroom. She did her business, then drank from the faucet, splashed water on her face. Whaley started pounding on the door. She took her time coming out.

"This is illegal, you know."

He waved her back into the cell.

"You must owe Hendrick a lot to put your career in danger like this. You can't just keep a person forever without charging them."

"Big talk for a lady that's committed multiple federal crimes."

"It's just moonshine."

"And kidnapping," he said. "Don't forget you took that girl against her will."

WHALEY DIDN'T BRING breakfast, or even coffee. When food finally did arrive, just before eleven, it was delivered by the last person she expected: Mary Lynn Rayburn, Lunk's sister.

She passed Stella a paper sack through the bars. "There's a ham sandwich, and some French fries, and a piece of chocolate cake—that might be messy, but I put in plenty of napkins."

The smell of food made her stomach sprout teeth. Stella dragged her cot close to the bars and tore into the sandwich. Mary Lynn pulled over a little stool and sat with a bottle of Coca-Cola on her lap and watched her eat.

Stella waved for the Coke. Mary Lynn passed it through, and Stella popped off the cap on a crossbar.

"How'd you know I was here?"

She hesitated. "Bobby mentioned he'd seen you last night. And this morning . . . I work just a few doors down, and I thought . . ."

"I'm glad you came. I was starving." She took a swig from the bottle, wondering about the timing. When did Bobby have time to see her? "I didn't know you two were friends."

Mary Lynn was still enough of a preacher's daughter to blush. "He doesn't know I'm here. I hope I don't get him in trouble—I waited till Sheriff Whaley drove off. Mavis let me in." Mavis was the department receptionist. "I can't stay long." Lord, she was nervous.

"I won't mention it to the sheriff," Stella said. She finished the sandwich, then started on the fries. She needed to ask Mary Lynn for a favor, but didn't want to spook her. "Thanks for this. Oh, and the flowers—thanks for those, too. You didn't have to do that."

"I meant what I said. I know Lunk loved you."

Suddenly the food was dry in her throat. Stella blinked hard, swallowed.

"I think you scared him, too. But he didn't stop adoring you. Those months when you wouldn't see him, they like to broke his heart," Mary Lynn said. "He just didn't understand. He said you'd stopped seeing him, stopped talking to him. But he never gave up. That last night he went to see you—"

"Mary Lynn. I need you to do me a favor. Something bad's happening tonight, and I have to get out of here. I need you to call Pee Wee Simms and Merle Whitt and tell them I'm here."

"I couldn't do that. Bobby would get in trouble."

"They won't say it came from you. I just need you to tell them I'm stuck here, and they need to bring bail." She didn't even know if Whaley would accept bail, seeing as how she wasn't formally arrested.

"I won't do that," Mary Lynn said. "I can't—I can't go against the law."

"This is important, damn it!"

The woman drew back in alarm. Tears had appeared in her eyes.

Stella said, "If you aren't going to help me, why the hell did you come?"

"Bobby says you're in bad trouble, may even go to federal

prison. Before you went away, I thought you might . . . I don't know. Tell me."

"Tell you what? Spit it out."

"I want to know what happened. The night he died."

*What happened.* Such an innocuous phrase.

"You know," Stella said. "Everybody knows."

Mary Lynn shook her head. "That story never made sense. I want to hear you tell it."

"I've got nothing for you. I told the police everything. It was in the papers."

"You lied to them, then. Or Motty did."

Stella realized she was standing. "Thanks for the lunch. Say hi to your folks for me."

"Tell me," Mary Lynn said, "and I'll help you."

"No you won't." She put a foot on the cot and pushed it back. Metal legs screeched on concrete.

"I know it was a lie," Mary Lynn said. "Lunk didn't go up to the cove to drink with you and Abby. Oh, I know he tried liquor. He tried it because you got him to. But he didn't like it. And he wouldn't have got so drunk that he crashed Daddy's car."

"You don't know that."

"Not on that night." She was angry now, glaring up at Stella. This was a side of her Stella had never seen. "No. Not on that night. Not unless something terrible happened."

"I don't know what you're talking about."

*"I saw the ring."*

Stella started to speak, couldn't find the words. What ring?

"He told me he was running away with you. He said you were going to get married. He swore me not to tell. Then he showed me the ring." The tears were running down Mary Lynn's cheeks, but she was oblivious to them. "He was so proud. It wasn't much of a diamond, but it was all he could afford."

For a long moment Stella couldn't speak. She'd seen the necklace, hanging around Sunny's neck.

"Please," Mary Lynn said, and Stella tried to focus on her face. "Tell me the truth."

Stella stared off to the side at the cinder block wall, but not seeing it.

"I didn't know he'd done that," she said.

Stella sat on the cot. All strength had left her body.

Mary Lynn said, "What did you do, Stella? Did you change your mind?"

"I never changed my mind," Stella said.

"But you—"

"Let me finish. You wanted the truth, sit still for it."

Mary Lynn set her lips in a hard line. The tears were still coming, though.

"I didn't change nothing," Stella said, "because I never loved him. Not like he loved me." She leaned forward and grabbed the bars. "My heart belonged to another."

Mary Lynn's eyes went wide. She glanced to her left, thinking hard.

"Doesn't matter who," Stella said. "None of your business."

Mary Lynn slowly shook her head. "Why would you lead him on, then? Why would you make him think you could run away together?"

"I wanted to escape the cove, and he was my way out."

Mary Lynn's tears had stopped.

Stella sagged against the bars. Cold iron pressed into her forehead. "That night, he finally saw me for what I was. I should have kept him away, Mary Lynn. I should have protected him. I got to live with that the rest of my life."

A silence opened between them. Stella could hear every breath in her throat.

"What about the baby?" Mary Lynn said finally. Her voice almost a whisper. "Were you carrying the child when you did this to Lunk?"

"Doesn't matter. What I told your father is the truth. Sunny's not Lunk's child. I'm sorry."

Mary Lynn seemed stunned. But she was finally taking it in.

"The girl's in trouble," Stella said. "Hendrick's letting her—making her do something dangerous. Something I went through as a kid. I lived through it, but I'm afraid she won't."

"What are you *talking* about?" Mary Lynn's confusion was so pure. "Are you saying Hendrick's some kind of . . . what?"

"I can't tell you. I'm sorry. But I'm asking you, even though she's not Lincoln's child, to help me. Help me get out of here, so I can go get her."

The door handle moved, and Mary Lynn jerked and stared at the door. "I can't—I have to go."

"I have to stop him," Stella said. "Mary Lynn. Please."

A female voice said, "Mary Lynn! The sheriff's back." It was Mavis, the receptionist. "You better scoot."

Mary Lynn stood up. "I'm sorry you got the girl into . . . whatever this is. But you don't get to do this, Stella. You don't get to run away and ten years later swoop back in and try to make up for all your—" She searched for the word. "Destruction."

She walked to the door, stopped.

"You killed him," Mary Lynn said. "You can tell yourself you didn't mean it, or it was an accident. But you need to own up to what you've done."

## 19

1938

THE WORLD WAS awash in scarlet. So much beauty, they thought. So much to be grateful for.

They made their way down the mountain, and when they reached the valley they encountered an animal blocking their way. It took some time for them to realize it was a human being. Four skinny limbs, balancing upright on two of them. So precarious. They gawked at its small, hair-covered head, its tiny eyes. Its toothy mouth moved, issuing squawks and squeals.

Then its name came to mind: *Lunk*.

A shift of balance, and then perspective: They were suddenly lying on the ground at Lunk's feet. Sunlight haloed his head. So, it was dawn. The world had kept spinning while they were in the cave.

Lunk knelt down beside them. "Stella! You're bleeding!"

*Stella.* Yes. That name was familiar, too.

"Can you stand? Oh my goodness. Oh my goodness. Let me . . ."

He looped one of his arms underneath their legs, another arm behind their back. He grunted and lifted their body. Stumbled and caught himself.

Ah, the world was so beautiful. The air smelled sweet.

Lunk looked down at the body in his arms, and she was that girl, the knowledge surfacing in her brain. She was Stella.

He carried her down the hill. They passed the empty pig-pen and she thought: Why are there no young pigs? There was something important she needed to remember, something she glimpsed in the God's mind. The shape of the thought was tiny, but as she reached for it it opened like a flower in her head.

*A child.*

Somehow Lunk managed to open the back door of the house without dropping her. He carried her down the hall and laid her on a bed.

Stella's bed. Yes. Her bed.

"What are you doing here?" she asked.

Lunk's face was twisted in some emotion she couldn't read. He was sweating despite the cool air. Breathing hard. There were bloodstains on his shirt.

"Let me get—where's Motty? Don't move, you're still bleed-ing. Just a second."

She gazed at the ceiling. Her mind was crowded with knife-edged thoughts. But every time she began to comprehend a shape it folded into a different configuration, became, abruptly, a mystery. Everywhere she turned in her mind's eye, shapes skit-tered away and transformed, as if desperately trying to escape her. Why was she so weak?

She screamed.

Lunk was there, wrapping a towel around her hand. "What happened? Is there glass? Did you cut yourself?"

When is now? June? No, sometime in the heart of July. She'd communed with the God so many times—and each time her mind had filled with his thoughts, and each time she came a little closer to knowing his true nature. It was as if the God himself was trying to climb into her mind. Last night she'd come the closest of all. And yet—failure. She was too small, or else resisting him without knowing it. Even now, less than an hour after the communion, his thoughts were collapsing inside her. By afternoon they'd be as small as dust, irretrievable.

She was filled, and she could not figure out how to stop the emptying.

She wasn't despairing, not yet. If she tried harder, if she remained conscious just a little while longer, she believed his knowledge would fill her like water. And then? She didn't know what happened next. Her mind would slip from her body and she'd float down from the mountain a new creature.

"You're smiling," Lunk said. "You're not hurt?"

"It hurts," she said. "But I'm not hurt."

"Mary Lynn told me you never went back to school."

What was there to say? There was nothing school could teach her, and nowhere it could take her. Everything she needed was right here.

"So I learned to drive." He smiled shyly. "It's my father's car. I never thought he'd give up the horse and buggy."

A silence grew between them. He looked toward the door. Motty still hadn't appeared.

Stella said, "Why'd you come here, Lunk?"

"I just . . . I wanted to . . ." It took him several more false starts before he arrived at, "I came to apologize."

"For what?"

He seemed frustrated that she'd asked, as if she was being coy. "For what happened on the mountain."

She thought a moment. That night on the blanket. It seemed ages ago. "That doesn't have to do with anything."

"If I crossed a line . . ."

"No lines," she said. "Not any I didn't want to cross."

"I want to make it up to you. When you stopped talking to me I about died. You're the one, Stella. I know you're the one for me. If I had you I know everything in my life would work out."

She let him run on like that for a while. Finally she said, "I'm sorry."

"What?"

"That's not going to happen."

*"Why?"* He was near tears.

She didn't know how to explain. She'd become a different person. Her heart belonged to someone else. Her life belonged to someone else.

"Just tell me," Lunk said. "Did I drive you to it?"

He was so sad. She wanted to touch his face to soothe him, but her hands were for holy work now.

"Go home, Lunk. Find a girl, get married, become a preacher. Don't come back."


STELLA STOOD at the fence, her bandaged hands crossed on the top rail. Summer flies buzzed over the empty pen.

"It's time to buy a sow," Stella said. She'd heard Motty come up behind her.

"I ain't buying no pigs."

"The message ain't coming from me," Stella said.

Motty stared at her. "God damn it," she said. "You've been to see him again."

Stella didn't bother denying it. The bandages were proof enough. "I don't know why it wants one, but it does. I could see it in its mind—clear as a commandment."

"I was hoping we were done," Motty said.

Stella could remember the night, two years ago, a month after her first communion. The gunshot. Motty covered in blood.

"Last time," Stella said. "You failed."

"You don't know what the hell you're talking about."

"Don't you doubt me." When Stella did her first communion, the God's thoughts evaporated almost immediately. Now she could hold on to the ideas and concepts for days, long enough to describe them aloud, as if she were two Stellas, speaking in tongues and translating at the same time.

"It's dying, Motty. It's old, yes, but also there's a . . . something toxic in it. Or around it."

"One body, ever blooming," Motty said tiredly. "So that the poison of the world—"

"I know, I know. But this ain't a metaphor, this ain't spiritual. It's actual. Something's killing it, but it's—"

"Stop calling him *it*."

Stella closed her eyes, trying to wrangle one of the God's thoughts—or rather, her memory of the thought as it had traveled through her. "The poison's in the air. The rocks. It's seeping into it." Nefarious chemicals, she thought. "I can feel the death like it's happening to me. When I'm communing with it, it's like I'm inside it, looking down at myself."

Motty made a small noise.

Stella asked, "Did you not feel that way?"

Motty slowly shook her head.

"It's not what we think it is," Stella said. "It's not some spirit. It's meat and bone. Like the Cherokee gods. Spearfinger had to eat and breathe, and the God—"

"Shush. This is Abby's fault. He's full of stories. I should have kept him away from you."

*Shush.* If only Motty knew all the things Stella wasn't saying. The things she only spoke to herself. Well, she'd find out soon enough.

"I want to talk to Hendrick," Stella said.

"Why?" Meaning, *Why now?* Hendrick had been wanting to

come back to the farm for weeks, and Stella had said she wouldn't meet with him. She was doing her own work, and didn't need or want him. Motty had respected her wishes.

"Tell him I've been doing communions."

"He'll explode," Motty said.

"Maybe. But I want him to know what I've done. Tell him I'm going to keep communing, but I'll let him record them. *If.*"

"Here we go," Motty said.

"He's got to let me read the other books. Not just the typed-up books—the originals, the handwritten transcripts. I need the source material to do my work—everything that was said, not what he decided to record."

"But the whole transcript *is* in the books, he just types it out. That's our tradition."

"Maybe, maybe not. Hendrick does seem to love every last scrap of the God's word, but he might have been tempted to leave something out. I need to know that—and that's why I need the originals."

"That ain't going to happen. He already said no just to giving you the books, never mind the first scriptures!"

"I did that wrong. I asked him in front of the Uncles. You were right, you can't embarrass a man, he won't think straight. But I know he wants to know everything about the God. He's as devoted as I am, in his way."

Motty never agreed that it would work, but she said she'd invite Hendrick back to the farm. Something had shifted in their relationship since Stella started her own communions. Motty had starting acting respectful, but it could be that she'd just grown scared of Stella.

Stella said, "Meanwhile, I'll try to find out more from it about the pigs."

"You can't go in again so soon!" It was strange to hear Motty so worried for her. It was almost sweet. "Stella, please. You just went two nights ago."

Stella hadn't told her that Lunk had carried her home. She didn't want Motty to panic.

"Don't you worry about me," Stella said. "The Ghostdaddy would never hurt me."

SHE FOUND Uncle Hendrick and Motty in the kitchen, despite the summer heat. The oven was on, and there was corn bread in the oven. Hendrick loved her corn bread.

Stella was carrying the scientific notebook Merle had given her. Hendrick hopped up and turned on his smile, as if the last time they'd seen each other he hadn't threatened to tie her down. He reached for her hand and stopped himself. The bandages were small, just a pad over each palm with a layer of cloth wrap holding them in place, but they shocked him. They were proof she'd been communing.

"It's so good to see you, Stella."

They took seats facing each other. The green leather case sat upright next to Hendrick's chair.

"I want to apologize," he said. "I didn't hear you out and I let things get out of hand."

Motty grunted in amusement.

Stella said, "You brought them?"

He lifted the case onto his lap and opened it. "We've never let a Revelator read all the books because, well, all the reasons I said before. However . . ."

He held out *The Book of Selena*. She tucked the notebook aside and took it. The book was thicker than Clara's and Esther's books combined. How many times did Lena commune, to fill so many pages? Or did she just have more to say?

THE BOOK OF SELENA

*Being the Fourth Volume of a New Revelation*
*From the God in the Mountain*
*To Selena Birch, Recorded by Hendrick Birch, her Uncle*
*with Commentary and Clarifications*
*by Hendrick Birch*

"You recorded the words *and* wrote the commentary? How generous that you didn't call it *The Book of Hendrick*."

"It was amazing to hear the words as they were spoken," Hendrick said, declining to take offense. "I believe it clarified my thoughts as I wrote the commentaries. When I sat down, later, I was—"

"Where are the other books? Motty's. Mine."

"Ah. Well." He nodded as if he'd given it great thought. "Why don't we start with hearing about communions? If that goes well, I'm sure I'll bring more books on my next visit."

"You were supposed to bring all of them—and the original transcripts. That was the deal."

"There was no deal—Motty should have told you, bringing the transcripts is impossible. They never leave the safety of my care. It's my most sacred responsibility."

"See?" Motty said to Stella.

"It was worth a shot." To Hendrick Stella said, "I'm honestly surprised you brought even Lena's book. It kills you to even let one of them go."

"As I tried to explain—"

"Listen, Hendrick. Just listen. I know you love the word of God more than anything else. Even if I don't trust anything else about you, I trust that. That's why I brought you here."

This was news to Motty. Stella kept her focus on Hendrick.

"The old Revelations are obsolete," Stella said. "Everything you've told me, about the God, your beliefs, is wrong. Wrong or incomplete. You think the God loves you and is going to grant you eternal life, here on Earth."

"That's right," Hendrick said. "On the day the God emerges from the mountain, we shall all be transformed, and the world will know that a new kingdom is here. And I—well, all of us, really—will be there to announce his presence, like John the Baptist."

"John the Baptist got his head cut off," Motty said.

Hendrick was undeterred. "The modern world has lost its faith, because of war and disease and machinery. But when shown proof of the God, *irrefutable* proof of the God, the old governments will fall away, and his children—"

"Hold on." Stella was shaking her head. Hendrick frowned at the interruption. "I'm sorry, you're making all that up. That's not what the God is talking about." There were so many things Hendrick didn't understand, starting with the fact that he thought the God never came out of the cave. "It don't care about governments, or end times. This is about its own end. It's dying."

Motty was staring hard at her. Was she furious? Afraid? Maybe both.

"The world is killing it," Stella said. "It doesn't care about you. It only cares about its children."

"But we are his children," Hendrick said. "In *The Book of Esther* it says that all who—"

"*The Book of Esther* doesn't mean shit."

Well. That shut them up.

Stella opened her own notebook. The pages were almost all filled. She'd recorded everything she remembered from her visits with the God, and everything that happened during the night of the sow. She hadn't been writing to herself. She was describing these miracles to an unknown audience, years in the future, maybe a girl like herself, the next Revelator. Something about inscribing those words in black ink gave them a power that worked on her like X-rays, making tiny changes.

Hendrick and Motty were watching her.

"We have to be clear what the God really wants," Stella said. "What it needs." Her voice was level but she was ready to bolt if they rushed her. The hallway was at her back. "The whole focus of the church has to change, to concentrate on helping it."

"And you alone know what that is," Hendrick said.

"I've communed with it seven times since you were here last spring."

Motty gasped. She'd had no idea how often Stella had gone out there. And Hendrick's face was pure consternation. Seven times! That was more than all of Stella's communions that Hendrick had witnessed.

"This notebook is my Revelation," Stella said. "It's the record of what it said to me."

Hendrick's face had gone pale. "You kept it? You kept the words?"

Motty glared at Stella. "What are you doing?"

"It's all there," Stella said. "Everything I could remember."

Hendrick's face contorted, and he put a hand to his eyes. Stella realized he was crying. "Oh, thank goodness. Oh, thank you, thank you." He breathed out, and then laughed. "I've been so worried. I can't tell you. I thought you'd never go in again, but this!" To Motty he said, "Did you know about this?"

Motty did not. The look on her face was as hard as tombstone.

"We can't just keep this secret," Stella told them. "I want this made part of the Revelations. I want it printed and published."

"Of course, though—I'll try. There might be issues, the commentary might—but if it's what you say, of course it will be included."

"It's too important not to," Stella said. "The next task is to move the God."

She could feel the authority in her voice, hear that preacher cadence that Hendrick and Elder Rayburn had deployed on her—and she could see its effect on Hendrick. It thrilled her. She felt like she'd finally become a person in his eyes.

"The park will make it impossible for it to stay here," she said. "We have to find a new home, a new Jerusalem, so that it can accomplish its great work."

"Great work?" Hendrick's eyes lit up. "What is it? What has he told you?"

So many things, Stella thought. Most of them she didn't understand herself, not completely, but she wasn't about to express doubt in front of Hendrick. One idea, however, was clear.

"It's trying to create a child," Stella said. "A child of its own that can survive here."

"When you say create a child . . ." Hendrick was barely keeping up. "Do you mean actually impregnate a woman, or—?"

"The God ain't male. It ain't female, either. Those were just words we put on it, trying to make sense of it. All that matters is that it *is*, do you see? It is, and it wants to make more like itself. It's been trying to grow something of its own that will survive in this world. Something adapted to it. So far none of them have lived, or . . ." This was a foggy concept. In the God's thoughts, none of its children had *thrived*; none had lasted long enough to be what it needed. She was confident that with more communions, its exact needs would become clear.

She told him what she did understand. "They withered," she said. "They failed. But the God's going to try again, it's going to keep trying, over and over, until it succeeds."

"What's she talking about, Motty?"

"Tell him," Stella said to Motty. "Tell him about the sows."

"The *sows*?" Hendrick asked.

"The next—"

The punch knocked her to the floor. Stella lay on her side, gasping. Her vision had gone starry.

Motty plucked the notebook from her hand. Turned toward

the iron stove and opened the firebox. The logs were in full flame.

Hendrick shouted. Tried to reach past Motty. She shoved him away, sent him stumbling backward. Pushed the book into the flames and slammed the firebox door.

"That's priceless!" Hendrick said. "You can't burn the word of God!"

"Get out of my house, Hendrick."

He looked at Motty's hands, then down at his chest where she'd pushed him. Across the white shirt, a bloody smear.

THE HEADACHE WOULD not abate. Stella lay on her bed, curled into a ball, eyes closed. Every time she tried to open them her vision wavered and the pain in her head spiked. Her cheek where Motty had smashed her felt hot. The pain ebbed and flowed.

Motty had spanked her countless times, and striped her butt with a switch when her offense had been more serious, but she'd never struck her with a closed fist. This was new. A violation.

After Hendrick drove off, Motty stomped to her bedroom and slammed the door, leaving Stella on the floor. She picked herself up. Winced at the brightness of the fire. Slunk off to her own room.

I'm alone, Stella thought. Motty had shown herself to be jealous and weak, a spurned Revelator who'd rather burn the truth than accept Stella's leadership. Hendrick could only be trusted to follow his path to religious glory. And Abby was useless—so reluctant to take a stand against the Birches that he couldn't stand for her. He'd go to his grave with blinders firmly in place. And Merle and Lunk? She'd fooled them, and that made them useless to her. They cared for her only because they didn't know her true nature. They loved an imaginary Stella.

None of them understood what she did, the thing that she had not written down, because it was too much for them to bear: they were all, Stella included, expendable. Humans were as common as June bugs. Not only was the God unique on this Earth but its life was centuries long, and so many times more precious than their own. The difference between Stella and Hendrick—and Motty and every Birch who'd come before her—was that Stella understood this, and accepted it. Better to sacrifice yourself for a higher purpose than to live a long life scrabbling in the dirt.

There was only one soul she cared for in the world, and one soul who knew her for what she was.

Stella climbed out of the bed. Her limbs felt heavy, and her head was awash in dizziness. She leaned against the wall until she thought she could walk, then passed out of the house, into moonlight. The cold air shook her awake.

She walked between the dark trees until she reached the chapel. Her head pounded but she ignored the pain. Pushed the cave's door out of the way.

"I'm here," she called out. "I'm alone."

She closed her eyes and let her feet and hands guide her down the steps and into the mountain. When her fingers touched the stone table she breathed deep, until the latest wave of pain passed, and then climbed up onto the surface.

"I'm here," she said again, and lay back on the rock.

The walls were still. The only thing she could hear was the sound of her breathing. Her head throbbed with pain. The minutes crawled by.

"Please," she said.

The table sucked the heat from her body. She began to shiver. And then the God descended.

## 20

1948

WORRY STRETCHED the afternoon into an endless staircase—she'd never reach the top. Every minute she spent in this cell was a minute closer to Sunny entering the cave. A minute closer to her being erased.

Stella should have just lied to Mary Lynn and told her, Sure, Lunk was the love of my life; Sunny's his daughter! The Rayburns would have jumped to help Stella. Now she was stuck under Whaley's thumb. He wasn't about to let her out, not until Hendrick achieved his wet dream and saw his god with his own eyes.

Stella couldn't understand what Sunny had told the Uncles. What crazy lie let them think the little girl could commune with the Ghostdaddy—on her *first time*—and convince it to come out to get its fucking picture taken? When Stella communed, there was never a moment when she felt like she could demand anything from it. There was nothing she could tell it, no words it would listen to. It wanted nothing from her but obedience. The great lie about communion was that it wasn't a union at all. Every experience was a one-way street. The Ghostdaddy filled her with its thoughts, over and over, until she burst. And then, when she'd proved to be a failure, it stopped talking to her altogether. Just like it had stopped talking to Motty, and then Lena. The Revelator wasn't good enough for it, so it moved on to the next child.

Sunny was more gifted than Stella, for sure. The way she'd controlled the filaments with that mouse—that was like nothing Stella had ever been capable of. But she was still just a child. And she was going into the cave alone. The weight of the God's will would crush her.

SHERIFF WHALEY CAME into the building at just after 4:00 p.m. Stella was standing at the bars by the time he reached her cell.

"About time," she said. "My bladder's about to burst." She held the Coke bottle behind her back.

Whaley shook his big sad face. "You know you're going to prison, don't you?" He was holding the key to her cell but hadn't made a move toward the lock. "It's just a matter of time."

"At least prison has a john in the cell. Can I pee, please?"

He winced, as if hearing a woman discuss urination offended him. He put the key in the lock. Swung open the gate. "I wouldn't take too—"

He'd just seen the bottle in her hand. His eyes widened.

"You know, if this were the movies," Stella said, "this is the part where I break this thing against the bars, hold the jagged end to your throat, and use you as a hostage as I make my escape."

Whaley stared at her.

She handed him the bottle. "Could you throw this out for me?"

"Get the hell out of here."

She raised an eyebrow.

He waved at the open door. "I said, get the hell out of my jail."

And if this were the movies, she thought, this is the part where he shoots me for "escaping."

She walked out in front of him, unable to shake the tingling at the back of her neck, into the breezeway between the cinder block building and the department proper. There she saw Pee Wee and Merle, standing beside a white man she didn't recognize, and suddenly felt a wave of relief.

This time it was Merle who stepped forward to hug her. Stella soaked it in, grateful.

Pee Wee said, "Marcus, this is Stella Wallace. Stella, Marcus Ruvolo."

There was a time Stella didn't know what a truly first-class suit looked like. There was no doubting Ruvolo's: a custom-tailored pearl-gray pinstripe with high-waisted pants. The pleats were as long and sharp as scimitars.

She shook hands with him. "I'm guessing you're a lawyer?"

"Better than that," he said. "I'm *your* lawyer."

RUVOLO WANTED TO take her to his office up in Knoxville, but Stella didn't have time for that, so the four of them drove her to Merle and Pee Wee's house. The lawyer wanted to discuss legal strategy. Sheriff Whaley had never formally charged her but claimed he was getting around to it. The state gave the police a lot of leeway in that regard. He'd already impounded her car and seized the farm, and had threatened to go after her other personal property.

Stella thought of the five hundred dollars she'd hidden under the car's seat. That was gone now.

"There will be rough days ahead," Ruvolo warned her.

"Just keep me out of jail," she said. "For a few more days."

She left him in the living room. It was almost sunset, and the ceremony would take place after dark.

She went into the bathroom. Peed, and then splashed water in her face. She didn't look at that porcelain tub.

Merle was waiting for her on the other side of the door. "Care to let me in on what's going on?"

"I've got some things I got to do. You don't have a cigarette, do you?"

"Always." Merle produced a pack of Luckies, lit one for her. "It's suppertime. Stay and talk with me, stay the night. Your old bed's free, if you give me a minute to clear off some books."

"I wish I could." That was the truth. If there was a place on this Earth she felt safe, it was here. Even more than her own house.

She didn't know exactly how much Merle and Pee Wee knew about the Birch family religion. When they took her in, Stella had told them nothing. She could scarcely bear to talk at all. That first month she spent days straight in the spare bedroom they'd given her, curtains pulled, lights off. They thought she was in despair over Lunk's death—which was true enough. They told her that his death wasn't her fault—which was kind, but dead wrong. Merle fed her and kept her clean.

It took Stella some time to get there, but one night she finally realized, It's time to be done with this mopery. What was the point of lying around, waiting to feel better? There was no God to forgive her. Nope. Better to take arms against the sea of troubles.

Merle found her in the bathtub, her wrists open. The idea had been to cut the badness out of her, and die clean.

They could have had her committed, but Pee Wee drove her home from the hospital while Merle held her in the back seat. They took turns at her bedside for weeks, until Stella could do a decent impersonation of a normal person. She went on with that impersonation for the next three years. In all that time, Stella never let on that the Ghostdaddy was in her head. She never mentioned its name. Not when she was awake, anyway. She had no control what she screamed in her nightmares, and those came every night for a long while. She'd wake up with her throat sore and the echo of her own voice in her ears, Merle sitting on the bed beside her with a stricken expression—pretty much the same one she wore now.

So. Even though Stella had told Merle and Pee Wee almost nothing about the Ghostdaddy, they probably knew plenty.

"I'm worried about you," Merle said. "I can see you holding on by your fingertips."

"There's nothing for it," Stella said. "I got to go make things right. You were right the other day—I been walking away from my responsibility. I got to make up for that."

"Take responsibility tomorrow."

"Sorry, can't wait. Maybe after this is over, we can sit down and I can explain everything. But right now I need to use your telephone."

A WOMAN ANSWERED the line. Her hello was a challenge.

Stella said, "Mrs. Bowlin? This is Stella Wallace. I was wondering if—"

"You said you were gone." Mrs. Bowlin's voice was harsh. "You promised I'd never hear from you."

I said you'd never *see* me again, Stella thought. But arguing with Alfonse's mother would get her nowhere.

"I'm so sorry," Stella said. "I am. Please don't hang up."

A deep male voice spoke from somewhere on the other side. Mrs. Bowlin said, "Stay out of this, Antoine." Alfonse's dad. Mrs. Bowlin came back on the line. "We've got nothing to say to you."

"I just want to talk to Alfonse."

"You're a little late for that."

Stella stood in Merle's living room—stood because the couch

and chairs were occupied by books, sweaters, packing boxes. She could hear Pee Wee, Merle, and Ruvolo talking in the kitchen, not twenty feet away. She turned and bent over the receiver. "Did the police get him? Bobby Reed told me he left town before they got here."

"No thanks to you."

"Did he say where he was going?"

The line went silent, except for a faint hiss. Stella listened for any stray breath in that static.

Then Mrs. Bowlin said, "He may have mentioned Myrtle Beach."

"Oh." Stella straightened. "I . . . hear it's nice."

"For hurricanes. Goodbye, Miss Wallace."

"Wait! Please. Alfonse was going to get something for me. A souvenir."

"I don't know anything about that."

"I was just hoping that—when he gets back—he'd drop it off at the cove. Could you let him know that? I need it right away."

"My boy is not going into the cove, not for anybody."

"I wouldn't ask if it wasn't—"

"*Anybody*. You're a hurricane yourself, Miss Wallace."

The click was loud.

Fuck me, Stella thought. She needed Alfonse's help. But now he'd gone to ground, and she had only herself to blame.

Stella walked into the kitchen. The three of them looked at her.

"I need to borrow a car," Stella said.

Merle looked at Pee Wee. The lawyer suddenly became interested in the window.

Stella felt terrible. Nobody had been so unreasonably kind to her as these two. When she was a teenager, Merle had lured her back into the world with books like a trail of bread crumbs. Pee Wee had taught her the moonshine distribution business, taking her with him on deliveries, showing her accounting, all the things that Abby never had to mess with because he had Pee Wee. And when she started making her own shine Pee Wee had not only staked her but become her first bootlegger, introducing her product to rich clients he'd cultivated for years. She couldn't ask anything more from them, yet she had to.

Merle said to Stella, "Are you going to get it into a shoot-out?"

"I can't guarantee I won't."

"Take Pee Wee's then."

Pee Wee laughed, said, "Come on, then." Walked Stella out to the garage and his Sequoia Cream Buick Roadmaster. She was less than six months old and goodness gracious, she was beautiful.

"I was about to make a trip west with the latest batch," Pee Wee said. "Just let me unload."

"No. Keep it in the car."

Pee Wee raised a devilish eyebrow. That moonshine was worth a lot of money, to both of them.

"I'll make it up to you," Stella said.

"It's your liquor," he said.

"I meant the car."

"Ah! Be careful with her!"

She drove east, with the setting sun pushing her into the mountains.

## 21

1938

**H**ER BODY WOKE HER. The sound it was making was so odd—a high, soft wail. As soon as she concentrated on it, it stopped.

This was the wrong body. She could feel it, arrayed around her. The wrong number of limbs. The wrong size. Wrong everything.

The eyes opened, revealing wood beams and a ceiling that seemed very far away. The room glowed with a frosty white light. She waited. Listened to the body breathing. Slowly lifted a hand, marveling that it obeyed her. The hand touched her face, and she felt the wet. Tears.

Then she realized she was alone, and the body made that keening sound again.

A human voice spoke to her. She didn't want to look, didn't want to be alone. She closed her eyes again, and fled.

SHE AWOKE AGAIN to a light so bright it burned. She tried to sit up, but fell back against the mattress. Rolled onto her side.

After some time she was able to get her legs over to the side of the bed. She stood, and immediately her knees buckled and she fell to the floor. The pain seemed very far away.

The door opened, and a voice said, "What are you trying to do?" Motty. The woman reached under her arms and heaved. Pulled her backward until the bed was under her again.

Stella looked around. The room was so bright. "Where is it?" she asked.

"Sit here, don't try to get up. Your legs are weak."

Stella's body was weeping again. "It was here. I—we were here, together."

The God's thoughts, sharp as razors. It had wounded her to try to hold them. But it had been glorious. She'd become glory.

She was dizzy, and her stomach felt hollow. Every breath scraped her throat.

Motty stared at her. She was frightened.

"How long?" Stella asked.

"Six days."

Six. Stella tried to fathom that. The time had disappeared.

"I want to see the sow."

"That can wait," Motty said. "You lay down, and I'll—"

"Get out of my way!"

The force of the shout startled Stella. Motty too.

"Hold on, hold on."

Motty put socks and boots on her feet. Helped her into a coat.

Stella breathed, told herself she felt stronger. When she got to her feet Motty stood close.

Outside, the summer had disappeared. How many times had Stella communed since Motty burned her Revelation—twenty, twenty-five? For weeks she lived half in the God's thoughts. And then for six days, entirely swallowed up.

The sow was huge. She was only four months old, but she looked bigger than any hog they'd ever owned.

"This is the way it is," Motty said. "This is the job. We go into the mine and come back with the truth, because we're the only ones who can do it."

"What truth?"

Motty's eyes widened a fraction. "You don't remember."

Stella felt the panic rising in her chest. What did she say while she was in bed? What babble had spilled out of her mouth?

"It's coming," Motty said. "There's going to be a child."

SNOWFLAKES FLOATED DOWN from the clear night sky, one by one, like moon dust.

The door scraped open behind her. Abby called her name, twice: once in surprise, then in alarm. Stella sat on a stump, her arm outstretched, hand open. Each snowflake melted as it touched her palm.

"How long you been out here? Where's your coat? It's November, Star, you could've froze to death!"

She allowed him to steer her inside the cabin and set her in front of the fireplace. "You're all wet! Oh, Stella." Abby found a rabbit-skin blanket and draped it over her shoulders. He kept asking questions. The Russian boar grinned at her. The host of petrified animals regarded her with their glass eyes.

Her body began to shake. He knelt behind her and wrapped his arms around her. "Oh, Star, I'm so sorry. I've been worried about you."

It had been two days since she left the bed. So over a week since her last communion. She was so alone.

"Motty wouldn't let me come inside the house," Abby said. "You know what she's like when her mind's set. She said you were feeling poorly, didn't want me in the house. But . . . are you all right? Should I have gone in?" He smelled of woodsmoke and old sweat, with a tang of formaldehyde. He smelled like Abby. Of course he'd gone to bed drunk and was drunk still—she could smell the moonshine on his breath and hear it in that tumble of words. He only got loquacious when he was sauced. "Talk to me, little girl. Why were you just sitting out there?"

She hadn't meant to go to Abby's shack. She'd climbed the hill to the chapel, her legs trembling the entire way, only to find a new lock on the door. Motty's doing. Stella was furious. She grabbed the lock, yanked at it.

The cold of the metal shocked her. She let go. Looked at her palm.

No, she thought. No.

She'd walked across the ridge to Abby's place. She was afraid to knock on the door, so she sat on the stump and told herself, If he opens the door, I'll tell him.

"Are you sad about that boy?" Abby asked. "I heard you had a fight. Don't worry, he'll come around. I know he's over the moon about you."

Abby thought she was heartsick. Well, she thought, I am.

Abby squeezed her and said, "That boy loves you. If you talked to him, he'd come back."

A noise escaped her. Oh, Abby. Not Lunk. How could you be so ignorant?

"I guarantee it," he said. "I can see it when he talks to you."

Stop talking, she thought. Ask me what happened with the God.

He went on about the fickleness of young men, how they didn't know their own hearts. He told her how they couldn't see what was perfect even if it was right in front of them.

Finally Stella said, "Did you love Lena?" She was shivering, and her jaw was tight.

He eased away from her. His hands gripped her arms, but his belly was no longer pressed against her back. Then, as if to make up for this withdrawal, he rubbed the fur that covered her arms. Drying her, petting her.

"Sure I did. She was like a daughter to me."

"When I was little . . ." Stella said. It was hard to talk with her chest so tight, so little air in her lungs. But she was grateful they were both staring at the fire—she couldn't have said a word if he was looking at her. "When I was little, and I first saw that picture—you and Lena and Ray Wallace . . ."

He said nothing.

"I used to think, you were my father. You were taking care of me in secret, because of some vow you'd made to Lena, and that's why Ray never came back."

"Aw, Stella, that ain't—"

"I know it ain't true. I know. I was just wishing."

"Ah, fuck me," he said. He rested his forehead on her shoulder. "I wouldn't mind if I was. That wouldn't be such a bad thing, would it?"

"No. Not so bad." But it wouldn't have made any difference. Not if they'd stayed here in the cove. The God would have called to her. The way it still called to her.

She'd stopped shaking. He rose to one knee and kissed the top of her head. "Let's keep the fire going." He got both feet under him.

"Motty says she lay in bed five weeks," Stella said.

He grunted. Walked around her and picked up his makeshift poker, a length of narrow pipe that could have been a worm for a still. He said, "That was the worst time of my life."

"Do you know what killed her?"

"They said it was TB."

"No," Stella said. "That's a lie."

He wouldn't look at her.

"You know what happened to her," Stella said. "You didn't do anything."

"I wish I had," Abby said. "Even if it would've done no good, I sure wish I had."

He looked at the poker, not sure what to do with it. Leaned it against the wall. "I'm going to make up a pallet for you," he said. "You can stay right here by the fire, sleep as long as you like."

"I'm afraid to sleep," Stella said.

"Don't you worry about that. In the morning it'll all be clear. And there's one thing we know already—that Lincoln Rayburn's a damn fool."

TWO NIGHTS LATER she heard the faint rumble in the distance. She sat up, and abruptly it stopped.

It was near midnight, but she was awake, and her bedroom was awash in a quavering light—the moon shining through the frost-glazed window. She could hear everything, as if the walls were paper; the fire snapping in the woodstove, Motty's wheezy snore, the ticking of the clock in the front room. And outside, the wind scraping at the trees. The crunch of heavy steps on the icy, brittle grass.

A shape appeared in her window. A voice softly called her name.

Stella slipped out of bed. The air was cold. She took her robe from the hook and walked out to the front porch.

"I'm here," she said.

A moment later he appeared from around the side of the house. Lunk, looking tall in his black coat, his face serious.

"I heard your car," she said.

He glanced behind him. He'd parked it down the road, out of sight.

"I need to talk to you," he said. "Without Motty."

Motty was snoring away. Still, she closed the door. She asked, "Did Abby send you?"

"He talked to me, yes, but he didn't send me. I been waiting to come." He put a foot on the bottom step, looking up at her. "I been sick ever since you told me to leave you alone. I can't sleep, I can't eat."

"I'm sorry," she said. "That was cruel."

"Oh!" He seemed ready to burst into tears. "Abby said . . . but I didn't know. After the last time, you seemed so . . . I couldn't understand it. You were so different. It was hard to hear."

"I'm sorry," she said again.

"Stella, don't apologize for a thing. You told me how you felt, and I tried to understand. But when Abby said, maybe, that you'd . . . well, I came to tell you—I'll wait for you. If you're here in the cove, that's where I'll be, too. If you go to college—any college, any town—I'll follow if you'll let me. I'll find work. I'll do anything. I'll dig ditches!" He laughed, amazed at the words spilling out of him. "I love you, Stella Wallace. My life ain't worth anything without you."

"Don't say that."

"It's true. I can't help it, but it's true. I don't know how you feel about me, right now, but—"

"I know," she said.

"You . . . ? What do you . . . ?" He lost his balance, righted himself. He was so beautiful like this, fear and hope and love and confusion, all bubbling away under high heat, and him trying to contain himself, trying to drive home his case when the case was already settled.

"Tomorrow night," she said.

"Tomorrow?"

"I don't care where we go. We can drive to California if you want."

"Tomorrow!"

"If I don't leave here," she said. "I'll die."

## 22

1948

STELLA PUSHED the Buick as hard as she could, but even though it was brand-new, the Roadmaster was no undercover race car like her Ford or Alfonse's souped-up Chevy; Pee Wee preferred comfort over speed. The accelerator was sluggish, the brakes mushy. It was like driving a four-thousand-pound mattress.

She reached the park after an achingly long time, then came to the T. East to Motty's, west to Abby's.

She thought, I can't do this alone. And Abby has my shotgun.

A quarter mile west she jammed the wide vehicle between two trees, onto the dirt track. Last time she'd gone this way, in her own car, she'd driven slow and careful. Not this time. She launched the Buick up the road, counting on momentum to get her over rocks and roots. The car bucked wildly, and her headlights skidded from tree to tree. She whipped around the hairpin turn that marked the three-quarter point, then—

The Buick slammed to a stop. Stella's body kept moving. Her chest caromed off the steering wheel and she fell sideways, onto the passenger's side floorboards. The car was listing to starboard.

The engine clunked to a halt. For a long moment she lay on the floor, wincing in pain, sipping spoonfuls of air. Her sternum felt like it'd been whacked by a ball-peen hammer.

You'll live, she told herself. Get moving.

She climbed back onto the ridiculously padded seat, restarted the engine, and pressed the gas. The car roared but didn't move. She killed the engine but kept the headlights on. Climbed out, bones complaining.

The front axle was hung up on a log, the driver's side wheel in the air. What the fuck was a log doing in the road? She could try to rock the car off it, but she didn't have time. The Uncles would be done with supper, and they could be taking Sunny to the chapel this very minute.

She'd have to go the rest of the way on foot. She started moving through the trees in a stuttering run, cutting straight over the hill rather than following the road. A rib stabbed her side every other step. In ten minutes she'd reached Abby's yard.

The cabin door hung open. The inside was dark. Stella took a moment to catch her breath, and then called, "Abby?"

He didn't answer. She called his name again, louder. Went to the doorframe. And then, on instinct, said, "Sunny?"

No answer.

She went in. The fireplace was cold, not even an ember. The room was empty and dark. And the bedroom door was open. The bedroom door was never open.

She went to the doorway. The room was windowless and much darker than the main cabin. She lowered her voice. "Abby? It's Stella."

The air smelled of harsh chemicals, the preservatives and glues he used in the taxidermy. Her eyes slowly adjusted to the dark. She could make out a narrow bed, and something that could have been a stack of buckets.

"Abby?"

A figure lay on the bed. She leaned close. "Hey. It's me."

Her hand touched the bed where his head should be, and it was sticky. A small noise escaped her throat. She dug into her pocket and found her Zippo.

It was Abby, but his face was hard to make out in the tiny flame. Then she realized he was masked in blood. His mouth hung open.

"Oh God. Abby." She touched his neck. She pressed her face close to his, almost kissing him. Both his eyes had swelled shut, and his jaw was misshapen. "Please," she said.

A faint rasp came from his open mouth.

Was he choking? She put two fingers in his mouth. He lurched when she touched his broken teeth. Her fingers came away wet. She'd felt no blockage.

He made a sound like air leaking out of a tire. Was he trying to say Sunny, or Stella?

"Sorry," he said. "So, so . . ."

"Abby. What happened? Did Hendrick do this to you?"

He breathed out, heavily. "She okay?"

"Hold still, just a second." She left the bedroom, looked around frantically, finally found a lantern by the sink, and returned to him.

His shirt was open to his breastbone. She moved her hands over his body, fearing gunshot wounds. There were bruises on his arms, cuts on his hands. When she touched his ribs he gasped. It looked like they hadn't shot him, though—just beaten him within an inch of his life. Every exhalation sounded like he was breathing through mud.

"I tried," he said. "Tried."

The blood on the bed was dried and tacky. They'd done this to him hours ago, then. Maybe last night, when they came looking for Sunny.

She knelt beside the bed. "Abby. Listen to me." She was having trouble breathing herself. Tears had sprung into her eyes. "I need to go get Sunny. But I'm going to come back for you, okay? I'll get you to a doctor. Pee Wee's car is down the back way, at the turn."

"I can get up."

"Don't get up! I'll be back for you."

A sigh escaped him.

"I'm sorry, I need to know," she said. "Do you still have the shotgun?"

He moved his head slightly. Whispered, "Took it."

"Fuck."

"I tried. I didn't tell 'em. I didn't . . ."

"I know," she said. "I know. I'll be back for you."


SHE TOOK the high ridge trail. Ran, trying to ignore the pain in her chest. Fell into the chapel yard with the bright moon behind her.

Veronica stood in front of the chapel door, peeking in through a gap, her curls lit up by a bright light spilling out. Those fucking movie lights.

Veronica didn't hear Stella, either, thanks to the growling Delco generator.

Stella tapped her on the shoulder and she spun about, shocked.

"Get away from the door."

"I thought you were in jail!" Then: "What happened? I couldn't believe it when I heard."

"I know what you did, Vee. I should have known you was always your daddy's girl. Now move."

Still Veronica didn't step from the door. "I don't know what you're—Stella!"

Stella grabbed the front of Veronica's dress, bunched the cloth in her fist, and yanked her close. "I *said*." Pushed her sideways.

"Daddy!" Veronica shouted. "Daddy! Rickie! Come out here!"

Behind the generator, leaning against the wall next to the gas cans, the excavation tools: a short-handled shovel, a long-handled one, a pickax. Stella hefted the long shovel. It was out of balance, not made for swinging at skulls, but it would have to do.

The door opened, and a robed figure stepped out. Rickie, all dressed up. He looked at Veronica and said, "What are you doing? They're in the middle of the thing!"

Veronica pointed. Rickie turned, threw up an arm. The shovel hit him in the elbow and he yelped, went down on one knee. "What's the *matter* with you?"

Hard to tell through a long handle, Stella thought, but it sure *felt* like bones had fractured.

Rickie gingerly touched his elbow and swore, loudly. Veronica backed away, a hand at her mouth.

Stella strode into the chapel.

At the far end of the room, a ring of tripods surrounded the hole in the floor like sentries. One of the set of lights, however, had been swiveled to illuminate the girl in the chair. Sunny sat in profile, perched on what looked like the same cane-back chair Stella had occupied a dozen years ago. Hendrick knelt before her, holding the copper bowl. His fancy robe had swallowed his legs and feet so that he looked like a munchkin offering Dorothy a treat. This tableau was being filmed by the skinny man, and tape-recorded by a new soundman, a replacement for the bald man who'd died in the cave. They wore robes, too, though much plainer than Hendrick's gold-threaded wonder. And in the pews, half a dozen more robed men.

Every face had turned toward Stella.

One of the men in the front row abruptly ducked, reached for something under the pew. "Cut!" Hendrick shouted. "Stop filming!"

Another man, closer to Stella, stepped into the aisle, blocking her way. He was one of the Georgians, a round, heavy-jowled man. "Women aren't allowed in here."

She gripped the shovel with both hands. "You think I won't bash your brains in? I grew up on a *farm.*"

The man hesitated. Then a voice behind him said, "Step away, Brother Jerome." The man plopped down, relieved.

Brother Paul stood at the end of the aisle, pointing a shotgun at her. Not just any shotgun—her family's Winchester 97. "You want to put down that shovel?"

"Not really." She kept walking, measuring the distance between them. His face was hard to make out against the halo framing him, but it was clear one of his eyes had been blackened, a recent mark. It was the most color she'd ever seen on his face.

Paul worked the shotgun's slide.

Stella stopped, took a breath. Ten feet remained between them. "Fine." She let the shovel fall with a clatter.

Behind Paul, Hendrick said, "What are you doing here, Stella?"

Paul eased out of the way, lifting the gun slightly to clear the back of the pew. His aim never strayed from Stella's gut. On the platform, Hendrick had gotten to his feet. The bowl sat on the floor between him and Sunny's feet.

"Sunny, I need you to listen to me," Stella said, ignoring Hendrick. "You don't know what's going to happen in that cave." The girl regarded her calmly. She wore a pale yellow dress and white shoes, with lace-topped ankle socks. Veronica—it had to have been Veronica—had woven small white flowers through Sunny's hair like a crown. It was harvest time, but she was dressed for Easter.

Stella said, "Did they tell you what they did to Abby?"

Sunny glanced at Hendrick. She didn't know.

"Tell her," Stella said.

He had the decency to look embarrassed. "Couldn't be helped. He wouldn't get out of the way."

"They beat him within an inch of his life," Stella said. "Nearly killed him."

"I will say this," Brother Paul said. "He put up a good fight."

Up close, she could see that the whole side of Paul's face had turned greenish blue. "I bet he did," Stella said. Absalom Whitt was a big man. Slow to anger, but he knew how to take care of himself—and his girls. He'd tried to keep his promise to her.

"So he's alive?" Sunny asked.

Stella walked forward, slowly. The barrel of the gun was at her back now. "Yes, barely," she said. "They could have tied him up if they didn't want him to warn me. But they hurt him, bad, and left him to die."

"It's okay," Sunny said. "We'll take care of him, after."

"That's right," Hendrick said. "As soon as the world knows of the God's existence, all will be taken care of."

"Holy hell," Stella said. "Would you stop with the bullshit?"

"You're the one who's been—"

"You just breathe it in and breathe it out. You're adapted to it, like some kind of swamp animal."

"Is that Lena?" a voice loudly asked. Morgan Birch talking to John Headley beside him. Both of them in their nineties and deaf as posts. "I always liked her."

"Jesus Christ," Stella said. "How's that eternal youth working out for you two?"

Morgan smiled a toothless smile.

Stella stepped closer to the platform and Brother Paul barked a warning. "Whatever they told you, they don't know what they're talking about," Stella told Sunny. "The Ghostdaddy's not going to come out. It's dying."

"That's ridiculous," Hendrick said. "This is the day we've all been—Stanley! I said cut!" The skinny man lowered his camera. The man beside him punched buttons on the reel-to-reel, clearly confused.

Stella kept her eyes on Sunny. "They can't force you. You're in charge here. They can't go in without you, nothing happens without you."

"That's enough," Hendrick said. "Take her out of here."

Stella ignored them. "Sunny, I don't care what you did to Motty. I know it was an accident."

"What?" Hendrick said. "What are you talking about?"

A hit. Hendrick had no idea that this little girl had murdered his sister. Of course he'd never suspected. She was a little girl.

"There's things you don't know," Stella said to him. "Let's just slow down. No need to rush off into the cave."

"You're lying," Hendrick said. "You're just trying to delay us."

Fuck yes, I'm delaying, Stella thought. She needed the time to get Sunny to doubt him. To get all of them to doubt him.

"The God ain't coming out of the mountain," she said, loud enough so even the old men could hear. "You think it's going to risk everything, for what you want? When I was a girl, Uncle Hendrick told me about the government, how they'd come down on us like a swarm of locusts. It was true then and true now. If they find out about the Ghost—"

"Shut up!" Sunny yelled.

Stella held up her hands. "Sunny, I'm sorry if you're upset. But you can't go in there alone. It's too dangerous."

"Shut her up!" the girl yelled.

Brother Paul pressed the barrel of the shotgun against her back.

She looked over her shoulder. "What are you going to do, Brother? Shoot an unarmed woman in front of a child?"

"I'll do what's necessary," he said, and she believed him.

Sunny stood up. "I can't wait anymore."

Stella said, "Please! Don't do it, Sunny. You're not—"

Pain shot up her neck and she fell onto hands and knees. Stars fired behind her eyelids. He'd hit her with the butt of the shotgun.

"Stay down," Paul said.

"The God in the Mountain's waiting," Sunny said.

"You've ruined it," Hendrick said to Stella. "The ceremony's ruined."

"He's lying," Stella said through gritted teeth. The pain was an ongoing surprise. "His plan won't work."

"Aw, Stella Wallace," Sunny said. "This ain't *his* plan."

The girl took two steps, then descended into the hole. In a moment she had disappeared.

No one spoke or moved.

Then Hendrick shouted at the skinny cameraman, "Did you get that? Did anybody get that?"


BROTHER PAUL HAULED Stella to her feet.

She thought, I'm an idiot. She'd misunderstood everything since she'd driven back into the cove almost a week ago. Sunny had been playing her like a fiddle—and Hendrick, too, and all these Georgia boys, and the ancient Uncles. It had been Sunny's idea to call the God out, and Sunny who promised she could do it.

Motty was the only one who'd figured it out. She recognized the danger, and ordered Abby to pave over the entrance. And Sunny had killed her for it.

Hendrick didn't believe the girl could have done such a thing, because he was a man, a human man. "Take her back to the house," he said.

Paul blinked. "I—we agreed I'd be here. In the room."

"We can't have her interrupting, and you're, well . . ." He gestured at the shotgun. ". . . best suited."

"With all due respect, no."

"Brother Paul?" Uncle Hendrick was frazzled—he was losing all control of the Big Night.

"*With all due respect*, I've financed this church, Pastor Hendrick, and I've waited too long and sacrificed too much to sit idly by. I'm sorry, I will not." He turned. "Brother Jerome!"

The man who'd blocked Stella a minute ago stood up, confused. He was sweating, despite the cold. He carried rolls of fat on his neck like a bunched carpet.

Paul shoved the shotgun into his hands. "Take her."

"But I don't want to miss, either."

"God damn it!" Hendrick yelled. "When the God comes out, y'uns'll see him, sooner or later! It's not a God damn contest! Now go! Take her to the house and tie her the hell up!"

Stella had never heard Hendrick swear—certainly not three times in one breath.

Jerome said, "Is there rope?"

"What?"

"Is there rope, in the house?"

"*I* don't know. Veronica!" Veronica and Rickie stood by the door. Rickie cradled his wounded arm, and blood had soaked the sleeve. "Go with them, find some rope!"

"But, Daddy—"

"Would *somebody* listen to me?!"

Brother Jerome nudged Stella with the gun. "Let's go."

She thought, I can't leave. I have to get Sunny out of that cave.

"Come *on*," Jerome said.

He was itching to blow a hole through her. She walked out of the chapel, pushed by that gun. Veronica and Rickie joined their group.

Stella said to Veronica, "Your daddy's making a mistake."

Jerome said, "Hush up. You've talked enough tonight."

They walked downhill, through the dark. Rickie said, "Did you hear something?" He stopped walking, then Veronica. Jerome said, "Come on, the faster we get her tied up, the faster we can all get back here."

Veronica said, "Is that—?"

A huge shape came out of the trees. It barreled into Jerome, knocking him to the ground.

Abby Whitt, his face dark and bulbous as a gourd. She didn't know how he could see out of those swollen eyes.

"Let her go," he said. His voice anguished.

Rickie ducked his good shoulder and rammed Abby in the gut, drove him back, and then Abby slammed into the trunk of a tree. He groaned.

Rickie tried to pull away, but Abby's arm was around his throat.

"Hey!" Rickie said. "Let me—"

Abby brought his fist down on the back of Rickie's head. The sailor collapsed at Abby's feet, boneless. Veronica ran down the hill, trailing screams.

Jerome had rolled onto his back. Somehow he'd kept his grip on the Winchester. The barrel was pointed at Abby's chest. Stella could see the murder, as if it were a frame stuck in a movie projector, melting at the edges. Jerome, wincing in anticipation of the recoil, his fingers tight on the trigger. And Abby, half blind, a monster about to be brought down.

The air around her turned violet. Stella opened her fists.

## 23

**1938**

A N HOUR AFTER SUNSET, the screaming started. It sounded human, but Stella recognized it for what it was: the sow, in pain.

Stella had been holed up in her room all day, avoiding her chores—and Motty. Stella felt like she was vibrating at a strange frequency, a sharp, jittery feeling that could have been excitement, joy, or dread. Lunk was coming that night, and the cove would be a memory. Motty, Hendrick, and the Ghostdaddy could go to hell.

Her first problem, though, had been finding luggage. She didn't want to start her new life carrying a pillowcase full of clothes like some hobo. The cardboard suitcase she'd arrived with when she was nine was split down the side, useless. So when Motty was out of the house Stella slipped into her room and dug under the bed for the ancient carpetbag. It may not have been the one Esther used in her escape, but Stella would claim it for her own.

She stuffed the bag with the few clothes she liked, and even fewer keepsakes. The handkerchief Lunk had given her. Her

Bible. Her science journals. Nancy Drew's *The Secret of the Old Clock*. She hesitated over *The Book of Clara* and *The Book of Esther*. Take them because they were part of her history, or leave them behind for the same reason?

She made a disgusted noise and threw them in. She could always burn them later.

Last was her prized possession: the photo of Abby and her parents, looking so young, all of them in their cowboys-and-Indians getup. She felt weak in her stomach and sat down. Something about the picture unsettled her. Maybe it was the way Ray Wallace and Abby looked so oblivious. Maybe it was how her mother, tiny and small-boned and clear-eyed, stared out with a sad smile, as if she knew her daughter were out there on the other side of the camera, invisible, untouchable.

Stella thought, The God nearly killed us both.

She wrapped the frame in one of her dresses and tucked it into the bag. How terrible that everything she owned fit in one ancient carryall. God damn she was tired of being poor. Soon it would be different. She promised herself that, no matter what Lunk did for a living, preacher or typewriter repairman, she'd make her own money, and keep it, too.

The sun went down, and fear rattled. She paced the small room, unable to place the emotion anywhere, unable to dispel it.

Then she heard the screaming, like a woman being murdered.

THE SOW LAY on her side, legs thrashing. Motty was bent over the animal, struggling to hold it in place. She looked up at Stella and, "For goodness sake, help me!"

The pig lay atop an old wooden gate inside the old horse stall, surrounded by fresh hay. Four lanterns had been set atop the stall—a country operating theater. Motty's .22 squirrel rifle leaned against a wall.

"Tie her legs down," Motty said.

"Are you going to shoot her?"

"Not yet. Better if she stays breathing long as possible."

The pig screamed and screamed.

Stella threaded rope through the slats of the gate. Looped it around one rear leg. The pig went into a frenzy; the sharp hooves cut through Stella's sleeve and sliced her arm. She ignored it and cinched the back legs together. The front legs were easier.

"Make sure they're pulled tight," Motty said. "I need a clear space." She'd unrolled a leather cloth. On it were three knives, a large pair of shears, a small pair of scissors, and a long, thin metal tube. She picked up the medium-weight knife and with her other hand felt along under the pig's chin to the top of the swollen teats. Rested the point of the knife there—not lower on the belly where Stella would have expected.

Motty looked at Stella. "Are you staying?"

Stella took a breath. Nodded.

"Let's put her down." Motty tapped her own forehead. "Right there. Can you do that?"

The pig had no name. Stella had learned early never to name an animal they'd be eating. But she'd been the one to feed her every day, and muck out her pen, and make sure she had water. The sow deserved one last act of kindness.

Stella picked up the rifle. Checked the safety. Then she pressed the barrel to the front of her skull and fired. The sound in the small space was deafening. The pig went still.

"All right," Motty said. "We got to work fast."

Motty knelt and made her first cut, a long one. Liquid gushed out of the animal—not blood, but gummy and pale. It splashed out like warm water from a tipped bathtub, soaking both their laps. The air steamed.

Motty waited calmly for the rush of liquid to abate, and then made her second cut. She put both hands inside the animal. "Reach in there, between my hands. I'm holding open the womb."

Stella thought, I'm not supposed to be here. I'm supposed to be gone.

Motty shouted, "Reach in, damn it!"

Stella pushed up the sleeve of her right arm. She rested her left elbow on the sow's huge, bristled neck, pushed her hand in. She felt something that was thick, yet yielding.

"Feel for the cord," Motty said. "Do you feel a cord?"

Stella didn't know what she felt. Everything was warm and slippery. Her hands felt coated in jelly. Then she touched something hard. A head? No, flatter. A shoulder, maybe. She moved her hand down. Felt something thick as a sausage. Moved her thumb along it.

"I think I have the cord." She was trying to steady her breathing. "It feels so big."

"Get your second hand in there. You want to find its neck, make sure the cord's not wrapped around it. You have it?"

"I don't know!" She was terrified.

"Bring it out."

The fetus was encased in a waxy gel, and beneath that, its skin was red as wine. It looked like a baby. A human baby.

"It's not moving," Stella said. "It's not moving!"

"Shush." Motty hooked a finger into its tiny mouth, pulled out some black matter. Her finger was bleeding now. Inside the mouth were tiny white teeth. The child already had *teeth*?

Its eyes remained closed. The little barrel chest wasn't moving. Its arms and legs, skinny and human-looking, hung limp. Motty snipped the umbilical cord and tied a string around it. So fast, like she'd done it a hundred times.

Motty breathed into its mouth, and the child's chest moved in response.

Stella burst into tears. Please live, she thought. Please. She didn't know who she was praying to. Only Motty and Stella were here to save it. Stella touched its head, studying that narrow nose as sharp as any Birch woman's. Those delicate hands with their tiny, perfect fingernails. Except for that red skin, it looked like a normal human child. It was a wonder.

"Oh my God."

Stella looked up at the voice. Lunk stood a few feet away, staring at the child. He looked like he was going to burst into tears. "What *is* that?"

Stella glanced down. "I . . ." She didn't know what it was, or what to call it.

Lunk stepped forward. The baby coughed, and suddenly began to wail.

Lunk jerked back. He dropped a small box he was holding. His hand went to his mouth. Then he turned, and ran.

"Stop him," Motty said. The child was still in her arms, alive, alive and bawling. *"Stop him."*

LUNK WAS RUNNING pell-mell for the road. He was taller than she was. Maybe faster. She shouted his name but he kept running. Then he reached the end of the gravel drive and cut right. His feet slipped on the pavement and he almost went down. Caught himself. Glanced back and saw her chasing him, and the look of terror on his face broke her heart.

When Stella got to the road, he was thirty yards away, making for a car parked along the ditch—his father's new car. Lunk had tucked it under the trees, where it couldn't be seen from the house. Later, she'd realize he must've gone to her window, and when she failed to come out, he'd crept toward the lights in the barn. And then he saw the bloody child, delivered out of the body of a sow.

Lunk was pelting along so fast he had to put out his arms to stop himself from crashing against the trunk of the car. He yanked open the driver's side door. Froze. Looked up.

The God in the Mountain loomed out of the dark. It strode into the roadway, its white torso swinging under a profusion of tall, tall limbs. Legs unfolded before it, scissored, retracted. It halted in front of the car.

Lunk screamed.

Stella stopped running and looked up in wonder. The God reared back, so that the torso stood on end, like a human's. The air throbbed like a beating heart.

It knew her. It needed her.

The dread she'd carried with her all day fell away. The false bravery. The imaginary future. All she wanted was one more communion. One more hour with its thoughts spilling into her head, whispering to her. All she wanted was to be its daughter.

Stella opened her arms, letting the vibration run through her.

Lunk was screaming. She felt so sorry for him. He didn't know how lucky he was.

Lunk threw himself backward, fell onto the cold pavement, scrambled back up. He sprinted toward Stella. His eyes were wild, like a pony running from a fire.

"Stella! Run!"

"Don't," she said softly.

"We have to go!" He grabbed her arm and moved past her. She was yanked along for a few feet. She seized his wrist with her other hand, set her feet. He jerked to a stop, surprised at her strength.

He screamed again. Now in pain.

Her palms were open now. A thrill like icy air ran across her skin. The air had turned violet.

He looked down, and she followed his gaze. Her fists were open. From her left hand floated a bundle of white filaments, undulating as if underwater. And from her right, another flowering of strands—and these connected her palm to Lunk's wrist.

She could feel everything Lunk felt. His fear. His confusion. And his love for her, yes, that too, but it was tiny compared with that fear, a tiny raft on an ocean of terror. He wanted, more than anything, to run. Run and keep running, until he found someone to save him. He had to tell everyone what he'd seen. Satan was real. Every rumor swirling around the Birch women—that they were pagans, devil-worshippers, witches—was true. He'd given his heart to a demon.

"You can't go," Stella heard herself say. "You can't tell."

He couldn't tear his eyes from the threads. Blood seeped from the perforations, but the threads themselves were beautiful. They didn't feel foreign to her; they belonged to her, simple as that. How stupid of her that she hadn't suspected. All those years, she thought the God was reaching out to her. Instead, it had been drawing these out of her. Showing her herself.

"Please," Lunk said.

"I'm sorry." She understood, now, how the God felt toward her. She was a mayfly, and incapable of containing everything it wanted to give her. She was its damaged, broken child, but no less precious for all that. It had to let her go, it had to reject her, before it shattered her.

Lunk reached with his free hand and gripped the tendrils.

"No," she said. "Don't. Let me—"

He yanked the strands from his wrist. Blood sprayed from a dozen tiny holes; each filament had found some length of a vein. In Stella's altered vision Lunk's skin was red as hot coals but his blood burned even hotter, bright yellow. It sprayed into the air and fell across the road like molten gold.

Lunk sank to his knees. His expression melted from fear to bewilderment. He didn't recognize her. She'd become something else.

The God eased forward on its many legs until it stood over her. The vibration set her bones to humming. She could feel its thoughts press upon her. She'd done something terrible, but she could not hold on to what it was: the God bathed her in love. Love, and pity, and sadness, but most of all love, an adoration so deep it was almost wonder.

## 24

**1948**

S HE KILLED Brother Jerome with a touch.

He fell back, and his head smacked the ground. The shotgun slipped from his arms. His body, in her violet-hazed vision, burned orange. She couldn't help but see Lunk: scared, mystified, stunned by her transformation.

She cried out and stepped back from the body. The threads withdrew from the man, but the tips hovered over his chest, as if seeking another way in.

"Stella," Abby said. His voice was hoarse. "It's okay."

No, nothing was okay. She'd promised herself she'd never murder again. And now she'd done it, easy as reaching for a glass of water.

The strands twisted through the air, as if trying to braid into a rope. She concentrated and managed to pull them back into herself. A splotch of blood, bright as a sunflower, marked each palm. Whatever trick Sunny's body possessed to stitch the hole back together, Stella's had never acquired it. She'd spent ten years hoping to never see these things again.

The red haze over her vision dissipated, and darkness swept in.

"Stella," Abby repeated. She turned, and he slid down the tree and thumped to the ground. Rickie lay beside him, snoring.

"Abby!"

She crouched down. He looked at her with his nearly closed eye, his face like a bloody fist. "I'm okay." Expelled a ragged breath. "You?"

"No." Then: "You knew."

He didn't have to answer. "Go get her," he said.

She went to Brother Jerome and picked up the Winchester. The chapel was near enough she could see the light coming through the open doorway, splintered by the intervening leaves.

"Rest here," Stella told him. "I'll be back with her."

She thought about striding through that church door, one more time. She had a shotgun now, but the math remained bad: two shells in the Winchester and thirty feet of aisle between the door and Brother Paul's pistol. She gave herself even odds of killing him before he killed her. But that left the rest of the Georgians, and Uncle Hendrick.

Then she realized what she had to do.

She edged up to the chapel, staying out of sight of the door and that white light. Squatted next to the generator and ran a hand along its side, then the back of it. There, above the power cord: a switch.

She flipped it. The engine coughed and stopped. The lights inside went out.

Hendrick angrily commanded someone, anyone, to go outside and refill the generator. Stella stepped back behind the door. A figure stepped out, bent over the machine. It was the skinny cameraman. She slowly reached out with the gun and touched the barrel to the back of his head.

"Run," she said.

His hands went up. He didn't dare turn his head to look at her.

"Quiet," she said.

He stood up. Turned, slowly, and then walked down the trail toward the house. When he was a dozen yards away, he began to run. Stella thought, One down.

Inside the chapel, Hendrick argued with someone else—probably Brother Paul. "Stanley!" he yelled. Stella waited. The men went silent.

Hendrick called out, "Stella? Is that you?"

They wouldn't be sending out any more deacons. She figured there were eight men left in the sanctuary: two ancient Uncles up front, three deacons in the pews, one soundman, and Uncle Hendrick and Brother Paul.

She could think of only one way to reach the hole alive.

She set the Winchester on the ground and opened her palms. The strands slid out of her, tasted the air. A gauze of milky scarlet settled over her vision.

She thought, Time to run across the pews.

SHE SLIPPED THROUGH the door and ducked to her right. A gun fired, and the wall beside the door splintered. They'd seen her shadow cross the doorway. She wouldn't give them that shot again.

The men burned bright, fiery against the cool red that filled the room. She had no trouble distinguishing them. Hendrick stood on the platform behind Brother Paul; Paul's arm straight, the pistol appearing to her as a cold, inky blot. His hand moved, unable to find her in the dark. The soundman had backed into the corner, still holding the microphone.

She ran up the side of the chapel, between the pews and wall. One of the Georgians stood in her way, though he didn't know it; he was swiveling his head, trying desperately to spot her.

The strands shot forward and slipped between his ribs. *No!* Then, *I'm sorry.* She moved to catch him but his body thumped to the floor.

Brother Paul turned, fired at the sound.

The tendrils licked at the body's neck and face. She yanked them toward her, and they reluctantly slipped out of his body. She ducked between the pews, and the filaments trailed behind, thrashing. "Everyone get the fuck out!" she shouted. "Run, and I won't kill you."

Paul fired again and the bullet smacked the pew in front of her. The strands whipped around her body in a frenzy.

"Where is she?" Hendrick yelled. "For God's sake, shoot her!"

"Shut up," Brother Paul said.

Stella concentrated, tried to calm the tendrils. She couldn't control them like Sunny. Back in the Acorn Farm, the girl had killed that mouse gracefully, and the strands had retracted obediently. She was the next Revelator. Stella was last year's model, in as much control of the strands as of her heartbeat.

She peeked over the top of the pew. Paul was walking slowly across the front of the sanctuary, gun arm moving. He was too far away for her threads to reach.

On the other side of the room, two Georgians decided they'd had enough, and scrambled through the door, robes flapping. Thank God, she thought. The pews were empty now, except for Morgan Birch and John Headley Martin. If the old men didn't move—and why would they?—they might survive the night.

Hendrick called out Stella's name. "This is ridiculous. The God is coming. This is what you wanted, too!"

To her right and three rows ahead of her, the fiery figure that was Brother Paul tilted his head, studying the shadows between the pews.

"Just talk to me," Hendrick said. He dropped to his knees, looking for something on the floor. "If you're worried about

Sunny, I'm sure we can figure something out." Trying to distract while he searched for something. Stella wondered if the sound-man was recording this.

Paul moved to the next pew. He was only ten feet from her now. The strands whispered as they slid over each other. Stop it, she thought. Obey me.

"You don't have to worry about Sunny," Hendrick said. "The world will adore her. They'll absolutely . . ."

A light flicked on. Hendrick had found a flashlight. The beam swept the sanctuary. Flickered across her eyes.

The gun fired. The bullet struck her, knocked her sideways. Paul stepped to the end of the pew and leveled his gun. "What in God's na—"

A hundred long needles entered his face. Paul's body remained standing for several seconds. Then the gun arm drooped, and his body fell forward, onto her. The flashlight beam roved the wall.

"Brother Paul?" Hendrick called. "Brother Paul!"

Stella shoved Paul off her. The tendrils dripped into his body, tearing the robes. "Enough," Stella said. *"Enough."*

She didn't know who or what she was talking to. Another Stella, perhaps, who'd always lived inside her. But the tendrils ceased their probing.

Something was wrong with her right arm. Her shirt was soaked with blood, a hot, orange color. It was impossible to tell whether it was Paul's or her own. She pulled herself up with her left hand, and the strands there gripped the top of the pew, sup-porting her.

Hendrick's light found her. Stayed on her as she walked toward him. Her right arm hung at her side, an electric ache pulsing from shoulder to wrist. The strands, though, were alive, and dancing.

As Stella grew closer, the light began to twitch. Hendrick couldn't hold his hand steady.

"What *are* you?" he asked.

He sounded so afraid. She couldn't fathom his weakness. He'd come here to see a god. Now that he'd finally witnessed a miracle he couldn't bear it.

"You never knew?" Stella asked. "Never suspected?"

He shook his head. All the Revelators he'd known, and he'd only seen what he wanted to see.

"You can't go in there," Hendrick said. He stood in front of the hole. "I won't let you interrupt this."

"Won't?"

"Why are you doing this?" His voice climbed. "Just let it happen, for God's sake! This is the most important thing that's happened to the world in two thousand years. The world is about to change."

"I don't care a whit for the world. Or your god. I'm here for Sunny. She's my responsibility."

"She hates your guts."

"True enough. Still."

"Let her do what she wants! Let her *become* what she wants."

"Can't do it," Stella said. She was six feet from him. "I made a promise."

"To who? For *what*?"

It was too much to explain. She was done explaining anything to Uncle Hendrick.

She held out her left hand. The threads danced like fireflies trailing silk. "Step aside."

Hendrick lowered the flashlight. "No. I won't let you ruin this. I will see the God. I'll be the one to announce his presence. I've waited my whole life for this moment."

"I know," she said.

Threads pierced his robe, his skin. They slipped through muscle, over and under his ribs, sewing through him, and found his heart.

. . .

SHE STOOD AT the lip of the cave, trying to steady herself. The muddy odor wafting out of the hole was as familiar as the smell of her own body. When she was a girl, she'd never hesitated to enter this place, not from the first day she found her way inside. That should have told her something. But a child doesn't know from normal. What the world shows you, that's what the world is. All the times she'd walked in here, even that last time, ten years ago, she'd never felt fear. She felt it now.

"What's going on?" a voice asked. In the front row, Morgan Birch and John Headley Martin stared into the dark with wide eyes, like two children waiting for the start of a magic show.

"Get them out of here," Stella said.

The soundman had pressed himself against the back wall, hoping the darkness would hide him. He'd remained still throughout the killing, holding his microphone like a talisman. He didn't move now.

"Drop the equipment," she said.

He slowly unslung the reel-to-reel machine and set it on the floor. Placed the microphone next to it.

"If you tell anyone about this, I will hunt you down. Do you understand?"

He didn't answer.

"Do you *understand*?"

"Yes."

Stella stepped down, into the hole.

## 25

1938

MOTTY WAS TRYING to feed her. A hunk of corn bread, a bowl of steaming soup beans. The smell made her stomach clench.

"Just let me sleep," Stella said. "Please."

She'd barely left the bed for three days. A couple of visits to the outhouse, with a blanket draped around her, because of the remaining needs of this body. She lived inside a heavy machine that she didn't have the strength to turn off. Not yet.

Motty held the spoon to her mouth. "Come on now. One bite." Stella allowed a dab of the oily juice to pass her lips. She didn't lift her bandaged hands.

"Did I miss the funeral?" Stella said.

"You ain't going. You're in no condition."

Stella didn't want to go to the service—she wanted to know when it was over. Some time ago, maybe yesterday, she'd heard Elder Rayburn's voice, speaking to Motty. She didn't try to make out their words.

"The police will be coming over here soon to talk to you."

Motty had told her this before. Five times? Six? "You need to get straight in your head what happened."

Stella closed her eyes.

"Lincoln came to see you," Motty said. "It was six or six-thirty, after supper. You went up to Abby's and sat around the fire, talking. The three of you started drinking. Say it back. Stella? Come on now."

Her eyes stayed shut. Motty went through it three times, finally gave up. Stella heard the scrape of her stool as she stood.

"What about the baby?" Stella asked.

"Don't say nothing about the baby."

SHE COULD HARDLY keep her eyes open all day but that night she found herself wide-awake. It was snowing, making the light coming through the window tremble. She stared at whatever the moonlight showed her: the spines of books, her jacket on its hook like a patient stranger, the picture on the dresser.

Motty had found the carpetbag. Unpacked it and put her belongings back in place, because there couldn't be any clue that she was planning on leaving town with Lunk. The story was the story.

The brightest object in the room was the glass covering the picture.

Stella slipped out of the bed. The floor was cold against her bare feet. She took down the frame. In this light it was hard to make out the figures in the photograph, but she saw them clearly in her mind's eye; she'd memorized every detail years ago. The proud men in their cowboy suits. The skinny, delicate Lena Birch.

She turned over the frame. Her hands were clumsy in the bandages, but she managed to slip the picture free. The penciled words on the back were too faint to read, but she'd memorized those, too: *Cherokee NC Feb 3 1924*. Not once in all those years gazing at the picture in Abby's cabin did she wonder at that date. Not even when Abby gave her the picture on her birthday. March 15. Stella was born six weeks after that picture had been taken.

Lena wasn't her mother. Ray Wallace wasn't her father. And Abby Whitt, he wasn't anything at all.

Stella slowly tore the picture down the middle. Tore each half again, and kept going, until the pieces were too small and the white tatters fell through her fingers.

She went into the hall. Followed small sounds to the kitchen.

Motty looked up as if she'd been caught in a devious act. She sat at the table, the baby in her arms, feeding it with an Allenbury bottle shaped like a banana. The tiny child sucked at the rubber nipple, its eyes half closed. Its skin was aswirl with white and scarlet.

"You want to try?" Motty asked.

Stella shook her head.

"You're going to have to learn."

Stella sat across from them and watched it feed. The wooden stove was burning, and the air was warm and moist. The child grew sleepy, but its mouth kept working the nipple.

Motty dabbed at the child's chin. "We'll have to keep her hid while the police are here," she said. "And for a few months after that. Keep you out of sight, too."

"And then what?" Stella asked.

"Then she'll be yours."

And Lincoln's, Stella thought. That's what everyone would think.

"You have to give her a name," Motty said.

"No. You do it."

"It's your right. I named Selena, and she named you."

The child's eyes closed, and its mouth stopped moving. Motty set down the bottle and wiped the white mixture from its lips. "Why don't you hold her?"

Stella didn't move. Motty shook her head in disappointment. She laid the sleeping child in a crate lined with blankets. Went to the sink and started pumping, but no water came. The pipe was frozen. Motty cursed.

Stella said, "Show me your hands."

"What?"

"You owe me that much."

Motty stared hard at her for a moment. Then she held out her arms. Opened her fists. Her palms were deeply fissured, ringed by hard, pale calluses. A lifetime of work.

"All the way," Stella said.

Motty's eyes narrowed, her lips pressed tightly together. She was embarrassed, Stella realized. The old woman said, "I'm not like you."

"I need to see."

Motty closed her eyes. Her fingers spread slightly. The flesh of one palm cracked open.

Two black threads emerged. Blood welled around them. Each thread was stiff and only an inch or so long. Motty sighed and three more pushed their way out.

Stella touched one of them, and Motty flinched.

"I can't give it what it wants," Motty said. "I was never good enough. But Lena, she had so much more to work with than I did, her communion so clear and strong."

"So she kept going back."

"That's the way it goes with us. Every generation gets a little closer."

"Closer to what?"

"What it needs. Someone who'll understand it, full and complete. I was flawed, and Lena was better. But you, you were near to perfect."

*Near to.* That week Stella lost, after her last communion, she'd been out of her head, not knowing where the God ended and she began. And yet, she wasn't able to hold on. She'd failed. Of course the God would move on to the next vessel.

"Most of them die," Motty said. She closed her fists. "I can't tell you the number of dead things I've pulled out of them sows. But once in a long while, one of us lives."

One of us. Esther. Motty. Lena. Stella. And now this child. All daughters of the God in the Mountain.

Motty wiped her hands on a dish towel. "I won't forget the night Lena and I delivered you. There was a cold snap, and the wind cut through the barn timbers like a knife. But you, you were *so* alive. You came out fighting mad." Motty seemed anxious to tell her the story, at last. Blasphemy made into something beautiful.

"I always wondered why I was never afraid of it," Stella said. Then: "You should've told me."

"I knew you'd find out on your own. That's a hard day. To find out you'll never be like them. That boy was never going to love you. Lena ran off with Ray Wallace, thinking she could play house with him, keep you like you were her own. Hope nothing ever jumped out of your hands. She knew if he ever found out, he wouldn't look at her the same way. Or you."

Stella understood this already. She'd known it the second Lincoln looked at her on the road, saw his face opening in terror to revulsion. He was right to fear her. When the moment came to choose him or her god, her body knew who it belonged to.

And now, another child. She seemed perfect. But only the God would know if she was good enough for her purpose.

"It's been making children for a hundred years," Stella said. The thoughts that had been inside her made a little more sense. "Or trying to."

"He puts his essence into the sow," Motty said. "Lets it grow there. Borrowing the womb." And Stella thought, Not just its own essence.

It took from the Birch women, too. Taking from the old to make the new.

"What are we?" Stella asked. "Are we even people?"

"What we are," Motty said, "is sisters."

THE UNIFORMED MEN TROMPED in the next morning, talking loud. Their ungainly bodies filled up the front room, surrounded her. Once again she was the center of attention.

She recognized only Tom Acherson, the one-armed man who worked for the park. He seemed embarrassed to be there. "You don't have to worry," he said. "We know this isn't your fault. We just need you to tell us what happened that night."

She looked into their faces. They were treating her like a frightened little girl. Like a human being. Motty stood nearby, watching.

"Lincoln came over around six," Stella said. "Maybe it was six-thirty."

Nothing she told them was a surprise. Everything jibed with the story Abby had told them when he turned himself in. He'd given Stella and Lincoln the liquor he'd brewed himself. At the end of the night he sent them down the mountain.

"What's going to happen?" Stella said.

"Nothing to you, honey," one of the policemen said. "Nothing to you."

They were buttoning their coats when the first church bell rang, and were still chatting when it rang again. On the third bell Tom quieted the other men, and Stella realized what was happening. The policemen held their hats in their hands, stared at their shoes.

Tom was looking at Stella, his eyes full of pity. Was she supposed to be feeling something? There was nothing in her but a granite heaviness.

The bell tolled again, and again, again. She didn't like the side glances of the men and stood up from her chair. Went to her bedroom, counting. Twelve. Thirteen. She closed the door but it made no difference in the sound: each toll resonated down the valley through winter air and penetrated the cabin walls like they were paper. Each louder and clearer than the last. Each a pronouncement.

The seventeenth bell rang. The sound hung in the air, incomplete and unfinished, waiting to be drowned out by the next bell.

THAT NIGHT, Stella lay awake, listening, until finally the baby stopped crying and Motty fell asleep. She sat on the edge of her bed and unwrapped her hands. The wounds had scabbed over. She quietly put on her coat and laced her boots.

The crate sat on the floor at the foot of Motty's bed, the baby nestled in the blankets. Stella picked up the child, holding it below rump and neck the way Motty did, and carried it out of the room. In the kitchen, Stella opened her coat and tucked the baby against her chest. It curled against her instinctually.

She buttoned the coat over it. There. It was almost as if she were pregnant.

She walked out into the cold, headed up between the trees. The baby stirred but didn't awaken.

The chapel door was splintered, the lock burst apart, where the God had pushed its way out. The panel covering the stairs had been tossed aside. Stella cradled the child with one arm and stepped down.

After so many visits, Stella knew the way through the mountain, even in darkness. Soon she put out her free hand and there was the stone table, rising like a flattened mushroom out of the stone floor. She backed up to it, shielding the baby, and then levered herself atop it.

She'd stood atop this stone many times, arms out, waiting for the Ghostdaddy to come to her. She wasn't going to wait this time. She cinched the belt of the coat tight, under the child's butt. It lay snug against her, tight as skin.

Stella opened her hands. A sharp pain, like a serrated knife dragging across her palm, and the threads emerged. Her vision misted as it had on the road outside. The darkness turned red.

"Show me," she said. The white tips of the threads brushed the face of the stone, then began to slip higher. There: a lip of stone that could support her weight. There, a bulge of rock to grab next.

She began to climb.

There were long seconds when she could see no way forward and her arms began to ache. And then the strands would find a crevice or a ridge and she'd pull herself up. The ceiling seemed to recede from her. Gaps appeared, as if the rock was slipping aside, widening just enough for her body. She thought, The mountain is opening its arms for us.

She climbed higher, and when she reached for a projection of rock she found instead a hole, a little wider than her shoulders. She drew her threads into her, and inched inside, one arm covering the baby.

The tunnel gradually widened, and soon she could crawl, moving awkwardly with one arm across her belly, holding the child in place. Twenty yards on she could stand. The passage turned, turned again, corkscrewing up into the mountain, until she emerged in faint golden light.

She stood in a vaulted cavern. The light glowed from recesses in the floor. There were twenty or thirty of these holes scattered across the space, like pools of honey. Stella walked to the closest. The cavity was lidded in amber. A dark shape nestled inside, curled like a question mark.

Stella crouched, holding the baby, and with her free hand touched the glassy surface. Despite the light it was as cool as the stone. She leaned closer.

A sound escaped her, and she jerked back.

It was a child. Or something that could have been a child, if it had lived. If it had been more human.

She looked around the cavern at the dozens of recesses. She walked to the next one, a few feet away. Her heart beat fast. Inside lay another tiny body, cradled in jellied light. This one's head was very large, but its short limbs ended with fingers melded into blunt hooves.

She was sobbing now, so hard she was struggling to get breath. She dragged herself to the next hollow, and the next. One body after another. Some looked human. Some looked like no creature she'd ever seen. All were dead.

And all were her sisters—as much a sister as the newborn she held now. Generations of the God's children, born from the bodies of pigs. All delivered back to the Ghostdaddy by their survivors, Lena and Motty and Esther—and Stella. She was part of this, too. Her hands were not clean.

She drew a breath, and shouted. "Show yourself!" Her echo mocked her.

Then, high up in the ceiling, something moved. A pale shape slowly unfolded from the rock. One flat, mantis limb eased down, seemed to test the floor. Then another. Its bulbous torso swayed as it descended, finally settled. Its body seemed to lock into place.

"You can't do this anymore," she said. Her voice was shaking. She wiped the tears from her cheeks. "You hear me?"

It remained mute. As always. If it could speak, it wouldn't need a Revelator.

Stella unbuttoned her coat with one hand. Held the child with the other. The child stirred and made a sound like a mouse.

"This girl is the last one. No more, do you hear me? No more . . . *experiments*."

The Ghostdaddy didn't move, but she could feel its attention on her. She moved close to it. "You don't get to use her," Stella said. "There can't be any more. It has to stop. And I'll make sure there aren't any more."

The bulging belly looked perfectly smooth, but she knew that it was dusted with minuscule perforations, a thousand tiny mouths. It breathed through these, and smelled and ate and heard through them. Beneath that skin was where it lived, the same way Stella lived behind her eyes. This world was anathema to it. The air was poison; the soil, poison; the sun, too. It was losing the battle, but it could live for a hundred more years. She didn't know how to kill it. And it could kill her with a gesture.

The Ghostdaddy eased forward, creaking.

"Stop," she said.

Stella didn't know how to kill it. But the Bible had taught her how to negotiate with gods. All you had to do was be willing to murder what you loved.

She opened her right hand. The threads floated out of her, and there was no pain this time. A few of them would be all it would take. The newborn was tiny. Fragile. Stella could strike before the God moved.

"I'm leaving the cove," she told it. "If I ever find out you've touched this girl, I'll kill her."

It gave no sign it heard her. God never answered Abraham, either.

"If you ever make another child, I'll kill it, too," Stella said. "I'll kill every last one."

## 26

1948

**T**HE THREADS CARRIED Stella into the heart of the
mountain, as they'd done ten years before. Her right arm
was slowly returning to her. She could lift it slightly, and
wiggle her fingers, though every movement brought pain.

The threads did much of the work. They found purchase in
the rock, hauled her up through the red darkness.

She was crawling through the most narrow passage when she
felt the low rumble she'd first experienced when she was a child,
like distant thunder. Then she stepped into the cavern and saw
them.

Sunny was communing with her god.

The girl knelt on the stone floor, her head thrown back, surrounded by lozenges of yellow light. Her arms were outstretched,
and hundreds of threads sprouted from each palm and connected
to the pale giant like a shimmering cat's cradle. The God and the
girl swayed together, their arms sawing in tandem. Dancing.

Stella recognized ecstasy. She'd never seen it from the outside,
but she remembered her body filling with jagged joy, as if the

Ghostdaddy were climbing inside her. It was no mystery why Sunny schemed and lied to get back to the cave. The God loved her and she loved the God. What was Stella to it but another failed vessel, someone too weak to do its divine work?

Stella strode across the stone floor, between the glassy recesses where her sisters—all those failed attempts—were preserved. The Ghostdaddy had never asked for permission to make them, and there'd never been a Birch woman or man with the sand to question it.

Stella was just as guilty. More so. It wasn't the Ghostdaddy that killed Lunk.

"Hey," she said. The rumble filled up the air, muffled her voice. Louder she said, "Sunny. *Hey.*" The girl's eyes were closed. Her mouth hung slack. Then she seemed to lose her balance, and the Ghostdaddy gently tugged her upright like a puppet.

Enough, Stella thought.

Stella ducked beneath the Ghostdaddy's outstretched limb, placing herself between the creature and the girl. The twined threads stretched out on either side of Stella as if she stood on a rope bridge.

The Ghostdaddy's bulging torso hung at eye level. It was from this belly that the low sound emanated, its only voice. Deep inside it were all the vitals that kept it alive.

It had to know that she meant the promise she'd made ten years ago, meant it with all her heart. And now, it could stop her from carrying it out, strike her down in an instant. All it had to do was release Sunny and spike one of its hard limbs into her.

"Do it," she said aloud.

If the creature released Sunny, and the girl saw her god murder Stella, maybe Sunny would run. Maybe she'd realize how little the thing cared for its daughters.

"Come on!" Stella screamed. "You think I won't do it?"

She turned and marched to Sunny. Gripped the girl by the throat with her left hand. "You think I won't sacrifice one more to stop this?"

Stop me, Stella thought. Stop me.

Sunny's mouth moved. Then sounds emerged. Babbling, not words at all. Then the babble became a hiss, and the hiss a word. "Stella."

Fuck.

She dropped her hand from the girl's throat.

Sunny's eyes remained closed. "Don't," Sunny said. "Not yet."

Stella thought, You stupid girl. Stupid as every Revelator who'd come before her.

Sunny kept repeating, "Not yet. Not yet." Her god gazed down. Its flower-like hands were wide open, each of Sunny's tendrils buried in the soft flesh there.

Stella touched the threads coming from Sunny's left hand. They were soft as oil. She could almost hear the creature's thoughts humming through them. "I'm sorry," she said. Then she closed her fist around the threads, and yanked. The threads popped free from the Ghostdaddy with a sickening, soft *pop*.

Sunny cried out and collapsed onto the vault floor. The needle-sharp tips in Stella's grip flailed about, seeking reconnection. Several sliced through Stella's shirtsleeve, raked her flesh. She shouted a curse and tossed them away from her. The filaments thrashed against the floor.

The Ghostdaddy reared back. The threads attached to its right limb were pulled taut and Sunny was dragged several feet across the stone.

Stella threw herself against that second bundle of strands, seized it with both hands, ignoring the pain in her arm. She jerked the threads from the creature's body.

Sunny fell onto her side, her entire body shaking. The thrumming abruptly stopped. The silence seemed to ring like a chime.

One of the Ghostdaddy's limbs was still outstretched, the petal fingers open. Stella threw open her own arms. "Well? *Well?*"

The limb swung down like a scythe and struck the floor at Stella's feet. The creature listed to the side. Then, very slowly, its huge body eased to the ground.

Stella screamed at it. She opened her fist, and her threads burst free. She touched them to a spot on its pale torso. There, she thought. Right there. Maybe it was possible to kill the creature after all.

The Ghostdaddy didn't pull away. Didn't move to defend itself. And her threads . . . felt nothing.

No pulse of its blood. None of the whispering sounds of its breathing.

The God she'd worshipped since she was nine years old was dead.

STELLA CARRIED Sunny up the stairs, the girl slack in her arms, unconscious. Stella's strands wrapped her body like spider silk.

Please be all right, Stella thought. Please. She didn't know if she'd stopped the communion in time. Sunny had taken more than a sip. No telling what it had done to her.

The sanctuary was empty except for the corpses. Hendrick. Brother Paul. The man she'd killed first, whose name she'd never learned. Morgan Birch and John Headley, however, had gotten out with the soundman. Good for them.

Abby was watching for them, just down the hill. He was burning like a torch in the violet air. Somehow he'd gotten back on his feet.

"Is she . . . ?" His voice high-pitched, plaintive.

"It's okay," Stella said. "She's just—" Stella sagged, and Abby caught her, her and Sunny. He took the girl from her.

Stella drew the strands back into herself. Her vision returned to normal. She was sorry to see the night grow so dark. God, she was tired.

Abby was alarmed at her bloody shirt. "What happened in there? I heard shots."

"Don't worry, the blood's not mine. Most of it."

She didn't know what to tell him. I murdered three men. The Ghostdaddy died. Sunny survived. Three monumental things that she didn't have the words to explain. Her only fear now was that the girl's mind had been scoured clean before the communion had been severed.

"Where's Rickie?" she asked.

"Woke up and left, with the rest of 'em."

They walked the ridge toward Abby's shack, moving slowly, Abby grunting every time a step jarred him, but he wouldn't put down the girl. Stella was sorry for how much this was costing him.

Finally they reached the hairpin where the Roadmaster's front whitewall was hung up on the log like a bear paw in a trap.

Abby said, "Who taught you to drive?"

"Funny story."

Stella opened the rear door and Abby laid Sunny down across the back seat. She was breathing easy, as if she'd nestled into a beautiful dream. The threads had rolled up inside her, and her hands were as unmarred as ever. No holes to even show the disciples.

Stella touched her head. The girl stirred. Opened her eyes sleepily. "Stella," she said.

Tears sprang into Stella's eyes. She spoke!

"It's okay," Stella said. "You can rest."

Sunny rolled onto her side.

"She okay?" Abby asked.

"She's fine," Stella said. The relief was like a blast of oxygen. She rubbed the wet from her cheeks.

Abby said, "We're going to need the jack."

Stella unlocked the trunk. The spare usually sat upright in its well, but Pee Wee had removed it to make room for the hooch, seventy gallons' worth. She hoped to hell he hadn't thrown out the jack, too. With her good arm Stella began lifting out brown jugs, and lined them up along the road. Abby leaned against a tree, breathing hard.

She found the jack tucked into the well, wrapped in its own leather case. She assembled it under the front bumper, ratcheted the car up with her good hand. Stella was sweating hard despite the cold, and her wounded arm burned.

Stella gingerly got behind the wheel, leaving the door open. The key was still in the ignition. She started the engine, put it in reverse, holding down the clutch. "Stand back," she said.

She gunned it. The car lurched and dropped onto the road, bouncing on heavy springs.

Sunny didn't even stir.

Stella climbed out. Walked over to one of the jugs, held it between her feet while she unscrewed the cap with her good arm. Offered it to Abby. "Do me the honors?"

He hesitated. His lip was split, his face still a mess. "I guess one pull couldn't hurt." He drank deep. Shook his head like a wet dog. "Goodness sake, Stella Wallace!"

"You can't complain, old man. That there's Uncle Dan's recipe."

"It sure is."

Stella took the jug from him and tipped it. Let the fire run down her throat. "I need you to take her to Merle and Pee Wee's," she said. "They're expecting her."

"You ain't coming with?"

"I've got some things to take care of first."

"Those Georgians, they'll be coming back with police."

"Maybe. Or maybe they're running for their lives."

"But sooner or later . . ."

"Sooner or later, they'll be looking for Sunny. You'll have to keep her hid."

"I know my job."

She went up on tiptoes and gently kissed his damaged cheek. "I know you do."

THE LANTERNS AND the fireplace had been left burning, but Motty's house had been abandoned. Stella went into the kitchen, peeled off the stiff, bloody shirt. The wound was a weepy mess but surprisingly small, the width of a nickel. The inside of the hole looked like raspberry jam. Maybe there was a bullet under there, maybe not. A problem for later.

She sat at the kitchen table with Motty's box of cast-off rags in front of her. This house had seen a constant need for bandages. She splashed moonshine across the wound, grimaced, then took a gulp for herself. She wrapped her arm, then held the end of the bandage in her teeth while she pinned it.

After, she gingerly pulled on one of Motty's old shirts. The cabin breathed as it always had in the winter, cold air outside, warm air within, the walls creaking like wooden lungs. The floors were seasoned with the sweat of generations of Birch women. How ridiculous that they thought these four rooms could some-day be known as a new Jerusalem.

She didn't know how long she had to wait. She mixed coffee with her whiskey to keep awake.

THE HEADLIGHTS SWEPT across the window sometime around three in the morning. The driver didn't shut off the engine, but Stella recognized that Chevrolet rumble. She walked out to the porch.

A figure stepped out from behind the wheel.

Stella said, "You got my message."

"My father passed it along," Alfonse Bowlin said. "My mother, well, she wasn't happy about me having any more dealings with you."

"Understandable."

He walked up to her and she put a hand on the back of his neck. Touched her forehead to his. "I appreciate this. I can't even tell you."

"It ain't nothing, Stella."

He unloaded three big duffel bags from his trunk. He uncinched one and took out a cardboard box stamped HERCULES POWDER COMPANY.

"This is the good stuff, fifty-percent mix," Alfonse said, showing her one of the sticks. "The strongest they come."

"And this'll do it?"

"You said you needed to drop some rock. This'll seal the deal."

"Okay, show me."

"Show you?"

"Show me how to do it. How to put it all together. You know I ain't afraid of a little fire." Stella was an engineer at heart—she'd laid out and welded every pot and pipe in the Acorn Farm—and while she was respectful around explosives, they didn't cause her to quake in her boots. Queen Bess, under high heat and creaking at the seams under the pressure of alcohol fumes, was a bomb-in-waiting, and she'd never lost sleep over it.

He laughed. "How about you let me take the lead in this, just this once."

"I don't want any of this to come back on you. I'm in serious trouble. There are . . . bodies."

"Plural?"

"Four."

"Well, fuck." He looked to the side. Nodded, taking it in. Then: "Is one of them that saltine cracker?"

"Brother Paul."

"That's him."

"As a matter of fact . . ."

"Then it would be my pleasure. Where's this cave of yours?"

"You're not going to like it."


"A *church*?" Alfonse shook his head. "No, this ain't right."

"It's not a real church," Stella said. "It's a fake. A front. If anybody asks, you said it was where some moonshiners were storing hooch."

"You don't say," Alfonse said. "Your uncle Hendrick, Brother Paul, and these other fellas, they were moonshiners who . . . what?"

"Got into a gunfight. Over money, probably. You know how criminals are."

"A greedy, violent lot."

Alfonse laid the tools and material on the chapel floor. A spool of green safety fuse, a pair of crimping pliers, heavy-gauge snips. A box of metal blasting caps. And the main prize: thirty full sticks of dynamite in three cardboard boxes. All of it purchased from his cousins working at the bauxite mine in Chattanooga.

Assembling each stick was painstaking work. Alfonse had to crimp a length of safety fuse into the blasting cap, then slide the cap into the body of the dynamite stick. Crimp the cap too close to its internal charge, he said, and you'd lose a hand, or worse, set off the whole damn chain of explosives. Stella tried to help by handing him tools, but with her lame arm she wasn't much help. In an hour he wired all thirty sticks. Each one trailed six feet of fuse.

"Now let's find the right places to set them."

"I'll have to do that."

"Stella, no. Place them wrong, and the tunnel won't col-lapse. Wire them wrong, and, well, you could blow yourself up. Plus . . ."

"What?"

"You're not looking good, Stella."

"I'm fine," she lied. Her arm ached. Sweat painted her neck, and she was on the verge of throwing up. She was also dying for a cigarette, but lighting up didn't seem wise.

"Think you could show me where the spot is?" he asked.

She thought, The Ghostdaddy's dead. If she never took him past the table room, he wouldn't see something that would give him nightmares.

"I can do it," she said. "Let's head down."

Alfonse ended up doing all the work, while she held the flash-light. His eyes kept asking questions, but she declined to answer. She tried not to think about the vault above her head. It was a tomb now. Let some far-future Howard Carter find it.

An hour later, Alfonse crimped the last strand of safety fuse onto the main cord. They stood in the small passage, surrounded by stone, and she thought, I should send him out of here, then set it off right here.

She'd known for a long time that she wasn't fit for human company. That much had been clear even before she found out she wasn't one of them. She'd murdered four people, one of them an innocent boy stupid enough to love her. If she stayed on this path she was on, she might have to kill more. Maybe that's what Lena understood, at the end. Ray Wallace couldn't abide what she was, and she couldn't stand what she was becoming.

Stella could end it now with one spark of the blasting cap. It wouldn't be a bad way to go. Instant death and burial, and her bones laid deep underground, secret as a meteorite.

Except: Sunny. Stella couldn't leave her alone in the world.

They backed out of the cave, letting the cord spool out behind them.

"One more thing," Stella said. Two of the generator's gas cans were still full. Alfonse splashed gas down the main aisle and across the platform.

Stella portioned out the gallon of hooch across the corpses. Thinking, Drink up, boys. You'll be thirsty in hell.

Out in the chapel yard she shook a cigarette from the pack of Lucky Strikes Merle had given her and lit up. She passed one to Alfonse. Together they enjoyed them for a moment, and then Alfonse stooped and handed her the end of the safety fuse.

She touched the tip to the fuse. Watched it burn, spitting and twisting, until it disappeared through the chapel door.

Waited a while longer.

She looked at Alfonse and said, "Is it . . . ?"

A *womp* and the ground shook. A second later came another muffled explosion, and another, and suddenly a chain of them like rolling thunder. The chapel door banged open, and the cigarette jumped from her fingers. A black cloud billowed from the doorway, scattering moonlight. Not smoke; dust. The mountain emptying its lungs.

Stella picked up her Lucky Strike. Still burning.

"Huh," she said aloud. She'd expected more. Then fire filled the doorway and she said, "There you go."

She wished they could stay to watch it burn.

IT WAS NEAR DAWN when they reached the top of Rich Mountain Gap. She and Alfonse got out of the Chevy and watched the sun come up over Thunderhead. Blue fog wreathed the mountains. The sunlight crept over the floor of the valley, and the autumn trees seemed to burst into flame along its path.

The smoke from the chapel fire was all but invisible, a thin twist of black smoke rising through the fog. The rangers were no doubt already there.

"Sure is pretty," Alfonse said. He lit a cigarette, passed it to her.

No wonder the Ghostdaddy had chosen this valley. No wonder the government wanted it. The cove was the prettiest place on Earth.

She was exhausted, and would have liked to watch for an hour. But no, she had one more thing to take care of, and a long drive ahead.

"You don't have to do this," Stella said for the third time.

Alfonse lit his own cigarette. "Get in."

## 27

## 1938

S TELLA STOOD in front of the house, her feet planted in the red dirt, her face turned toward the road. The afternoon sun threw hard shadows across the yard. The carpetbag sat at her feet.

"You'll be back," Motty said.

The old woman was hanging back on the other side of the screen door, holding the baby. No outsider would mistakenly see it, not until some plausible gestational period had elapsed. Then Motty would claim the baby was a girl cousin from North Carolina, knowing everyone would assume it was the child of Stella and Lunk. One lie could cover the other.

It was tradition. Everyone in the cove knew the Birch women were suspect: born out of wedlock, giving birth out of wedlock, a chain of fatherless daughters.

"Lena swore she'd never come back, too," Motty said.

Without turning around, Stella said, "I ain't Lena."

Stella had threatened a god. Promised to kill its next child. In the moment, she meant it—and meant it still. But years from now, when the time came, would she still have the strength?

Abraham was *willing* to sacrifice his child. God turned his son over to the mob. But she was no god, and no Bible hero.

She was a monster. Plain and simple. The only question was how long could she live with that knowledge.

A shiny sedan pulled into the yard. Stella picked up the carpetbag. It felt like a hundred pounds of river rock. There was nothing in it but a few changes of clothes—no books, no framed pictures. The only picture she'd ever owned she tore to pieces. Why march off to a new life holding on to a lie?

Motty said, "It's your right to name her."

"Call it what you like."

"I was thinking of naming her after you."

"Suit yourself."

Merle stepped out of the car, long-legged, broad-shouldered. Stella walked toward her and Merle brought her in close. A strong arm circled her shoulders.

"You okay?"

Stella pressed her forehead into Merle's shoulder. "Get me out of here."

Pee Wee opened the rear door and smoothly took the bag from her. "That's all you got, kiddo?"

Stella looked back toward the house. Motty stood behind the screen door, holding that bundle in one arm.

Stella slid into the back seat. Cigarette smoke on leather made her think of her pa, those long hours in the truck on their way here from Chicago. Maybe one day she'd forgive him for breaking his word to Lena and taking her back to the cove. Maybe one day she'd forgive him for failing to protect her. But she was grateful for one thing he'd done for her. He'd taught her how to leave.

## 28

**1948**

T HE ELECTRIC PERCOLATOR WAS such a tidy, efficient device. Stella liked everything about it: the little glass dome that showed the coffee bubbling, the cheerful red power light, the stainless-steel innards and the painted ceramic skin. It felt like the future.

She and Alfonse sat at the table, pouring cups for each other. They were both exhausted by a long night and a day of driving, but this, this imitation moment of domesticity, was sweet. Alfonse's Colt pistol lay on the table between them.

They were on their third cup when the front door opened in the distant living room. Veronica and Rickie were arguing in low, urgent voices. It was Aunt Ruth who entered the kitchen. She didn't see the strangers at first, and in that unguarded moment her face was a portrait of a lost woman: pale, hollow-eyed. Undone.

Then Ruth saw her husband's murderer sitting at her table, across from a Black man. To her credit she didn't scream, or cry. Her face hardened.

Stella put down her cup. "Howdy, Ruth."

The argument in the next room ceased. Stella waited.

Veronica crept in, her eyes wide. She looked about as wrecked as her mother. Rickie loomed behind her. His arm was in a sling. He saw Alfonse and went purple.

Alfonse stood up. "Ma'am."

Rickie bulled forward. "What the hell is a—?" He got as far as saying a word Alfonse didn't approve of. Alfonse punched him in the nose. A quick jab.

Rickie cried out, covered his nose with his free hand.

"Navy," Alfonse said under his breath.

Veronica burst into tears. "Stella! What are you doing here? What happened to Daddy?"

"Why don't y'all have a seat," Stella said.

Ruth trembled with bottled rage. "Get out of my house."

"I'm going to need something first."

"Rickie, throw these people out."

But Rickie was in no shape to throw anything. Veronica gripped his arm, trying to soothe him. He'd had a tough week. Shot full of splinters, hit by a shovel, knocked out by a mountain man.

"And call the police," Ruth added. "We know about the fire. You started it, didn't you? You murdered him."

Stella uncurled her fingers. Ruth stared at her open palms. Stella didn't know how much the men had seen in the chapel, or how much they'd passed on.

"Mother," Veronica said. "Please." Vee shut her eyes. Opened them. Between those two moments came a calculation.

"All right," Veronica said. "Tell us what you want."

"The Revelations. The original, handwritten ones, from Russell Birch on down."

"*What?*" Ruth was outraged.

"They're mine by right," Stella said.

"That's ridiculous," Ruth said. "They're not leaving this house. They're sacred."

Stella scraped back her chair and stood. "Take me to the safe, Vee."

Alfonse picked up his Colt.

Ruth's thin lips twisted into something like glee. "Only Hendrick knows that combination. Hendrick and myself. And I'll *never* let you lay your filthy hands on them."

Veronica turned and walked out of the room. Stella followed and Ruth shouted, "Veronica Louise Birch! Get back here!"

Rickie started to trail them and Alfonse said, "Ah ah ah. Let's just wait here."

Stella said to Alfonse, "This won't take long."

Hendrick's office was at the end of the hall. Stella had walked through the house when they'd arrived an hour ago and found it empty. Empty of people, anyway. Every room was overcrowded with furniture: end tables and armchairs, lamps and armoires. Hendrick's desk was a mighty rolltop that filled the room like an overturned lifeboat. The safe sat just behind it, beside Hendrick's green suitcase.

Veronica walked to the safe, knelt before it, and carefully dialed the combination. Stella suspected she was puttin' on. Vee had to have opened this safe a hundred times.

The stack of manuscripts inside was surprisingly small. "Put them in the case," Stella said.

Veronica started moving them to the suitcase, going slow and careful. Some had cardboard covers, like accounting ledgers; others were loose pages wrapped in string. She asked, "Is Sunny all right?"

"She will be."

"Thank goodness."

"Don't pretend like you care about her."

"You're wrong. I do care. If there's a Revelator to serve the God in the Mountain, the work goes on, one body, ever—"

"Your god's dead."

Veronica's face went still.

"You heard me."

Stella could sympathize. The Ghostdaddy's death was still a mystery to her. All those cryptic Revelations, the generations of women giving themselves to it, the endless promises of some immortal body resilient to the poisons of this world . . . and for what?

Veronica shook her head as if she was coming awake. "I don't believe you. You can't kill *God*."

"You ought to ask Jesus about that."

"He rose again."

"Which you know because of scripture," Stella said. "Because the Bible told you so." Stella slammed the lid shut. Turned out, one suitcase could contain an entire religion. She carried it to the doorway. Stopped. "One more thing."

Veronica sighed elaborately.

"I don't know how many copies Hendrick printed. I don't know where they're stored. But I advise you to burn them all. If I ever see a single copy out in the world, or find out you're trying to publish them? I will come back here and kill you all. You, your mother, Rickie. Everyone."

"You wouldn't." Her voice was a whisper.

"Tell me, Veronica. Tell me what I would or wouldn't do to protect my family."

"But, but, *we're* your—"

"No. You aren't. You never were."


ALFONSE DROVE THEM northwest until the sun was blasting the dirty windshield and the lines of the highway started to blur and jump.

"Go to sleep," Alfonse said. "I'll get you home."

But she couldn't rest. Not yet. The green suitcase lay on the floorboards.

"Could you pull over?" she said.

"There should be a gas station in a half hour," he said. "Least, one you can use."

"It ain't that. Up there's good." She pointed toward an empty field in a long, bare stretch of road.

Her arm ached. She'd smoked the last of her Lucky Strikes two hours ago. And she was bone tired. If she'd been driving alone she would have run off the road by now. And if Alfonse had been driving alone, he'd have been pulled over by now. Georgia cops were worse than the ones in Tennessee.

The car rolled to a stop. Stella opened the glove box and retrieved Alfonse's jar of moonshine. Took a long pull, grateful for that hint of sweetness, right before the long sawtooth burn.

She stepped out of the car, then reached back to pull the suitcase onto the seat. Opened it. On top of the pile was one of the newest notebooks, bound in bright leather. It had her name on it.

"Fuck me."

"You all right?" Alfonse asked.

"My cousin, fucking with me." Veronica had placed this book there, deliberately, Stella was sure of it. She opened it to the first page.

### THE BOOK OF STELLA
*Being the Fifth Volume of a New Revelation*
*From the God in the Mountain to Stella Wallace,*
*Recorded by Hendrick Birch, her Great Uncle*
*with Commentary and Clarifications by Hendrick Birch*

She turned the page—and jerked her hand away. This was poison. She didn't need those thoughts in her head.

She carried the suitcase out to the field. Unscrewed the lid of the Mason jar and poured it over the pages, dousing them.

Fuck you, Hendrick Birch. And fuck you, too, Ghostdaddy.

She reached for her matches.


SHE OPENED HER EYES as the headlights hit the WELCOME TO SWITCHCREEK sign.

"Nearly there," Alfonse said.

She pulled herself upright. She'd slept most of the way since burning the manuscripts. Alfonse cut the headlights, coasted into Merle's driveway, and stopped.

Stella said, "After this, I think you better head to Myrtle Beach for a while."

"Might be a good idea. When we get back we can figure out how to build a new still."

"I'm out of the moonshine business. But you have my blessing to keep going. You've got the recipe."

"That's crazy! I'm not going on without you. We make a good team, Stella. And we make damn good hooch. We'll just lay low for a while."

"Myrtle Beach won't be far enough for me—I'm headed out to sea. I don't know when I'll be back. Maybe never. I've got to take care of the girl."

He sat with that for a long moment, staring out the windshield.

"Well, shit," he said.

"Yeah."

"It was a damn good marriage."

"The best."

She leaned over to him. Kissed his cheek. "My Hooch Husband."

"My Whiskey Wife."

. . .

THE HOUSE WAS DARK. She went in quiet, without knocking, so as not to wake anybody, and stepped carefully. She'd spent many nights walking these rooms in the thin hours and knew that blundering into a stack of books could trigger an avalanche.

From the living room came a wall-rattling snore. Abby. The doors to Merle's bedroom and Pee Wee's bedroom were closed, but the one to Stella's old room was ajar.

Sunny lay in the bed under thick blankets, her long hair covering her face. Peaceful. Safe, for this moment at least. Stella had spent hours of the drive wondering how to protect her. They'd have to live somewhere as isolated as the cove had been. But nothing with caves—she wanted sunlight for the girl, sunlight and books and room to walk—yet so far away that she'd never run into a stranger. Wilderness like that was hard to come by. They might have to go west. Fuck, they might have to go to Alaska.

Stella eased onto the bed. She wanted to touch the girl but was afraid to wake her. Sunny had to think it was Stella who killed her god, and Stella didn't have the strength this minute to fight with her or try to explain. Stella didn't have any answers.

Something lay on the pillow next to her. It was a cross made of twigs and bound with yarn. No, not a cross. A stick figure.

Someone touched her shoulder. Merle. "That's one of her babies," she whispered. "She was making them all day."

They stepped into the hall. "She's been okay?" Stella asked. "She's not . . . hurt anyone?"

"Oh, Stella. No. No. She's fine. Quiet, but fine. How are you doing?"

"I'm fine, just tired. Is Abby . . . ?"

"My brother's come through worse. Pee Wee took him to the doctor this afternoon, they set his arm in a cast, wrapped his ribs. He passed out on the couch after supper."

"Okay, good. I . . ." She didn't know what to say next.

"Sweetie. Sweetie." Her tone was pitying. "Go in there and lie down next to Sunny. It's okay, she's been sleeping like a log."

Merle found her a nightgown. Stella moved the stick figure from the pillow and slipped into the bed. Sunny didn't stir. She breathed easily, her body throwing off warmth. A little girl in a big bed. Her sister.


SOMEONE WAS HUMMING.

Stella opened her eyes, winced. The room was bright with sunlight. She didn't know how long she'd slept, but it was not enough. Her body felt like it had been pummeled.

Sunny was sitting up next to her on the bed. She'd surrounded herself with a dozen of her little stick figures. She gazed at the one in her hand as if it were about to speak. Her humming was tuneless but happy, unmistakably happy.

She's beautiful, Stella thought. That skin, like ruby glass. Surely they could find a place for her.

Stella touched the girl's arm. "Hey."

The girl looked at her with those dark eyes. She put down her stick figure and gently touched Stella's cheek. Stella could feel the bump on the girl's palm, like a walnut under her skin.

"We forgive you," Sunny said. The words came out slow, as if she were translating from some more complex language. Her thumb caressed Stella's cheek. "We're here now. All the way here."

"Sunny?"

"Yes," she said. "And no." She leaned close to Stella's ear and whispered, "Can we tell you a secret?"

# Acknowledgments

Both sides of my family came out of Cades Cove, Tennessee, and my ancestors were among those bought out when they created the national park. My father, Darrell Gregory, was a direct descendant of Russell Gregory, who was murdered by North Carolina Rebels at the tail end of the Civil War. My dad loved the history of Cades Cove, and loved hiking the trails of the park. He died during the writing of this book, and I'm sad I didn't write faster so he could see it done.

My mother, Thelma Gregory, put many good books in my hand that led to this strange one. Especially useful were two books by A. Randolph Shields, *The Cades Cove Story* and *The Descendants of Robert and Margaret Emmert Shields of Cades Cove, Tennessee,* as well as *Born in a Split-Level House: Bert Garner and the Squirrels and Other Stories and Essays* by Leslie G. Walker. Mom and Dad brought me to the cove early and often, and it's why I love the place.

My uncle, Clinton Barbara, is a skilled taxidermist whose house is a wonder, crowded with the results of his craft. When I was ten, he gave me a stuffed raccoon head that hangs over my mantel today. My uncle is skilled in another craft that is central to this book. One afternoon in 2019, we sat down to sample his wares, and he shared an important recipe, revealed a few secrets of the trade, and told some stories about his brushes with the law.

Speaking of sampling wares, Jack Skillingstead and I spent many evenings at West Seattle's Whisky West and even more afternoons at Uptown Espresso ("Home of the Velvet Foam"), complaining about how very difficult it was to be a writer. I couldn't have written this book without him.

Liza Trombi had to put up with a lot from me during the writing of this book. She read many drafts, and early in the process she bought me the book *Cades Cove: The Life and Death of a Southern Appalachian Community 1818–1937* by Durwood Dunn, which was hugely valuable. Other folks read various drafts and offered their help when I needed it. My thanks to Nancy Kress, Chris Farnsworth, Stephanie Feldman, Dave Justus, Emma Gregory, Ian Gregory, and Ysabeau Wilce, as well as my Bay Area writers' group: Lisa Goldstein, Derrend Brown, Eliot Fintushel, Susan Lee, Lori White, Gary Shockley, and David Cleary.

A team of publishing professionals put the finishing touches on this book. Many of them are unknown to me, but I'd like to thank the copyediting and proofreading team of Lisa Silverman, Annette Szlachta-McGinn, and Jane Elias, who saved me from many mistakes, and the fine artist Dan Hillier, who created the artwork for the hardcover while listening to an audio version of the book. Dan, your work is beautiful.

Finally, many thanks to my literary agent, Seth Fishman, and my media agent, Flora Hackett, for their early enthusiasm for this book when I was still lost in the woods, and to Tim O'Connell, Anna Kaufman, and Robert Shapiro at Knopf, who pointed the way to daylight.

ALSO BY

# DARYL GREGORY

### SPOONBENDERS

Once they were The Amazing Telemachus Family, perform-
ers blessed with clairvoyance, telekinesis, and other psychic
abilities. But then a tragic event took the magic away, and
the powers that briefly made them stars of daytime TV suddenly seem more like a curse. Since their fall from grace
they've been trying to lead normal lives back home in
Chicago, but there's no such thing as normal for the
Telemachuses. When the CIA, the mafia, and an unrelent-
ing skeptic come calling, the family is forced to put their
past behind them and unite one more time. But will it be
enough to make them amazing again?

Fiction

VINTAGE BOOKS
Available wherever books are sold.
vintagebooks.com